Maps of the Ancient Sea Kings

# Maps of the Ancient Sea Kings

Evidence of
Advanced Civilization in the Ice Age

CHARLES H. HAPGOOD

*Revised Edition*

A DUTTON PAPERBACK

E. P. Dutton
New York

The author wishes to express his gratitude to the following for permission to reprint material in this volume:

Abelard-Schuman, Limited, New York, *Greek Science in Antiquity* by Marshall Clagett, Copyright © 1955.

`Little Brown and Company, Boston. *Admiral of the Ocean Sea* by Samuel Eliot Morison. Copyright © 1942 by Samuel Eliot Morison.

E. J. Brill, Ltd., Leiden, The Netherlands. *Hallucinations Scientifiques* (*Les Portolans*) by Prince Youssouf Kamal. Copyright © 1937.

E. J. Brill, Ltd., Leiden, The Netherlands, and the Editorial Board. *Encyclopaedia of Islam,* edited by M. Th. Houtsma, et al. Copyright © 1936.

Cambridge University Press, New York. *Science and Civilization in China, Vol. III* by J. Needham. Copyright © 1959.

Harvard University Press, Cambridge, Massachusetts. *Travel and Discovery in the Renaissance, 1420–1620* by Boies Penrose. Copyright © 1955.

The National Library, Ankara, Turkey. *The Oldest Map of America* by Dr. A. Afet Inan, translated by Dr. Leman Yolac. Copyright © 1954.

The Royal Danish Geographical Society, Copenhagen, Denmark. *Ptolemy's Maps of Northern Europe: A Reconstruction of the Prototypes* by Gudmund Schütt. H. Hagerup, Copenhagen, 1917.

The Map Collectors Circle, London, for the Buache map of Antarctica.

Twayne Publishers, Inc., New York, for the map of the St. Lawrence River in *Explorations in America Before Columbus* by Hjalmar R. Holand. Copyright © 1956.

The Huntington Library of San Marino, California, for permission to use the photograph of the Hamy-King Map.

Hutchinson & Co. Ltd, for a map of the Sahara, from *The Search for the Tassili Frescoes*, by Henri Lhote © 1959.

# Contents

# Illustrations

# Key to Sources of Maps

*N*   Nordenskiöld Periplus
*F*   Nordenskiöld Facsimile Atlas
*V*   Monumenta Cartographica Vaticana
*T*   Ptolemy World Atlas of 1513
*I*   Imago Mundi
*P*   Portuguesa Monumenta Cartographica
*B*   British Museum facsimile or MS

# Foreword

The geographer and geologist William Morris Davis once discussed "The Value of Outrageous Geological Hypothesis."* His point was that such hypotheses arouse interest, invite attack, and thus serve useful fermentative purposes in the advancement of geology. Mr. Hapgood will agree, I am sure, that this book records a mighty proliferation of outrageous cartographical and historical hypotheses, as luxuriant as an equatorial vine. His hypotheses will "outrage" the conservative instincts of historically minded cartographers and cartographically minded historians. But while those in whom conservatism predominates will react to this book like bulls to red rags, those of radical, iconoclastic bent will react like bees to honeysuckle, and the liberals in between will experience a feeling of stimulating bafflement.

A map dating from 1513, and by the Turkish Admiral, Piri Re'is, is the seed from which the vine has grown. Only the western half of the map has been preserved. It shows the Atlantic coasts from France and the Caribbean on the north to what Hapgood (following Captain A. H. Mallery) holds to be Antarctica on the south; and, of course, the proposition that any part of Antarctica could have been mapped before 1513 is startling. But yet more startling are the further propositions that have arisen from the intensive studies that Mr. Hapgood and his students have made of this and other late medieval and early modern maps. These studies, which took seven years, have convinced him that the maps were derived from prototypes drawn in pre-Hellenic times (perhaps even as early as the last Ice Age!), that these older maps were based upon a sophisticated understanding of the spherical trigonometry of map projections, and—what seems even more incredible—upon a detailed and accurate knowledge of the latitudes and longitudes of coastal features throughout a large part of the world.

In my opinion, Mr. Hapgood's ingenuity in developing his basic concept regarding the accuracy of the maps is fascinating and accounts for the book's most valuable contribution. Whether or not one accepts his "identifications" and his "solutions," he has posed hypotheses that cry aloud for further testing. Besides this, his suggestions as to what might explain the disappearance of civilizations sufficiently advanced in science and navigation to have produced the hypothetical lost prototypes of the maps that he has studied raise interesting philosophical and ethical questions. Had "Sportin' Life" in *Porgy and Bess* read this book, he would have been inspired to sing: "it ain't nessa ... it ain't nessa ... it ain't necessarily *not* so."

John K. Wright (ex-President, American Geographical Society)

* *Science*, vol. 63, 1926, pp. 463–468.

# Preface

This book is the story of the discovery of the first evidence that advanced peoples preceded all the peoples now known to history. In one field, ancient sea charts, it appears that accurate information has been passed down from people to people. It appears that the charts must have originated with a people unknown; that they were passed on, perhaps by the Minoans (the Sea Kings of ancient Crete) and the Phoenicians, who were for a thousand years and more the greatest sailors of the ancient world. We have evidence that they were collected and studied in the great library of Alexandria and that compilations of them were made by the geographers who worked there.

Before the destruction of the great library many of the maps must have been transferred to other centers, chiefly, perhaps, to Constantinople, which remained a center of learning through the Middle Ages. We can only speculate that the maps may have been preserved there until the Fourth Crusade (1204 A.D.) when the Venetians captured the city. Some of the maps appear in the west in the century following this "wrong way" crusade (for the Venetian fleet was supposed to sail for the Holy Land!). Others do not appear until the early 16th century.

Most of these maps were of the Mediterranean and the Black Sea. But maps of other areas survived. These included maps of the Americas and maps of the Arctic and Antarctic seas. It becomes clear that the ancient voyagers traveled from pole to pole. Unbelievable as it may appear, the evidence nevertheless indicates that some ancient people explored Antarctica when its coasts were free of ice. It is clear, too, that they had an instrument of navigation for accurately determining longitudes that was far superior to anything possessed by the peoples of ancient, medieval, or modern times until the second half of the 18th century.

This evidence of a lost technology will support and give credence to many other evidences that have been brought forward in the last century or more to support the hypothesis of a lost civilization in remote times. Scholars have been able to dismiss most of that evidence as mere myth, but here we have evidence that cannot be dismissed. This evidence requires that all the other evidence that has been brought forward in the past should be reexamined with an open mind.

To the inevitable question, are these remarkable maps genuine, I can only reply that they have all been known for a long time, with one exception. The Piri Re'is Map of 1513 was only rediscovered in 1929, but its authenticity, as will be seen, is sufficiently established. To the further question, why didn't somebody else discover all this before, I can only reply that new discoveries usually seem self-evident, by hindsight.

C. H. H.

## A Word of Appreciation

DISCOVERIES ARE often made by persons who, having fastened onto suggestions made by others, follow them through. This is the case with this book, which is the result of seven years of intensive research undertaken as the result of a suggestion made by someone else.

That person is Captain Arlington H. Mallery. He first suggested that the Piri Re'is Map, brought to light in 1929 but drawn in 1513 and based upon much older maps, showed a part of Antarctica. It was he who made the original suggestion that the first map of this coast must have been drawn before the present immense Antarctic ice cap had covered the coasts of Queen Maud Land. His sensational suggestion was the inspiration for our research.

It is therefore with deep appreciation that I dedicate this book to Captain Arlington H. Mallery.

# I The Treasure Hunt Begins

IN 1929, in the old Imperial Palace in Constantinople, a map was found that caused great excitement. It was painted on parchment, and dated in the month of Muharrem in the Moslem year 919, which is 1513 in the Christian calendar. It was signed with the name of Piri Ibn Haji Memmed, an admiral ("Re'is") of the Turkish navy known to us as Piri Re'is.

The map aroused attention because, from the date, it appeared to be one of the earliest maps of America. In 1929 the Turks were passing through a phase of intense nationalism under the leadership of Kemal, and they were delighted to find an early map of America drawn by a Turkish geographer. Furthermore, examination showed that this map differed significantly from all the other maps of America drawn in the 16th century because it showed South America and Africa in correct relative longitudes. This was most remarkable, for the navigators of the 16th century had no means of finding longitude except by guesswork.

Another detail of the map excited special attention. In one of the legends inscribed on the map by Piri Re'is, he stated that he had based the western part of it on a map that had been drawn by Columbus. This was indeed an exciting statement because for several centuries geographers had been trying without success to find a "lost map of Columbus" supposed to have been drawn by him in the West Indies. Turkish and German scholars made studies of the map. Articles were written in the learned journals, and even in the popular press.*

One of the popular articles, published in the *Illustrated London News* (1),† caught the eye of the American Secretary of State Henry Stimson. Stimson thought it would be worthwhile to try to discover the actual source Piri Re'is had used, a map which had supposedly been drawn by Columbus and which might still be lying about somewhere in Turkey. Accordingly, he ordered the American Ambassador in Turkey to request that an investigation be made. The Turkish Government complied, but no source maps were found.

---

* See the Bibliography, Nos. 1, 2, 5, 6, 23, 27, 28, 36, 40, 61, 78, 83, 104, 105, 106, 109, 115, 117, 154, 181, 187, 208, 215.

† Figures referring to specific sources listed in the Bibliography are inserted in parentheses throughout the text. The first number indicates the correspondingly numbered work in the Bibliography, and a number following a colon indicates the page in the work.

Piri Re'is made other interesting statements about his source maps. He used about twenty, he said, and he stated that some of them had been drawn in the time of Alexander the Great, and some of them had been based on mathematics. The scholars who studied the map in the 1930's could credit neither statement. It appears now, however, that both statements were essentially correct.

After a time, the map lost its public interest, and it was not accepted by scholars as a map by Columbus. No more was heard of it until by a series of curious chances, it aroused attention in Washington, D.C., in 1956. A Turkish naval officer had brought a copy of the map to the U.S. Navy Hydrographic Office as a gift (although, unknown to him, facsimiles already existed in the Library of Congress and other leading libraries in the United States). The map had been referred to a cartographer on the staff, M. I. Walters.

Walters happened to refer the map to a friend of his, a student of old maps, and a breaker of new ground in borderland regions of archaeology, Captain Arlington H. Mallery. Mallery, after a distinguished career as an engineer, navigator, archaeologist, and author (130), had devoted some years to the study of old maps, especially old Viking maps of North America and Greenland. He took the map home, and returned it with some very surprising comments. He made the statement that, in his opinion, the southernmost part of the map represented bays and islands of the Antarctic coast of Queen Maud Land now concealed under the Antarctic ice cap. That would imply, he thought, that somebody had mapped this coast before the ice had appeared.

This statement was too radical to be taken seriously by most professional geographers, though Walters himself felt that Mallery might be right. Mallery called in others to examine his findings. These included the Rev. Daniel L. Linehan, S.J., director of the Weston Observatory of Boston College, who had been to Antarctica, and the Rev. Francis Heyden, S.J., director of the Georgetown Universtiy Observatory. These trained scientists felt confidence in Mallery. Father Linehan and Walters took part with Mallery in a radio panel discussion, sponsored by Georgetown University, on August 26, 1956. Verbatim copies of this broadcast were distributed and brought to my attention. I was impressed by the confidence placed in Mallery by men like Walters, Linehan, and Heyden, and, when I met Mallery himself, I was convinced of his sincerity and honesty. I had a strong hunch that, despite the improbabilities of his general theories, and the lack, then, of positive proof, Mallery could well be right. I decided to investigate the map as thoroughly as I could. I therefore initiated an investigation at Keene State College.

This investigation was undertaken in connection with my classes at the college, and the students from the beginning took a very important part in it. It has been my habit to try to interest them in problems on the frontiers of knowledge, for I believe that unsolved problems provide a better stimulation for the intelligence and imagination than do already-solved problems taken from textbooks. I have also long felt that the amateur has a much more important role in science than is usually recognized. I taught the history of science, and have become aware of the extent to which most radical discoveries (sometimes called "breakthroughs") have been opposed by the experts in the affected fields. It is a fact, obviously, that every scientist is an amateur to start with. Copernicus, Newton, Darwin were all amateurs when they made their principal discoveries. Through the course of long years of work they became specialists in the fields which they *created*. However, the specialist who starts out by learning what everybody else has done before him is not likely to initiate anything very new. An expert is a man who knows everything, or nearly everything, and usually thinks he knows everything important, in his field. If he doesn't think he knows everything, at least he knows that other people know less, and thinks that amateurs know nothing. And so he has an unwise contempt for amateurs, despite the fact that it is to amateurs that innumerable important discoveries in all fields of science have been due.* For these reasons I did not hesitate to present the problem of the Piri Re'is Map to my students.

* The late James H. Campbell, who worked in his youth with Thomas A. Edison, said that once, when a difficult problem was being discussed, Edison said it was too difficult for any specialist. It would be necessary, he said, to wait for some amateur to solve it.

Figure 1. The Andreas Walsperger World Map of 1448. *N*

# II  Construction of the Piri Re'is Map

W HEN OUR investigation started my students and I were amateurs together. My only advantage over them was that I had had more experience in scientific investigations; their advantage over me was that they knew even less and therefore had no biases to overcome.

At the very beginning I had an idea—a bias, if you like—that might have doomed our voyage of discovery before it began. If this map was a copy of some very ancient map that had somehow survived in Constantinople to fall into the hands of the Turks, as I believed, then there ought to be very little in common between this map and the maps that circulated in Europe in the Middle Ages. I could not see how this map could be *both* an ancient map (recopied) and a medieval one. Therefore, when one of my students said this map resembled the navigation charts of the Middle Ages, at first I was not much interested. Fortunately for me, I kept my opinions to myself, and encouraged the students to begin the investigation along that line.

We soon accumulated considerable information about medieval maps. We were not concerned with the land maps, which were exceedingly crude. (Figs. 1 and 2.) We were interested only in the sea charts used by medieval sailors from about the 14th century on. These "portolan" maps ("from port to port") were of the Mediterranean and Black Seas, and they were good. An example is the Dulcert Portolano of 1339. (Fig. 3.) If the reader will compare the pattern of lines on this chart with that on the Piri Re'is Map he will see that they are similar. The only difference is that, while the Dulcert Portolano covers only the Mediterranean and the Black Seas, the Piri Re'is Map deals with the shores of the entire Atlantic Ocean. The lines differ from those on modern maps. They do not resemble the modern map's lines of latitude and longitude that are spaced at equal intervals and cross to form "grids" of different kinds. Instead, some of the lines, at least, on these old maps seem to radiate from centers on the map, like spokes from a wheel. These centers seem to reproduce the pattern of the mariner's compass, and some of them are decorated like compasses. The radiating "spokes" are spaced exactly like the points of the compass, there being sixteen lines in some cases, and thirty-two in others.

Since the mariner's compass first came into use in Europe about the time that

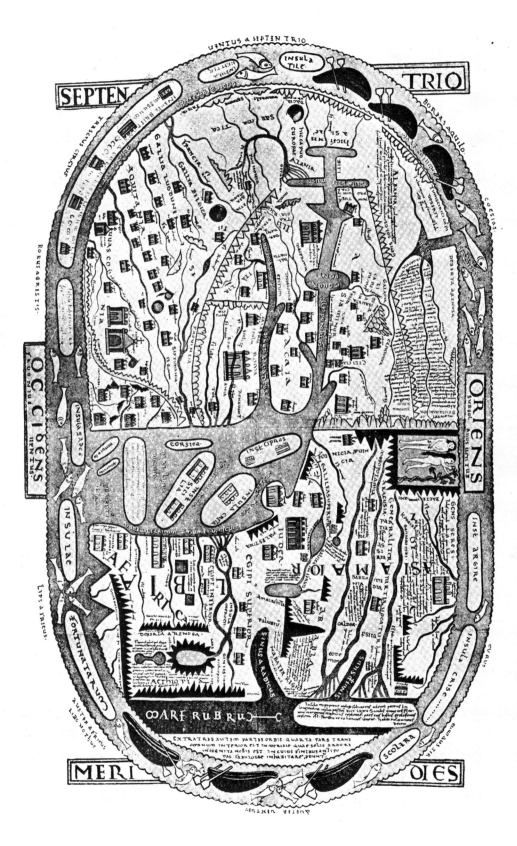

Figure 2. The S. Osma Beatus Medieval World Map. *V*

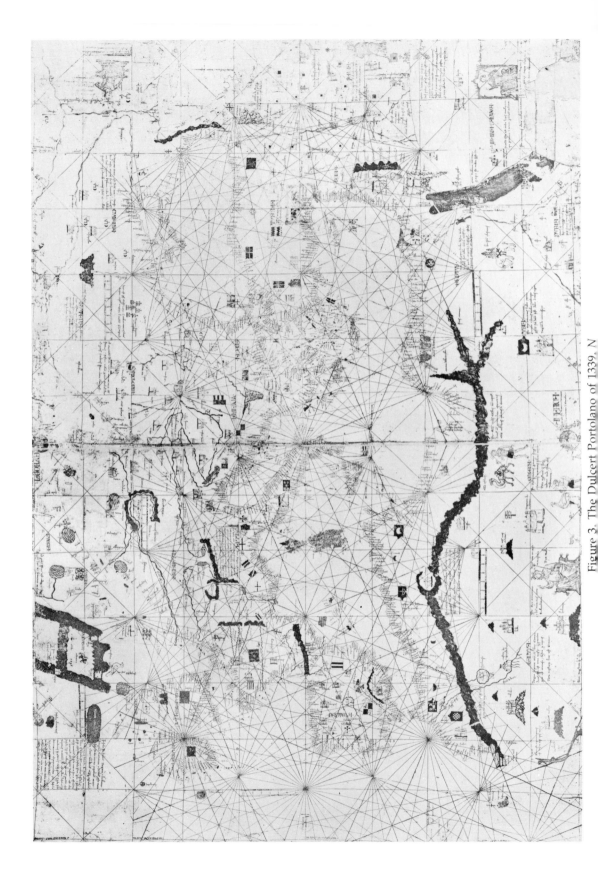

Figure 3. The Dulcert Portolano of 1339.

these charts were introduced, most scholars have concluded that the charts' design must have been intended to help medieval sailors sail by the compass. There is no doubt that medieval navigators did use the charts to help them find compass courses, for the method is described in a treatise written at the time (89, 179, 200). However, as we continued to study these medieval charts, a number of mysteries turned up.

We found, for example, that one of the leading scholars in the field did not believe that the charts originated in the Middle Ages. A. E. Nordenskiöld, who compiled a great Atlas of these charts* (146) and also wrote an essay on their history (147), presented several reasons for concluding that they must have come from ancient times. In the first place, he pointed out that the Dulcert Portolano and all the others like it were a great deal too accurate to have been drawn by medieval sailors. Then there was the curious fact that the successive charts showed no signs of development. Those from the beginning of the 14th century are as good as those from the 16th. It seemed as though somebody early in the 14th century had found an amazingly good chart which nobody was to be able to improve upon for two hundred years. Furthermore, Nordenskiöld saw evidence that only *one* such model chart had been found and that all the portolanos drawn in the following centuries were only copies—at one or more removes—from the original. He called this unknown original the "normal portolano" and showed that the portalanos, as a body, had rather slavishly been copied from this original. He said:

> The measurements at all events show: 1. that, as regards the outline of the Mediterranean and the Black Sea, all the portolanos are almost unaltered copies of the same original; 2. that the same scale of distance was used on all the portolanos (147:24). (See Note 22.)

After discussing this uniform scale that appears on all the portolanos, and the fact that it appears to be unrelated to the units of measurement used in the Mediterranean, except the Catalan (which he had reason to believe was based on the units used by the Carthaginians), Nordenskiöld further remarks:

> . . . It is therefore possible that the measure used in the portolanos had its ultimate origin in the time when the Phoenicians or Carthaginians ruled over the navigation of the western Mediterranean, or at least from the time of Marinus of Tyre . . . (147:24).†

Nordenskiöld inclined, then, to assign an ancient origin to the portolanos. But this is not all. He was quite familiar with the maps of Claudius Ptolemy which had survived from antiquity and had been reintroduced in Europe in the 15th Century.

---

* From which most of the maps in this book are taken.

†Marinus of Tyre lived in the 2nd Century A.D. and was the predecessor of the geographer Claudius Ptolemy.

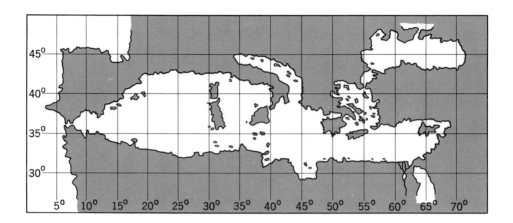

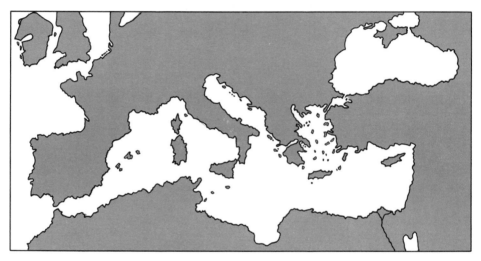

Figure 4. Nordenskiöld's comparison of Ptolemy's Map of the Mediterranean (top) with the Dulcert Portolano.

After comparing the two, he found that the portolanos were much better than Ptolemy's maps. He compared Ptolemy's map of the Mediterranean and the Black Seas with the Dulcert Portolano (Fig. 3) and found that the superiority of the portolano was evident.

Let us stop to consider, for a moment, what this means. Ptolemy is the most famous geographer of the ancient world. He worked in Alexandria in the 2nd century A.D., in the greatest library of the ancient world. He had at his command all the accumulated geographical information of that world. He was acquainted with mathematics. He shows, in his great work, the *Geographia* (168), a modern scientific mentality. Can we lightly assume that medieval sailors of the *fourteenth century*, without any of this knowledge, and without modern instruments except a rudimentary compass—and without mathematics—could produce a more scientific product?

Nordenskiöld felt that there had been in antiquity a geographic tradition superior to the one represented by Ptolemy. He thought that the "normal portolano" must have been in use *then* by sailors and navigators, and he answered the objection that there was no mention of such maps by the various classical writers by pointing out that in the Middle Ages, when the portolan charts were in use, they were never referred to by the Schoolmen, the academic scholars of that age. Both in ancient and in medieval times the academic mapmaker and the practical navigator were apparently poles apart. (See Figs. 5, 6, 7, 8.) Nordenskiöld was forced to leave the problem unsolved. Neither the medieval navigators nor the known Greek geographers could have drawn them. The Arabs, famous for their scientific achievements in the Early Middle Ages, apparently could not have drawn them either. Their maps are less accurate than those of Ptolemy. (See Fig. 5.) The evidence pointed to the origin of the portolanos in a culture with a higher level of technology than was attained in medieval or ancient times.

All the explanations of the origins of the portolan charts were opposed by Prince Youssouf Kamal, a modern Arab geographer, in rather violent language:

> Our incurable ignorance . . . as to the origin of the portolans or navigation charts known by this name, will lead us only from twilight into darkness. Everything that has been written on the history or the origin of these charts, and everything that will be said or written hereafter can be nothing but suppositions, arguments, hallucinations. . . . (107:2)

Prince Kamal also argued against the view that the lines on the charts were intended to facilitate navigation by the compass:

> As for the lines that we see intersecting each other, to form lozenges, or triangles, or squares: these same lines, I wish to say, dating from ancient Greek times, and going back to Timosthenes, or even earlier, were probably never drawn . . . to give . . . distances to the navigator. . . .
> The makers of portolans preserved this method, that they borrowed from the ancient Greeks or others, more probably and rather to facilitate the task of drawing a map, rather than to guide the navigator with such divisions. . . . (107:15–16)

In other words, the portolan design was an excellent design to guide a mapmaker either in constructing an original map or in copying one, because of the design's geometrical character.

Early in our investigation, three of my students, Leo Estes, Robert Woitkowski, and Loren Livengood, decided to take this question—the purpose of the lines on the portolan charts—as their special project. They journeyed to Hanover, New Hampshire, to inspect the medieval charts in the Dartmouth College Library. On their return, Loren Livengood, said he thought he knew how the charts had been constructed.

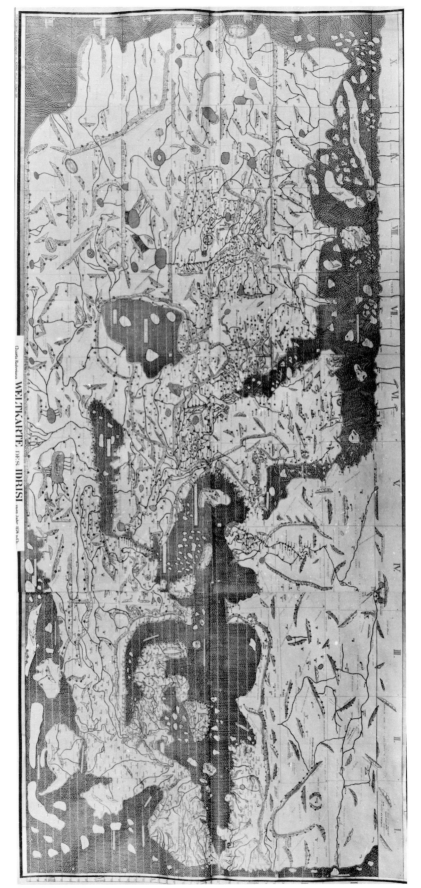

Figure 5. The World Map of Idrisi.

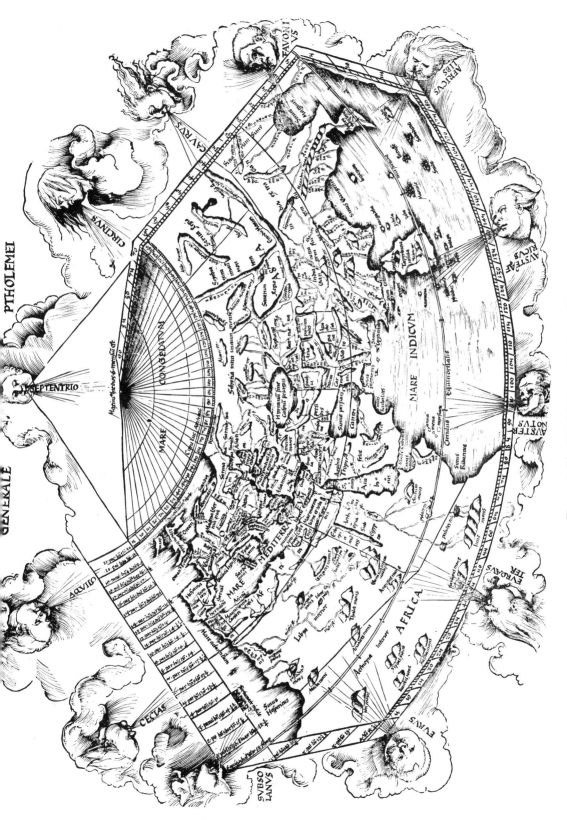

Figure 6. The World Map of Ptolemy. T

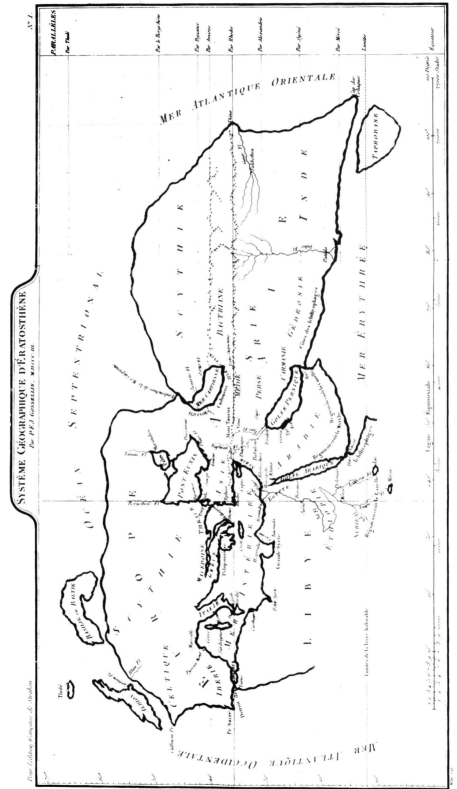

Figure 7. The World Map of Eratosthenes.

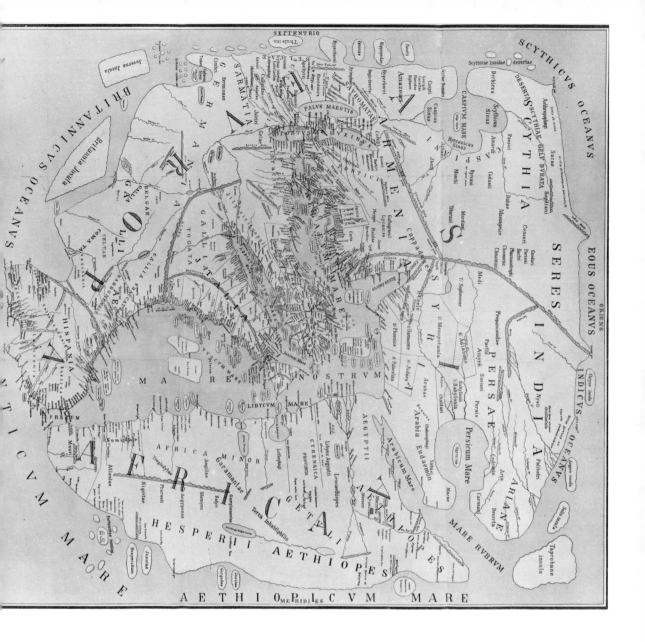

Figure 8. The World Map of Pomponius Mela.

The problem was to find out, from the lines actually found on the charts, whether it might be possible to construct a grid of lines of latitude and longitude such as are found on modern maps. In other words, the problem was to see if this portolan system could be *converted* to the modern one.

Livengood's approach was simple. Without actually realizing the importance of his choice, he put himself in the position of a mapmaker rather than of a navigator. That is, he saw the problem not as one of finding a harbor, but of actually constructing a map. He had never heard of Prince Kamal, but he was adopting the

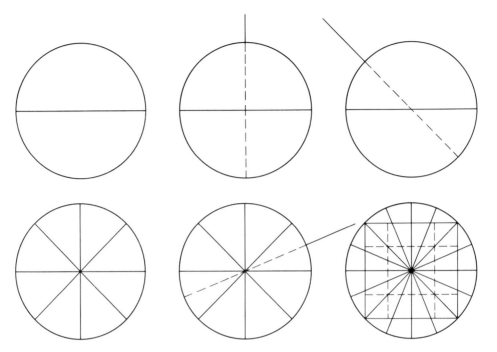

Figure 9. The Eight-Wind System of the Portolan Charts. *Rectangular grids could be constructed with the circular or polar type of projection used in the Piri Re'is and other portolan charts. In this diagram we see how Livengood, Estes, and Woitkowski solved the problem of the construction of the main grid of the Piri Re'is Map (see Fig. 12).*

Prince's view of the purpose of the lines. The probable procedure of the mapmaker, Livengood speculated, was first to pick a convenient center for his map and then determine a radius long enough to cover the area to be mapped. With this center and radius the mapmaker would draw a circle.

Then he would bisect his circle, again and again, until he had sixteen lines from the center to the periphery at equal angles of 22½°. (These could be further bisected, resulting in thirty-two points on the periphery, at angles of 11¼°.)

The third step would be to connect points on the perimeter to make a square, with four different squares possible.

The fourth step would be to choose one of the squares, and draw lines connecting the opposite points, thus making a map grid of lines at right angles to each other. (Fig. 9.)

Now, although the scholars agreed that the portolan charts had no lines of latitude and longitude, it stood to reason that if one of the vertical lines (such as the line through the center) was drawn on True North, then it would be a meridan of longitude, and any line at right angles to it would be a parallel of latitude. Assuming that a projection similar to the famous Mercator projection, in which all meridians and parallels are straight lines crossing at right angles, underlay these maps (see Fig. 10), then all parallel vertical lines would be meridians of longitude, and all horizontal lines would be parallels of latitude. (Notes 3 and 4.)

Applying this idea to the Piri Re'is Map, we could see that the mapmaker had selected a center, which he had placed somewhere far to the east of the torn edge of our fragment of the world map,* and had then drawn a circle around it. He had bisected the circle four times, drawing sixteen lines from the center to the perimeter, at angles of 22½°, and he had also drawn in all the four possible squares, perhaps with the intention of using different squares for drawing grids for different parts of the map, where it might be necessary to have different Norths.† It was Estes who originally pointed out to us that the portolan design had the potentiality of having several different Norths on the same map.

Now the next question was: Which was the right square for us? That is, which (if any) of the squares that could be made out of the design of the Piri Re'is Map was correctly oriented to North, South, East, and West?

Estes found the solution. Comparing the Piri Re'is Map with a modern map (Figs. 10, 11, 12) he found a meridian on the modern map that seemed to coincide very nearly with a line on the Piri Re'is Map—a line running north and south close to the African coast, in about 20° W longitude, leaving the Cape Verde Islands to the west, the Canaries to the east, and the Azores to the west.

Estes suggested that this line might be our prime meridian, a line drawn on True North. All lines parallel to this (assuming, of course, that the underlying projection resembled in some degree the Mercator projection) would also be meridians of longitude; all lines at right angles would be parallels of latitude. The meridians and parallels thus identified, provisionally, on the Piri Re'is Map, formed a rectangular grid, as shown in Fig. 12.

The only difference between this large rectangular grid actually found on the Piri Re'is Map and the grids of modern maps was that the latter all carry registers of degrees of latitude and longitude, with parallels and meridians at equal intervals, usually five or ten degrees apart. We could convert the Piri Re'is grid into a modern grid if we could find the precise latitudes and longitudes of its parallels and meridians. This, we found, meant finding the exact latitude and longitude of each of the five projection centers in the Atlantic Ocean, through which the lines of Piri Re'is' grid ran.

At the beginning of our inquiry I had noticed that these five projection centers had been placed at equal intervals on the perimeter of a circle, though the circle itself had been erased (Fig. 11). I had also noticed that converging lines were extended from these points to the center, beyond the eastern edge of the map. This, it seemed to me at the time, was a geometrical construction that should be

---

*The complete map included Africa and Asia. It was, according to Piri Re'is, a map "of the seven seas" (see Note 2). In addition to the eastern part, there was also originally a northern section.

†Since the earth is round, and the portolan design was apparently based on a flat projection (that is, apparently on plane geometry) which could not take account of the spherical surface, the parallel meridians would deviate further and further from True North the farther they were removed from the center of the map. The portolan design could compensate for this, however, as we shall see in the next chapter, by using different Norths.

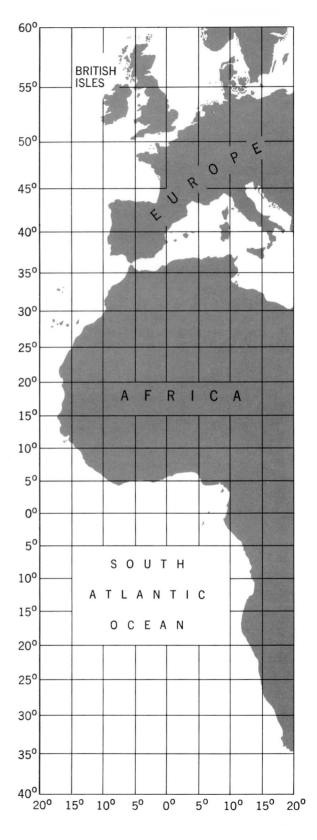

Figure 10. The Eastern Shores of the Atlantic on the Mercator Projection. *Compare the meridian of 20° W. with the "Prime Meridian" of the Piri Re'is Map (Fig. 18).*

soluble by trigonometry. I did not then know that, in the opinion of all the experts, there was no trigonometrical foundation to the protolan charts.

Not knowing that there was not supposed to be any mathematical basis for the potolanos, we now made the search for it our main business. I realized from the start that to accomplish this we would have to discover first the precise location of the center of the map, and then the precise length of the radius of the circle drawn by the mapmaker. I was fortunate in having a mathematician friend, Richard W. Strachan, at the Massachusetts Institute of Technology. He told me that, if we could obtain this information for him, he might be able, by trigonometry, to find the precise positions of the five projection points in the Atlantic Ocean on the Piri Re'is Map, in terms of modern latitude and longitude. This would enable us to draw a modern grid on the map, and thus check every detail of it accurately. Only in this way, of course, could we verify the claim of Mallery regarding the Antarctic sector of the map.

The search for the center of the map lasted about three years. We thought from the beginning that the lines extending from the five projection points probably met in Egypt. We used various methods to project the lines to the point where they would meet. Our first guess for the center of the map was the city of Alexandria. This appealed to me because Alexandria was long the center of the science and learning of the ancient world. It seemed likely that, if they were drawing a world map, the Alexandrian geographers might naturally make their own city its center.

However, this guess proved to be wrong. A contradiction appeared. The big wind rose in the North Atlantic looked as if it were meant to lie on the Tropic of Cancer. One of the lines from this center evidently was directed toward the center of the map. But we noticed that this line was at right angles to our prime meridian. This meant, of course, that it was a parallel of latitude. Now, the Tropic of Cancer is at 23½°N latitude, and therefore the parallel from the wind rose would reach a center in Egypt at 23½°N. But Alexandria is not at that latitude at all. It lies in 31°N. Therefore Alexandria could not be the center of our circle.

We looked at the map of ancient Egypt to find, if we could, a suitable city on the Tropic of Cancer that might serve as a center for the map. (We were still attached to the idea that the center of our map should be some important place, such as a city. Later, we were emancipated from this erroneous notion.)

Looking along the Tropic of Cancer, we found the ancient city of Syene, lying just north of the Tropic, near the present city of Assuan, where the great dam was built. Now we recalled the scientific feat of Eratosthenes, the Greek astronomer and geographer of the 3rd century B.C., who measured the circumference of the earth by taking account of the angle of the sun at noon as simultaneously observed at Alexandria and at Syene.

We were happy to change our working theory and adopt Syene as the center of the map. With the help of hindsight, we could now see how reasonable it was to place the center of the map on the Tropic, an astronomically determined line on the surface of the earth. The poles, the tropics, and the equator can be exactly determined by celestial observations, and they have been the bases of mapmaking in all

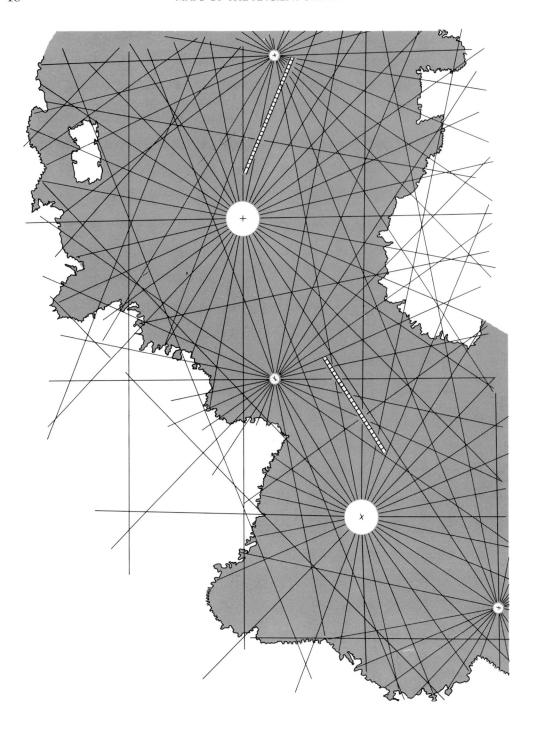

Figure 11. The Piri Re'is Map: the lines of the Portolan design traced from the Facsimile.

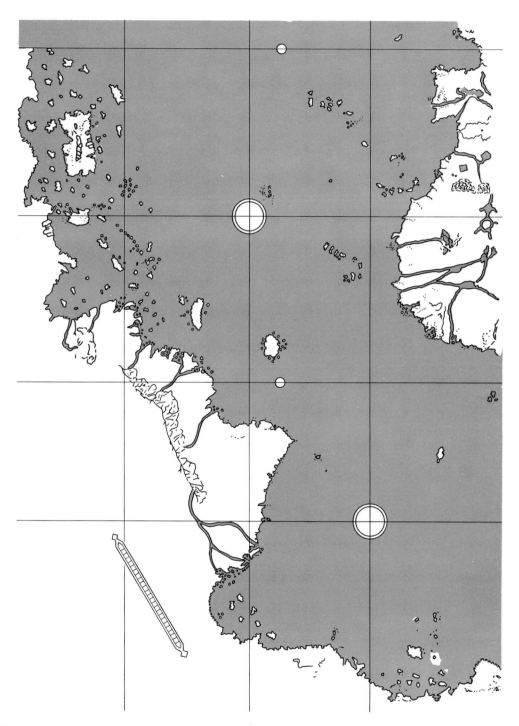

Figure 12. The Piri Re'is Map: the main grid of the Portolan design traced from the Facsimile.

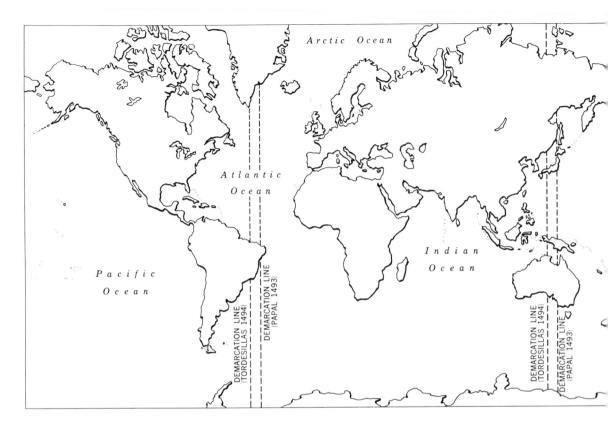

Figure 13. The Papal Demarcation Lines of 1493 and 1494.

times. Syene, too, was an important city, suitable for a center. A good "proof" of this center for the map was constructed by two students, Lee Spencer and Ruth Baraw. Only at the end of our inquiry did we find that Syene was not, after all, exactly the center.

The matter of the radius caused us much more trouble. At first, there appeared to be absolutely no way of discovering its precise length. However, some of my students started talking about the Papal Demarcation Line—the line drawn by Pope Alexander VI in 1493, and revised the next year, to divide the Portuguese from the Spanish possessions in the newly discovered regions (Fig. 13). On the Piri Re'is Map there was a line running north and south, passing through the northern wind rose and then through Brazil at a certain distance west of the Atlantic coast. This line appeared to be identical, or nearly identical, with the Second Demarcation Line (of 1494), which also passed through Brazil. Piri Re'is had mentioned the Demarcation Line on his map, and we reached the conclusion that this line, if it was the Demarcation Line, could give us the longitude of the northern wind rose and thus the length of the radius of the circle with its center at Syene.

The Papal Demarcation Line of 1494 is supposed to have been drawn north and south at a distance of 370 leagues west of the Cape Verde Islands. Modern scholars have calculated that it was at 46° 30' W (140:369). We therefore assigned this

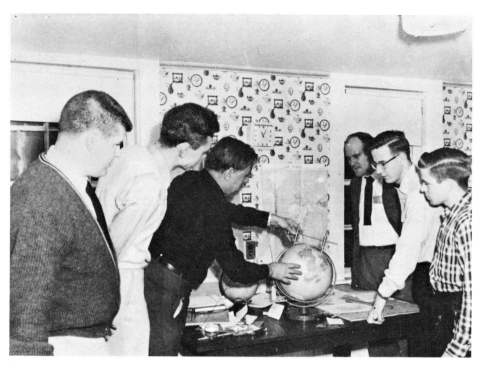

Figure 14. An Argument over the Piri Re'is Map: *left to right, Leo Estes, Frank Ryan, Charles Hapgood, Clayton Dow, John Malsbenden, George Batchelder.*

longitude to the northern wind rose, and thus obtained our first approximate guess as to the length of the radius of the circle. According to this finding the radius was 79° in length (32½ plus 46½). This result was wrong by 9½°, as we later discovered, but it was close enough for a starter.

At this stage, our findings were too uncertain to justify an attempt to apply trigonometry to the problem. Instead, we tested our results directly on an accurate globe provided by Estes. We made our test by actually drawing a circle, with Syene as the center, and the indicated radius, and then laying out the lines from the center to the perimeter, 22½° apart, beginning with one to the equator. The result seemed pretty good, and we were sure we were on the right track.

It was lucky that we got so far before we discovered that our interpretation of the Demarcation Line on the map was wrong. This fact was finally brought home to us by two other students, John F. Malsbenden and George Batchelder (Fig. 14). They had been bending over the map during one of our long night sessions when suddenly Malsbenden straightened up and exclaimed indignantly that all our work had been wasted, that the line we had picked out was not the right one. In an inscription on his map which we had overlooked Piri Re'is had himself indicated an entirely different line. It was the first line, the line of 1493, and it did not go through the wind rose at all. The mistake, however, had served its purpose. It was true enough that the line we had picked out on the Piri Re'is Map represented neither line; nevertheless it was close enough to the position of the Demarcation Line of 1494 to give us a first clue to the longitude.

Another error that turned out to be very profitable was the assumption we made, during a certain period of time, that perhaps our map was oriented not to true North, but to magnetic North. Later, we were to find that many, if not most, of the portolanos were indeed oriented, very roughly, to magnetic North. Some writers on the subject had argued, as already mentioned, that the lines on the portolan charts were intended only for help in finding compass directions, and were therefore necessarily drawn on Magnetic North. (89, 116, 143, 179, 199, 200, 223)

In the interest of maximum precision, I wanted to find out how the question of Magnetic North might affect the longitude of the Second Demarcation Line, which now determined our radius. If the Demarcation Line lay at 46° 30′ W at the Cape Verde Islands, it would, with a magnetic orientation, lie somewhat farther west at the latitude of the northern wind rose, and this would affect the radius. We spent time trying to calculate how much farther west the line would be. This in turn involved research to discover the amount of the compass declination (the difference between true and magnetic North) today in those parts of the Atlantic, and speculation as to what might have been the amount of the variation in the days of Piri Re'is or in ancient times. We found ourselves in a veritable Sargasso Sea of uncertainties and frustrations.

Fortunately, we were rescued from this dead end by still another wrong idea. I noticed that the circle drawn with Syene as a center, and with a radius to the intersection of the supposed Second Demarcation Line with the northern wind rose, appeared to pass through the present location of the Magnetic Pole. We then allowed ourselves to suppose (nothing being impossible) that somebody in ancient times had known the location of the Magnetic Pole and had deliberately selected a radius that would pass through it. Shaky as this assumption might have been, it was at least better than the Demarcation Line, since in ancient times nobody could have had an idea of a line that was only drawn in 1494 A.D. The Magnetic Pole is, however, very unsatisfactory as a working assumption because it does not stay in one place. It is always moving, and where it may have been in past times is anybody's guess.

In the middle of this I read Nordenskiöld's statement that the portolan charts were drawn on true North, and not on magnetic North (146:17). In this Nordenskiöld was really mistaken, unless he meant that the charts had *originally* been drawn on true North and then had been *reoriented* in a magnetic direction. But his statement impressed us, and then I observed, looking again at the globe with our circle drawn on it, that the circle that passed through the magnetic Pole also passed very close indeed to the true Pole. Now, you may be sure, we abandoned our magnetic theory in a hurry, and adopted the working assumption that perhaps someone in ancient times knew the true position of the Pole, and drew his radius from Syene on the Tropic of Cancer to the Pole. Again, hindsight came to our support. As in the case of the Tropic of Cancer, the Pole was astronomically determined: It was a precisely located point on the earth's surface.

It appeared to us that we had swum through a murky sea to a safe shore. We had now reached a point where it would be feasible to attempt a confirmation of the whole theory by trigonometry. We were proceeding now on the following assumptions: 1 The center of the projection was at Syene, on the Tropic of Cancer and at longitude 32½° East; 2 the radius of the circle was from the Tropic to the Pole, or 66½° in length, and 3 the horizontal line through the middle projection point on the map (Point III) was the true equator. By comparison with the African coast of the Gulf of Guinea, this line, indeed, appears to be very close to the position of the equator. Nevertheless, this was merely an assumption. We could not *know* that the ancient mapmaker had precise information as to the size of the earth, which would be necessary for correctly determining the positions of the poles and the equator. Such assumptions could be only working assumptions, to be used for purposes of experiment and discarded if they proved wrong. They were, however, the best assumptions we had been able to come up with so far, and assumptions we had to have to work with.

We could now give our mathematician, Strachan, the data he required for a mathematical analysis. He calculated the positions of all the five projection centers on the Piri Re'is Map to find their precise locations in latitude and longitude. (See Fig. 18 and Appendix.) He used our assumed equator as his base line of latitude. I have tried to explain this in Fig. 15. Here I have drawn the first radius from the center of the projection to the point of intersection of the assumed equator with the perimeter of the circle. I then have laid out the other radii at angles of 22½° northward and southward. In this way, our assumption that this equator is precisely correct controls the latitudes to be found for the other four projection points. The assumed equator is the base line for latitude, just as Syene is the reference point for longitude.

Strachan initially computed the positions of the five projection points both by spherical and by plane trigonometry. At each successive step, with varying assumptions as to the radius of the projection and the position of its center, he did the same thing, but in every case the calculations by plane trigonometry made sense—that is, plane trigonometry made it possible to construct grids that fitted the geography reasonably well, while the calculations by spherical trigonometry led to impossible contradictions. It became quite clear that our projection had been constructed by plane trigonometry. (See Note 5.)

Once we had precise latitudes and longitudes for the five centers on the Piri Re'is map, we could construct a modern type of grid. The total difference of latitude between Point I and Point V, divided by the millimeters that lay between them on our copy of the map (we used a tracing of our photograph of the map), gave us the length of the degree of latitude in millimeters. To check on any possible irregularities we measured the length of the degree of latitude separately between each two of the five points. We followed the same procedure with the longitude, as illustrated in Fig. 16. The lengths of the degrees of latitude and longitude turned out to be practically the same; we thus appeared to have a square grid. In doing

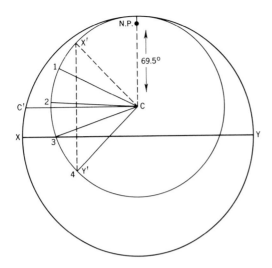

Figure 15. Diagram of the hypothetical Piri
Re'is Projection, based on the Equator. (*see
the calculations, p. 233*)
*x − y: equator according to Piri Re'is*
*c − 3: first rumb drawn from the centre*
*c − c': the Tropic of Cancer*
*x' − y': a meridian*

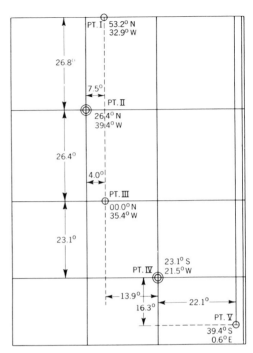

Figure 16. Mode of Calculating the Length of
the Degree for the Piri Re'is Map.

this we disregarded the scales actually drawn on the map, since there was no way
of knowing when or by whom they had been drawn, or what units of distance they
had represented.

The next step was to learn how to draw a grid, not at all an easy task. It was not a
particularly complicated task, but it demanded a very high level of accuracy and an
extreme degree of patience. Fortunately, one of my students, Frank Ryan, was
qualified for the job. He had served in the Air Force, had been stationed at Westover Air Force Base in Massachusetts, and had been assigned to the Cartographic
Section of the 8th Reconnaissance Technical Squadron, under a remarkable officer,
Captain Lorenzo W. Burroughs. The function of the unit at that time was to
prepare maps for the use of the United States Air Force's Strategic Air Command,
known as SAC. Later, it was attached to the 8th Air Force. Needless to say, the
personnel of that unit were competent to serve the demanding requirements of the
Air Force, as far as mapmaking was concerned, and Frank Ryan had been inten-
sively trained in the necessary techniques. He had had the experience of being
drafted into the Air Force: now he had the experience of being drafted again, to
draw our grid.

Later Ryan introduced me to Captain Burroughs, and I visited Westover Air
Force Base. The captain offered us his fullest cooperation in preparing a draft map
with the solution of the projection, and virtually put his staff at our disposal. The
co-operation between us lasted more than two years, and a number of officers and
men gave us very valuable assistance. Later both Captain Burroughs and his com-

manding officer, Colonel Harold Z. Ohlmeyer reviewed and endorsed our work (Note 19).

The procedure for drawing the grid was as follows: All the meridians were drawn parallel with the prime meridian, at intervals of five degrees, and all parallels were drawn parallel with the assumed equator, at intervals of five degrees. These lines did not turn out in all cases to be precisely parallel with the other lines of the big grid traced from the Piri Re'is Map, but this was understandable. The effect might have resulted from warping of the map, or from carelessness in copying the lines from the ancient source map Piri Re'is used. We had to allow for a margin of error here, for we could not be sure that no small errors had crept in when the equator or the prime meridian was recopied. Here, as in other respects, we simply had to do the best we could with what we had.

When the grid was drawn, we were ready to test it. We identified all the places we could on the map and made a table comparing their latitudes and longitudes on the Piri Re'is Map with their positions on the modern map. The errors in individual positions were noted and averages of them made (Table 1). The Table is, of course, the test of our solution of the Piri Re'is projection.

But I must not get ahead of my story. We found that some of the positions on the Piri Re'is Map were very accurate, and some were far off. Gradually we became aware of the reasons for some of the inaccuracies in the map. We discovered that the map was a composite, made up by piecing together many maps of local areas (perhaps drawn at different times by different people), and that errors had been made in combining the original maps. There was nothing extraordinary about this. It would have been an enormous task, requiring large amounts of money, to survey and map all at once the vast area covered by the Piri Re'is Map. Undoubtedly local maps had been made first, and these were gradually combined, at different times, into larger and larger maps, until finally a world map was attempted. This long process of combining the local maps, so far as the surviving section of the Piri Re'is Map is concerned, had been finished in ancient times. This theory will, I believe, be established by what follows. What Piri Re'is apparently did was to combine this compilation with still other maps—which were probably themselves combinations—to make his world map.

The students were responsible for discovering many of the errors. Lee Spencer and Ruth Baraw examined the east coast of South America with great care and found that the compiler had actually omitted about 900 miles of that coastline. It was discovered that the Amazon River had been drawn twice on the map. We concluded that the compiler must have had two different source maps of the Amazon, drawn by different people at different times, and that he made the mistake of thinking they were two different rivers. We also found that besides the equator upon which we had based our projection (so far as latitude was concerned) there was evidence that somebody had calculated the position of the equator differently, so that there were really two equators. Ultimately we were able to explain this conflict. Other important errors included the omission of part of the northern coast of South America, and the duplication of a part of that coast, and of part of the coasts of the Caribbean Sea. A number of geographical localities thus appear twice on the map, but they do not appear on the same projection. For most of the Caribbean area the direction of North is nearly at right angles to the North of the main part of the map.

As we identified more and more places on our grid, and averaged their errors in position, we found all over the map some common errors that indicated something was wrong with the projection. We concluded that there must still be errors either in the location of the center of the map, in the length of the radius, or both. There was no way to discover these probable errors except by trying out all reasonable alternatives by a process of trial and error. This was time consuming and a tax on the patience of all of us. With every change in the assumed center of the map, or in the assumed radius, Strachan had to repeat the calculations, and once more determine the positions of the five projection points. Then the grid had to be redrawn and all the tables done over. As each grid in turn revealed some further unidentified error, new assumptions had to be adopted, to an accompaniment of sighs and groans. We had the satisfaction, however, of noting a gradual diminution of the errors that suggested that we were approaching our goal.

Among the various alternatives to Syene as the center of the map we tried out, at one stage, the ancient city of Berenice on the Red Sea. This was the great shipping port for Egypt in the Alexandrian Age, and it, too, lay on the Tropic of Cancer. Berenice seemed to be a very logical center for the map because of its maritime importance. We studied the history of Berenice, and everything seemed to point to this place as our final solution. But then, as in an Agatha Christie murder mystery, the favorite suspect was proved innocent. The tables showed the assumption to be wrong, for in this case the errors were even increased. We had to give up Berenice, with special regrets on my part because of the beauty of the name.

Now we went back to Syene, but with a difference. The tables showed that the remaining error in the location of the center of the map was small. Therefore we tried out centers near Syene, north, east, south and west, gradually diminishing the distances, until at last we used the point at the intersection of the meridian of Alexandria, at 30° E, with the Tropic. This finally turned out to be correct.

Immediately hindsight began to make disagreeable noises. Why hadn't we thought of this before? Why hadn't we tumbled to this truth in the beginning? It combined all the most reasonable elements: the use of the Tropic, based on astronomy, and the use of the meridian of Alexandria, the capital of ancient science. Later we were to find that all the Greek geographers based their maps on the meridian of Alexandria.

Remaining errors in the tables suggested something wrong with the radius. We knew, of course, that our assumption that the mapmaker had precise knowledge of the size of the earth was doubtful. It was much more likely that he had made some sort of mistake. We therefore tried various lengths. We shortened the radius a few degrees, on the assumption that the mapmaker might have underestimated the size of the earth, as Ptolemy had. This only increased the errors. Then we tried lengthening the radius. The entire process of trial and error was repeated with radii

7°, 5°, 2°, and 1° too long. Finally we got our best results with a radius extended three degrees. This meant that our radius was not 66.5°, the correct number of degrees from the Tropic to the Pole, but 69.5°. This error amounted to an error of 4½% in overestimating the size of the earth.

A matter of great importance, which we did not realize at all at the time, was that we were, in fact, finding the length of the radius (and therefore the length of the degree) with reference mainly to longitude. I paid much more attention to the average errors of longitude than I did to the errors of latitude. I was especially interested in the longitudes along the African and South American coasts. Our radius was selected to reduce longitude errors to a minimum while not unduly increasing latitude errors. As it turned out, this emphasis on longitude was very fortunate, for it was to lead us to a later discovery of considerable importance.

With regard to the overestimating of the circumference of the earth, there was one geographer in ancient times who made an overestimate of about this amount. This was Eratosthenes. Does this mean that Eratosthenes himself may have been our mapmaker? Probably not. We have seen that the Piri Re'is Map was based on a source map originally drawn with plane trigonometry. Trigonometry may not have been known in Greece in the time of Eratosthenes. It has been supposed that it was invented by Hipparchus, who lived about a century later. Hipparchus discovered the precession of the equinoxes, invented or at least described mathematical map projections, and is generally supposed to have developed both plane and spherical trigonometry (58:49; 175:86).* He accepted Eratosthenes' estimate of the size of the earth (184:415) though he criticized Eratosthenes for not using mathematics in drawing his maps.

We must interfere in this dispute between Hipparchus and Eratosthenes to raise an interesting point. Did Hipparchus criticize his predecessor for not using mathematically constructed projections on which to place his geographical data? If so, his criticism looks unreasonable. The construction of such projections requires trigonometry. If Hipparchus himself developed trigonometry, how could he have blamed Eratosthenes for not using it a century before? Hipparchus' own books have been lost, and we really have no way of knowing whether the later writers who attributed trigonometry to Hipparchus were correct. Perhaps all they meant, or all *he* meant or said in his works, was that he had *discovered* trigonometry. He might have discovered it in the ancient Chaldean books whose star data made it possible for him to discover the precession of the equinoxes.

But this is speculation, and I have a feeling that it is very much beside the point. If Hipparchus did in fact develop both plane and spherical trigonometry, the Piri Re'is Map, and the other maps to be considered in this book, are evidence suggesting that he only rediscovered what had been very well known thousands of years earlier. Many of these maps must have been composed long before Hipparchus. But it is not possible to see how they could have been drawn as accurately as they were unless trigonometry was used.

*However, a knowledge of plane trigonometry has been attributed to Appolonius, an earlier Greek scientist, by Van der Waerden (216). The date of its origin appears, then, unknown.

We have additional confirmation that the Piri Re'is projection was based on Eratosthenes' estimate of the size of the earth. The Greeks had a measure of length, which they called the stadium. Greek writers, therefore, give distances in stadia. Our problem has been that they never defined this measure of length. We have no definite idea, therefore, of what the stadium was in terms of feet or meters. Estimates have varied from about 350 feet to over 600. Further, we have no reason to suppose that the stadium had a standard length. It may have differed in different Greek states and also from century to century.

A great authority on the history of science, the late Dr. George Sarton of Harvard, devoted much attention to trying to estimate the length of the stadium used by Eratosthenes himself at Alexandria in the 3rd century B.C. He concluded that the "Eratosthenian stadium" amounted to 559 feet (184:105)†

The solution of the Piri Re'is projection has enabled us to check this. Presumably, it proves the amount of the overestimate of the earth's circumference to be 4½% (or very nearly that). Eratosthenes gave the circumference of the earth as 252,000 stadia. We checked the length of his stadium by taking the true mean circumference of the earth (24,800 miles), increasing this by 4½%, turning the product into feet, and dividing the result by 252,000. We got a stadium 547 feet long.

Now, if we compare our result with that of Sarton, we see that there is a difference of only 12 feet, or about 2%. It would seem—again by hindsight—that we could have saved all our trouble by merely adopting Eratosthenes' circumference and Sarton's stadium. We could then have drawn a grid so nearly like the one we have that the naked eye could not have detected the difference.

The next stage, which came very late, was our realization that if Eratosthenes' estimate of the circumference of the earth was used for drawing Piri Re'is' source map, and if it was 4½% off, then the positions we had found by trigonometry for the five projection points on the map were somewhat in error both in latitude and longitude. It was now necessary to redraw the whole grid to correct it for the error of Eratosthenes. We found that this resulted in reducing all the longitude errors until they nearly vanished.

This was a startling development. It could only mean that the Greek geographers of Alexandria, when they prepared their world map using the circumference of Eratosthenes, had in front of them source maps that had been drawn *without the Eratosthenian error,* that is, apparently without any discernible error at all. We shall see further evidence of this, evidence suggesting that the people who originated the maps possessed a more advanced science than that of the Greeks.

But now another perplexing problem appeared. The reduction of the longitude errors left latitude errors that averaged considerably larger. Since accurate longitude is much more difficult to find than accurate latitude, this was not reasonable. There had to be some further undetected error in our projection.

We started looking for this error, and we found one. That is, we found an error.

---

†That is, there were about 9.45 Eratosthenian stadia to a mile of 5,280 feet, which figures out to 558.88 feet per stadium.

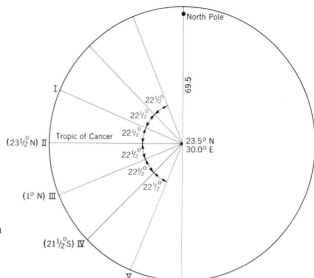

Figure 17. Diagram of the hypothetical Piri Re'is Projection, based on the North Pole. (*see the calculations, p. 234*)

It was not quite the right one; it did not solve our problem, but it helped us on the way. As already mentioned, we had found the positions of the five projection points by laying out a line first from the center of the projection to the intersection of the circle with the line on the Piri Re'is map running horizontally through the middle projection point, Point III, assuming this to be the equator. We had used this assumed equator as our base line for latitude. (See Fig. 15.)

When we laid out the projection in this way, we had not yet realized that the mapmaker was much more likely to have drawn his first radius from the center of the map directly to the pole and not to the equator. (See Fig. 17.) If he did this, since his length for the degree was wrong, then his equator must be off a number of degrees. This required new calculations, and still another grid. The new calculations showed that the line we had taken for the equator actually lay in 3.15°S. (See page 235.)

At first, this new grid seemed to make matters worse, especially on the coast of Africa. The equator seemed to pass too near the Guinea coast. My heart sank when this result became apparent, but I am thankful that I persisted in redrawing the grid despite the apparent increase in the errors, for the result was a discovery of the very greatest importance.

At first I thought that the African coast (and that of Europe) had simply been wrongly placed too far south on the projection. But I soon saw that if the African coast appeared too far south on the corrected projection, the French coast was in more correct latitude than before. There was simply, I first concluded, an error in scale. Piri Re'is, or the ancient mapmaker, had used too large a scale for Europe and Africa. But why, in that case, though latitudes were thrown out, did longitudes remain correct?

I finally decided to construct an empirical scale for the whole coast from the Gulf of Guinea to Brest to see how accurate the latitudes were relative to one another. The result showed that the latitude errors along the coasts were minor. It was obvious that the original mapmakers had observed their latitudes extremely well. From this it became apparent that those who had originally drawn this map of these coasts had used a different length for the degree of latitude than for the degree of longitude. In other words, the geographers who designed the square portolan grid for which we had discovered the trigonometric solution, had apparently applied their projection to maps that had originally been drawn with another projection.

What kind of projection was it? Obviously it was one that took account of the fact that, northward and southward from the equator, the degree of longitude in fact diminished in length as the meridians drew closer toward the poles. It is possible to represent this by curving the meridians, and we see this done on many modern maps. It is also possible to represent this by keeping the meridians straight and spacing the parallels of latitude farther and farther apart as the distance from the equator increases. The essential point is to maintain the ratio between the lengths of the degrees of latitude and longitude at every point on the earth's surface.

Geographers will, of course, instantly recognize the projection I have described here. It is the Mercator projection, supposedly invented by Gerard Mercator and used by him in his Atlas of 1569 (Note 4). For a time we considered the possibility that this projection might have been invented in ancient times, forgotten, and then rediscovered in the 16th century by Mercator (Note 13). Further investigation showed that the device of spreading the parallels was found on other maps, which will be discussed below.

I was very reluctant to accept without further proof the suggestion that the Mercator projection (in the full meaning of that term) had been known in ancient times. I considered the possibility that the difference in the length of the degree of latitude on the Piri Re'is Map might be *arbitrary*. That is, I thought it possible that the mapmaker, aware of the curvature of the earth, but unable to take account of it as is done in the Mercator projection by spherical trigonometry, had simply adopted a *mean* length for the degree of latitude, and applied this length over the whole map without changing the length progressively with each degree from the equator.

Strangely enough, shortly after this, I found that, according to Nordenskiöld, this is precisely what Ptolemy had done on his maps (see Note 7). In Nordenskiöld's comparison of the maps of the Mediterranean and Black Sea regions as drawn by Ptolemy and as shown on the Dulcert Portolano (Fig. 3), we see that he has drawn the lines of Ptolemy's projection in this way. This is, of course, another indication of the ancient origin of Piri Re'is' source map.

This is not quite the end of the story. We shall see, in subsequent consideration of the De Canerio Map of 1502, that the oblong grid, used by Ptolemy and found on the Piri Re's Map, has its origin in an ancient use of spherical trigonometry.

These successive discoveries finally enabled us to draw a modern grid for most of the Piri Re'is map as shown in Figure 18.

# III   The Piri Re'is Map in Detail

IN UNDERTAKING a detailed examination of the Piri Re'is Map of 1513, I shall break down the map into sections representing originally separate source maps of smaller areas, which appear to have been combined in a general map by the Greek geographers of Alexandria.

For each of the source maps, which I shall refer to as "component maps," since they are the parts of the whole, I will identify such geographical points as are evident in themselves, or are rendered plausible by their position on the trigonometric grid, and will find their errors of location.

Since in some cases the component maps were not correctly placed on the general map, we have two sorts of errors: those due to mistakes in compilation of the local maps into the general map and those due to mistakes in the original component maps. These can be distinguished because if a component map is misplaced, all the features of that map will be misplaced in the same direction and by the same amount. If the general error is discovered and corrected, then the remaining errors will be errors of the original local maps. We have discovered that in most cases the errors on the Piri Re'is Map are due to mistakes in the compilation of the world map, presumably in Alexandrian times, since it appears, as we shall see, that Piri Re'is could not have put them together at all. The component maps, coming from a far greater antiquity, were more accurate. The Piri Re'is Map appears, therefore, to be evidence of a decline of science from remote antiquity to classical times.

## 1.   The western coasts of Africa and Europe, from Cape Palmas to Brest, including the North Atlantic islands and some islands of the South Atlantic.

Longitudes, as well as latitudes, along the coasts are seen to be remarkably accurate (see Table 1). The accuracy extends also to the North Atlantic island groups as a whole, with an exception in the case of Madeira.

The accuracy of longitude along the coast of Africa, where it is greatest, might be attributed simply to our assumptions as to the center and radius of the projection,

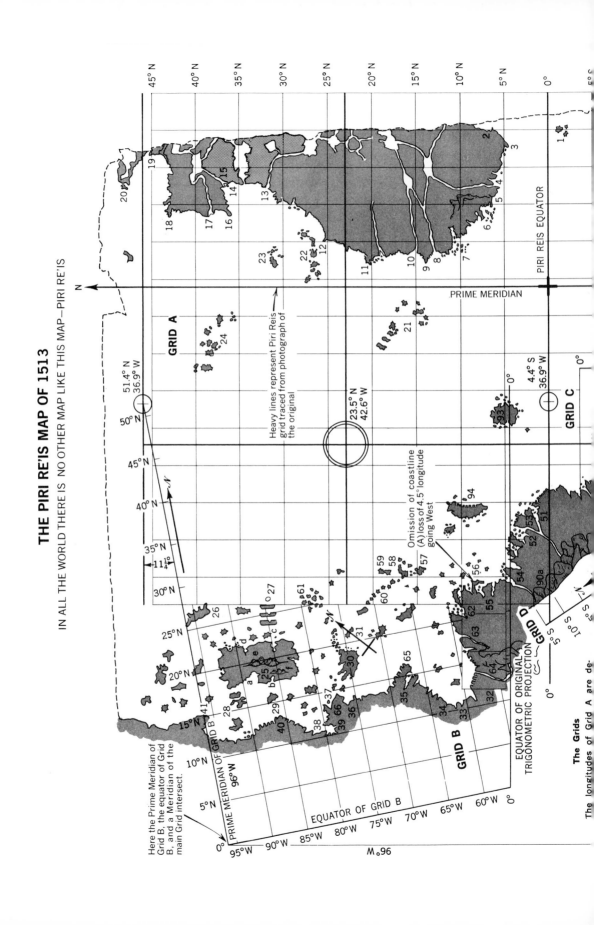

# THE PIRI RE'IS MAP OF 1513

IN ALL THE WORLD THERE IS NO OTHER MAP LIKE THIS MAP—PIRI RE'IS

GRID A

Heavy lines represent Piri Reis grid traced from photograph of the original

51.4° N
36.9° W

23.5° N
42.6° W

Here the Prime Meridian of Grid B, the equator of Grid B, and a Meridian of the main Grid intersect.

PRIME MERIDIAN

PIRI REIS EQUATOR

Omission of coastline (A) loss of 4.5° longitude going West

4.4° S
36.9° W

GRID C

0°

GRID D

EQUATOR OF ORIGINAL
TRIGONOMETRIC PROJECTION

GRID B

PRIME MERIDIAN OF GRID B
96° W

EQUATOR OF GRID B

96° W

**The Grids**

The longitudes of Grid A are de-

assumption that the horizontal line through Point III of the portolan design was supposed to be the equator; and (b) by the apparently arbitrary increase in the distance between the parallels, a device to take account of the curvature of the earth that has been attributed to Ptolemy (Note 9). These changes were no doubt the work of later geographers.

The northward shift of the geography of the main grid had the effect of pushing the geography of Grid B **westward** about 4°, thus increasing the longitude errors of that part of the map.

Grid B is determined both as to latitude and longitude by the trigonometry of the projection based on the pole. It may be considered as a part of the main grid that has been **swung** through an arc of about 78¾ degrees. Both the prime meridian and the equator of Grid B can be considered extensions of the lines of Grid A.

For a list of the numbered geographical points, see below. For a list of the numbered geographical points with comparative tables of their latitudes and longitudes, see Table 1.

Grids C and D represent errors in compilation, Grid C having an error in scale, and Grid D being unrelated to the trigonometric projection.

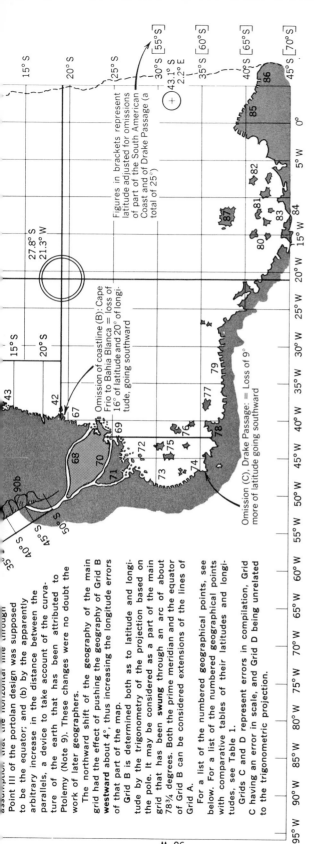

Omission of coastline (B): Cape Frio to Bahia Blanca = loss of 16° of latitude and 20° of longitude, going southward

Omission (C), Drake Passage: = Loss of more of latitude going southward

Figures in brackets represent latitude adjusted for omissions of part of the South American Coast and of Drake Passage (a total of 25°)

43.1° S
2.2° E

27.8° S
21.3° W

1. Annobon Islands
2. Cavally River
3. Cape Palmas
4. St. Paul River
5. Mano River
6. Freetown
7. Bijagos Islands
8. Gambia River
9. Dakar
10. Senegal River
11. Cape Blanc
12. Cape Juby
13. Sebu River
14. Gibraltar
15. Guadalquivir River
16. Cape St. Vincent
17. Tagus River
18. Cape Finisterre
19. Gironde River
20. Brest

21. Cape Verde Islands
22. The Canary Islands
23. Madeira Islands
24. The Azores
25. Cuba
  (a) Gulf of Guacanayabo
  (b) Guantanamo Bay
  (c) Bahia de Nipe
  (d) Bahia de la Gloria
  (e) Camaguey Mountains
  (f) Sierra Maestra Mountains
26. Andros Island
27. San Salvador (Watling)
28. Isle of Pines
29. Jamaica
30. Hispaniola
  (Santo Domingo, Haiti)
31. Puerto Rico
32. Rio Moroni
33. Corantijn River

34. Essequibo River
35. Orinoco River
36. Gulf of Venezuela
37. Pt. Gallinas
38. Magdalena River
39. Gulf of Uraba
40. Honduras (Cape Gracias a Dios)
41. Yucatan
42. Cape Frio
43. Salvador
44. San Francisco River
45. Recife (Pernambuco)
46. Cape Sao Rocque
47. Rio Parahyba
48. Bahia Sao Marcos
49. Serras de Gurupi, de Desordam, de Negro
50. The Amazon (No. 1)
51. The Amazon (No. 2) Para River
52. The Amazon (No. 2) western mouth

53. Island of Marajo
54. Essequibo (Demarara) River
55. Mouths of the Orinoco
56. Peninsula of Paria
57. Martinique
58. Guadaloupe
59. Antigua
60. Leeward Islands
61. Virgin Islands
62. Gulf of Venezuela
63. Magdalena River
64. Atrato River
65. Honduras (Cape Gracias a Dios)
66. Yucatan
67. Bahia Blanca
68. Rio Colorado
69. Gulf of San Mathias
70. Rio Negro (Argentina)
71. Rio Chubua
72. Gulf of San Gorge

73. Bahia Grande
74. Cape San Diego (near the Horn)
75. Falkland Islands
76. The South Shetlands
77. South Georgia
78. The Palmer Peninsula
79. The Weddell Sea
80. Mt. Ropke, Queen Maud Land
81. The Regula Range
82. Muhlig–Hofmann Mountains
83. Penck Trough
84. Neumeyer Escarpment
85. Drygalski Mountains
86. Vorposten Peak
87. Boreas, Passat Nunataks
90a,b Andes Mountains
91. Peninsula of Paracas
92. Valparaiso
93. Equatorial Island
94. 'Antillia' according to Piri Re'is
95. Fernando da Naronha

Figure 18

but for two considerations. First, the assumption regarding the length of the radius (that is, the length of the degree) was not reached with reference to the coast of Africa, but with reference to the width of the Atlantic and the longitude of the coast of South America. It will be seen from our map (Fig. 18) and from Table 1 that both these coasts, separated by the width of the Atlantic, are in approximately correct relative longitude with reference to the center of the projection on the meridian of Alexandria. This seems to mean that the original mapmaker must have found correct relative longitude across Africa and across the Atlantic from the meridian of Alexandria to Brazil.

It is also important that most of the islands are in equally correct longitude. The picture that seems to emerge, therefore, is one of a scientific achievement far beyond the capacities of the navigators and mapmakers of the Renaissance, of any period of the Middle Ages, of the Arab geographers, or of the known geographers of ancient times. It appears to demonstrate the survival of a cartographic tradition that could hardly have come to us except through some such people as the Phoenicians or the Minoans, the great sea peoples who long preceded the Greeks but passed down to them their maritime lore.

The accuracy of placement of the islands suggests that they may have been found on the ancient source map used by Piri Re'is. The "discoveries" and mapping of these islands by the Arabs and Portuguese in the 15th century may not, then, have been genuine discoveries. It is possible that the 15th century sailors really found these islands as the result of accidental circumstances (being blown off course, etc.). On the other hand, nothing excludes the possibility that source maps used by Piri Re'is, dating from ancient times, were known in some form to people in Europe. Possibly some of the early voyages to some of these islands, particularly the Azores, were undertaken to confirm the accuracy of the old maps. It is hardly, if at all, possible that these 15th century navigators could have found correct longitude for the islands. All they had to go by were rough guesses of courses run, based on the direction and force of the wind, and the estimated speed of their ships. Such estimates were apt to be thrown off by the action of ocean currents and by lateral drift when the ship was trying to make to windward.

A good description of the problem of finding position at sea is given by a 16th century writer quoted by Admiral Morison in his *Admiral of the Ocean Sea:*

> "O how God in His omnipotence can have placed this subtle and so important art of navigation in wits so dull and hands so clumsy as those of these pilots! And to see them inquire, one of the other, 'how many degrees hath your honor found?' One says 'sixteen,' another 'a scant twenty' and another 'thirteen and a half.' Presently they ask, 'How doth your honor find himself with respect to the land?' One says, 'I find myself forty leagues from land,' another 'I say 150,' another says 'I find myself this morning 92 leagues away.' And be it three or three hundred nobody agrees with anybody else, or with the truth." (140:321–322)

In the days of Piri Re'is no instruments existed by which the navigator at sea could find his longitude. Such an instrument did not appear for another 250 years, when the chronometer was developed in the reign of George III. It does not seem possible to explain the accuracy of longitude on the Piri Re'is Map in terms of navigational science in the time of Piri Re'is.*

The case for latitude is somewhat different. Latitude could be determined in the 15th and 16th centuries by astronomical observations. However, observations taken by trained people with proper equipment were one thing, and observations taken by explorers were quite another. Morison says that Columbus made serious mistakes in finding latitude. Speaking of the First Voyage he says: ". . . We have only three latitudes (all wrong) and no longitude for the entire voyage" (140:157). He describes one of Columbus' attempts to find his latitude as follows:

> On the night of Nov. 2 (1492) two days before the full moon, he endeavored to establish his position by taking the altitude of the North Star with his wooden quadrant. After applying the slight correction he decided that Puerto Gibara, actually in Lat. 21° 06'N, was in 42° N, the Latitude of Cape Cod (140:258).

For a long time after the four voyages of Columbus we find the latitudes of Cuba and Haiti wrong on the maps of the time. Almost all mapmakers put the islands above rather than below the Tropic of Cancer. (See Figs. 19, 20, 21, 23.)

To return to the problem of longitude, Morison remarks that the only method of finding longitude known in the 16th century was by the timing of eclipses, but that nobody was successful in applying it. He says:

> The only known method of ascertaining longitude in Columbus' day was by timing an eclipse. Regiomontanus's *Ephemerides* and Zacuto's *Almanach Perpetuum* gave the predicted hours of total eclipse at Nuremberg and Salamanca respectively, and if you compared those with the observed hour of the eclipse, wherever you were, and multiplied by 15 to convert time into arc (1 hour of time = 15° of Longitude) there was your longitude west of the Almanach maker's meridian. Sounds simple enough, but Columbus, with two opportunities (1494 and 1503) muffed both, as did almost everyone else for a century. (140:185–186)

Morison describes in an interesting manner the failure of an attempt to find the longitude of Mexico City in 1541 (twenty-eight years after Piri Re'is drew his map):

> At Mexico City in 1541 a mighty effort was made by the intelligentsia to

---

*However, longitude could be determined when the time of a predicted eclipse was calculated. Adrian Vance in a recent work (210a) shows how the ancients may have used a system of lunar-solar observatories to track the sun-moon interval variations at different locations during an eclipse, for an accurate determination of longitude. Capt. James Cook used such a method ("lunar distances") to fix the longitude of Pacific islands (53a, p. 5).

determine the longitude of the place by timing two eclipses of the moon. The imposing result was 8h 2m 32s (= 120° 38′ west of Toledo) but the correct difference of longitude between the two places is 95° 12′, so the Mexican savants made an error of 25½°, or 1450 miles! Even in the 18th Century Pere Labat, the earliest writer (to my knowledge) who gives the position of Hispaniola correctly, adds this caveat: "I only report the longitude to warn the reader that nothing is more uncertain, and that no method used up to the present to find longitude has produced anything fixed and certain" (140:186).

With this backwardness of the 16th century science of navigation, I cannot see how the accuracy of the Piri Re'is Map can be explained, either as to latitude or longitude.* Figures 19–24 illustrate the poor qualities of the maps that were drawn at this time.

In this part of the Piri Re'is Map the average latitude error of 22 places was only 0.7°, and the average longitude error 1.8°. Madeira was not included in averaging the latitude errors because it was apparently left in alignment with the trigonometric equator when the rest of the map was shifted. The longitude errors were bunched, places on the Gulf of Guinea averaging about 4° too far east, and places on the coasts of France and Spain about 2° too far west. The Cape Verde, Madeira and the Azores Islands were in correct longitude, which is remarkable.

With regard to latitude there are several inconsistencies in the different parts of the map. It is evident that it went through many stages of compilation, when ancient maps derived from different periods were combined. Most of the map is in agreement with the equator as found in Fig. 15, and we have therefore used this for the main grid of the map. However, several parts of it (such as Madeira) appear to have latitude based on the trigonometric projection (Figs. 17, 18.) There were other errors made in combining different source maps, some omissions and some duplications. We shall point out these as we go along.

To sum up, this part of the Map suggests that Piri Re'is had a source map of Africa, Europe, and the Atlantic islands, based on maps probably drawn originally on some sort of trigonometric projection adjusted to the curvature of the earth. By default of any alternative, we seem forced to ascribe the origin of this part of the map to a pre-Hellenic people—not to Renaissance or Medieval cartographers, and not to the Arabs, who were just as badly off as everybody else with respect to longitude, and not to the Greeks either. The trigonometry of the projection (or rather its information on the size of the earth) suggests the work of Alexandrian geographers, but the evident knowledge of longitude implies a people unknown to us, a nation of seafarers, with instruments for finding longitude undreamed of by the Greeks, and, so far as we know, not possessed by the Phoenicians, either.

---

* W. H. Lewis, in his *The Splendid Century* (Doubleday, 1957, pp. 227–228), quotes an extract from the memoirs of the Abbé de Choisy (1644–1724) on the difficulty of finding longitude a century and a half after Piri Re'is: "Father Fontenay lectures on navigation, and shows that not only is longitude undiscovered, but why it is undiscoverable. . . ."

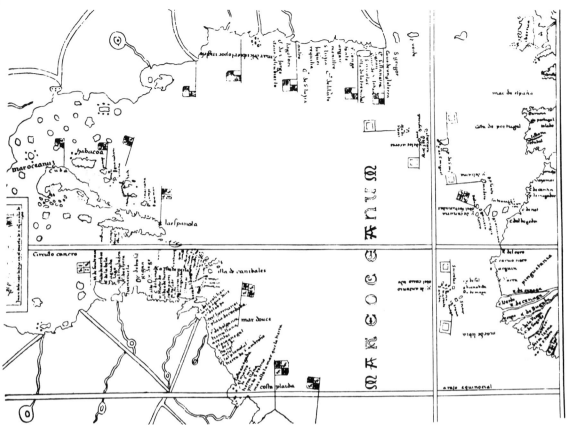

Figure 19. The Juan de la Cosa Map of 1500.

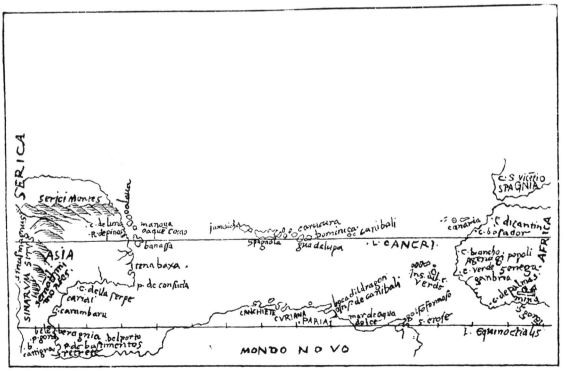

Figure 20. The Bartholomew Columbus Map.

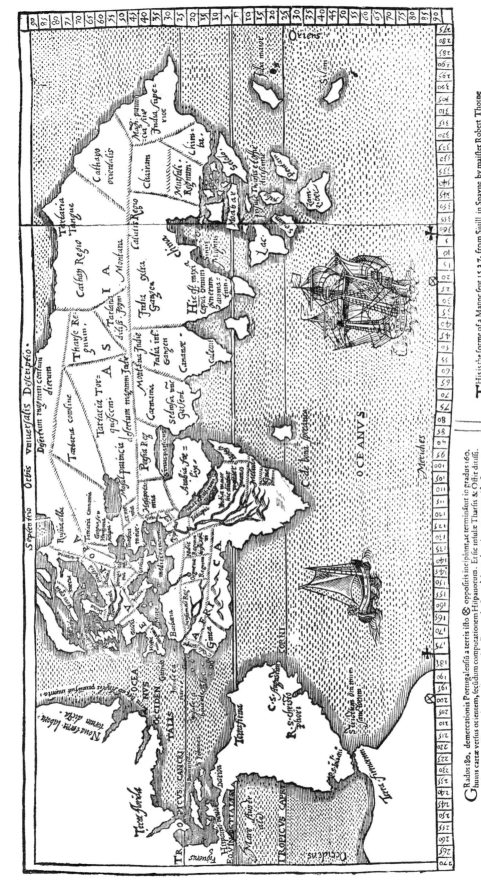

Figure 21. The Robert Thorne Map of 1527. V

Figure 22. Ptolemaeus Basilae Map of 1540. F

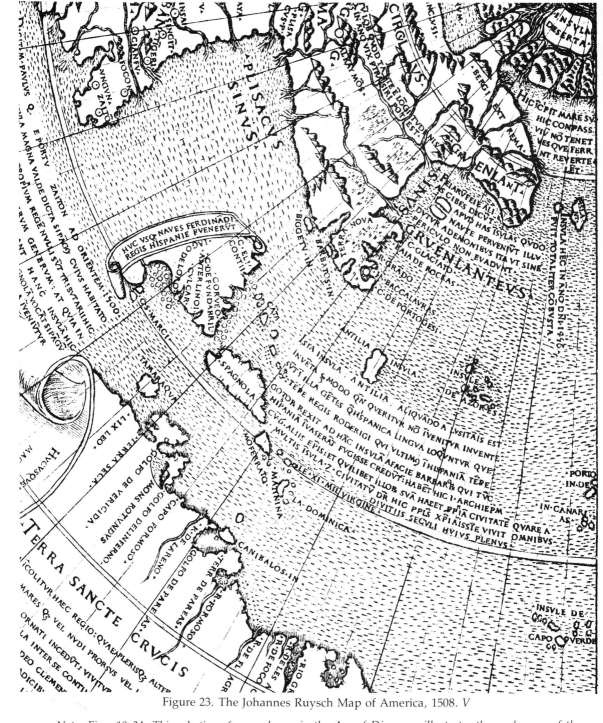

Figure 23. The Johannes Ruysch Map of America, 1508. *V*

*Note, Figs. 19–24: This selection of maps drawn in the Age of Discovery illustrates the weaknesses of the cartographic science of the period. So far as relative distances, land shapes, and particularly longitude are concerned these maps are much inferior to the Piri Re'is Map. None of these maps suggests the use of trigonometry.*

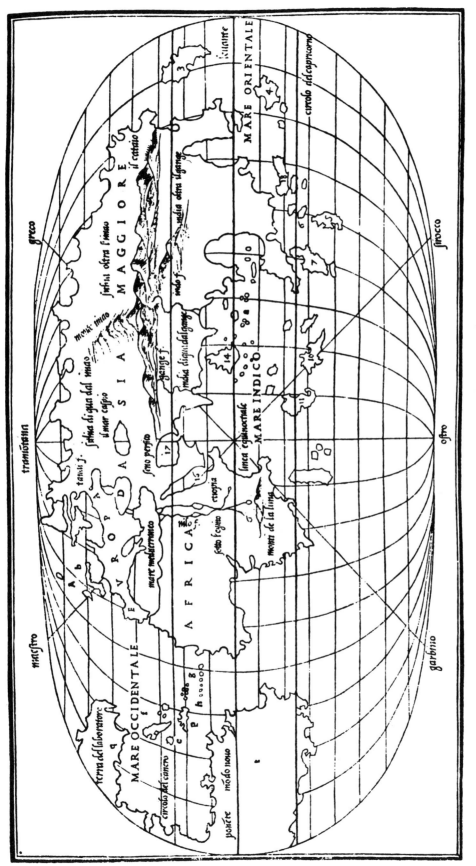

Figure 24. The Benedetto Bordone Map of 1528.

## 2.   A special projection in the Caribbean, including part of the coast of South America.

The Caribbean part of the Piri Re'is Map offered the greatest difficulties. It seemed entirely out of line. The coast appeared to trend entirely the wrong way. It looked at first like some of the very worst mapmaking imaginable. From our studies of the portolan projection, however, I was prepared to accept the possibility of there being more than one North on this map. Estes had pointed out that the portolan design permitted a change of North from one part of a map to another, if and when it became desirable to move from one square, or grid, to one of the others that the design made possible.

I was looking at the map one day when I suddenly found that by twisting my head far to one side, I could make some sense of the Caribbean section. I saw that there was indeed another North in this area. I assumed to start with that it might be integrated with the mathematics of the world projection. It had already become evident to us that it was theoretically possible to take any one of the map's projection points, whose positions were now known, and repeat the portolan design by drawing a circle with this point as a center, and then constructing a grid within it exactly as with the world projection. This would be a satellite grid, and any North line could be chosen to suit the mapmaker's convenience.

To solve this problem it was necessary to locate a North line, that is, a prime meridian. By identifying on the map a number of geographical localities which lay at the same latitude on the modern map of the Caribbean, I drew a rough parallel. I then looked for—and found—a line on the Piri Re'is projection at right angles to this. The line I found came down from Projection Point I at the top of the map and bisected what looked like the Peninsula of Yucatán. The angle of this line to the meridians of the main part of the map was 78¾°; this meant that it lacked one compass point (11¼°) of being at a right angle to the north of the rest of the map.

Gradually it became possible to extend the mathematical system of the whole projection to this part of the map. The common point was Projection Point I, which we had located at 51.4° N and 36.9° W. We assumed this point to be at the same latitude in both parts of the map. Since the length of the degree was (by assumption) the same, we could lay out parallels of latitude at five-degree intervals down to zero, which was, then, the equator of this special projection. Latitude was thus integrated mathematically with the world projection.

We found, after a number of tests, that the Ptolemaic spacing of parallels had also been applied in this component map.

The longitude problem presented much greater difficulty. Our first solutions were largely guesswork. Finally, the problem was solved by dropping a line, from the intersection of the prime meridian of our Caribbean section with the equator of that section, to the bottom of the map, where it intersected the register of longitude of the main grid extended westward. The longitude of the point of intersection at the bottom of the map became the longitude of our local prime meridian, and thus both the latitudes and longitudes of the Caribbean section were determined (See Fig. 18).

Now, if the reader will visualize the entire Caribbean grid as suspended from Point I, hanging down with no place to put its feet, and then *swung* through an arc of 78¾°, he should get the idea. Since the swing of the projection is so exact, and since, as the tables show (Table 1), the latitudes and longitudes of the identifiable places around the Caribbean are remarkable accurate, we are sure that the accuracy of this special projection is not a coincidence.

Perhaps the reader may wonder at the mapmaker's reason for resorting to this device. The only answer I am able to suggest is that he may have had ancient maps (maps ancient *then*) of the Caribbean area, with ample notations of latitude and longitude, but drawn, like a modern map, on some sort of spherical projection. Perhaps because he was unfamiliar with spherical trigonometry, he may have been forced to treat the round surface of the earth as a series of flat planes. He therefore had to have different norths in areas that were too far removed from each other in longitude. He was clever enough to work out a scheme by which he could preserve the accuracy of latitude and longtiude in the Caribbean. He had to find just the right angle for North that would achieve this purpose, and he did so. But it is probable that he did not achieve the full accuracy of his ancient sources.

Strong support for this hypothesis is provided by a comparison of the Piri Re'is Map with a modern map of the world drawn on a polar equidistant projection (see Figs. 25, 26, 27). This map was drawn for the use of the Air Force during World War II. It was centered at Cairo, Egypt, because an important U.S. air base was located there. Since Cairo is not far from the center of the Piri Re'is world projection, this modern map gives us a good idea of what the world would look like on a projection of this kind centered on Egypt. If we look at Cuba on this equidistant map, we notice that it appears to run at right angles to a latitude line drawn through Cairo. In other words, if we regard the map as representing a flat surface, then Cuba runs north and south, just as it seems to run with reference to the main projection of the Piri Re'is Map. Furthermore, in both cases we see Cuba much too far north.

How is this to be explained? What else can we conclude but that the mapmaker, confronted by a spherical projection he did not understand, had to translate his geographical data (latitudes and longitudes of places in the Caribbean) into terms of a flat surface? This contains the implication, of course, that spherical trigonometry must have been known ages before its supposed invention by Hipparchus in the second century B.C. It also raises another question: How did it happen that a world map, apparently drawn ages before Hipparchus, was centered on Egypt? Can we ascribe such advanced knowledge to the early Egyptians? It seems that perhaps we can. Evidence bearing on this will be presented in Chapter IX.

To sum up, then, our mapmaker was faced with the problem of indicating True North both for the Atlantic and for the Caribbean area, which extends much farther west. Since the portolan projection is a rectangular projection and the earth is

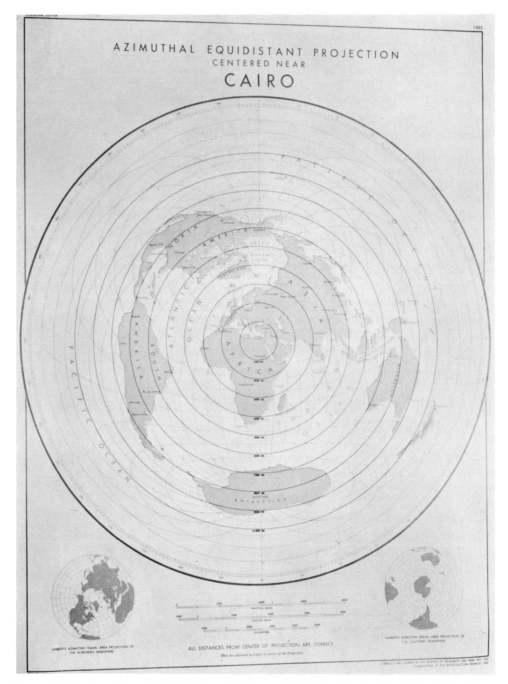

Figure 25. Modern Map of the World on the Bonne Projection Centred at Cairo (*U.S. Air Force*)

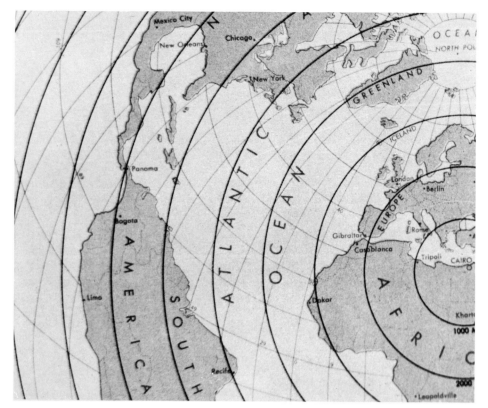

Figure 26. Part of the Bonne Projection for comparison with the Piri Re'is Map.

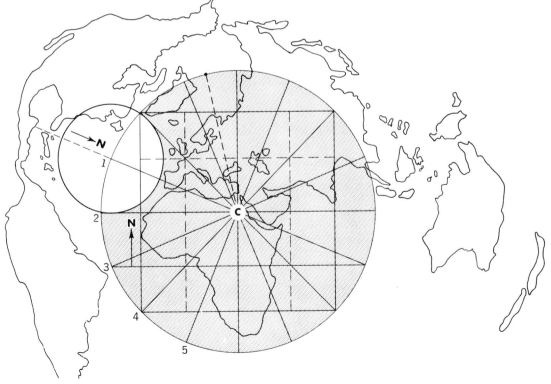

Figure 27. The Piri Re'is Projection, including the Special North of the Caribbean Grid.
imposed on the Bonne projection. (*B on Fig. 18*)

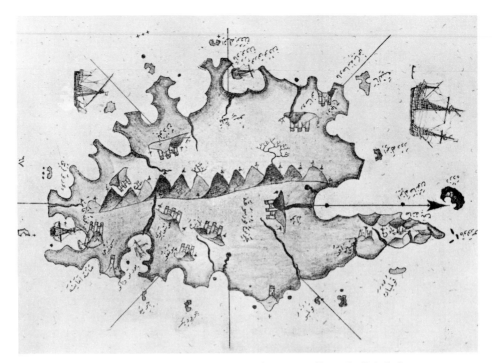

Figure 28. The Piri Re'is Map of Corsica. (*from the Bahriye*)

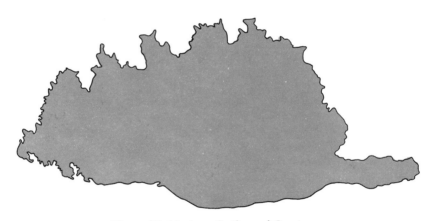

Figure 29. Modern Outline of Corsica.

round, it is evident that you cannot extend it through many degrees of longitude without getting to a place where the meridians will not point north at all. The geometrical scheme of the portolan projection, with several possible Norths, was the only way to solve this problem. But there had to be mathematical calculations. It seems that only by trigonometry could the correct angle for the Caribbean prime meridian have been found.

The peculiar projection for the Caribbean area permits some conclusions as to the probable history of the map as a whole. In the first place it is clear that Piri Re'is could not have constructed this part of his world map. Such a thing as two Norths on the same map was unheard of in the Renaissance. To Piri Re'is, the idea of changing the direction of north in the middle of the ocean would be lunacy, and all

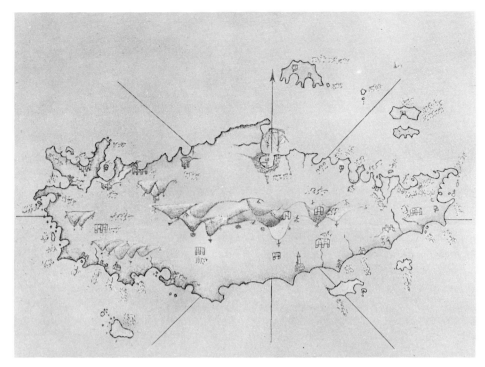

Figure 30. The Piri Re'is Map of Crete. (*from the Bahriye*)

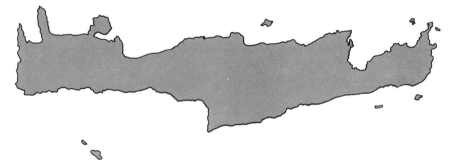

Figure 31. Modern Outline of Crete.

the mapmakers of the age would have looked at the matter the same way. But even if he had the idea, even if he knew some trigonometry (of which there is no evidence) he still could not have drawn the map, because neither he nor, as far as is known, anyone else at that time had any information as to the longitudes of places in the Caribbean.*

* Fortunately we possess, in Piri Re'is' extensive treatise on the geography of the Mediterranean, the "Kitabe Bahriye" (145a), a large number of maps personally drawn by him. Their characteristics are most interesting. Like Arab maps generally, they are good pictures. But they lack any sort of projection. They do not even carry scales of distance. They do not show the compass directions of the portolan charts. (See Figs. 28–31.)

What applies to Piri Re'is applies also to Columbus. Columbus could not have drawn any part of the map included in the special grid because for him, as for Piri Re'is, there could be only one North on a map. It is possible, however, that this special grid may provide a solution to one of the problems of Columbus' first voyage.

Let us suppose that Columbus had a copy of this map of the Caribbean, as it appears on the Piri Re'is Map. (Piri Re'is himself believed this was the case.) Perhaps the map showed the Azores, or even some part of the European coast, so that by simple measurement Columbus was able to get an idea of the scale of the map and the distance across the ocean to the Caribbean islands.

We know he had some sort of map and that he had an idea of how soon he would find land. But we also know that he did not find land where he expected to find it. Instead, he had to sail about one thousand miles farther and was faced with a threatened mutiny of his crew. Finally he made a landfall at the island of San Salvador (Watling Island) or some other island nearby.

Now, if you look at San Salvador on our map (Fig. 18) and note its longitude on the main grid of the map, you will see that it lies about 63° W on that grid instead of at 74½° W, where it actually should be. But if you swing the map around and find the longitude of the island on the special Caribbean grid, it turns out to be at 84.5° W. The trouble that Columbus ran into may now be understood. His error in not understanding the map he had may have led to a mistake of about 22° or about 1290 miles in his estimate of the distance across the Atlantic, and thus nearly caused the failure of his expedition.

Let us consider the probabilities of Columbus' having carried with him from Spain a copy of this component map of the Caribbean. He need not have had with him the entire source map used by Piri Re'is, including South America. The evidence is that he did not suspect that a continent lay to the south of the Caribbean until he ran into the fresh water of the Orinoco out at sea.

We have seen that Piri Re'is, in all probability, had ancient maps at his disposal in Constantinople. It is quite possible that copies of some of these had reached the West long before his day. Greek scholars fleeing from the Turks brought thousands of Greek manuscripts to Italy before the fall of Constantinople in 1453. Much earlier still, in the year 1204, a Venetian fleet, supposedly intended to carry a crusade to the Holy Land, attacked and captured Constantinople. For about sixty years afterward Italian merchants had access to map collections in Constantinople.

We have reason to believe that good maps of the St. Lawrence River were available in Europe before Columbus sailed in 1492. In Fig. 32 we see a map of the river and the islands near its mouth that the mapmaker Martin Behaim placed on a globe he made and completed before Columbus returned from his first voyage. Columbus was not an ignorant mariner, as some people seem to imagine. He was quite at home in Latin, which indicated some education, and he was a cartographer by trade. It is known that he travelled widely in Europe, always on the lookout for maps. His voyage was not a sudden inspiration; it was a deeply settled objective, one followed with perseverance for many years, and it required, above all, maps.

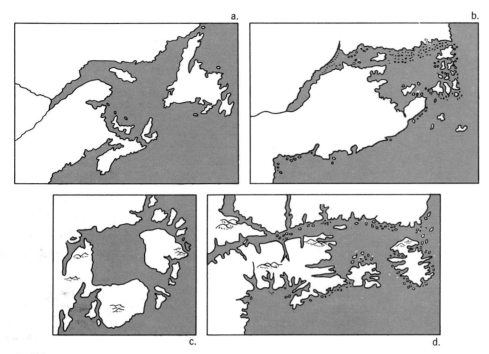

Figure 32. Martin Behaim's Map of the mouth of the St. Lawrence, drawn in 1492 before the return of Columbus from his first voyage, as compared with later maps, (a) modern map, (b) Sebastian Cabot, 1544, (c) Behaim Globe, 1492, (d) Lescarbot map of 1606. *After Hjalmar R. Holand, in "Explorations in America Before Columbus," New York, Twayne, 1956.*

The historian Las Casas said that Columbus had a world map, which he showed to King Ferdinand and Queen Isabella, and which, apparently, convinced them that they should back Columbus.

Many have thought that this map may have been the map said to have been sent to Columbus by the Italian scholar Toscanelli (see Fig. 33). But a Soviet scientist has presented a strong argument against this, including evidence that the Toscanelli letter to Columbus, accompanying the map, was a forgery (209). In any case, the Toscanelli Map, whether Columbus had it or not, is a very poor map.

Cuba on the Piri Re'is Map presents some very interesting problems.

In the first place, Cuba was wrongly labeled *Espaniola* (Hispaniola, the island now comprising Haiti and the Domincan Republic) by Piri Re'is. This error was accepted by Philip Kahle who studied the map in the 1930's (106). Nothing could better illustrate how ignorant Piri Re'is was of his own map. The mislabelling of Cuba also clearly shows that all he did was to get some information verbally from a sailor captured by his uncle, or from some other source, and then try to fit the information to a map already in his possession, a map he may have found in the Turkish Naval Archives, which possibly inherited it from the Byzantine Empire. In Figures 34, 35 I have compared the island I have identified on the Piri Re'is Map as Cuba with a modern map of that island.

50

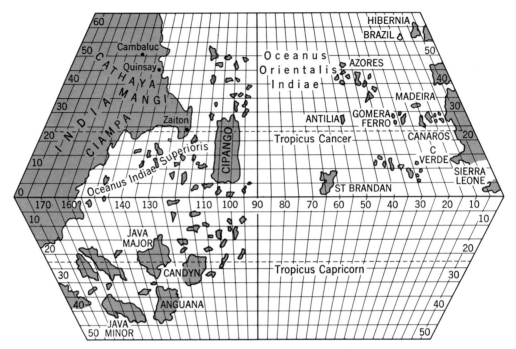

Figure 33. The Toscanelli Map of 1484.

This comparison shows that what we have in this island on the Piri Re'is Map is a map of Cuba, but a map only of its eastern half. We can identify a number of points around the coasts and in the interior. The western half is missing, but, as if to compensate for this, the island is shown at twice the scale of the rest of the map, so that it subtends about the correct amount of longitude for the whole island. Oddly enough, there is a complete western shoreline where the island is cut off, as if when the map was drawn, all of western Cuba was still beneath sea level. We observe that some islands are shown in the west in the area now occupied by western Cuba. (Fig. 18).

There is good evidence that a map of a thus truncated Cuba was well known in Europe before the first voyage of Columbus. In Figure 36 I have compared the Cuba of the Piri Re'is Map with the island labeled "Cipango" on the Behaim Globe (completed before Columbus' return from his first voyage), and on the Bordone Map of 1528. (See also Fig. 33).

It seems quite clear that Bordone's island, which of the three most closely resembles the Piri Re'is island, was not inspired by the current information on Cuba. Cuba on the maps made by the 16th century explorers in no way resembles the island on the Piri Re'is Map. (See, for example, Fig. 37, the Piri Re'is Map of 1528. Here Piri Re'is represents Cuba in a form typical of the other maps of the day. He had evidently abandoned his ancient maps.)

In view of the possibility that an ancient map of the eastern half of Cuba may have been circulating in Europe before Columbus' first voyage, it becomes increas-

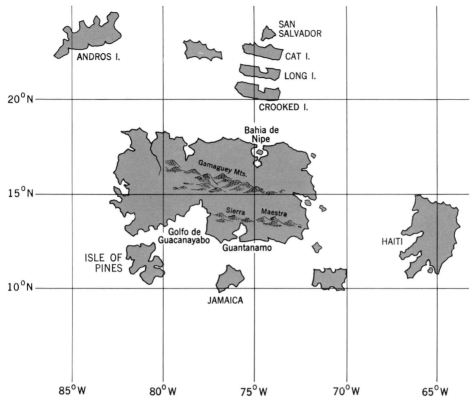

Figure 34. Cuba according to the Piri Re'is Map.

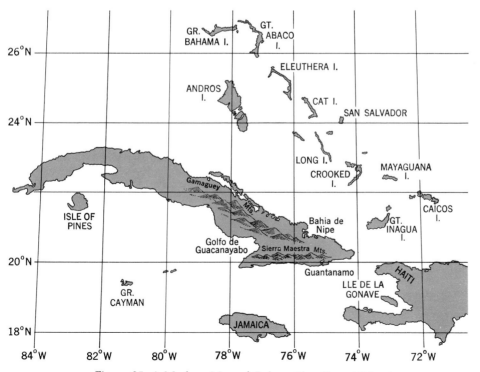

Figure 35. A Modern Map of Cuba with adjacent Islands.

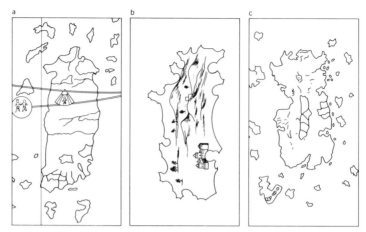

Figure 36. "Cipango" on the Behaim Globe (a) and on the Bordone
Map of 1528 (b), and Cuba on the Piri Re'is Map (c).

ingly easy to accept the idea that Columbus may have found a good map, at least
the Caribbean section of the Piri Re'is Map, and that this may actually have led him
to America. In view of these facts one of my students, Lee Spencer, revised the old
verse:

In Fourteen Hundred Ninety Two
Columbus sailed the ocean blue.
With maps in hand drawn long before
He headed straight for Cuba's shore.
Much fame he gained, so I am told,
For he proved true the maps of old.

The Piri Re'is representation of Cuba suggests that the Caribbean section of his
map was itself a compilation of originally separate local maps. One of these may be
identified in the map of Hispaniola.

Here we have still another North. The arrow on our map (Fig. 18) indicates the
direction of north for Hispaniola and some adjacent islands. It does not agree with
the Norths either of the main grid or of the Caribbean grid; it is not, so far as we can
see, integrated with the trigonometric projection. Columbus could not have placed
it on the map (assuming he had it) because, if there was one thing Columbus could
determine, it was north, and he would therefore have aligned Hispaniola with the
rest of the Caribbean islands on the main grid of the map.

A point of considerable interest in this Caribbean map is the shape of the Atrato
River (Fig. 18, No. 64). According to our grid the river is shown for a distance of 300
miles from the sea, and its eastward bend at 5° North Latitude corresponds to the
geographical facts. This implies that somebody explored the river to its headwaters
in the western cordillera of the Andes sometime before 1513. I have found no
record of such an early exploration.

Figure 37. Fragment of the Piri Re'is Map of 1528.

### 3. A map of the Atlantic coast of South America, from Cape Frio northward to the Amazon, with an error in scale.

On the Piri Re'is Map, South America consists of a compilation of various local maps differing in scale and in orientation. This particular component map is on too small a scale, as shown by the inset grid, Fig. 18, but is in correct longitude. It is possible that we can partially reconstruct the story of this map.

It was, in the first place, an accurate map of the coast. But it seems that the mapmaker may have been operating under the impression that Point IV of the world projection pattern lay on the Tropic of Capricorn, and he placed this component map so that its southern end lay on this assumed tropic. This left its northern end too far south, because of an error in the scale. The mapmaker, however, may

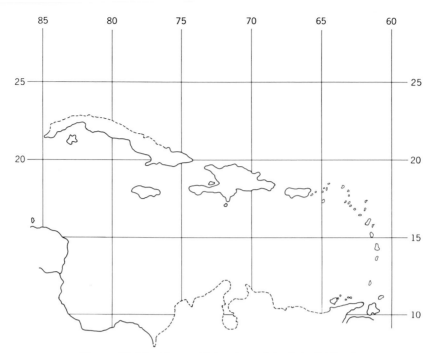

Figure 38. The Coasts Columbus visited. (*solid lines*).

have been unaware of this because of a failure to identify the river shown there as the Para River, one of the mouths of the Amazon. According to my interpretation, the map does show the course of the Amazon coming down to its Para River mouth, but it does not show the Island of Marajo. The map would suggest that it may come from a time when the Para River was the main or only mouth of the Amazon, and when the Island of Marajo may have been part of the mainland on the northern side of the river. If the mapmaker knew of the Island of Marajo as existing in his time he might not identify the river on his source map with the Amazon. We shall see evidence shortly that he did know of the existence of the Island.

The evidence for my interpretation of this part of the map is in the agreement of the inset grid in Fig. 18 with the topography, as shown in Table 1.

## 4. A map of the Amazon and the Island of Marajo, correctly placed on the equator of the trigonometric projection.

One part of the Piri Re'is Map that seems to date without modification from that remote time when a trigonometric projection was used to compile a world map is a map of the Amazon with a very good representation of the Island of Marajo. Here both mouths of the Amazon are shown. The upper one, the mouth of the Amazon proper, is shown about 10° north of the river suggested as the Amazon, on the inset grid of Fig. 18. It lies just below the equator of the trigonometric projection.

Interestingly, both the duplications of the Amazon suggest the actual course of the river, while all the representations of it in the later maps of the 16th century bear no resemblance to its real course. Moreover, the excellent representation of the Island of Marajo is quite unique. Nothing like it can be found on any map of the 16th century until after the official discovery of the island in 1543. Where could Piri Re'is have gotten his accurate conception of this island? If he had somehow obtained the information as to its shape, how could he have placed it correctly both in latitude and longitude, using a mathematical projection of which he was almost certainly ignorant? This part of the map is certainly ancient.

This Island of Marajo did quite a bit of drifting after Piri Re'is day. It turned up on Mercator's 1569 Map of South America, but here we find it placed at the mouth of the Orinoco! (See Fig. 39).

## 5.   The Atlantic Island

A great island, No. 93 in Fig. 18, is one of the major mysteries of the Piri Re'is Map. It does not look like an invention. It does not have the artificial look of the nearby island, No. 94, which Piri Re'is labelled "Antillia." No. 94 indeed has the look of the legendary islands of the Atlantic (21) but there are good reasons for a different conclusion about No. 93.

In the first place, the details of the island are convincing. Some reproductions of the colored facsimile (but unfortunately not all of them) suggest by a deeper shade around the coasts that there were coastal highlands or mountains surrounding a great central plain. The harbours and the islands off the coast are inviting. They are carefully drawn. There seems to have been an effort to achieve accurancy. This island, if it really existed, would have been ideally suited by climate and location for agricultural and commercial development. An ideal home for a sea people! A secure base for a maritime empire: whose ships would have had easy access to commercial ports in the Caribbean, in South America, in Europe, in Africa, and even, perhaps, in Antarctica! Here, in this island, there might have developed the people who made these maps!

A second consideration is the location of this island directly on the equator of the mathematical projection of the map and right over the sunken Mid-Atlantic Ridge where some tiny islands, the Rocks of Sts. Peter and Paul, now exist. These islands are the top of a mountain rising from a plain now submerged to a depth of a mile and a half. The plain is a plateau on the top of the Mid-Atlantic Ridge. The mountain is not a volcanic, but a folded mountain, which suggests that it is structurally part of the Ridge.

There are two other maps which independently testify to the real existence of this island. One of these is attributed to the French geographer, Philippe Buache, who presented it to the French Academy of Sciences in 1737 (Fig. 40.) The map shows South America, Africa and various islands in the Atlantic. It is a traverse of the Equatorial Atlantic, taken at an angle of 25° to the equator, and it shows not only the islands *but the ocean bottom*.

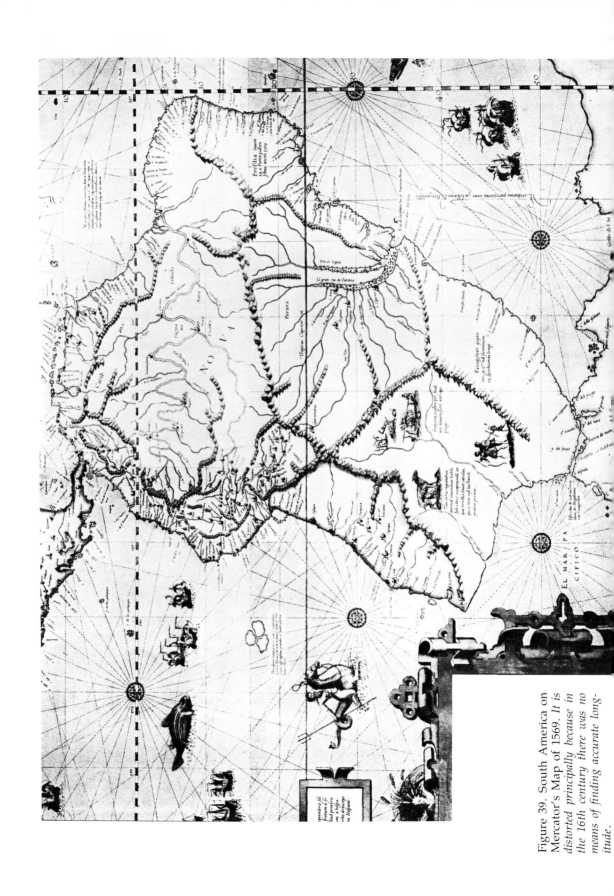

Figure 39. South America on Mercator's Map of 1569. *It is distorted principally because in the 16th century there was no means of finding accurate longitude.*

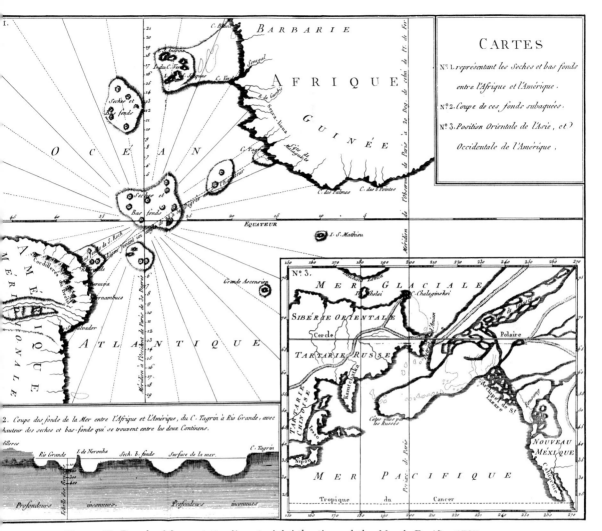

Figure 40. Buache Maps of the Equatorial Atlantic and the North Pacific, 1737.

In the center of the Atlantic, at the very side of the tiny islands of Sts. Peter and Paul, Buache has a very large island, but it is not shaped at all like the Piri Re'is island. The island is only outlined, it is not drawn in detail. Inside the outline a number of small islets are indicated, suggesting clearly that a large island had submerged leaving the islets as remnants which later disappeared.

Half way between this large island and the African coast another island is indicated in the same general way, also including within some islets, and this feature is placed directly over the Sierra Leone Rise, a mountain range on the floor of the Atlantic Ocean. Farther north another large island is outlined enclosing five or six more islets, while the Cape Verde Islands are shown connected with the African mainland. Still another now non-existent island is suggested due south of the central island.

So far the detail of this map, while interesting, is not by itself proof of anything

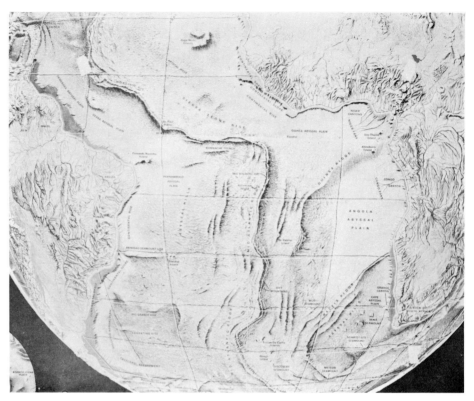

Figure 41. Bathymetric Map of the Atlantic. *The rocks of Sts Peter and Paul are located on the Equator over the Mid-Atlantic Ridge.*

except that it is evidence in support of the real existence of the island on the Piri Re'is Map. What is truly amazing, however, is the bathymetric traverse of the bottom of the ocean. The traverse is not accurate in detail, but it does show both the Mid-Atlantic Ridge and the Sierra Leone Rise. Who in the year 1737 knew anything about the bottom of the Atlantic? The Buache Map is now in the Bibliothek Nationale. Perhaps Buache left other documents that might throw light on this matter.

Some readers may suppose that Buache was just another Atlantis enthusiast. But before 1737 Atlantis was not a very hot subject. And Atlantis is supposed to have been located in the Azores, not on the equator. And if he was describing Atlantis why doesn't he say so? It is true that later in the century an Atlantis enthusiast, Count Carlo Carli (44) did make use of the map, but he did not invent it.

In an inset map Buache shows the North Pacific with a land mass extending from Alaska nearly to Kamchatka, and including the Aleutian Islands. This might be evidence of land subsidence. The map shows some signs of antiquity. It is hardly what one would have expected from the cartographers of 1737. On the one hand the coasts of China and Japan are very badly drawn, which one would expect, but on the other the Aleutians are very well drawn, and here the mapping is far too scientific, considering that navigators at this time still had no means of ascertaining their longitude.

The third map that bears on the question of Piri Re'is' great equatorial island is the Reinel Chart of 1510 (Fig. 74) which, however, we will examine later on. It shows a large island in precisely the same location as the islands on the Piri Re'is and Buache maps. It seems that the maps are independent of each other. There is no indication that they stem from a common source. One would suppose, on the contrary, that the original prototype maps must have been drawn at very different times: one when the island fully existed, one when it was half submerged, and the third when it had submerged but the islets were still above sea-level. But they all agree precisely as to its location.

The most significant fact is that the island on all three maps is located right over the Mid-Atlantic Ridge. Some years ago Dr. René Malaise, a Belgian scientist, reached the conclusion that the Mid-Atlantic Ridge, or at least parts of it, was still above sea-level at the end of the ice age. He examined sediments taken from the top of the Ridge, and found specimens of diatoms of fresh water species that must have lived in a fresh water lake when the Ridge was above sea-level. The species were all recent species, indicating that the fresh-water lake was in existence within the last 10,000 or 15,000 years.

## 6.   The Andes on the Piri Re'is Map

Another component map, which may be briefly dealt with here, shows the mountainous area on the western side of Piri Re'is' South America. This component map was added to the general map, but it was not integrated with the trigonometry of the projection. There are errors both in scale and in orientation, as shown in Figure 18.

It seems that the mountains shown here must have been intended for the Andes. However, Kahle, one of the earlier students of the map, rejected this on the ground that the Andes were not yet discovered when Piri Re'is drew his map. On this controversial point the following considerations may be pertinent:

First, what is the probability that a cartographer, by pure invention, would place an enormous range of mountains on the western side of South America, *where one actually exists?*

Second, the various rivers, including both Amazons on Piri Re'is' map of South America, are shown flowing from these mountains, which is correct.

Third, the drawing of the mountains indicates that they were observed from the sea—from coastwise shipping—and not imagined.

Fourth, the general shape of the coast on the map agrees well with the South American coast from about 4° S down to about 40° S. It is between these latitudes that the Pacific cordillera of the Andes closely parallel the coast. There is even a suggestion on this coast of the Peninsula of Paracas.

## 7. The Caribbean Islands: The Leeward and Windward Groups, the Virgin Islands, Puerto Rico on the main grid of the map; more questions about Columbus.

These islands are more accurately placed on this map, in reference to latitude and longitude, than they are on any other map of the period.

Piri Re'is wrote, in his long inscription about Columbus, that this part of the map was based on a map Columbus drew. Here the two different grids overlap to some extent: some islands are on the special grid already discussed, and some are on the main grid. I have pointed out that one of Columbus' errors may have been due to not understanding the special grid. The Leeward and Windward Islands, which Columbus discovered, are on the main grid on this component map. Nevertheless, it is hardly possible that he could have added them to the map, as Piri Re'is supposed. For we see them in remarkably correct latitude and longitude on the trigonometric grid. Not understanding the grid, not even dreaming of its existence, and not being able to find either correct latitude or correct longitude, how could Columbus have correctly located the islands? Piri Re'is gives names to these islands, and says that they are the names given by Columbus, yet the names are wrong! (140:408–409) It looks as if Piri Re'is here depended upon hearsay information and did not really see a map drawn by Columbus.

One group of islands on the Caribbean part of the map, the Virgin Islands, are so far out of position, so badly drawn, and so far out of scale that they might well have been added to the map by Columbus or interpolated by Piri Re'is on the basis of some contemporary report.

One of the most unusual features of this part of the map is that some features can be interpreted as two different localities, according to the grid one uses.

## 8. The lower east coast of South America from Bahia Blanca to Cape Horn (or Cape San Diego) and certain Atlantic islands on the main grid of the map.

Two of my students, Lee Spencer and Ruth Baraw, discovered that about 900 miles of the east coast of South America were simply missing from the Piri Re'is Map, two different source maps having apparently been erroneously put together on the general compilation. Earlier students of the map—Kahle, Goodwin, Mallery—had all assumed that the map was continuous and complete as far as it went.

Kahle's assumption of an unbroken coast required a rather forced interpretation of the map. On this assumption it was necessary to conclude that the mapmaking here was very bad. However, it seems that someone before Kahle had had the same idea. Fig. 42 shows how that interpretation actually fits the oblong grid of the map. The equator is different from both that of the trigonometric projection and

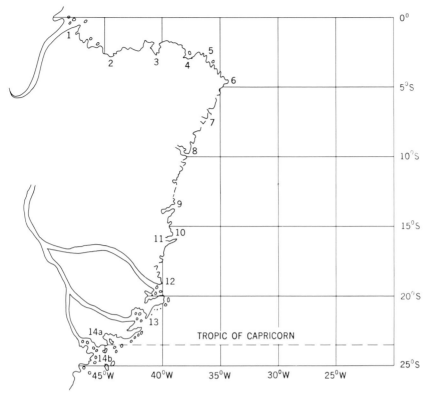

Figure 42. Alternative Grid for the Coast of South America on the Piri Re'is Map. (*see table 15*).

that of the main grid, but the length of the degree of latitude has been increased in the same way. The new detail serves to support our impression of the long and complex history of this map. There is no way of knowing how many peoples of how many epochs had their fingers in the pie.

The method used by Spencer and Baraw to verify their observation of the omission of the coastline was to try identifying localities by comparison with the modern map, first from one end of the coast, and then from the other. They started first with Recife and went all the way down the coast from point to point. Everything went well as far as Cape Frio, but south of Cape Frio they thought the Piri Re'is Map ceased to correspond with the modern map at all. Then they started from the bottom, from what we assumed to be Cape Horn, or Cape San Diego (No. 74, Fig. 18), and went northward identifying localities. Here again everything seemed to agree very well with the modern map until they came to a point just below Cape Frio. Farther than this they could not go. The missing coast lay in between. Our grid assisted us very much in the final verification of the break, for it gave us its value in degrees.

The omission of the coast between Cape Frio and Bahia Blanca apparently resulted in a loss of about 16° of S latitude and about 20° of W longitude. Therefore, in Table 1, I have added these amounts of latitude and longitude to the ones found by our grid. When this is done, the positions of the identified localities are correct to an average error of less than a degree. More important is the fact that they are correct relative to each other.

It appears significant that Piri Re'is, who stuck names taken from explorers' accounts on much of his map (making numerous errors), did not attempt to place any names on the southern part of this coast of South America. The reason offers itself: *There were no explorers' accounts.* That coast had not been explored by 1513.

The Falkland Islands appear in this section of the map at the correct latitude relative to this lower east coast, but there is an error of about 5° in longitude. The Falklands are supposed to have been discovered by John Davis in 1592, nearly eighty years after Piri Re'is made his map (68:869). (Though some have given the credit to Amerigo Vespucci.)

South of Cape Horn, or Cape San Diego, the coast on the Piri Re'is Map appears to continue unbroken, but here we have been able to identify another break, or rather omission.

## 9.   The Antarctic.

Proceeding as in the case of the break in the east coast of South America, we first identified localities down to the vicinity of Cape Horn (including specifically Cape San Diego), then jumped to the next cape to the eastward, assuming as a working hypothesis that it was the Palmer or Antarctic Peninsula as claimed by Mallery. This assumption would require that the sea between the Horn and the Antarctic Peninsula had been omitted by the mapmaker. This assumption appeared to be supported by our identification of the Shetland Islands. These islands are not far off the Antarctic coast. The omission of the sea between (Drake Passage) automatically would put the South Shetlands too far north by the width of the strait, which happens to be about 9°. If the reader will compare the positions of the Falklands and the South Shetlands on a globe with their positions on the Piri Re'is Map, as we have identified them, (Fig. 18) he will see how the Antarctic coast seems to have been simply pushed northward, and Drake Passage omitted.

Interestingly enough, we find that the same mistake was made on all maps of the Renaissance showing the Antarctic. When we come, in the next chapter, to the examination of the map of Oronteus Finaeus, we shall discover the probable reason for this error.

The extraordinary implications of Captain Mallery's claim that part of the Antarctic Continent is shown on the Piri Re'is Map demand unusually thorough verification, considering that the continent was supposedly discovered only in 1818. This is no slight matter. Important questions, for geology as well as for history, depend upon it. We may begin with a brief survey of the historical background.

A good many world maps of the 16th century show an antarctic continent (206). As we shall see, Gerard Mercator believed in its existence. A comparison of all the versions suggests that there may have been one or two original prototype maps, drawn according to different projections, which were copied and recopied with

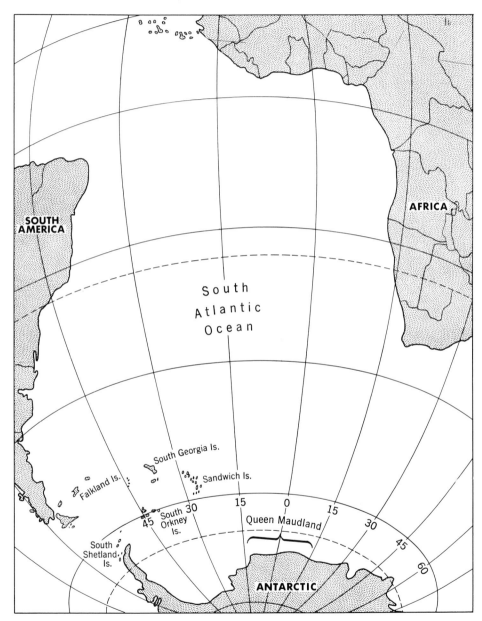

Figure 43. Relative Longitudes of the Guinea Coast of Africa and the Queen Maud Land Coast of Antarctica, for comparison with the Piri Re'is Map.

emendations according to the ideas of different cartographers.

The belief in the existence of the continent lasted until the time of Captain Cook, whose voyages into the South Seas demonstrated the non-existence of a southern continent at least in the latitudes where one appears on these maps (112). The idea of an antarctic continent was then given up, and geographers began to explain the maps as the work of geographers who had felt the need to have a land mass at the South Pole to balance off the concentration of land in the northern hemisphere. This seemed to be the only reasonable explanation, for in the first place there apparently was no such continent, and in the second place there was no reason to suppose that anyone in earlier times (Romans, Greeks, Phoenicians) could have explored those distant regions.

When we began our study of the southern sector of the Piri Re'is Map our first step was to compare it carefully, not with a flat map of the Antarctic, but with a globe. Fig. 43, traced from a photograph of a globe, shows a striking similarity between the Queen Maud Land coast and the coastline on the Piri Re'is Map. (We took this step because flat maps distort geography in one way or another, and unless we found a map on precisely the right projection we could not be sure of a good comparison.) It should be especially noted that on the modern globe the Queen Maud Land coast lies due south of the Guinea coast of Africa, just as the coastline referred to by Mallery does on the Piri Re'is Map.

This was an encouraging beginning. We went on to make a thorough examination. We asked ourselves, first, how does the coast in question on the Piri Re'is Map compare in its extent, character, and position, with the coasts of Queen Maud Land? (These coasts are named the Princess Martha and Princess Astrid Coasts.) With the gradual development of the mathematical grid we could answer two of these questions.

In the first place, we found that the Piri Re'is coast, according to our grid, extends through 27° of longitude as compared with 24° on the modern map, a very remarkable degree of agreement. At the latitude of the coasts (about 70° S) a degree of longitude is only about 20 miles, so that the error was not great. The grid also showed the coast in good position; only about 10°, or 200 miles, too far west.

With regard to latitude, we must take account of the omissions we have noted above—part of the South American coast and Drake Passage. Together these omissions account for about 25° of S latitude. When these degrees are added to those found by the grid for the Queen Maud Land coast, the coast appears in correct latitude (see Fig. 18 and Table 1.)

We have noted that the omission of the South American coastline resulted in a loss of about 16° of West Longitude. The omission of Drake Passage resulted, we found, in adding about 4° to this, making 20° to be accounted for. This, with the 10° westward error of the Queen Maud Land coast, creates a deficit of some 30° between that coast and the Antarctic Peninsula. This appears to be made up for by the fact that the Weddell Sea, as we have identified it on the map, extends through only 10° of longitude, instead of 40°, as would be correct.

Now it might be argued that this result is artificial, and that we have deliberately

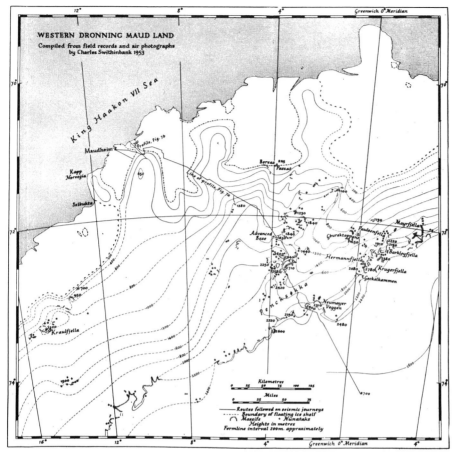

Figure 44. Route of the Norwegian-British-Swedish Seismic Survey Party across Queen
Maud Land, 1949, (*see Note 8. The Geographical Jour. June 1954*)

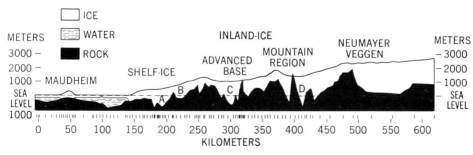

Figure 45. Profile of the Queen Maud Land ice cap, showing the sub-glacial topography:
*Note the extensions of the ice cap below sea level, A, B, C, D. Compare with the islands
and bays of the Antarctic sector of the Piri Re's Map (Figure 18). (After Schytt)*

twisted the evidence to support the conclusion, but this is not the case. My students, Lee Spencer and Ruth Baraw, had already established the omission of 900 miles of the South American coast without any thought of Antarctica. They were not interested in the bearing of their discovery on the question of the Queen Maud Land coast. We did not even see the connection until long afterwards, when the grid was·worked out, and the same is true of the omission of Drake Passage. The omission is obvious from the map itself: the strait simply isn't there. In the case of both omissions we were able to measure approximately the amounts of latitude and longitude involved.

There is in addition the comparison of the character of the Queen Maud Land coast, as shown on the ancient and on the modern map. It is plain, from the modern map, that this coast is a rugged one. Numerous mountain ranges and individual peaks show up above the present levels of the ice. The Piri Re'is Map shows the same type of coast, though without any ice. The numerous mountains are clearly indicated. By a convention of 16th century mapmaking heavy shading of some of the islands indicates a mountainous terrain.

Coming to greater detail, Mallery's chief argument was the striking agreement of the map with a profile across Queen Maud Land (see Figs. 44, 45 and Note 8) made by the Norwegian—British—Swedish expedition of 1949. The reader will note that the profile shows a rugged terrain, a coastline with mountains behind the coast and high islands in front. The points of the profile below sea level coincide very well with the bays between the islands on the Piri Re'is Map. This amounts to additional confirmation. The identification of specific features of the coast, as shown in Table 1, appears further to strengthen the argument.

If the Piri Re'is Map stood alone, it would perhaps be insufficient to carry conviction. But it does not stand alone. We shall shortly see that the testimony of this map regarding the Antarctic can be supported by that of several others.


## 10.   Evidence of the Subsidence of the Azores.

The Azores are an archipelago that, like the great equatorial island of the Piri Re'is, Buache and Reinel Maps, is located right over the Mid-Atlantic Ridge. One of my students at Keene State College, Ronald Bailey, made a careful comparison of these islands on the Piri Re'is Map and on the modern map and concluded that there had been considerable subsidence since the original source map was drawn. In April, 1959, Bailey wrote:

> An interesting map appeared in *Time* magazine for September 11, 1958 which shows a profile of the Atlantic depths (Fig. 46.) The Mid-Atlantic Ridge, which runs from the Arctic to the Indian Oceans, passes through the Azores. Along this ridge is a rift valley which is an earthquake epicenter line. Rift mountains enclose the valley on each side. The Azores are bisected by this epicenter line. Flores and Corvo are west of the valley. These islands have subsided greatly

according to a comparison of the Piri Re'is Map with the modern hydrographic chart. The island of Faial rises from the bottom of this rift valley. Faial also has subsided according to this comparison. The island is located on the epicenter line. All other islands lie to the east of the epicenter line. These islands have shown less change in size. Position with regard to the epicenter line seems to determine the amount of subsidence and can perhaps explain the difference between the Piri Re'is and the modern charts, adding support to the validity of the ancient map.

It appears from Table 18 and from Fig. 47 that the whole archipelago has subsided greatly, with Corvo and Flores showing the greatest subsidence. The fact that the amount of longitude occupied by the islands on the Piri Re'is Map is not grossly exaggerated makes it very difficult to explain why the individual islands are so much larger. It is clearly not a matter of any mistake in scale. It is of course possible that a cartographer like Piri Re'is, not possessing instruments capable of drawing such small features to scale on a map of the world, might have had to increase their size. But their shapes are very different, and the islands are different in number. There are no such differences in Piri Re'is' maps of the Canary and Cape Verde Islands.

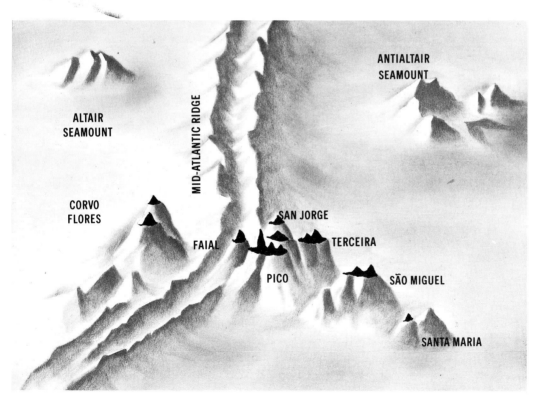

Figure 46. Bathymetric Map of the Azores and the Mid-Atlantic Ridge.

   The correct placing of the Azores in latitude and longitude on the geometric grid suggests that the map of the Azores is of great antiquity. It may have been this very map (in another version or copy) that led the Portuguese to the discovery of the islands in 1431. It is unreasonable to suppose that they could have mapped them in their correct positions when they had no means of finding longitude and when graduated sailing charts were not introduced until about the year 1500. But even the Portuguese would hardly have drawn the islands with so little regard to their present shapes.

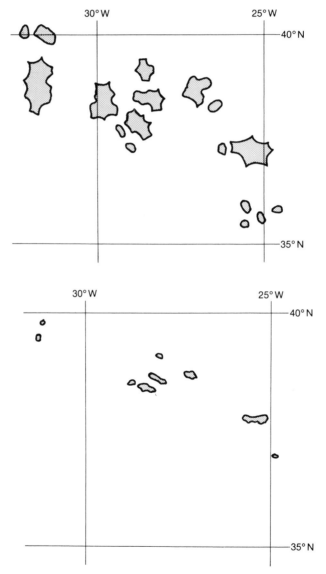

Figure 47. Comparison of the Piri Re'is Map of the Azores(b) with the modern map(a).

# IV The Antarctic Maps of Oronteus Finaeus and Mercator

## 1. Oronteus Finaeus.

A PART of our Piri Re'is investigation, quite naturally, was a search for other portolan charts of the Middle Ages and the Renaissance that might show Antarctica. Quite a number of these turned up, for, as we have mentioned, many cartographers of the 15th and 16th centuries believed in the existence of a southern continent.

In the course of this investigation I arranged to spend some time in the Library of Congress during the Thanksgiving recess of 1959. I wrote ahead to the Chief of the Map Division asking if all the old maps of the periods in question could be brought out and made ready for my inspection, especially those that might show the Antarctic. Dr. Arch C. Gerlach, and his assistant, Richard W. Stephenson, and other members of the staff of the Map Division were most co-operative, and I found, somewhat to my consternation, that they had laid out several hundred maps on the tables of the Reference Room.

By arriving at the Library the moment it opened in the morning and staying there until it closed in the evening, I slowly made a dent in the enormous mass of material. I found many fascinating things I had not expected to find, and a number of portolan charts showing the southern continent. Then, one day, I turned a page, and sat transfixed. As my eyes fell upon the southern hemisphere of a world map drawn by Oronteus Finaeus in 1531, I had the instant conviction that I had found here a truly authentic map of the real Antarctica. (Notes 9, 10).

The general shape of the continent was startlingly like the outline of the continent on our modern map (see Figs. 48, 49). The position of the South Pole, nearly in the center of the continent, seemed about right. The mountain ranges that skirted the coasts suggested the numerous ranges that have been discovered in Antarctica in recent years. It was obvious, too, that this was no slapdash creation of

Figure 48. The Oronteus Finaeus Map of 1532. *F*

somebody's imagination. The mountain ranges were individualized, some definitely coastal and some not. From most of them rivers were shown flowing into the sea, following in every case what looked like very natural and very convincing drainage patterns. This suggested, of course, that the coasts may have been ice-free when the original map was drawn.

At the beginning of our study we made a comparison of the proportions of Antarctica as this map shows them with those shown on modern maps. I measured two traverses across the continent on modern maps and compared their ratio with the ratio of the same traverses on the map of Oronteus Finaeus. We measured from the beginning of the broad part of the Peninsula because study seemed to show that the upper, narrow part of the Peninsula was omitted from the Oronteus Finaeus Map, as it apparently also had been from the Piri Re'is Map. These traverses were (a) from the Antarctic (Palmer) Peninsula at 69° S and 60° W to the Sabrina Coast of Wilkes Land at 66° S and 120° E; and (b) from the Ross Sea (Queen Maud Range) at 85–88° S and 180° E/W, to the Muhlig-Hofmann Mountains, in Queen Maud Land, at 72° S and 0° E/W, measuring in centimeters. On the Oronteus Finaeus Map (a small one) I measured in millimeters (since the ratios alone counted) with the following results:

### The Modern Map

Palmer Peninsula to the Sabrina Coast . . . . . . . . . . . . .    78.5 cm.
Ross Sea to Queen Maud Coast . . . . . . . . . . . . . . .    38.0 cm.

### The Oronteus Finaeus Map

Palmer Peninsula to the Sabrina Coast . . . . . . . . . . . .    129.0 mm.
Ross Sea to the Queen Maud Land Coast . . . . . . . . . .    73.0 mm.

$$\text{Thus we have:} \quad \frac{38:78.5}{73:129} = \frac{2.06}{1.76}, \text{ or a ratio of 8:7.}$$

It is improbable that this close agreement is accidental.

Examining this map of Antarctica on the grid of latitude lines drawn by Oronteus Finaeus, we observed that he had extended the Antarctic Peninsula too far north by about 15°. At first I thought he might simply have placed the whole continent too far north in the direction of South America. Further examination, however, showed that the shores of his Antarctic Continent extended too far in all directions, even reaching the tropics! The trouble, it would seem, therefore, was with the scale. By using an oversized map the compiler was forced to crowd the Antarctic Peninsula up against Cape Horn, squeezing out Drake Passage almost entirely. Furthermore, the mistake must have been made far back, for we find the identical error in all the Antarctic maps of the period, including that of Piri Re'is. It is possible, indeed, that this mistake may account for the omission at some ancient period, on the source map used by Piri Re'is, of a large part of the coastline of South America: There was simply no room for it!

As our study continued, it gradually began to appear tha Oronteus Finaeus' network of parallels and meridians did not fit the Antarctic as shown on his world

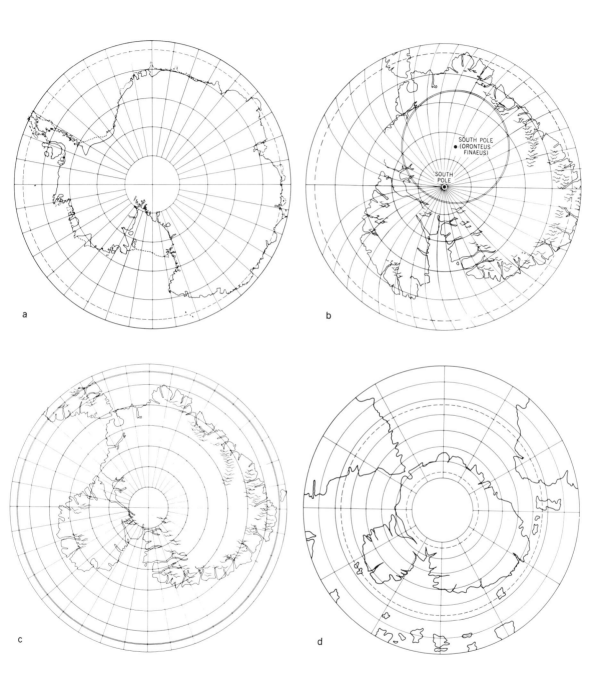

Figure 49. Four Maps of Antarctica: (a) the modern map, (b) the Oronteus Finaeus Map, (c) the Oronteus Finaeus Map redrawn on the modern equidistant projection, (d) Antarctica from the Schöner Globe of 1523–24, also on a polar type of projection. *The Schöner Globe suggests that more than one version of the ancient map of Antarctica may have survived.*

map. Apparently a projection had been imposed by him on a source map originally drawn with a very different kind of map grid. How were we to discover the nature of this original network of parallels and meridians?

The first step seemed obvious. It was simply to remove the network of lines applied to the map by Oronteus Finaeus. We made a tracing of the map, leaving off these lines but retaining, for the moment, his position for the South Pole, and his Antarctic Circle. Since he could have had no way of knowing the position of the pole in the interior of the continent, we considered that his source map must have shown the pole.

The position of the pole looked quite correct at first glance, as I have mentioned, but, as our study and comparison of the old map with modern maps continued, we could see that the mapmaker had apparently made a mistake of a few degrees in locating the pole. We found what seemed a truer position by measuring across the continent in several directions and finding the position that would divide all the diameters of the continent in approximately the same ratio as shown on modern maps. This was, of course, an extension of our first measurement. It was only an empirical experiment, but it seemed to give a more satisfactory result in terms of the latitudes of identifiable places.

With our adjusted pole as a center, I now constructed a grid on the supposition that the original projection might have been the equidistant polar projection, one that is said to have been known in ancient times (see Fig. 25). In this system the meridians are straight lines radiating from a pole. The parallels of latitude are circles. In order to fix the latitudes I had to find one circle at a known distance from the pole. The obvious thing to do was to locate the Antarctic Circle, which is approximately 23½° from the pole, by comparing the old map with the new. It so happens that Antarctica is circular and lies almost within the Antarctic Circle. It was comparatively easy to draw about the continent on the old map a circle that would pass at about the right distances from the various coasts, as compared with a modern map. This was, in fact, one method we used to relocate our pole.

Since the Antarctic Circle is 23½° from the pole, it was now possible to measure out one degree by dividing the distance to the pole on our draft map by 23½. With the length of the degree thus determined, we could then lay out circles 10° apart: the 80th and 70th parallels of latitude. Now we had the parallels necessary for our grid.

When it came to the meridians, we had to deal with another problem. It did not seem to us at first that the continent was properly oriented in relation to the other continents. To get correct longitude readings for our Antarctic coasts on the old map we naturally had to line it up with the meridians on the modern map. It was possible, of course, that, if we were dealing with an authentic map of Antarctica that had survived for several millennia, somebody could have placed it askew on a world map. We thought it looked as if the continent ought to be rotated about 20° to the east to bring it into correct relationship to the other continents. We selected empirically what looked like a reasonable "prime meridian" and then laid out the other meridians at five-degree intervals, thus constructing our grid.

At this point we made a vital discovery. I noticed that the circle we had drawn for the 80th parallel was almost exactly the size of the circle Oronteus Finaeus had drawn on his map and labelled *Circulus Antarcticus*—Antarctic Circle. The true Antarctic Circle follows a path in the sea off the Antarctic coasts; this Antarctic Circle of Oronteus Finaeus, on the other hand, was in the center of the continent. This suggested that Oronteus Finaeus, or a predecessor, in interpreting some old source map may have mistaken for the Antarctic Circle a circle upon the map intended to represent the 80th parallel. This mistake would have exaggerated the size of Antarctica about four times. Since every Renaissance map of the Antarctic seems to reflect this mistake, it is highly likely that the error goes back to Alexandria, or to some earlier period.

A very extraordinary aspect of this matter is that, with the correction of scale, the size of the Antarctic Continent on the map of Oronteus Finaeus is correct, by modern findings. The reader may check this matter by comparing the distribution of the land masses inside and outside the Antarctic Circle as it is shown on the ancient and modern maps (see Fig 49.)

The reader may well ask how it could happen that an ancient map, a map ancient even in classical times, could have had parallels of latitude indicated at ten-degree intervals, when this method of counting by tens and using a circle divided into 360 degrees was supposedly only applied to maps in the Renaissance. This question will be answered in connection with another matter. Meanwhile, the presumption that the ancients had a correct idea of the size of the Antarctic Continent suggests that they may also have had a correct idea of the size of the earth, knowledge that appears, indeed, to be reflected in the Piri Re'is Map.

Once we had a grid constructed, as I have described above, we tried to identify, by comparison with modern maps, as many places on this map of Antarctica as possible. The result was electrifying. All the errors of the location of places that we had identified on Oronteus Finaeus' own grid were greatly reduced. Some of the tentative identifications we had made on the basis of his grid had to be given up, but many new places were identified, so that our list of identified geographical features in Antarctica was increased from sixteen to thirty-two. For this grid we abandoned our empirically derived 80th parallel and simply used Oronteus Finaeus' own so-called *Circulus Antarcticus* as our 80th parallel. We found that by doing this we improved the accuracy of the grid. In other words, it seemed more clear than ever that the circle, misnamed by some early geographer, had originally been intended to be the 80th parallel and nothing else.

However, notwithstanding the amazing accuracy in the positions of many places, there were still numerous errors. We continued to experiment with rotating the continent a few degrees one way or the other, and changing by ever so little the position of the pole, but there were still plenty of discrepancies.

Then it appeared that this ancient map of Antarctica was put together, like the Piri Re'is Map, from a number of local maps of different coasts, and perhaps not put together correctly. An analysis of the errors in our tables showed that, so far as longitudes were concerned, the errors differed in direction in different parts of the

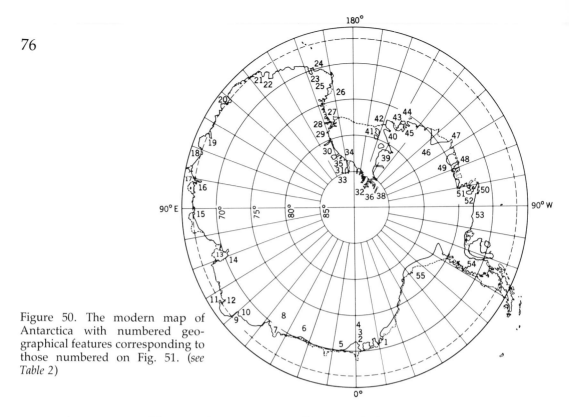

Figure 50. The modern map of Antarctica with numbered geographical features corresponding to those numbered on Fig. 51. (*see Table* 2)

map. The average of longitude errors in Wilkes Land, for example, was easterly, while in the Ross Sea area and Victoria Land it was westerly. I had a transparent overlay made of the Oronteus Finaeus Map, so that we could place it over a modern map, and shift it around as we pleased. We found that the Oronteus Finaeus Map could be aligned remarkably well with a modern map, but we had to shift it around to different positions to make the individual segments of the coasts fit. It seemed impossible to make all the coasts fit at once. It seemed clear that we had in hand a compilation of local maps made by people who were not as well acquainted with the area as those who had originally mapped the separate coasts.

As I have mentioned, we worked for a long time on the assumption that the original projection, on which the compilation had been made, was of a sort that had meridians that were straight lines. But, on this basis, we were never able to get a satisfactory alignment of Antarctica with other continents. I was therefore finally forced to consider the possibility that the meridians might have been curved like those that actually appear on the Oronteus Finaeus Map. And so it turned out. With a grid redrawn on this basis (see Fig. 51) the identified places on the map were increased in number from thirty-two to fifty, and the averages of errors again were reduced, as shown in Table 2.*

* This finding, of course, affects very much our visual comparison of the ancient and modern maps. Since they appear to have been drawn on different projections they would naturally look different, even if they were identical. Therefore, the agreement of the two may actually be greater than it appears. Table 2 indicates this. Fig. 49 shows the Oronteus Finaeus Map on a projection using straight meridians. This makes a better comparison with the modern map.

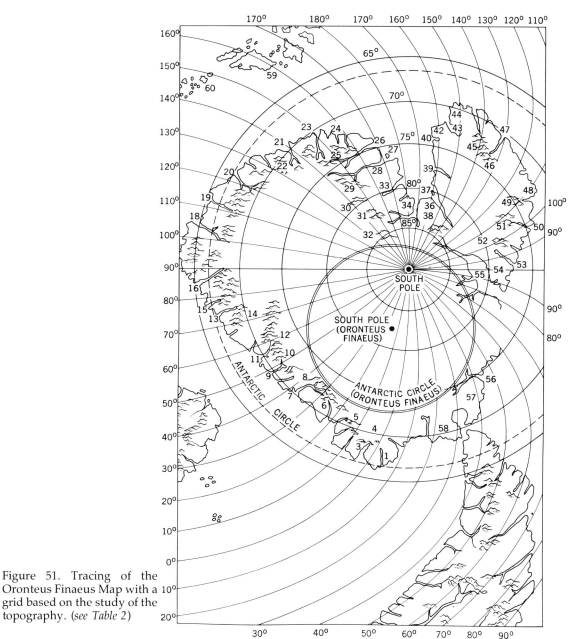

Figure 51. Tracing of the Oronteus Finaeus Map with a grid based on the study of the topography. (*see Table* 2)

At this point we should pause to consider in somewhat greater detail the obviously serious question of the ice cap which now covers the whole continent. We are not here concerned with the geological problem of accounting for a warm period in Antarctica within the lifetime of the human race. Rather, we are concerned with just what the map shows. It would appear that the map shows non-glacial conditions extending for a considerable distance inland on some of the coasts. These coasts include, it seems, the coasts of Queen Maud Land, Enderby Land, Wilkes Land, Victoria Land (the east coast of the Ross Sea), and Marie Byrd

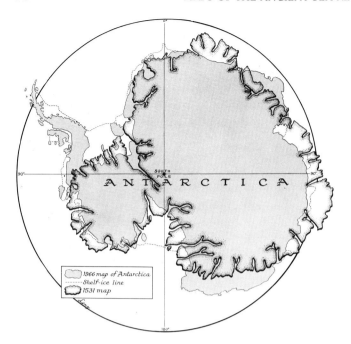

Figure 52. The Oronteus Finaeus Map of Antarctica redrawn on the modern equidistant azimuthal polar projection, compared with the modern map of Antarctica on the same projection (*Christian Science Monitor*)

Land. Notably lacking in definite identifiable points are the west coast of the Ross Sea, Ellsworth Land, and Edith Ronne Land.

A comparison of the Oronteus Finaeus Map with the map of the *subglacial* land surfaces of Antarctica produced by survey teams of various nations during the International Geophysical Year (1958) seems to explain some of the apparent short-comings of the Oronteus Finaeus Map, and at the same time throws some light on the question of the probable extent of glacial conditions when the original maps were drawn.

Figure 52 shows that the IGY teams discovered the actual land forms under the present Antarctic ice cap to be. It is noticeable that, contrary to surface appearances, there is no western shore to the Ross Sea; rather, the rock surface of the continent is below sea level straight across from the Ross Sea to the Weddell Sea, and most of Ellsworth Land is also below sea level. If the ice cap melted, all these areas would be shallow sea—not land.

It is plain, of course, that if the western coast of the Ross Sea and the coast of Ellsworth Land are, in fact, non-existent, the absence of definite physical features in these sections of the Oronteus Finaeus Map is well explained. But, it seems that the ice cap may already have been in existence at least in West Antarctica when the original maps were drawn, for the interior waterways connecting the Ross, Weddell, and Amundsen Seas are not shown.

The Antarctic (Palmer) Peninsula presents a point of special interest. As already noted, only the base of the Peninsula can be identified on the Oronteus Finaeus Map. The upper part of the Peninsula is missing. We find, now, from the results of the IGY investigations, that there is, in fact, no such peninsula. There is, in fact, what would be an island if the ice cap melted. It would seem, then, that even if a great deal of ice was already in existence when the original map of this portion of the Antarctic was drawn, the ice cap had not yet covered the area of shallow sea between the continental shore and this island.

It must, of course, be remembered that thousands of years may have elapsed between the drafting of the earliest and latest of the original maps of different parts of Antarctica. We cannot therefore draw the conclusion that there was a time when there was a great deal of ice in East Antarctica and none in West Antarctica. The maps of East Antarctica may have been drawn thousands of years later than the others.

Another very extraordinary map may serve to throw some light on this. Buache, the 18th century French geographer already referred to, left a map of Antarctica that may show the continent at a time when there was no ice at all (see Fig. 53). Compare this with the IGY map of the land masses (Fig. 52). If an apparent error in Buache's orientation of the continent to other land masses is disregarded, it is quite easy to imagine that this map shows the waterways connecting the Ross, Weddell, and Bellingshausen Seas.

When we discovered that the meridians of the original map were curved as Oronteus Finaeus had constructed them, it was no longer necessary to rotate his map of the Antarctic eastward in order to bring it into agreement with the other land masses. Instead, it became apparent that this source map of South America and his source map of Antarctica probably came to him in one piece. Their relative longitudes were correct.

The eastern hemisphere on the Oronteus Finaeus Map of 1531 in no way compares with the Antarctic and South American parts. Here Finaeus seems to have based his Mediterranean, for example, on the inaccurate Ptolemy maps rather than on the portolanos. (Notes 9, 10, 19).

Among the most remarkable features of the Oronteus Finaeus Map is the part we identify as the Ross Sea. The modern map indicates the places where great glaciers, like the Beardmore and Scott Glaciers, pour down their millions of tons of ice annually to the sea. On the Oronteus Finaeus Map (Fig. 48), fiord-like estuaries are seen, along with broad inlets and indications of rivers of a magnitude that is consistent with the sizes of the present glaciers. And some of these fiords are located remarkably close to the correct positions of the glaciers (see Table 2).

The open estuaries and rivers are evidence that, when this source map was made, there was no ice on the Ross Sea or on its coasts. There had also to be a considerable hinterland free of ice to feed the rivers. At the present time all these coasts and their hinterlands are deeply buried in the mile-thick ice cap, while on the Ross Sea itself there is a floating ice shelf hundreds of feet thick.

The idea of a temperate period in the Ross Sea in time so recent as is indicated by this map will, at first acquaintance, be incredible to geologists. It has been their view that the Antarctic ice cap is very ancient, perhaps several million years old, although, curiously enough, it seems that previously in the long history of the globe the climate of Antarctica was often warm and sometimes even tropical (85:58–61). (See Chap. IX).

Figure 53. The sub-glacial topography of Antarctica, according to Buache. (*from R. V. Toole*

In answer to this possible objection I can cite, in addition to the map itself, only one further piece of evidence, but it is a very impressive piece of evidence indeed. In 1949, on one of the Byrd Antarctic Expeditions, some sediments were taken from the bottom of the Ross Sea, by coring tubes lowered into the sea. Dr. Jack Hough, of the University of Illinois, took three cores to learn something of the climatic history of the Antarctic. The cores were taken to the Carnegie Institution in Washington, D.C., where they were subjected to a new method of dating developed by the nuclear physicist Dr. W. D. Urry.

This method of dating is called, for short, the ionium method. It makes use of three different radioactive elements found in sea water. These elements are uranium, ionium, and radium, and they occur in a definite ratio to each other in the water. They decay at different rates, however; this means that when the sea water containing them is locked up in sediments at the bottom of the ocean and all circulation of the water is stopped, the quantities of these radioactive elements diminish, but not at the same rate. Thus, it is possible, when these sediments are brought up and examined in the laboratory, to determine the age of the sediments by the amount of change that has taken place in the ratios of the elements still found in the sediments.

The character of sea-bottom sediments varies considerably according to the climatic conditions existing when they were formed. If sediment has been carried down by rivers and deposited out to sea it will be very fine grained, more fine grained the farther it is from the river mouth. If it has been detached from the earth's surface by ice and carried by glaciers and dropped out to sea by icebergs, it will be very coarse. If the river flow is only seasonal, that is if it flows only in summer, presumably from melting glaciers inland, and freezes up each winter, the sediment will be deposited somewhat like the annual rings in a tree in layers or "varves."

All these kinds of sediments were found in the cores taken from the Ross Sea bottom. As you will see from the illustration (Fig. 54) there were many different layers of sediment in the coring tubes. The most surprising discovery was that a number of the layers were formed of fine-grained, well-assorted sediments such as is brought down to the sea by rivers flowing from temperate (that is, ice-free) lands. As you can see, the cores indicate that during the last million years or so there have been at least three periods of temperate climate in Antarctica when the shores of the Ross Sea must have been free of ice. (Note 12).

This discovery would indicate that the glacial history of Antarctica may have been roughly similar to that of North America, where we have had three or more ice ages in the last million years. Let us remember that, if most geologists cannot imagine how Antarctica could have had warm climates at short and relatively recent geological intervals, neither can they explain how North America could have had arctic conditions at equally short intervals and just as equally recently. Ice ages remain for geologists an unsolved mystery (85:35).

The date found by Dr. Urry for the end of the last warm period in the Ross Sea is of tremendous interest to us. All three cores agree that the warm period ended

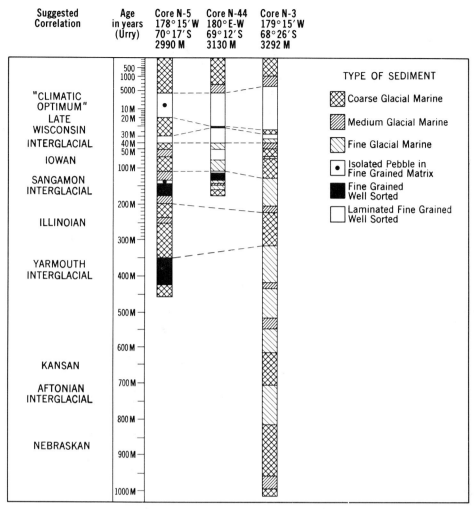

| Suggested Correlation | Age in years (Urry) | Core N-5 178°15'W 70°17'S 2990 M | Core N-44 180°E-W 69°12'S 3130 M | Core N-3 179°15'W 68°26'S 3292 M |
|---|---|---|---|---|

**TYPE OF SEDIMENT**

⊠ Coarse Glacial Marine

▨ Medium Glacial Marine

◫ Fine Glacial Marine

• Isolated Pebble in Fine Grained Matrix

■ Fine Grained Well Sorted

☐ Laminated Fine Grained Well Sorted

"CLIMATIC OPTIMUM"
LATE WISCONSIN
INTERGLACIAL
IOWAN
SANGAMON INTERGLACIAL
ILLINOIAN
YARMOUTH INTERGLACIAL
KANSAN
AFTONIAN INTERGLACIAL
NEBRASKAN

Figure 54. The Ross Sea Cores, *after Hough (96)*.

about 6,000 years ago, or about 4000 B.C. It was then that the glacial kind of sediment began to be deposited on the Ross Sea bottom in the most recent of Antarctic ice ages. The cores indicate that warm conditions had prevailed for a long time before that.

An important fact about the Oronteus Finaeus Map is that all the rivers on it are shown flowing from mountain ranges near the coasts, except those near the southern tip of South America. No rivers are shown in the deep interior. This suggests that, very possibly, when the source maps were made, the interior was already covered by the ice cap. In that case, the ice cap was an advancing continental glacier that had not yet brimmed the encircling mountain ranges to reach the sea, nor had it yet stopped the flow of rivers on the seaward side of the mountains.

Let us connect this situation for a moment in regards to the Princess Martha Coast as we have identified it on the Piri Re'is Map. It would seem that the ice cap had not yet crossed the mountains that stretch along behind that coast. Supposing the ice cap to have advanced from the direction of the South Pole, which area would it have reached first—the Princess Martha Coast or the Ross Sea? It would have reached the Ross Sea first, and the shores of that sea would no doubt have been glaciated quite a good deal earlier than the Princess Martha Coast, in fact, possibly some thousands of years before. If this was the case the ancient voyages to the Princess Martha Coast that may be reflected in the Piri Re'is Map may have been made as recently as about 1000 B.C. While this may go a little way to relieve the historian of the problem of accounting for the mapping of that particular coast, it does nothing to help him in the Ross Sea area, for there it seems that the mapping would have to have been done at least 6,000 years ago.

So far, then, we find that this map of Oronteus Finaeus is based on an authentic ancient source map of Antarctica compiled from local maps of the coasts drawn before the Antarctic ice cap had reached them. The individual maps of the different coasts are fairly accurate, taking account of the differences that may be attributed to the presence of the ice cap now over the coasts. In addition, the general compilation, which successfully placed the coasts in correct latitudes and relative longitudes and found a remarkably correct area for the continent, reflects an amazing geographical knowledge of Antarctica such as was not achieved in modern times until the twentieth century. The minor error in the location of the pole was perhaps subsequent to the date of compilation of the general map, or it might reflect a change in the position of the pole. A theoretical explanation of the climatic change in Antarctica is presented in Chapter IX.

This map appears to confirm our impression as to the presence of a part of the Antarctic coast on the Piri Re'is Map. We have been successful, it would seem, in the quest for supporting evidence.

## 2.   The remarkable map of Hadji Ahmed.*

In some respects this Turkish map of 1559 is one of the most remarkable I have seen (see Fig. 55). There is a striking difference between the drawing of the eastern and western hemispheres. The eastern hemisphere seems to have been based on the sources available to geographers of the time, mostly Ptolemy, and to be somewhat ordinary. The map of the Mediterranean is still evidently based on Ptolemy instead of on the much better portolan maps. The African coasts do not compare in accuracy with the same coasts on the Piri Re'is Map of 1513 or on other maps to be discussed shortly.

But if this is true of the eastern hemisphere, it is an entirely different story in the west, and here it is evident that the cartographer had at his disposal some most extraordinary source maps. The shapes of North and South America have a surprisingly modern look; the western coasts are especially interesting. They seem to be about two centuries ahead of the cartography of the time. Furthermore, they

---

* For a discussion of this map see bibliographic source 19.

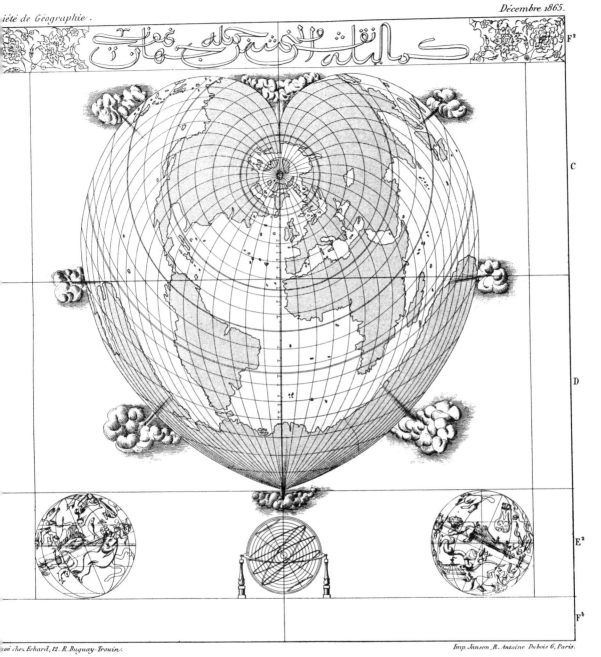

Figure 55. Hadji Ahmed World Map of 1550.

appear to have been drawn on a highly sophisticated spherical projection. The shape of what is now the United States is about perfect.

This remarkable accuracy of the Pacific coasts of the Americas, and the difficulty of imagining how they could have been drawn in the middle of the 16th century,†

† More than two centuries before the solution of the problem of longitude.

adds significance to another detail of the map: the suggestion of a land bridge connecting Alaska and Siberia.** This land bridge actually existed in the so-called Ice Age. The map suggests that the land bridge was a broad one, perhaps a thousand miles across.

In case the reader is drawing back at this moment, in a state of amazement mingled with horror, I am forced to remind him that this bit of evidence is only a link in a chain. We have completed a study of the Piri Re'is Map of 1513, and have concluded that it may contain a representation of part of the Antarctic coast drawn before the present ice cap covered it. We have examined the 1531 Oronteus Finaeus Map of Antarctica and have come to much more far-reaching conclusions. We cannot estimate, of course, the lapse of time implied by these remarkable maps of Antarctica. But we have presented evidence that the deglacial or unglaciated period in the Antarctic cannot have come to an end later than 6,000 years ago and must have existed for a very long time before that. The warm period in the Antarctic may, then, have coincided with the last glacial period in North America. If this is true it follows that this map need be based on maps no older than the maps already discussed.

A more detailed examination reveals further interesting facts. The grid drawn on the map enables us to check accuracy. This particular projection has all the eridians curved except one, which we refer to as the prime meridian. The reader can see the prime meridian on this map, running from the North to the South Poles, and passing near the coast of Africa. The other meridians are all spaced ten degrees apart, as are the parallels of latitude from pole to pole. The prime meridian on this map appears to coincide closely with the 20th meridian of West longitude on modern maps. Thus, to find the longitude of any place, we will start with this line as 20° West and count by tens, adding longitude westward and subtracting it eastward. In Table 3 I have listed a number of places and compared their positions on this map and on modern maps. Table 3 is in two parts; the first part deals with places that are fairly close to, and the second part with places that are far from, the prime meridian. Note that both latitude and longitude are surprisingly accurate for places near the meridian, the accuracy of longitude being especially noteworthy. But that accuracy declines rapidly with distance from the meridian.

This increased inaccuracy with distance from the prime meridian indicates an error in the projection, but not necessarily in error in the drawing of the coasts that seem too far off. It may merely be another case of imposing a projection on a map that was originally drawn on an entirely different projection.

Some of the apparent exaggerations of the size of Antarctica on the map of Hadji Ahmed can, of course, be attributed to the same error we found on the Oronteus Finaeus Map, namely the confusion of the 80th parallel of latitude with the Antarc-

** Mr. Derek S. Allan, a British scientist from Oxford, further comments on this map: "It would seem, perhaps, that either the sea-level was lower, or that the land has sunk since the original map was drawn. The Laptev sea area—including the New Siberian Islands?—appears as dry land (this may well be correct since the sea bottom today is the extraordinary mammoth graveyard), and it seems that Novya Semlya was joined to the Siberian Coast . . . One might note with astonishment that there appears to be no indication of ice cover in the area."

tic Circle. But even considering this, the continent on this map seems too large, and its shape is hardly recognizable.

To understand the cause of the extreme distortion of the map, let us consider the polar regions on any Mercator map. It is difficult to find a modern Mercator world map showing Antarctica, but anyone who has seen a Mercator world map cannot have failed to notice how the projection exaggerates the northern polar regions. On such maps Greenland, for example, appears to be about the size of South America. This results from the fact that on this projection the meridians are parallel straight lines that never meet. The whole line across the top or bottom of such a map represents the pole, and the geography is distorted accordingly.

What I am suggesting is that some of the ancient source maps of Antarctica may have been drawn on a projection resembling the Mercator at least in this respect of having straight meridians parallel to each other. Such a projection existed in Greek times and was, according to Ptolemy, the projection used by Marinus of Tyre (39:69). If ancient source maps survived on two different projections—some on a circular projection such as we have apparently found on the Oronteus Finaeus Map and some on a straight-meridian projection like that of Marinus of Tyre or Mercator—the appearance of this map would be readily explained.*

## 3.   Mercator's maps of the Antarctic.

Gerhard Kremer, known as Mercator, is the most famous cartographer of the 16th century. (Note 13). There is even a tendency to date the beginning of scientific cartography from him. Nonetheless, there never was a cartographer more interested in the ancients, more indefatigable in searching out ancient maps, or more respectful of the learning of the long ago.

I think it is safe to say that Mercator would not have included the Oronteus Finaeus Map of Antarctica in his *Atlas* if he disbelieved in the existence of that continent. He was not publishing a book of science fiction. But we have further reason to know he believed in its existence: He shows Antarctica on maps he drew himself. One of his maps of the Antarctic appears on Sheet 9 of the 1569 *Atlas*. (See Fig. 56.) At first glance I could see little relationship between this Mercator Map and that of Oronteus Finaeus, and I had little reason to suspect that it could be a good map of the Antarctic coast. But careful study showed that a number of points could be clearly identified (see Fig. 57). Among these were Cape Dart and Cape Herlacher in Marie Byrd Land, the Amundsen Sea. Thurston Island in Ellsworth Land, the Fletcher Islands in the Bellingshausen Sea, Alexander I Island, the Antarctic Peninsula, the Weddell Sea, Cape Norvegia, the Regula Range in Queen Maud Land (as islands), the Muhlig-Hofmann Mountains (as islands), the Prince Harald Coast, the Shirase Glacier (as an estuary) on Prince Harald Coast, Padda Island in Lutzow-Hölm Bay, and the Prince Olaf Coast in Enderby Land. In some cases these features are more distinctly recognizable than on the Oronteus Finaeus Map, and it seems clear, in general, that Mercator had at his disposal source maps

* Note similarity between Hadji Ahmed's South America and Mercator's (Fig. 39).

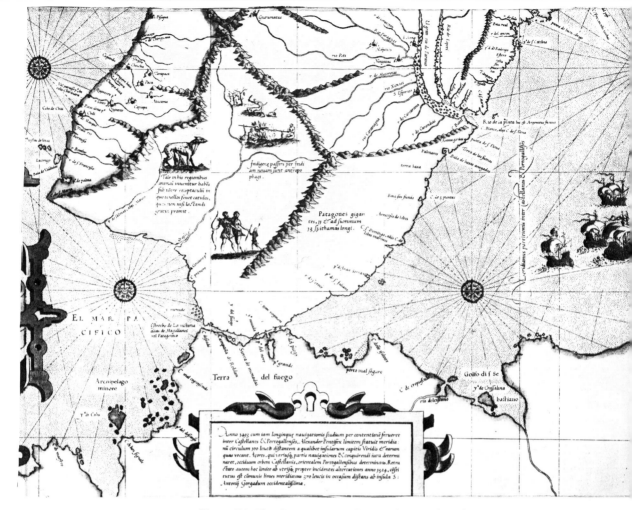

Figure 56. The Antarctic on Mercator's Map (1569). *I*

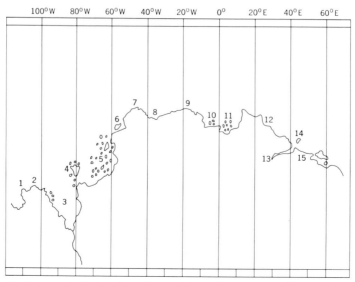

Figure 57. Mercator's Antarctic with meridians drawn according to his own projection.

other than those used by Oronteus Finaeus.

The projection on Mercator's map of Antarctica is the one that is named after him. It has straight meridians that run parallel from pole to pole, and these, of course, enlarge the polar regions very much, as already explained.

I thought at first that Mercator might have drawn his map of Antarctica to fit his projection; in which case its large size might be thus explained without recourse to any other considerations. To test this, I traced the map and drew parallel meridians on it at ten-degree intervals, converting his longitude figures into East and West Greenwich longitude (Fig. 57). Mercator, accepting the cartographical convention of his time, counted 360° from a meridian off the west coast of Africa, approximately in what we now call 23° W longitude. This is indicated on his world map of 1538, which also shows the Antarctic (Figs. 59, 60).*

In order to correlate his system with ours, it is necessary to find a point common to both. I picked the meridian of Alexandria as this common point because I saw that Mercator's 60th meridian (1528 World Map) passed through Alexandria, which, in our system, is the 30th meridian of E longitude. Thus his 30th meridian, we might suppose, should be equivalent to our zero meridian (the meridian of Greenwich). To convert his longitude to our system, accordingly, it seemed that we should merely have to subtract 30° going eastward. His zero meridian and his 360th meridian coincided, and should be, according to this, equivalent to our meridian of 30° W. But, as we have seen, this is not the case. His zero/360th meridian actually coincides fairly closely with our meridian of 23° W. The discrepancy amounts to about 7°.

I should perhaps explain at this point that the exact location of Mercator's zero/360th meridian depends on the accuracy of his placing of the Cape Verde Islands, the Canary Islands, and the Azores in longitude. He has his zero meridian running through the easternmost of the Cape Verde Islands, missing the westernmost Canaries by a degree and a half, and passing through the easternmost Azores, so that he has the easternmost islands of the Cape Verdes and of the Azores on the same meridian. But they are actually not on the same meridian. For this reason I thought it best to take a definite point, like Alexandria, as a common point for converting his system into ours. However, we have just seen that this will not precisely do, either. There is a descrepancy.

What is the matter? This brings up a most important point. Mercator is rightly regarded as a great cartographer. We forget that he had to work within the limitations of his age. Since he did not know the true circumference of the earth, he had to take the best guess going. We have seen that when we start counting degrees from Alexandria by his system and by our own we do not end up in the same place. We find ourselves 7° too far west. On the other hand, if we start counting from our 23rd meridian, converting that to Mercator's zero meridian, we are going to find Alexandria at 37° E longitude, 7° too far east. The actual longitude difference between the meridian of 23° W and Alexandria is 53°. A simple calculation shows that 7° is 13% too short.

---

* Mallery maintained that this map of Mercator must have been based on an authentic ancient source map (131).

With regard to Mercator's 1569 map, my first step was to pick a reference point for longitude. It seemed to me that our zero meridian, which intersects the Queen Maud Land Coast between the Regula Range and the Muhlig-Hofmann Mountains, might be a good point to start with, experimentally. I took no account of the difference in the length of the degree, but drew my meridians the same distance apart as Mercator did, numbering them after our modern system. The errors in the longitudes thus found for the various points convinced me that Mercator had not redrawn his source map; apparently he had simply taken a map constructed on quite a different projection and transferred it bodily to his own map.

I conjectured that the original projection may have been a polar type of projection with straight meridians. In this case the parallels of latitude would be circles. To test the matter, I listed the identifiable points on the map with their latitudes. As the reader can see (Fig. 58), the localities are distributed in a semicircle. They are, nevertheless, closely in the same latitudes, averaging about 70° S, as this list shows:

| | | | |
|---|---|---|---|
| Cape Dart | 73.5 S | Cape Norvegia | 71.0 S |
| Cape Herlacher | 74.0 S | Regula Range | 72.0 S |
| Amundsen Sea | 72.0 S | Muhlig–Hofmann Mts. | 71–73 S |
| Thurston Island | 72.0 S | Prince Harald Coast | 69–70 S |
| Fletcher Island | 73.0 S | Shirase Glacier | 70.0 S |
| Alexander I Island | 69–73 S | Padda Island | 69.0 S |
| Bellingshausen Sea | 71.0 S | Casey Bay | 67.5 S |
| Antarctic Peninsula (truncated) | 70.0 S | Edward VIII Bay | 67.0 S |
| Weddell Sea | 72.0 S | | |

The indication is that the parallels of latitude on this map were originally circles. I found it possible with a pair of compasses to draw a circle that would pass close to all of them. A series of experiments finally located a point for the South Pole that gave me a satisfactory parallel of 70° S latitude, with respect to most of the localities. Having the pole and the 70th parallel, it was a simple matter to find the length of the degree of latitude and then measure out the 80th, 75th. 70th, and 65th parallels. We could then check the latitudes and longitudes of the various points as shown in Table 4; we found our grid fairly well confirmed (Fig. 58).

These findings indicate that Mercator had a real map of the Antarctic, though he was unable to transfer the points on it to his own projection. The errors of longitude are less than they seem, since, as we have already mentioned, the degree of longitude is very short at the high latitudes of Antarctica.

Earlier, in 1538, Mercator drew a world map that also showed Antarctica, as we have seen. Its similarity to the map of Oronteus Finaeus is obvious, but there are important differences. Mercator has the Antarctic Circle inside the continent, as Oronteus Finaeus does, but not at the same distance from the pole. In other words, Mercator seems to have changed the *scale*. On the Oronteus Finaeus Map, as we have seen, the so-called *Circulus Antarcticus* seemed to be a mistaken interpretation of the 80th parallel of the source map, as confirmed by the agreement of the geography with the grid drawn on that assumption. By shifting this, Mercator

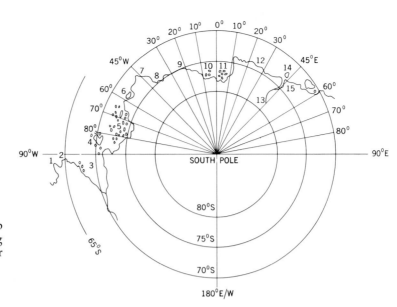

Figure 58. Mercator's Map of the Antarctic, tracing with super-imposed Polar Projection. (*see Table 4*).

destroyed the original scale. Therefore, it is impossible for us to reconstruct a grid of latitudes on this map, as we did for the other map. Longitudes, however, are remarkably accurate (Table 5).

It seems that Mercator made constant use of ancient source maps available to him. What eventually happened to these maps we do not know, but we are able to distinguish, in a number of cases at least, where he depended on them and where he was influenced by contemporary explorations.

For the Antarctic, of course, he had to depend on the ancient sources. (Since the continent was not "discovered" until 250 years later.) The source maps here may have come to him through Oronteus Finaeus, who may have found them in the library of the Paris Academy of Sciences, now part of the Bibliothèque Nationale; or he may have had others of his own. For Greenland he used the Zeno Map of the North, (Fig. 79) with the mountain ranges conventionalized. So far as his 1569 map of South America is concerned (Fig. 39), a number of interesting points emerge.

First, with regard to the northern coast, it is clear that he depended on ancient maps as well as modern explorations. He has the Amazon misplaced with regard to the equator, just as it appears on the Piri Re'is Map, but the course of the Amazon is conventionalized with a number of snakelike meanders. The Island of Marajo, correctly delineated on the equator of the mathematical projection of the Piri Re'is Map, is here confused with the Island of Trinidad, off the mouth of the Orinoco. Trinidad is therefore shown as much too large. The southeast coast of South America, from the Tropic of Capricorn to the Horn, is very badly drawn, evidently from the accounts of the explorers, while the west coast is completely out of shape.

Oddly enough, in his map of 1538, thirty years earlier, Mercator had represented the west coast of South America much more correctly (Fig. 59). How is this explained? I suggest that in his first map he depended on the ancient sources, while on his map of 1569 he depended on the modern explorers, who, since they could find no accurate longitude, could merely guess at the trends of coasts.

Figure 59. Mercator's World Map of 1538. *F*

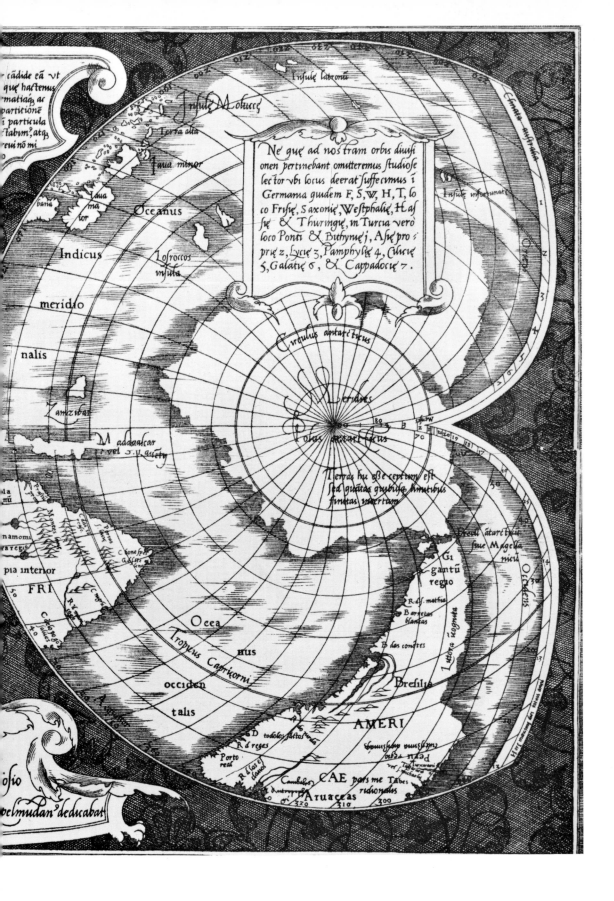

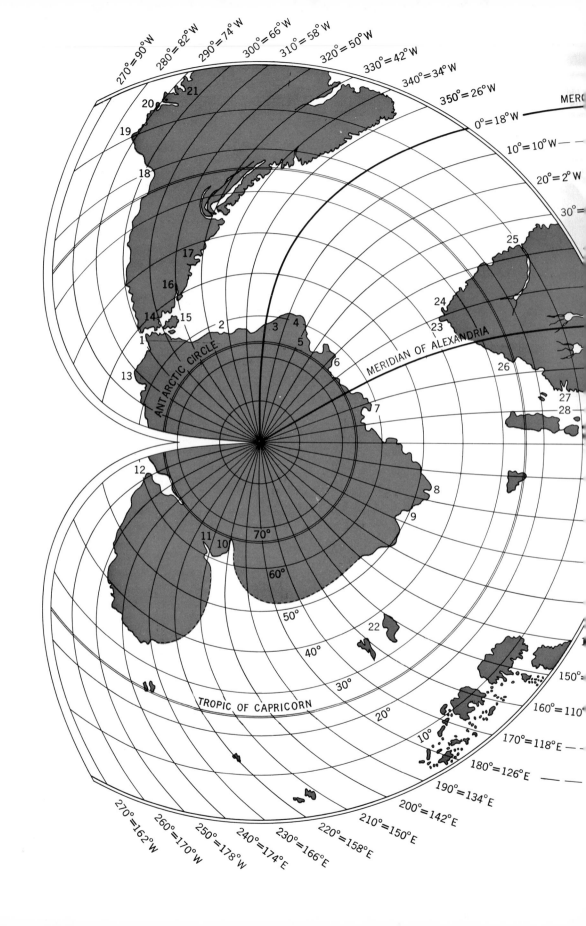

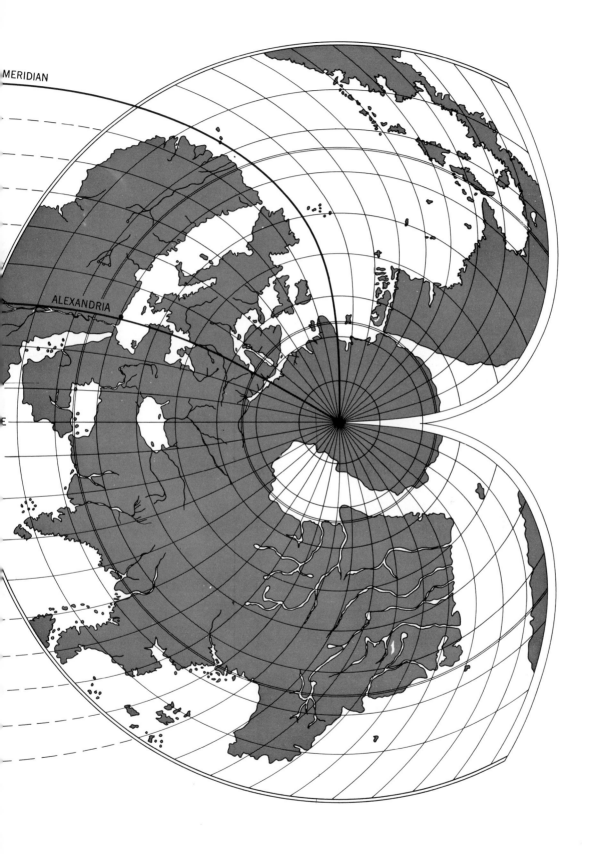

MERIDIAN

ALEXANDRIA

Figure 60. Mercator's World Map of 1538 converted to Greenwich Longitude.

# V   Ancient Maps of the East and West

WE HAVE already noted that Nordenskiöld in his essay on the portolan charts stated that they were too accurate to have originated in the Middle Ages. He found evidence that they probably existed in classical times, along- side the inferior maps of Eratosthenes, Pomponius Mela, and Ptolemy. He even hinted that he thought they were of Carthaginian origin. It is our purpose now to examine a number of these charts, to see how accurate they really are, and how far they may be related to a possible worldwide system of sophisticated maps deriving from pre-Greek times.

## 1.   The Dulcert Portolano of 1339.

The Dulcert Portolano of 1339 is an early version of the "normal portolano"—the highly accurate map that appeared suddenly in Europe in the early 14th century, seemingly from nowhere. This kind of map did not evolve further but was simply copied and recopied during the rest of the Middle Ages and during the Renais- sance (see Fig. 3).

In Fig. 61 I have worked out the grid of this map. I began with the assumption that the grid would be a square grid. I identified a number of geographical points around the map and from these discovered how much latitide and longitude was covered by the map. Dividing the number of degrees into the millimeters of the draft map, I found the length of the degree. It did appear that there was a square grid.

It was necessary to lay out this grid from some definite point. For a first experi- ment I selected Cape Bon, in Tunisia, close to the ancient site of Carthage. I was influenced here by the idea that perhaps this map had been drawn in ancient times by the Carthaginians, using Carthage as a center. I drew my first grid on the assumption that the vertical line (or prime meridian) through the center of the portolan projection was drawn on true North (see Fig. 3). The resulting table revealed errors that indicated that the map was not oriented to true North, but

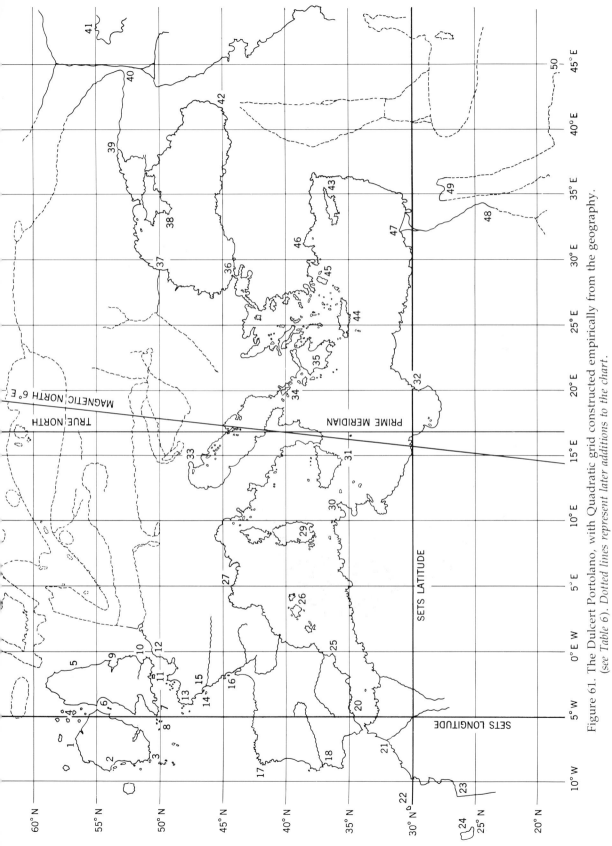

Figure 61. The Dulcert Portolano, with Quadratic grid constructed empirically from the geography. (see Table 6). Dotted lines represent later additions to the chart.

about 6° to the east. It appeared that 6° was probably just about the amount of the compass declination in the Mediterranean at that time. A grid drawn on this basis, however, revealed yet further errors, which seemed to indicate that Alexandria, not Cape Bon, might be a better reference center for the map. A new grid, based on Alexandria, proved to be very satisfactory with respect to latitude, but about 2° off with respect to longitude. A final grid was drawn with latitude based on the parallel of Alexandria, and longitude based on the meridian of Gibraltar, and this proved extremely satisfactory (see Table 6).

The grid applied to this portolano reveals some very interesting facts. First, it appears that the geographical information contained in the chart is much greater than can reasonably be expected from medieval sailors and cartographers. The map falls into three parts: a very accurate map of the Mediterranean and Black Sea regions and of the coasts of Europe as far north as the Hebrides; a very inaccurate map of the Baltic region; and a very inaccurate map of the eastern regions, embracing the Persian Gulf and the Indian Ocean. It seemed that the inaccurate parts of the map were simply tacked onto the portolano proper. They would seem to reflect the true state of medieval geographical knowledge. The portolano proper, on the other hand, is a truly scientific work.

Exclusive of the Black Sea area the latitudes of forty places are correct to within an average error of 0.9°, and the longitudes to within an average error of 0.8°. In the Black Sea latitude errors average 4.5° too far north but (except for the Danube which is anomalous) the longitudes are correct to within 2.0°. This suggests that the Black Sea on this map was aligned with the upper equator of which we have found evidences on the Piri Re'is Map and of which we shall find further evidences in maps to be considered in Chapter VII.

We find that the longitudes of the map are more correct on the average than the latitudes. It appears that the ancient cartographer had very accurate information on the latitudes and longitudes of places scattered all the way from Galway in Ireland to the eastern bend of the Don in Russia. Nordenskiöld would seem to have been quite right when he said no medieval mapmaker could have drawn this map; not even Mercator could have done it.

Another point calls for mention. How could it have been possible to draw so accurate a map of the vast region covered by the Dulcert Portolano (one thousand miles north and south, almost three thousand miles east and west) without the aid of trigonometry? Let us remember that the mapmaker's problem was to transfer points on the spherical surface of the earth to a flat plane in such a way as to preserve correct distances and land shapes. For this, the curvature had to be calculated and transferred to a plane by trigonometry. That this probably was done for the Dulcert Portolano will be shown a little later.

In conclusion, we may remark that, since the Dulcert Portolano represents essentially Nordenskiöld's "normal portolano," we have evidence here that all the portolanos stemmed from a common origin in remote times.

## 2.   The De Canerio Map of 1502.

Before it was torn in two, the Piri Re'is Map had included the whole continent of Africa as well as Asia. In view of this, and in view of the probability that other copies or versions of the source map Piri Re'is used for Africa (or that were used by the Alexandrian compilers) might have survived, we continued a search for a map of Africa drawn on the same projection. We finally found what we thought was such a map.

My first glance at the De Canerio Map of 1502 (see Fig. 62), gave me a feeling that our search had been successful. The South African part (from the equator southward) looked astonishingly modern. I felt fairly confident that this was an authentic ancient map in Renaissance dress.

The abundance of easily identifiable points on the coasts made it easy to work out the scale and construct an empirical grid, and their positions with reference to the grid indicated that the mapmaker had achieved considerable accuracy in both latitude and longitude. The errors of latitude averaged only 1.6° and those of longitude only 1.4°. We thought it remarkable that longitudes seemed more accurate than latitudes.

For some time it was not possible to connect the map directly with the Piri Re'is Projection, nor to solve the mathematical structure that, I still confidently felt, underlay it. Finally, the discovery of the magnetic orientation of the Dulcert Portolano furnished the key.

In the center of Africa, there appears a very large wind rose, obviously the center of the portolan design. It had not appeared to me to lie on any significant parallel or meridian, and I had therefore been unable to link it up with the projection of the Piri Re'is Map until it occurred to me to find out whether this map was oriented to magnetic North. Experiment indicated that the map was, in fact, oriented about 11¼° east of north. It was a simple matter to rotate the map, on its center, westward to true North. Fig. 63 shows how this was done and how, with this shift, the center of the map turned out to lie on the equator—and *on the meridian of Alexandria!*

This was an extraordinary discovery. It constituted as good proof as might be necessary to establish the Alexandrian derivation of the map. It demonstrated, too, that the original map had been drawn on true North, and that the magnetic orientation was probably introduced by De Canerio or some other geographer of the relatively modern period. Why that geographer gave the map an orientation more than twice too far to the east is difficult to imagine. It would, of course, have rendered all compass courses hopelessly wrong. The same error appears in numerous other portolanos.

Now that the exact center of the map had apparently been established, it occurred to me that it might be possible to solve its mathematical structure and to construct a grid based on trigonometry.

This proved easier than I had expected. A number of minor projection points appeared at equal intervals on the map, obviously arranged on the perimeter of the

Figure 62. Africa and Europe on the Nicolo de Canerio World Map of 1502. *B*

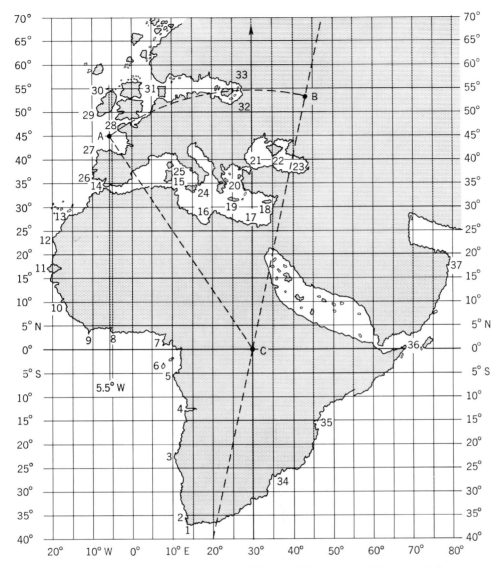

Figure 63. Part of the Canerio Map with an oblong grid constructed by spherical trigonometry.
(*see Table 7, and the calculations p. 236*).

circle of the portolan projection. The trigonometric solution would depend on finding the exact length of the radius of the circle. For this all that was needed was the exact position of one of these minor projection points in latitude and longitude. Fortunately, one of these points lay just off Land's End, England, as near as we could estimate in latitude 50° N and longitude 5.5° W. We now had the two co-ordinates necessary for a trigonometric calculation.

From our experience with the Piri Re'is Map, we assumed at first that plane trigonometry would be involved, and found the length of the radius to be about 61.3°. This gave us the latitudes of the two projection points located on the perimeter, where the latter was intersected by the prime meridian, and we thus obtained the length of the degree of latitude. Since we had not then discovered the oblong grid of the Piri Re'is Map, we assumed that the lengths of the degrees of latitude and longitude would be the same, and drew a square grid for the map. Some remarkable facts now emerged.

The most sensational development was what the grid revealed in the Mediterranean and Black Seas. It was obvious, by comparison with the Dulcert chart, that the De Canerio Map was based on the "normal portolano," though it did not show such fine detail. This was natural enough, considering the much vaster area covered. This part of the De Canerio Map, however, was evidently an integral part of the map of Africa; it had not been just tacked on. It would seem that it had been drawn originally on the same trigonometric projection. This is shown by what follows.

A table of thirty-seven geographical points, as found by our square grid, revealed the extraordinary accuracy of the map as to latitude and longitude. We found, for example, that the average error in the latitudes of eleven places (Gibraltar, the northern coasts of Sardinia, Sicily, Cyprus, and Crete; Cape Bon, Bengazi, Lesbos, the Bosphorus, Sevastopol, and Batum) was only one half of one degree. The longitudinal distance between Gibraltar and Batum was correct, proportionate to the latitude, suggesting that there may have been no considerable error in the original source map, as to the size of the earth. It seemed that the trigonometric solution of the De Canerio Map carried with it the implication that trigonometry underlay the normal portolano and, in fact, the whole group of portolan charts.*

The other parts of the De Canerio Map were not as accurate as the Mediterranean and Black Sea areas. The eastern section (including the upper part of the African coast of the Indian Ocean and Arabia) was evidently plastered onto the accurate source map by De Canerio or somebody else. It did not fit the grid, and it seemed to have been derived from Ptolemy. Another section in the far north, covering the Baltic, also appeared to have been originally a separate source map which at some time had been incorrectly compiled with the principal part of the map.

Other errors appeared within the limits of the trigonometric chart itself. Points on the west coast of Africa from the Cape of Good Hope to the delta of the Niger averaged about 4° too far south. Points from Freetown to Gibraltar averaged about 3.6° too far north. The total latitude error from the Cape of Good Hope to Gibraltar was 5.5°, implying an error in the length of the degree of latitude of about 8%. Latitude errors continued to increase northward on the coasts of Europe as far as northern Ireland.

At first I supposed this might imply an error in the scale of the source map, but

---

* An exception must be made for the earliest of the maps called portolanos, the Carta Pisana. This apparently dates from the 13th century. In this case the typical portolan design was applied to an extremely inferior map, such as might have been drawn in the Middle Ages or very sloppily copied from an accurate portolano. The latter supposition is supported by the fact that the mapmaker made a botch of the portolan design. This consisted of two circles, but the mapmaker made them of different diameters, and hardly a line in the design is straight.

corresponding longitude errors were not found. An error in scale would carry with it proportional errors in both latitude and longitude. There were larger longitude errors, it is true, along the African and European coasts than in the Mediterranean, but they did not suggest an error in the length of the degree of longitude. From the Cape of Good Hope to Walvis Bay, on the west coast, the average error was 3.5° W. From the Congo to Cape Three Points it was 3.5° E. From Cape Palmas to Gibraltar longitude errors were negligible. On the European coasts, from Cape St. Vincent to Londonderry, they averaged 3.5° E. There was no indication here of any error in scale, and, in view of the distribution of latitude errors in the Mediterranean, very little suggestion of any error in the orientation of the continent. We did, however, change the orientation later, making the shift from the magnetic orientation 12° instead of 11¼°.

The apparent increase of latitude errors with distance from the equator gained added significance with our discovery of the oblong grid on the Piri Re'is Map. If no error in scale was responsible, perhaps it was a question of an original projection that might have taken account of the curvature of the earth by spreading the parallels with distance from the equator, as in the modern Mercator Projection. Hints were found, although not confirmed, of a possible knowledge of the principle of the Mercator Projection in medieval Europe and in ancient China. Accordingly, we decided to find out whether there could be any truth in this. Charles Halgren, of the Caru Studios, was kind enough to construct a Mercator grid for the map, and this was then examined by William Briesemeister. Unfortunately, it turned out that there was very little basis for supposing that the original source map had been drawn on anything resembling Mercator's projection.

We now came back to the point from which we had started: the question of the alternatives of plane versus spherical trigonometry. I decided to draw a grid based on spherical trigonometry to see whether that would solve our problem. Three different persons—Richard Strachan, Professor E. A Wixson, of the Department of Mathematics of Keene State College; and Dr. J. M. Frankland, of the Bureau of Standards—independently used spherical trigonometry to calculate the length of the degree, and agreed on essentially the same result: 58.5° for the radius of the projection. The diagramme in Fig. 63 shows that, by this calculation, the degrees of latitude and longitude *differ* and that, as a result, we have an oblong grid, as we found empirically to be the case with the Piri Re'is Map. This grid, based on spherical trigonometry, solved our problem of latitude errors, as can be seen by an examination of Table 7. The following paragraphs summarize the general results:

1. Longitude in the Mediterranean and Black Seas: The average of the errors of longitude of twelve places from Gibraltar (5.5° W) to Batum (42° E) is about one-fifth of a degree or about 12 miles. Over a total longitudinal distance of 47½° (about 3,000 miles) between Gibraltar and Batum, we find an error of only 1°, equal to about 2 per cent of the distance.

2. Latitude on the Atlantic Coasts: From the Cape of Good Hope (35.5° S) to Londonderry, Ireland (55° N), over a total latitude distance of 90½°, the error is 1°, about 1% of the distance. There are larger latitude errors at many points in be-

tween, but these may represent distortions of local geography introduced by careless copyists. The accuracy of longitude east and west in the Mediterranean, and of latitude north and south in the Atlantic, suggests the basic accuracy of the grid based on spherical trigonometry.

3. Latitudes in the Mediterranean and Black Seas: There seems to be a southward error of about 3° applying to this whole area. The relative latitudes of places however, are accurate. Deviations from the standard, error of 3° average less than 1°. It would seem probable that the general error was introduced by the compilers who originally combined maps of the Mediterranean and of the Atlantic coasts with the map of Africa on the trigonometric projection.

These findings with regard to the De Canerio Map affect rather deeply our views with regard to the Piri Re'is Map and other maps to be considered later. It would now seem that the source maps used by Piri Re'is for Africa and Europe, and perhaps also for the American coasts, as well as all the portolanos, may originally have been based on spherical trigonometry.

The De Canerio Map of 1502, showing, as it does, both the Atlantic and the Indian Ocean coasts of Africa, raises another problem, especially for those who are anxious to attribute its origins to the Portuguese and other explorers of the 15th century. An investigation of the history of the discovery of the African coast in the century before the drawing of this map reveals no solid basis for believing that the explorers could have drawn the map or even supplied cartographers at home with the data necessary for drawing it.

To begin with, it appears that by 1471, only thirty-one years before the map was drawn by De Canerio, the Portuguese had not even reached the mouth of the Niger, four degrees north of the equator on the west coast. The Portuguese scholar Cortesao (54) says:

> . . . The whole of the Gulf of Guinea was discovered by the Portuguese during the third quarter of the 15th Century, and Rio de Lago, where the present Lagos, the capital of Nigeria, lies, not far from Ife, was reached for the first time in 1471.

Lagos is in 6° N latitude and 3.5° E longitude, and there is 100 miles or more of coast between Lagos and the mouth of the Niger. Boies Penrose, in his scholarly account of the Age of Discovery, gives a chronology of the discovery of the African coast and states that by 1474 the Portuguese had just reached Cape St. Catharine, two degrees below the equator (162:43). It is plain from this that only a quarter of a century before the De Canerio Map was compiled the Portuguese had not even begun the exploration of the west coast between the equator and the Cape of Good Hope, to say nothing of exploring the eastern coast.

To understand how impossible it would have been for Portuguese or other western explorers to have accurately mapped these coasts, even if they had explored them, we have only to understand that sea charts with graduated scales of degrees, subdividing the multiples of them into equal smaller units, were not in use by navigators until after 1496. Until then, therefore, even if the navigator could have found longitude—which was impossible—he could not have entered any notations of longitude on the charts, and the same is true for latitude. Penrose describes the state of nautical science just before 1502 in the following passage:

> King John [of Portugal] was very interested . . . in cosmography and astronomy, and he had a committee of experts—the Junta—headed by the brilliant Jews, Joseph Vizinho and Abraham Zacuto, to work on the problem of finding position at sea. Zacuto had written in Hebrew in the previous decade his Almanach Perpetuum, the most advanced work yet to appear on the subject, and one containing full tables of the sun's declination. But its technical nature, coupled with the fact that it was written in a language but little understood by the average skipper, rendered it quite impractical. Vizinho, therefore, translated it into Latin (printed at Leiria, 1496) and later made an abridged version. . . . One result of this technical research was the expedition of Vizinho in 1485 along the Guinea Coast as far as Fernando Po, for the purpose of determining the declination of the sun [the Latitude] throughout Guinea. . . . The observations made by the Vizinho expedition led to the introduction of graduated sailing charts into Portugal. . . . (162:44–45)

The story of the exploration of the coast from 1496 when graduated sailing charts were introduced to 1502 gives no basis for supposing that the De Canerio Map of 1502 resulted from it. An important explorer, Diogo Cão, discovered the Congo, reaching a latitude of 13° S, and returned to Portugal in 1484 (162:45–47). On his next voyage he explored the coast for nine degrees farther south and returned to Portugal in 1487. This was fifteen years before the drawing of the De Canerio Map, and there were still about 800 miles of unexplored coast lying between the point reached by Diogo Cão and the Cape of Good Hope.

It is true, of course, that Bartholomew Diaz rounded the Cape of Good Hope in 1488, but his was not a mapping expedition. He did not follow the coast down to the Cape. Instead, just south of Caboda Volta (Lüderitz) in 27° S latitude, he was blown off course and around the Cape, making his landfall 250 miles to the East! He returned to Portugal in 1489 (162:47).

After Diaz, the next expedition was that of da Gama, who left Portugal in 1497 and returned in 1499. This expedition may have carried graduated sailing charts, for it was very carefully planned. Penrose says:

> Four ships were constructed under the supervision of Bartholomew Diaz. . . . Bishop Diogo Ortiz supplied the fleet with maps and books, and Abraham Zacuto provided astronomical instruments, and made tables of declination, and trained the ships' officers in the art of making observations. . . . (162:50)

This fleet might have produced some accurate observations of latitude along the coast, but this was not its purpose. Its destination was *India*. Therefore, da Gama plotted his course to *avoid the coast*. He followed it a short way, and then made for the Cape Verde Islands. From there he steered a "circular course far out into mid-ocean to the southwest, to escape the doldrums and the currents of the Gulf of Guinea" (162:51). He reached St. Helena, on November 8, 1497, a few days later set to sea again, and rounded the Cape of Good Hope without touching at any other port. His first landfall after rounding the Cape was at Mossel Bay, 300 miles to the east of the Cape. He touched at a few other points before heading out across the Indian Ocean to India, but the African coast was out of sight most of the time and therefore could not have been mapped. He might have found the latitudes of his ports of call, but he could not, at any point, have determined longitudes.

We can conclude that neither da Gama, nor Diaz, nor any of their predecessors, could have done the accurate mapping of the west and east coasts of Africa that we find on the De Canerio Map.

It is an interesting point that on this map there is no suggestion of a second equator such as we have found on the Piri Re'is and Dulcert maps.

## 3.    The Venetian Chart of 1484.

Among the most noteworthy of the portolan charts is one drawn, or at least found, in Venice in 1484 (see Fig. 64). This chart is remarkable for its accuracy and because it is based both on trigonometry and the so-called "twelve-wind system" known to the ancients. In the last particular it appears to be unique among the known portolan charts. We will consider these points in reverse order.

The usual portolan design, with which the readers of this book have now become familiar, is one in which the circle is bisected a number of times to make angles at the center of 180°, 90°, 45°, 22½°, and 11¼° (and occasionally with still another bisection into angles of half of 11¼°). This has already been explained (see Fig. 9). There also was in antiquity the so-called "twelve-wind system." My student, Alfred Isroe, who illustrated the eight-wind system, has also illustrated the more sophisticated twelve-wind system (Fig. 65). Instead of requiring only the bisecting of angles this calls for the trisecting of the hemisphere, which, in turn, requires a knowledge of the ratio of the circumference of the circle to its diameter. This system produces angles of 60°, 30°, 15°, and 5° and appears related to the 360° circle, known from ancient times but not used, at least for navigation, in the Renaissance.

Various writers refer to the use of the twelve-wind system among the ancients. According to one (199:54), it was employed by the Greek geographer Timosthenes, an immediate predecessor of Eratosthenes. The latter is said to have abandoned it in favor of the eight-wind system, because it was too difficult· for mariners (39:124–125). (Note 14). The system continued to be the one preferred by the Romans, who were not much interested in the sea. It was known in the Middle Ages and is said to have been used in the earliest editions of Ptolemy's maps when they were recovered in the 15th century.*

* Professor Carl Weis noticed that there are twelve faces representing winds on Ptolemy's Map (Fig. 6) and pointed out that they might have some connection with the twelve wind system.

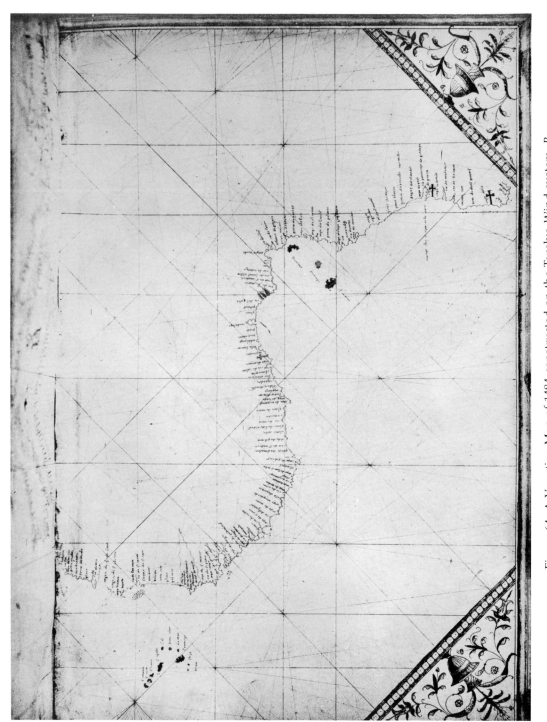

Figure 64. A Venetian Map of 1484 constructed on the Twelve-Wind system. *B*

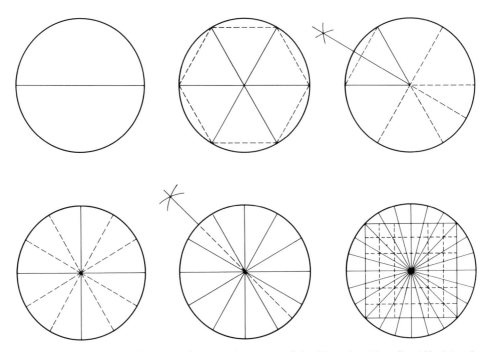

Figure 65. Diagram of the Twelve-Wind system of the Venetian Map (*by Alfred Isroe*)

When I first examined the Venetian chart, what struck me most was that, more distinctly than any other chart I had seen, it showed a square grid, dominating the portolan design, which appeared to be drawn on true North. Only after long examination did I discover that it was, in fact, oriented about 6° to the east. Obviously this map has a grid of lines of latitude and longitude. The diagonal lines were less emphasized than on most other portolanos. Examination now suggested the possibility of finding a solution of this map by trigonometry.

The first step was to make a careful comparison of this map with a good map of the African coast. This revealed that previous scholars, who seem to have assumed that the map showed the coast from the Strait of Gibraltar to the Cape of Good Hope, or to a point near the Cape, were apparently in error. It appeared that the map extended on the north only to about 26° or 27° N latitude, while on the south it extended only a few degrees below the equator.

The intervals of the twelve-wind system made it simple to draw an equilateral triangle with its apex on the 27th parallel and its base on the equator, and solve for the length of the degree with trigonometric tables. A square grid, based on the length of the degree found in this way, seemed to give very good results, at least so far as latitude was concerned. It seemed that the latitudes of all identified points on the coast were accurate to within one-third of one degree, or about 20 miles.

Longitude findings, however, were not as accurate. Errors averaged about one degree. This was not very bad, excepting that they were distributed in such a way

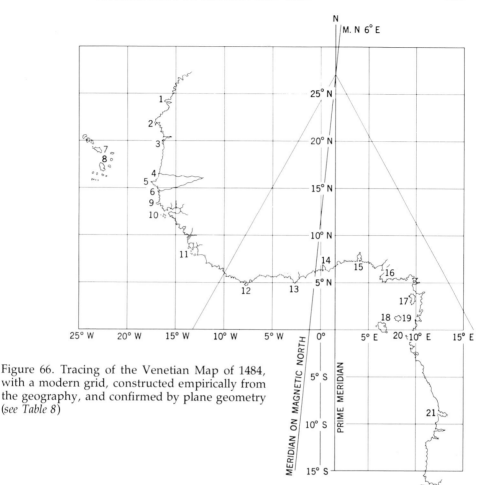

Figure 66. Tracing of the Venetian Map of 1484, with a modern grid, constructed empirically from the geography, and confirmed by plane geometry (*see Table 8*)

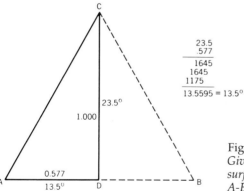

Figure 67. The Trigonometry of the Venetian Map. *Given an equilateral triangle, A-B-C-D, on the earth's surface between a point at 23½° N and the Equator, A-B, with the length of C-D given (23½°). Problem: to find the length of A-D in degrees, to find the length of the degree of longitude on the draft map. (The ratio 1.000:0.577 is taken from "Natural Trigonometric Functions," in Chemical Rubber Company Tables, C. D. Hodgman, ed. Cleveland: 1956, p. 107)*

as to imply an error of some kind in the projection. The easternmost points were too far east, the western points too far west, so that it was a question of the length of the degree of longitude. Were the degrees of latitude and longitude really equal, as we had assumed?

In this situation it seemed best to set aside the trigonometry and try to work out a grid empirically to see whether the degrees of latitude and longitude were equal. The reorientation of the map to true North revealed that the top of the map was not at 26° or 27° N, but at 24° N. On this basis, measurements showed that the degrees were not quite equal. The degree of latitude was, it appeared, slightly *shorter* than the degree of longitude. Surprisingly, however, the length of the degree of longitude found empirically now turned out to be precisely the same as the length of the degree found by trigonometry (see Fig. 67 and Table 8). It is one thing to work out the grid of a map that has already been drawn, but quite another to draw the map in the first place. Our work indicated that the map must have been originally drawn on a plane trigonometric projection. The fact that the apex of the triangle was found to be at 24° N also was interesting, in view of the fact that the Greek geographers (Eratosthenes, Hipparchus, and their successors) accepted that as the Tropic, for the sake of simplicity even though they knew better. It seems then, that the map was intended to be fixed astronomically between the Tropic of Cancer and the equator.

There is evidence that at the southern end of the map some 15th century navigator added some coastline. The errors of latitude increase sharply from Cape Lopez southward to the Congo and Benguela; they are of the sort to be expected from 15th century navigators. Disregarding the added coast, latitude errors for the map average only 0.7°, and longitude errors only 0.2°.

Another detail should attract our attention in passing. An extra island appears near São Tomé on the equator. The fact that the second island (No. 19, in Fig 66) has the same relationship to the equator of the projection oriented to Magnetic North that the other island we have identified as São Tomé has to the true equator suggests that No. 19 is an addition by somebody exploring Africa's equatorial coast with the map already oriented to 6° E. This would mean, of course, that the original explorers were using true North, not magnetic North. The 15th century navigator, sailing by the compass, may have had with him this map already showing the island, but at its correct place on the sidereal grid. And so he added the second island.

But why weren't these explorers honest enough to admit they were exploring these coasts with the help of maps many times better than they could draw for themselves? Or if the Portuguese were using trigonometry and the twelve-wind system, and had a means of finding longitude, why didn't the facts leak out? King John II of Portugal must have had a very efficient security system!

## 4.   The De Canestris Map of 1335–37.

Our discovery of the twelve-wind system in the Venetian Map of 1484 led us into

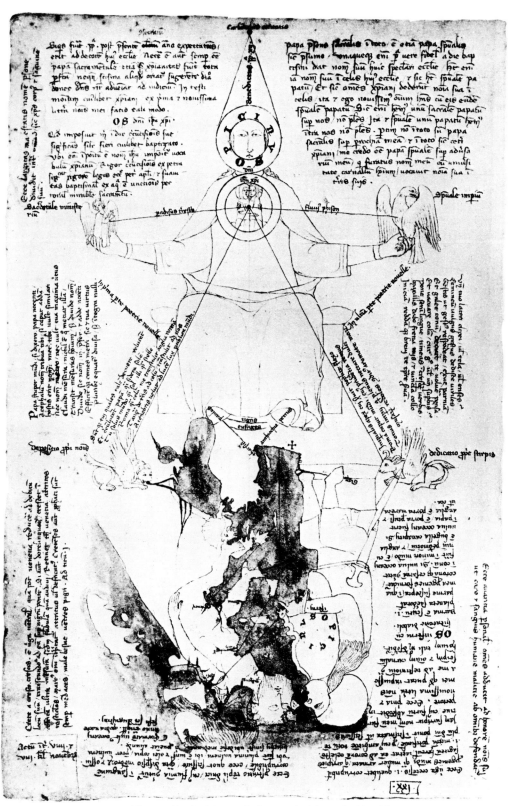

Figure 68. Opicinus di Canestris Map of 1335–38.

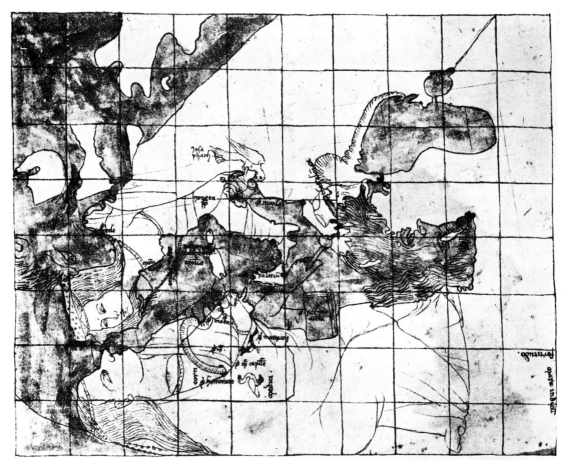

Figure 69. Section of the Canestris Map, with original square grid. *This grid suggests one of the projections attributed by Nordenskiöld to Ptolemy or Marinus of Tyre. One of the meridians and one of the parallels intersect at the site of Alexandria (see Fig. 73). Assuming the interval to be about 5°, the map shows surprising accuracies in the latitudes and longitudes of many geographical localities.*

a search for other such maps. Various persons collaborated in this search. Richard W. Stephenson, of the Map Division of the Library of Congress, went through the map collections in that library; Dr. Alexander Vietor, Curator of Maps at the Yale University Library, also made a search for us, without success. Finally, Alfred Isroe detected the twelve-wind system, in a very dilapidated form, in the De Canestris Map of 1335–37 (see Fig. 68).

At first glance this looks like many medieval maps, presumably originating in the peculiar ideas and limited knowledge of the time. Most ingenious work was

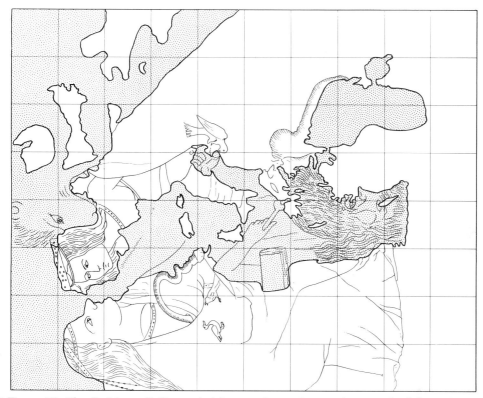

Figure 70. The Opicinus di Canestris Map, section redrawn. *An example of the medieval imagination. How many figures can the reader find?*

done in adapting the geography to animal and human forms—including those of a man and a woman (who are seen in lively dispute). This anthropomorphism appears to have been accomplished without distorting the geography to any noticeable extent.

Among the various irregular lines on this map (many of them introduced to complete the human forms), Isroe noticed a few straight lines that suggested the survival of parts of an original pattern resembling that of the portolanos. Measurements with a protractor showed that, while the angles between them were not precisely those of the twelve-wind system, they were much closer to those than to the angles characteristic of the eight-wind pattern.

Taking this suggestion of Isroe's, I thought I would try to reconstruct the possible original pattern. I straightened the two lines emanating from the projection center at the left of the map, on the assumption that they might have been intended originally to represent one straight line. This involved only a slight change. With this change all the other angles of the intersections of the lines traced

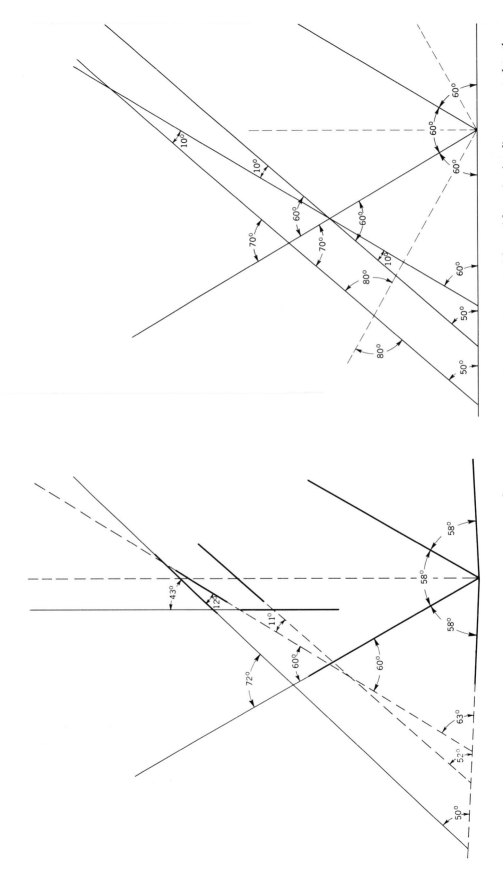

Figure 71. Opicinus de Canestris Map, tracing of projection lines.

Figure 72. Canestris Map with projection lines corrected to the Twelve-Wind system.

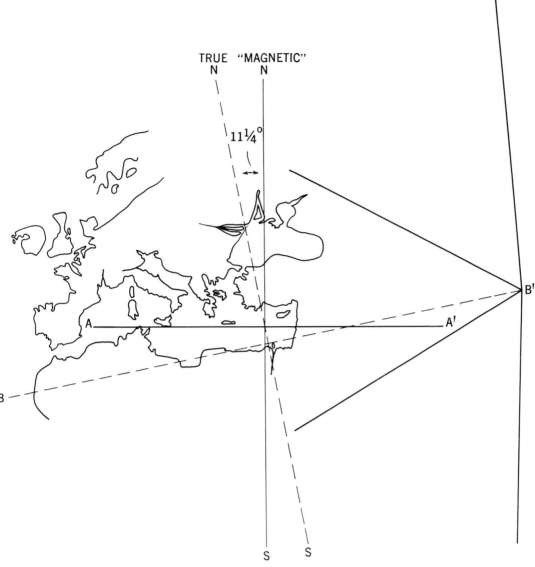

TRUE "MAGNETIC"
N      N

11¼°

B'

A                                    A'

B

S    S

Figure 73. Canestris Map, reoriented from Magnetic to True North.

by Isroe from the photograph of the original map fell into agreement with the twelve-wind system (see Figs. 71 and 72).

In addition to these indications of an original twelve-wind system on this map, I discovered a straight line in the Mediterranean that suggested a parallel of latitude of the original source map. Comparing this line with the present geography of the Mediterranean, I observed that it indicated an orientation of the whole map about 11½° or 12° east of true North, as on so many of the maps recognized as portolanos. It would seem, then, that this map, and a whole family of other maps from this period of the Middle Ages, are, in fact, not so much original productions of the Middle Ages as degenerated versions of ancient maps, very possibly drawn originally by the geographers of the School of Alexandria, or coming from even more remote times.

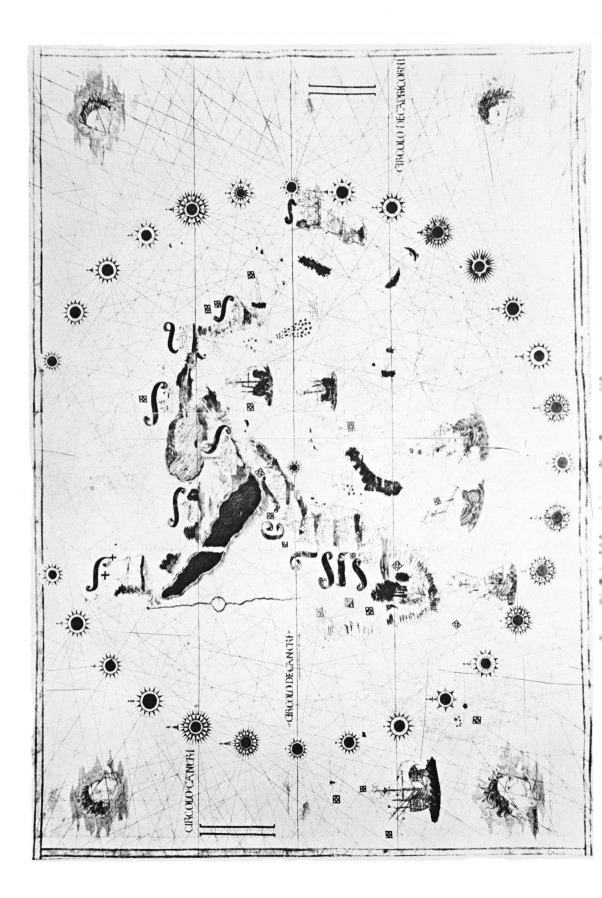

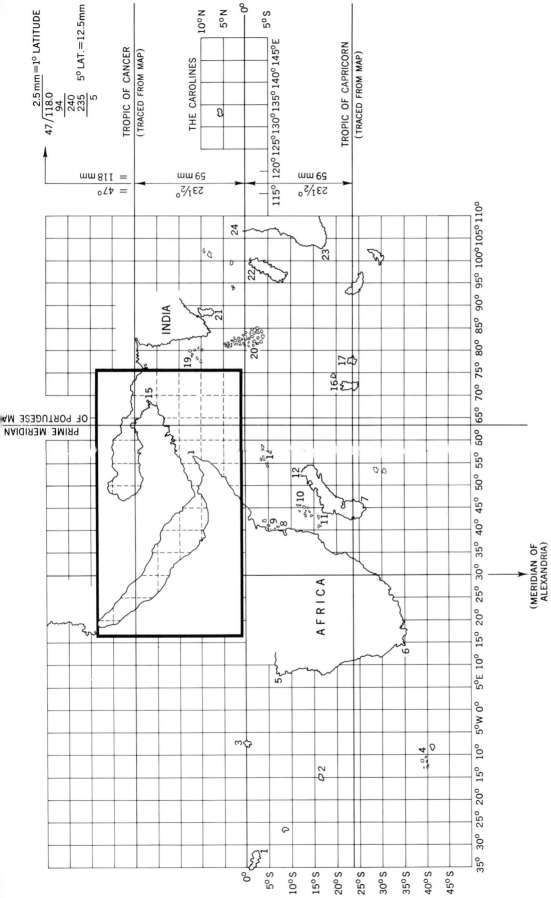

Figure 75. Reinel Map with a square grid, constructed on the basis of the degree as measured between the two tropics. *The area within the frame is interpolated from a Ptolemaic map and is grossly incorrect. (see Table 9)*

## 5.   The Reinel Chart of the Indian Ocean

I felt it important to see whether, having found a map of Africa that seemed to be based on ancient mathematical cartography, it might not be possible to extend the system to Asia. Thus I might be able to determine whether the ancient cartographers of a vanished race had extended their system farther east. With this in mind I examined what is considered to be the earliest Portuguese chart of the Indian Ocean (Fig. 74). Fortunately, this map shows both the tropics. Since the distance between them is just 47° it was a simple matter to find a value for the degree of latitude. I assumed an equal value for the degree of longitude and drew a grid as shown in Fig. 75, which proved accurate as shown by Table 8. I discovered that the map, besides displaying remarkable knowledge of the archipelagoes of the Indian Ocean, shows a number of islands in the Atlantic, including a large one on the very site of the equatorial island of the Piri Re'is and Buache maps, the Caroline Islands of the Pacific and a part of the coast of Australia. The longitude of the grid was based on the meridian of Alexandria, as found from the east coast of Africa.

As I continued to examine this map, I saw that the trend of the Australian coast was wrong, as was its latitude. This reminded me of the Caribbean area of the Piri Re'is Map. Was it possible that we had here another example of a satellite grid, with a different north, integrated with the Piri Re'is world projection? A comparison of the map with the world map drawn by the Air Force centered on Cairo (see Fig. 25) was extremely thought-provoking. A glance at a tracing of this map with the Piri Re'is projection superimposed on it (Fig. 27) showed that the design of the Piri Re'is projection was capable of being used to cover this area just as well as it was used to cover the Caribbean.

Table 8 shows that latitudes for the map as a whole exclusive of Australia and the Carolines are remarkably accurate, the average of the errors of twenty places coming to 1.1°. Longitudes for the Atlantic and Africa are also very good, the errors averaging 2.5°. Longitudes for the Indian Ocean, however, have been badly thrown out by the interpolation of the Ptolemaic sector. Here the average of longitude errors is 12° eastwardly. We shall find the same magnitude of eastward errors on the Hamy-King Ptolemaic chart of 1502–4 (Chapter VII.) It seems evident that the Reinel chart shows much more geographical knowledge than was available to the Portuguese in the first decade of the 16th century, and a much better knowledge of latitudes and longitudes than could be expected of them.


## 6.   The Yü Chi Fu Map

In the effort to see whether the system of ancient maps extended farther east than the Indian Ocean, I examined the available Chinese and Japanese maps. Despite the splendid co-operation of the staff of Japan's great Diet Library (the equivalent of our Library of Congress), which sent me many old Japanese charts, I was not able to discover any maps that bore apparent relationships to the western

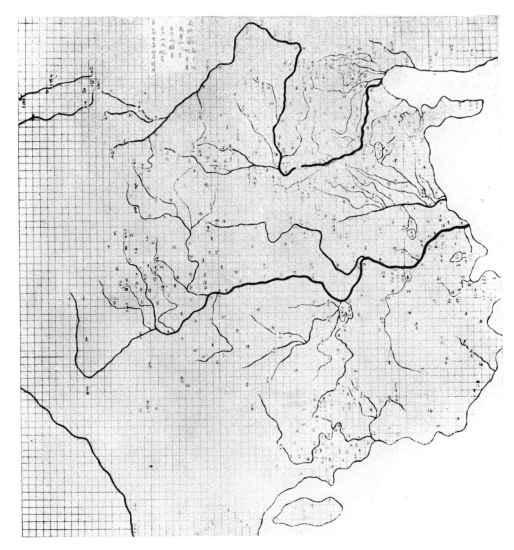

Figure 76. A Twelfth Century Map of China: The Yü Chi Fu. (145)

portolanos, except maps of a comparatively late date which might have been influenced by western cartography.

I had much better luck in China. This was owing entirely to the availability of Needham's great work on *Science and Civilization in China* (145). In Volume III of that work he reproduced a very remarkable map that had been carved in stone in China in the year 1137 A.D. It is referred to as the *Yü Chi Fu,* or *Map of the Tracks of Yü the Great* (see Fig. 76). Although it was carved in 1137, it is known to have been in existence for an indefinite period before that. Its real date of origin is unknown. Therefore it is wrapped in the same mystery as are the portolanos of the West. A comparison of the river system shown on this map with that on a modern map of China shows a remarkable accuracy (see Figs. 77 and 78). This map was evidently drawn with excellent information as to longitudes, such as we find on the portolanos, but do not find on the classical maps of Greece and Rome, and which was certainly not typical of the cartography of medieval China or Japan.

Needham, and presumably the Chinese scholars who have studied this map, apparently assumed that its square grid was the original grid on which it had been drawn; this was a perfectly natural conclusion for them. On the other hand, I had just recently discovered that the square grid inherent in the plane trigonometry of the portolan projection was evidently *not* the original grid on which some of the source maps used by Piri Re'is and other mapmakers had been drawn. I had just come to believe, on the contrary, that Piri Re'is' source map had originally been drawn with an oblong grid of some kind. Therefore I decided to test the grid of this Chinese map.

I began by trying to find the length of the degree of latitude on a tracing of the map. As before, the procedure was to pick a number of geographical features that were easily and clearly identifiable and find their latitudes on a modern map. These were distributed from the northernmost to the southernmost parts of China. I extended lines from these points to the margins of the tracing and found the length of a degree of latitude by dividing the number of millimeters on the tracing from north to south by the number of degrees of latitude between the identified points.

Then I repeated the process to find the length of the degree of longitude I supposed it would probably come out the same, but nevertheless a sense of excitement gripped me as I noted the longitudes of identifiable places across the map and drew lines from these to the bottom of the tracing. I used a number of geographical points in each case, for finding the lengths of the degrees of latitude and longitude, to ensure against the risk that any one of the chosen points might be out of place because of a local error in the map. Thus, if I depended only upon two positions, at either extreme of north and south or east and west, an error might be made in the length of the degree.

When I finished the measurement of the degree of longitude on the map I was truly electrified, for I found that it was unmistakably shorter than the degree of latitude. In other words, what revealed itself here was the oblong grid found on the Piri Re'is Map, found on the Ptolemy maps, and found, through spherical trigonometry, on the De Canerio Map. The square grid found on the map was, then, clearly something superimposed on the map in ignorance of its true projection. This, together with the fact that the square grid was similar to the square portolan grid, created an altogether astonishing parallel, a parallel that suggested an historical connection between this map and the maps of the West. If I may be allowed to speculate here, I may suggest that perhaps we have here evidence that our lost civilization of five or ten thousand years ago extended its mapmaking here, as well as to the Americas and Antarctica.

The square grid imposed on the map is evidence of the same decline of science we have observed in the West, when an advanced cartography, based on spherical trigonometry and on effective instruments for determining latitudes and longitudes, gave way to the vastly inferior cartography of Greece—and when, later in the Middle Ages, even the geographical science known to the classical world was entirely lost. In China, the square grid was apparently imposed on the map by people who had entirely forgotten the science by which it was drawn.

There are other indications that the map was drawn in its present form in an age of the decline of science in China. Despite the extraordinary accuracy of the geographic detail of the Chinese interior, the coasts are hardly drawn in at all; they are only schematically indicated. This suggests to me that the map was carved in stone in an age when China had no interest in the outside world, but an enormous interest in the great river system that carried the internal commerce of the fabulously rich empire. The original map may have shown the coasts in detail; but in the 12th century they were apparently of interest to nobody.

The map shows some of the rivers flowing in directions different from those of the modern map. This does not necessarily mean that there were inaccuracies in the ancient map. The rivers of China—particularly the Hwang Ho, or Yellow River—have the habit of changing their courses with the most disastrous consequences. The Yellow River is, in fact, called "China's Sorrow." It has changed its course three times in the last century and a half. The ancient map shows it following a course to the north of its present course, but that course, in one of the northern valleys, is perfectly reasonable.

I subjected the grid I had constructed for this map to the most rigorous testing. Using the grid, I identified a large number of additional geographical localities, mostly the intersections of major rivers, rejecting any that appeared in the least dubious. I have listed these localities, with the discrepancies in their positions, in Table 10, a, b, c. I grouped the localities in the northwest, northeast, southwest, and southeast quadrants of China. In each quadrant in turn I averaged the discrepancies, or errors, in the latitudes and longitudes of places, with the following results.

**Table 10a (summarized)**

| Quadrant | Number of Localities | Average Errors |
|---|---|---|
| 1. Northwest | 8 | 0.4° Lat.<br>0.0° Long. |
| 2. Northeast | 10 | 0.0° Lat.<br>0.0° Long. |
| 3. Southwest | 9 | 1.3° Lat.<br>1.2° Long. |
| 4. Southeast | 7 | 0.8° Lat.<br>1.2° Long. |

Here we have evidence that when this ancient map of China was first drawn, mapmakers had means of finding longitude as accurately as they found latitude, exactly as was the case with the portolan charts in the West. The accuracy of the map suggests the use of spherical trigonometry, and the form of the grid, so like that of the De Canerio Map, suggests that the original projection might have been based on spherical trigonometry.

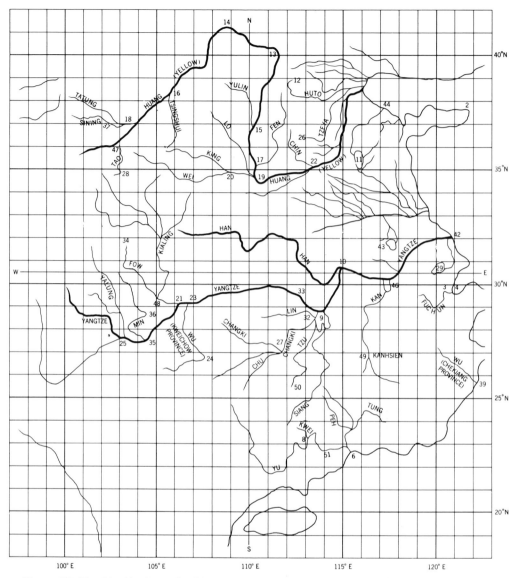

Figure 77. The Yü Chi Fu with oblong grid constructed empirically from the geography.
*For numbered geographical features see Table 10.*

As a further test of the grid I had drawn for the map, I listed separately all the northernmost and southernmost places identified on the map and averaged their errors in latitude. I also listed all the easternmost and westernmost places and averaged their errors in longitude (Tables 10b and 10c). The average error of latitude on the north was less than one-half of one degree (or 30 miles!), and the average error on the south balanced out to zero (with four localities 1° too far south and four 1.2° too far north). So far as longitude was concerned, the errors both on the east and on the west balanced out to zero. There was no indication, therefore,

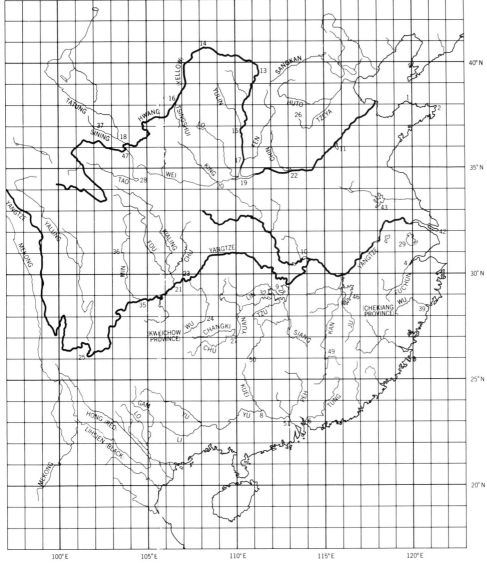

Figure 78. A modern map of China, with numbers corresponding to those in No. 77.

that the grid constructed for the map was seriously in error.

It seems to me that the evidence of this map points to the existence in very ancient times of a *worldwide* civilization, the mapmakers of which mapped virtually the entire globe with a uniform general level of technology, with similar methods, equal knowledge of mathematics, and probably the same sorts of instruments. I regard this Chinese map as the capstone of the structure I have erected in this book. For me it settles the question as to whether the ancient culture that penetrated Antarctica, and originated all the the ancient western maps, was indeed worldwide (see also 135a).

# VI   The Ancient Maps of the North

W E HAVE seen that the analysis of a number of maps has led to surprising conclusions and implications. They appear to call in question not only the accepted ideas of ancient history, and especially the history of cartography, but also fundamental conceptions of geology. We have seen, in the maps already considered, suggestions of voyages to America and Antarctica that must have occurred in times preceding the oldest of our historical records—voyages accomplished by a people or peoples whose memory has not survived. The Oronteus Finaeus Map appears to document the surprising proposition that Antarctica was visited and perhaps settled by men when it was largely, if not entirely, non-glacial. It goes without saying that this implies a very great antiquity. In this chapter we shall consider additional reasons for supposing that the evidence of the Oronteus Finaeus Map takes the civilization of the original mapmakers back to a time contemporaneous with the end of the ice age in the northern hemisphere.

Facts do not stand alone. A given statement may mean more or less depending upon the context. The maps we are now to consider cannot be considered *in vacuo.* They should be evaluated with some reference to what we have already learned. If they suggest an enormous antiquity for the cartographic tradition their evidence cannot be so easily dismissed as it might be if it stood alone.

## 1.   The Zeno Map of 1380.

The Zeno Map of 1380 was supposedly drawn by two Venetians, Niccolo and Antonio Zeno, who made a famous voyage to Greenland and perhaps Nova Scotia in the 14th century (Fig. 79). Two hundred years later a descendant of these Zenos found the map among his family papers and copied it. Whether he made any changes in it we do not know.

A study of the map itself shows that it could not have been drawn by the earlier Zenos. In the first place, though they are supposed to have visited only Iceland and Greenland the map also shows the coasts of Scandinavia and Scotland.

In the second place, a polar projection applied empirically to the map (Fig. 80) shows surprisingly correct latitudes and longitudes for many places scattered all over it, though there are a good number of major errors. It was remarkable that, when I made the initial assumption that the original cartographer had accurate knowledge of longitude across the Atlantic and used this as the basis of my polar grid, then I found many accurate latitudes. (See Table 11a.)*

In the third place, further analysis of the map showed that it was a compilation of four originally separate maps drawn with different scales and oriented to different norths (Fig. 81 and Table 11b.)

A suggestion of a vast antiquity for the map is conveyed by a feature to which Captain Mallery first drew attention. He pointed out that the Zeno Map (Fig. 7a) shows Greenland with no ice cap (130). It correctly shows the extremely mountainous character of northern and southern Greenland, together with a flat central region. In our discussion of the Oronteus Finaeus Map we have presented evidence of a temperate period in Antarctica contemporaneous with the ice age in North America. In Chapter VIII we will discuss the geological questions in more detail, but here I will state that the theory I have used to explain the temperate period in Antarctica also explains why Greenland had a temperate or semi-glacial climate at the time this map was drawn. Fig. 82, a sub-glacial map of the present Greenland, drawn by seismic surveying through the ice, fully explains the flat area shown in central Greenland, if we simply assume that the inland sea on the Zeno Map was already frozen over because of the fall in temperature that has led to the present very thick ice cap. Mallery was in possession of earlier seismic data gathered by the French Paul-Emile Victor Polar Expeditions of 1947–49. Their findings indicated a sub-glacial strait clear across Greenland at the latitude in which the National Geographic map shows the inland sea.

Each of the maps presented new and special problems, but the Zeno Map was especially difficult. Since my solution was achieved by a step-by-step process, and can only be clearly understood if followed chronologically, I will try to reconstruct each step in the process in turn, as it actually occurred. I must emphasize that when I started on the analysis of this map, I had not the slightest idea what it would reveal. I was not optimistic that it would reveal anything. I had been discouraged by the fact that the portolan type of design, which I supposed must have originally been on the map, had apparently been replaced by the 16th century Zeno with a more modern sort of grid, ending the possibility of a solution along the lines of the Piri Re'is Map. My students had failed to solve the problem, and so had the cartographers of the Air Force. Therefore, we just put the map away, and I intended to ignore it.

---

* It is worth recalling that the astrolabe, reputedly invented by Hipparchus or Apollonius in ancient times, was reintroduced into Europe only in the beginning of the 15th century, after the Zeno brothers had made their trip. The sextant, like the chronometer, was not available until 300 years later. We have seen that Columbus, in 1492, was unable to find accurate latitude with his quadrant. The cross-staff was available to the Zenos, with inaccurate tables of the sun's altitude, but they could have recorded no latitudes owing to the absence of graduated sailing charts for a hundred years after their voyage.

Figure 79. Zeno Map of the North (1380). *F*

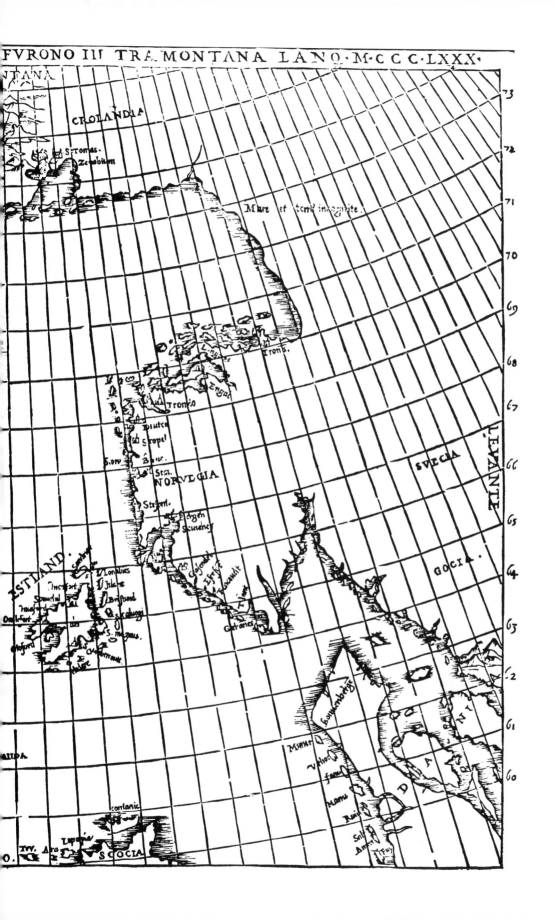

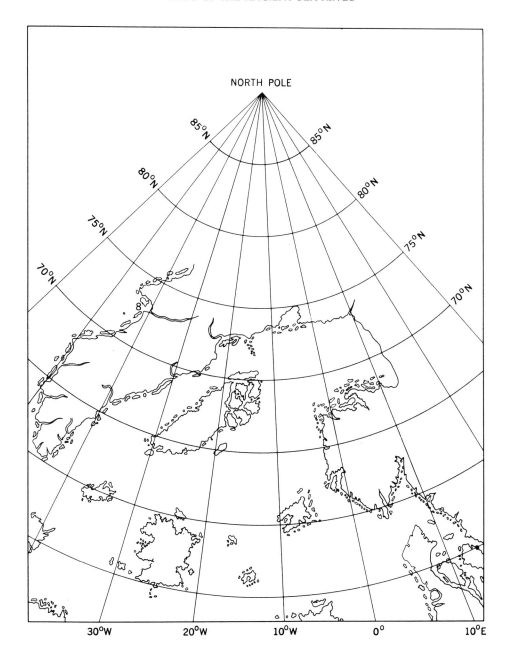

Figure 80. The Zeno Map with Reconstructed Polar Projection. (*see Table 11a*)


The map had been studied by Mallery in his book, *Lost America,* but we were not in agreement with his conclusions. He had noted the accuracy of the ancient map,

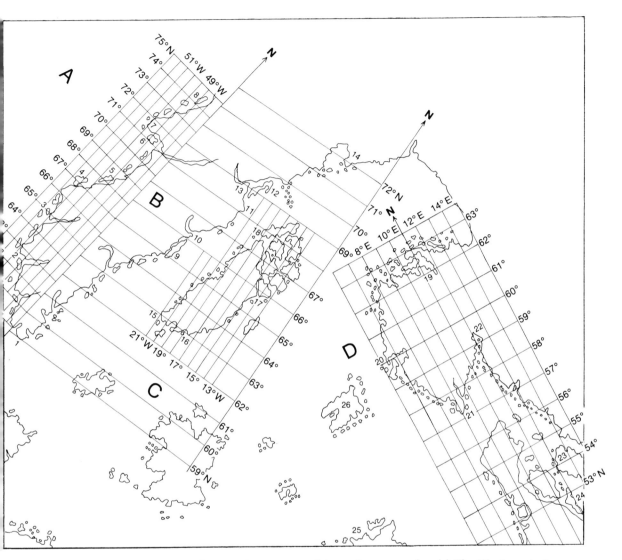

Figure 81. The Zeno Map with oblong grids constructed from the geography. (a) The West coast of Greenland misplaced 2° West; (b) The East coast of Greenland misplaced 1° South, latitude scale only; (c) Iceland with the same latitude as (b), but unrelated longitude; (d) Europe. Note ratio of degrees appropriate to high latitudes.

with respect to many points in Greenland, by drawing a grid of his own, based on the geographical points themselves, but not extending to the whole map. He assumed further that the large island to the east of Greenland on the Zeno Map was not meant to be Iceland. In his opinion this island represents Gunnbiorn's Skerries, islands that reportedly existed in medieval times along the Greenland coast, but now are partly subsided beneath the sea and partly covered by the Greenland ice cap. We could not agree with this.

In March, 1964, during the preparation of the first edition of this book, I decided to take one last look at the map and to review carefully just what Mallery had done, in order to see whether it was really as accurate as he claimed. I had run across an article by the geologist William H. Hobbs (93), who knew his Greenland and who said that the map was remarkably accurate. Therefore, I got out the map, looked at it, and collected and laid out a number of modern maps of the same general area—maps of the North Atlantic and of the Arctic.

First I noticed that the grid actually on the map was a sort of circular, polar one. By comparison with modern maps, I could see the sense of this. After all, this was a polar area. It seemed that the square or oblong grids of most of the other ancient maps would never do here. Meridians in Greenland pointing north could not be parallel to meridians in Norway pointing north. The meridians had to converge at the poles.

Was it possible that this was, after all, the original projection, as the 14th century Zenos had found it?

I analyzed the projection farther. Assuming that each space between the meridians and the parallels represented one degree, I counted the degrees to see how much longitude there was across the Atlantic. I picked two recognizable places, Cape Farewell at the tip of Greenland and Cape Lindesnës at the tip of Norway. These places were nearly at the same latitude. Since Cape Farewell is at longitude 44° W, and Lindesnës is at longitude 5° 30' E, the total longitude difference equaled 49½°. On the Zeno Map, however, counting each meridian as one degree, the longitude difference was only 30°, obviously very far off.

I played with the idea that perhaps the 16th century Zeno had made a mistake. He might have misinterpreted the grid. Perhaps each interval equaled two degrees of longitude, instead of one. This idea was not really satisfactory either, because it would give 60° across the Atlantic, instead of the correct 54½°. Furthermore, the curvature of the parallels of latitude across the Atlantic did not seem to me to be sufficient for the high latitude of Greenland. A comparison with modern maps of the polar region showed the difference in curvature. It seemed to me that the degree of curvature on the Zeno Map would be appropriate to a much lower latitude.

Finally, it was evident from the geography itself that the grid did not accurately represent north for either Greenland or Norway; there should be a much sharper convergence of the meridians. If the meridians as shown on the map are projected to the point of meeting, the pole so found is much too far north of Greenland (the northernmost point of which is actually only about six degrees from the pole) and the island thus is pushed much too far south.

I concluded that somebody had made a mistake, at some time or other, in applying this sort of projection to the map. It might well have been the sixteenth century Zenos, but hardly the earlier Zeno brothers, for no one in the 14th century drew grids of latitude and longitude on circular projections.

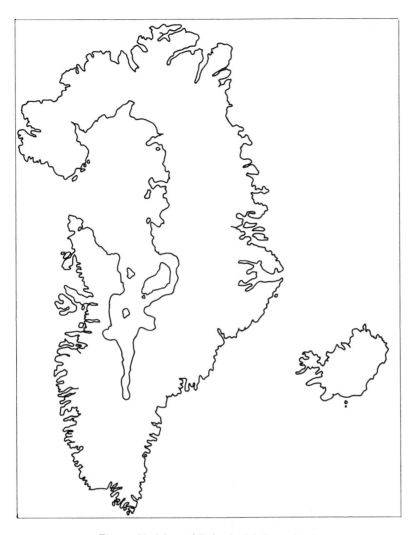

Figure 82. Map of Sub-glacial Greenland.

There was nothing to do but start afresh and draw a projection to fit the map—not just to fit Greenland, but to fit the map as a whole. The first problem was to find the right location for the North Pole. My first step was to find two localities on opposite sides of the Atlantic in about the same latitude. Finally, I found Cape Farewell in Greenland at 60° N, and Oslo in Norway at the same latitude. These are both very clearly shown on the Zeno Map. I now sought to draw a curved line, to represent the 60th parallel of north latitude, from Cape Farewell to Oslo. To do this I began by finding what seemed the direction of north in Greenland and also in Norway on the Zeno Map and drawing lines running due north until they met at a point representing the pole. The first experiment did not work because, when I described a circle with this point as a center and with a radius to Cape Farewell, it did *not* pass through Oslo. I then experimented in raising and lowering the polar point, and moving it slightly this way and that, until I found a point from which I could describe a circle that would intersect Greenland and Norway at the latitudes of Cape Farewell and Oslo. Then it was a simple matter to divide the radius by thirty (the number of the degrees between the 60th parallel and the pole) to find the length of the degree and draw a grid. This grid, it is true, did resemble very much the grid of the original map, though it was differently oriented and the parallels curved more sharply. Meridians could now be easily drawn at five-degree intervals from this pole, starting with Cape Farewell in 44° W longitude.

The first grid drawn in this way, when tested, did not prove sufficiently accurate. It indicated that my pole was too low, because of some mistake in finding the direction of north in Greenland and Norway. There were too many degrees of longitude between Cape Farewell and Oslo. Nevertheless I thought it worthwhile to assume that the ancient cartographer had known the relative longitudes of Greenland and Norway, and I therefore raised the pole enough so that the meridians from Cape Farewell and Oslo would meet at the pole at the angle of 54½°, the correct longitude difference. This meant a very considerable change in the length of the degree of latitude as well as in that of longitude. It was therefore with real anxiety that I drew a new grid on the map, as shown in Fig. 80, and tabulated the positions of the localities. To my astonishment I found that with the revision of the degree of longitude the accuracy of the map in latitude was notably increased!

However, there was still a good deal of inaccuracy in the map and I eventually discovered that it had been compiled from four originally separate maps, each with its own grid and a different north (see Fig. 81 and Table 11b.) The western and eastern coasts of Greenland were drawn with differences in scale and in orientation.

The map of the western coast of Greenland is perhaps the oldest part of the map. If the reader will compare it with Fig. 82, the subglacial map of Greenland, he will note the map extends northward only to the point where the sub-glacial strait existed when there was no icecap in Greenland. This supports Mallery's observation that the map shows evidence of having been drawn in a temperate age.

Iceland on the Zeno Map also offers food for thought. It is shown much larger than it is today. The geological history of the island supports the possibility that the island once had the extent it is given on this map. Mallery had presented a good deal of evidence to support this.

Mallery quotes a number of sources of Icelandic history, including G. W. Dacent, *Iceland* (1861), R. A. Daly, *The Changing World of the Ice Age* (1934), Cornelius Worford, *Floods and Inundations* (1875–1879) (published by the Statistical Society of London) and an account of the volcanic history of Iceland by T. Thoroldsen, published in the Icelandic language in 1882. It would appear that between 1340 and 1380 A.D. *several provinces* of Iceland were submerged following a series of terrific volcanic explosions. Subsidences continued to occur during the 15th century.

It would seem to be highly probable that the Iceland we see on the Zeno Map is the greater Iceland that existed before the Zeno brothers visited Iceland. A comparison with the modern map of Iceland, however, suggests that the land changes included both subsidence and uplift. The peninsulas on the southern and western coasts suggest uplift.

It is remarkable that the cartographer who tied these component maps together, though he made mistakes in combining them, nevertheless did place their connecting point, Cape Farewell in Greenland, in nearly correct latitude and longitude compared to southern Norway. It is interesting further to note that oblong grids of the component maps in Greenland, Iceland and Europe all show a high ratio of the latitude to the longitude degrees appropriate to the high latitudes involved in the map. We shall examine another grid of this sort in the next chapter.

## 2.   The Ptolemaic Map of the North.

One of the great events of the 15th century was the recovery of the works of Claudius Ptolemy, the last great geographer and cartographer of classical antiquity, who lived in the 2nd century A.D. The works included a treatise on geography, still of great interest, tables of latitudes and longitudes of known geographical localities, and a large body of maps.

The maps published in the 15th century, although attributed to Ptolemy, are not considered to have been actually drawn by him. Some authorities have considered that they were reconstructed from the tables sometime during the Middle Ages, or even in the 15th century. Others, on the other hand, feel that no one in the Middle Ages (or 15th century) was capable of reconstructing the maps in such detail from the tables left by Ptolemy. Among the latter is the Danish scholar Gudmund Schütt, author of a treatise on Ptolemy. Schütt writes:

> It is well known that the study of geography decayed lamentably after the close of the Roman period, or even earlier. How, then, could ignorant copyists in medieval times have undertaken the enormous task of constructing a detailed atlas on the base of the Ptolemaic text, and have carried it out so remarkably well? Such an idea cannot be entertained. The manuscript atlases, as we have them, at the first glance are proved to be copies of a classical original, executed by an expert who . . . represented the highest standard of geographical science of the classical era. (186)

Schütt adds more evidence to support his conclusion, showing in some detail that the manuscript atlases of Ptolemy recovered in the 15th century are closer in style to other surviving works of the 4th century A.D. than they are to those of the 5th and 6th centuries. This would suggest that the maps we have were the work of someone who lived within two centuries of the lifetime of Ptolemy even if they were not drawn by him. It is entirely possible that they were good copies of maps he drew.

Ptolemy himself worked at the Library of Alexandria, and had at his disposal not only the contemporary information on the geographical features of the known world (see his World Map, Fig. 6) but also the works of preceding geographers,

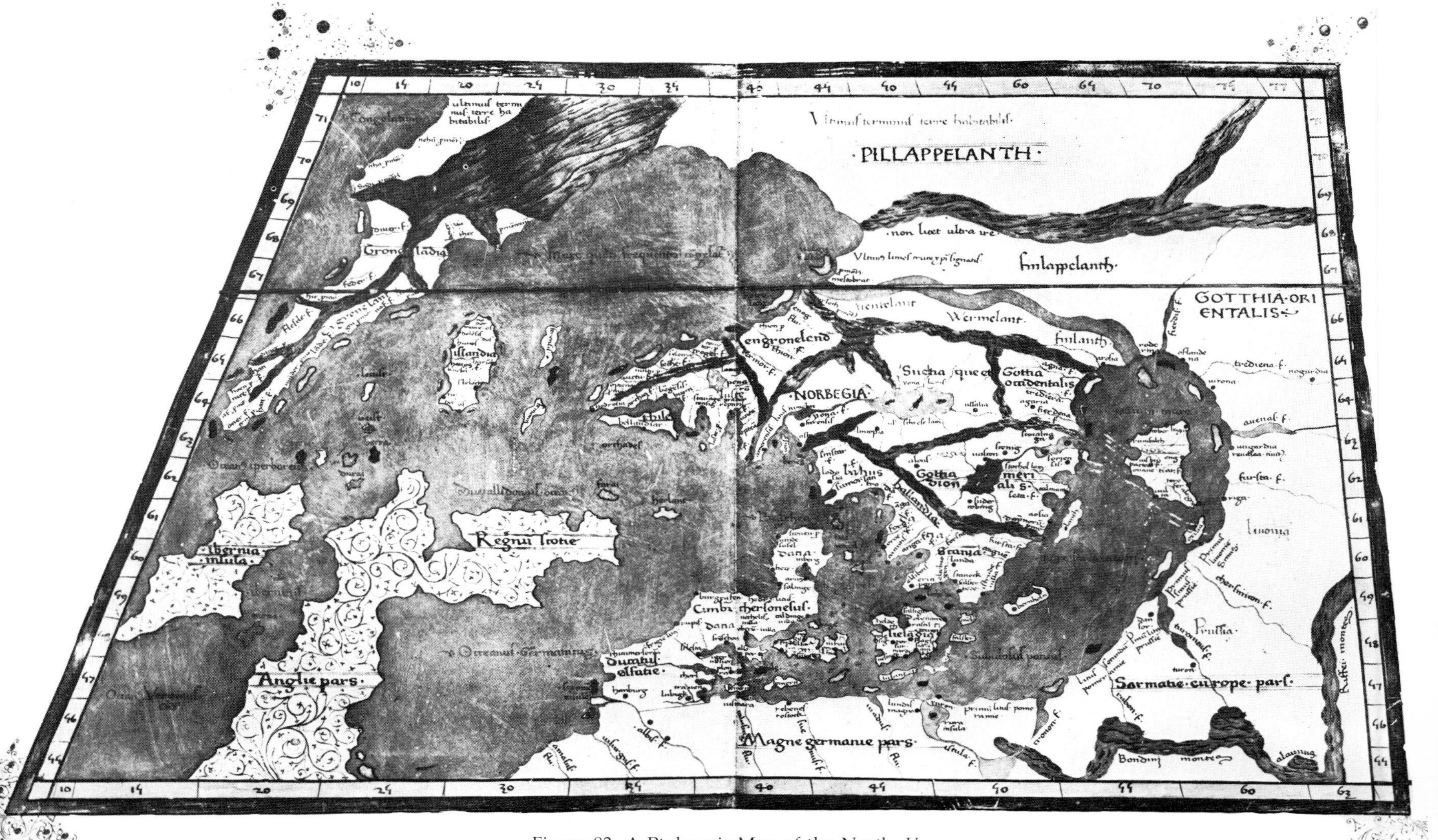

Figure 83. A Ptolemaic Map of the North. V

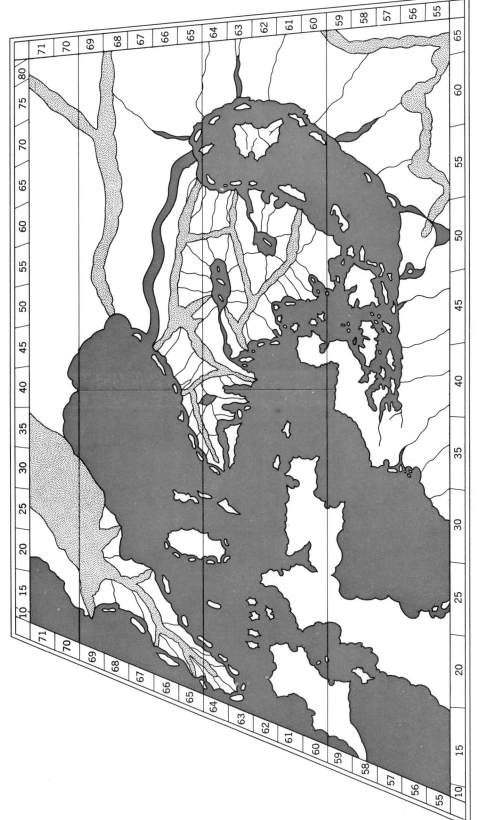

Figure 84. A redrawing of the Ptolemaic Map of the North.

Figure 85. Physiographic Map of Southern Sweden.

such as Marinus of Tyre, and the maps that had been accumulated during the library's five centuries of existence. It can be considered likely that he saw the prototypes of some of the maps we have been studying in this book, though he may not have realized the aspects in which they were superior to the cartography of his own time.

The map we are now to consider is similar in style to those published in all the Ptolemy atlases in the 15th century. It reflects, as they do, considerable information on the latitudes of places but exceedingly poor conceptions of longitude. Ptolemy had to depend on travelers' itineraries and similar information for his estimates of distances in the Roman Empire, for there was little geographical information derived from stellar observations. What there was dealt with latitudes only, since there was no scientific way of determining the longitudes of places. As a result, the shapes of countries and seas were sadly distorted on the Ptolemy maps, as we saw in the comparison Nordenskiöld made of his Mediterranean map with the Dulcert Portolano (Fig. 4).

In Ptolemy's Map of the North (Figs. 83, 84) we see these characteristics. Our version of the map seems to be the work of two different copyists. The part including Britain and Ireland is Ptolemaic in outline, but it is decorated with an artistic scroll device of geometrical character and has no internal details. The rest of the map is more typical of Ptolemaic maps in general, and shows a number of authentic geographical details, such as the lakes of southern Sweden.

The most remarkable detail of the map is the evidence it appears to contain of glaciation. It shows Greenland largely, but not entirely, covered by ice. The shape of the island suggests that of the Zeno Map and may come from the same ancient source. The ice is artistically suggested—there even seeming to be a sheen such as might be produced by the reflection of sunlight from the ice surface. There is a suggestion that when the map was drawn the ice cap was much smaller than it is now.

If we turn our attention to southern Sweden we see further evidence of what seems to be glaciation. Although there are still glaciers in Scandinavia, there is none in this part of Sweden. But the map shows features drawn in the same style as the Greenland ice cap. Unbelievable as it may appear, they actually do suggest the remnant glaciers that covered this country at the end of the last ice age, about 10,000 years ago. Some fine details strengthen the impression. Lakes are shown suggesting the shapes of present-day lakes, and streams very much suggesting glacial streams are shown flowing from the "glaciers" into the lakes. To me, there is a strong suggestion here of the rapid melting of the glaciers during the period of the withdrawal of the ice. It goes without saying, of course, that no one in the 15th century, no one in earlier medieval times, and no one in Roman times ever had any suspicion of the former existence of an ice age in northern Europe. They could not have imagined glaciers stretching across southern Sweden—and they would not have invented them.

Additional details deserve notice. Features of the same type—some of them following the ridges of mountain chains, but some not—can be observed on this map behind the German and Baltic coasts. They begin in the Erz Gebirge, or Hartz Mountains, in Germany, in correct longitude relative to southern Sweden, and stretch eastward across the Riesen Gebirge (the Sudeten Mountains) to the main range of the Carpathians, where they turn sharply southward, in the direction of the axis of the mountain range. Then the map shows the glacier turning northward, where it seems to follow quite accurately the highlands of Western White Russia (bordering Poland on the east) and ending in the Livonian Highlands in about 57° N, in correct latitude compared to southern Sweden.

I do not think that these features should be dismissed as merely representing mountains, even although the 15th century copyist can only have assumed they were mountains. It is natural enough that the glaciers of the end of the ice age should have lingered longest in the mountainous areas, but there are no mountains in southern Sweden, and there are no mountains in Poland or Livonia. Figure

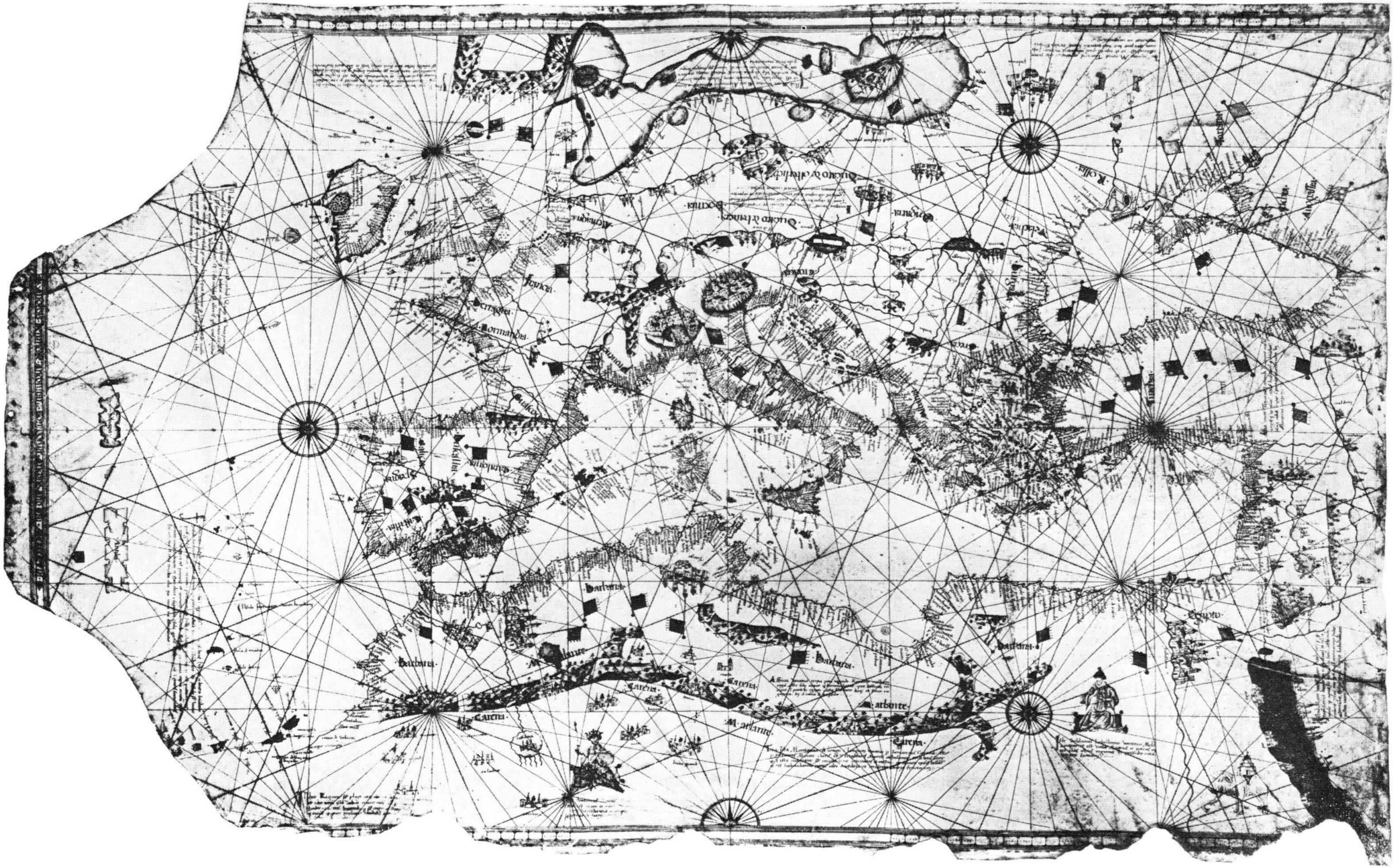

Figure 86. Andrea Benincasa Map of 1508. *V*

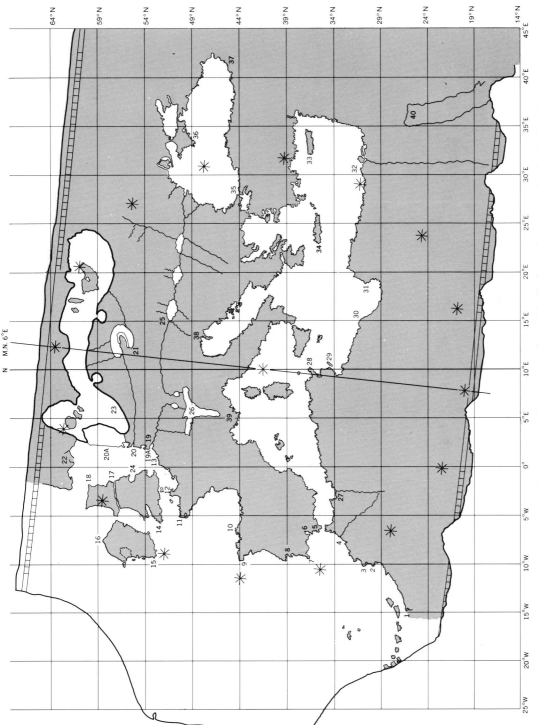

Figure 87. Benincasa Map with square grid constructed empirically from the geography (*see Table* 12).

85 shows the present topography in southern Sweden.

Comparing the Ptolemy Map of the North with the Zeno Map, we can see that they are related, but that they must have derived from sources dating from different times. If the original source of the Ptolemy Map came from the end of the ice age, that of the Zeno Map may have originated much earlier.

## 3.    The Andrea Benincasa Map of 1508.

This is one of the best of the portolan charts (see Fig. 86). Examination revealed that it was oriented to magnetic North, about 6° E.

To draw a grid for this map we first found the length of the degree of longitude by measuring the distance on the map in millimeters between known points at either end of the map—in this case Gibraltar and Batum—and dividing the millimeters by the number of degrees of longitude between them. The length of the degree of latitude was found in the same way separately by using points on the Atlantic coast from Cape Yubi to Ireland, and points on the east from Cairo to Yalta. On our draft map, we found the longitude degree to be 7 mm, the latitude degree on the Atlantic to be 9 mm, and the latitude degree on the east to be 5 mm. As the longitude degree was intermediate, we took this as the basis for our grid. There were not enough points (and not enough total latitude) on the east to give us a reliable measure for the degree (Fig. 87). The grid had to be tied to some geographical reference point for longitude, and for this we first chose Cape Ben, near the former site of Carthage, for it was central and well delineated on the map. Subsequently we discovered an error of about 1° affecting the whole map and moved our meridians one degree to the east. We based latitude on the latitude of Alexandria. The resulting grid revealed a remarkable accuracy for the map as a whole. The average of longitude errors for 35 places scattered from Gibraltar to Batum in the Caucasus (a distance of 3,000 miles) was about half a degree. Latitude errors for Africa and Spain averaged 0.8°, for France and Britain 1.8° for the Mediterranean 1.0°, and for the Black Sea about 4°, the sea being placed that much too far north. In this it resembled the Dulcert Map, and suggested an effort on the part of some cartographer to align the map with the higher equator indicated in the Piri Re'is Map. (See Table 12.)

In order to evaluate this map's most remarkable feature it is necessary to emphasise the fact that it is one of the most accurate of all the portolanos in the details of the coasts. At the same time it shows in its accuracy of latitude and longitude that, like some of the other maps, it can only have been drawn originally with the aid of spherical trigonometry. It is therefore a scientific product in the true sense of that term.

The feature in question is at the north, and looks at first glance like a very bad representation of the Baltic. A comparison with a modern map shows that the Baltic runs nearly north and south, while on this otherwise so accurate map it runs east and west. There is no evidence of the existence of the upper Baltic or of the

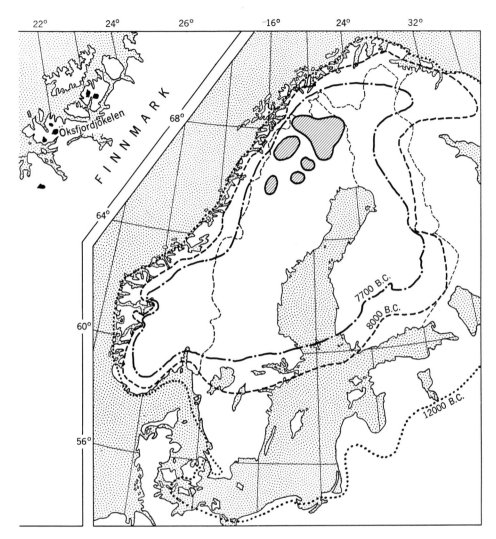

Figure 88. Glacial Map of the Baltic.

Gulfs of Bothnia and Riga. What could be the reason for this? This map is dated 1508, when the Baltic was, in fact, very well known. For nearly three centuries before this date it had been a highway of commerce, dominated by the merchant ships and navy of the Hanseatic League. Furthermore, its shape was better known to Ptolemy, as is shown by the map we have just discussed.

As we look at this feature on the Benincasa Map we note details that differ considerably from other representations of bodies of water on maps of the 15th and 16th centuries. Is this large feature really the Baltic—*or is it a mass of ice?* Are those blobs along the southern edge supposed to be harbors along the Baltic coast of

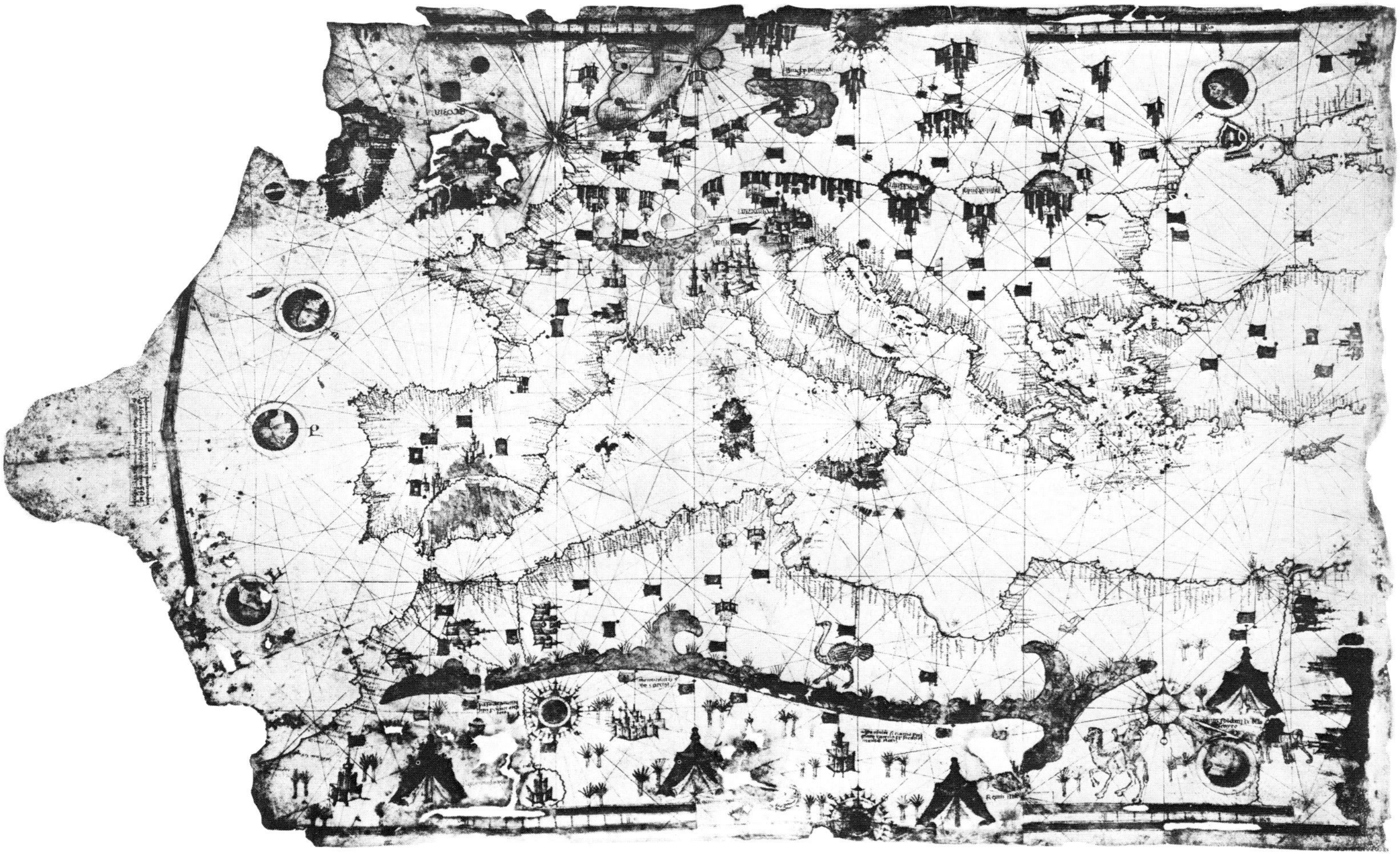

Figure 89. The Portolano of Ibn ben Zara, 1487.

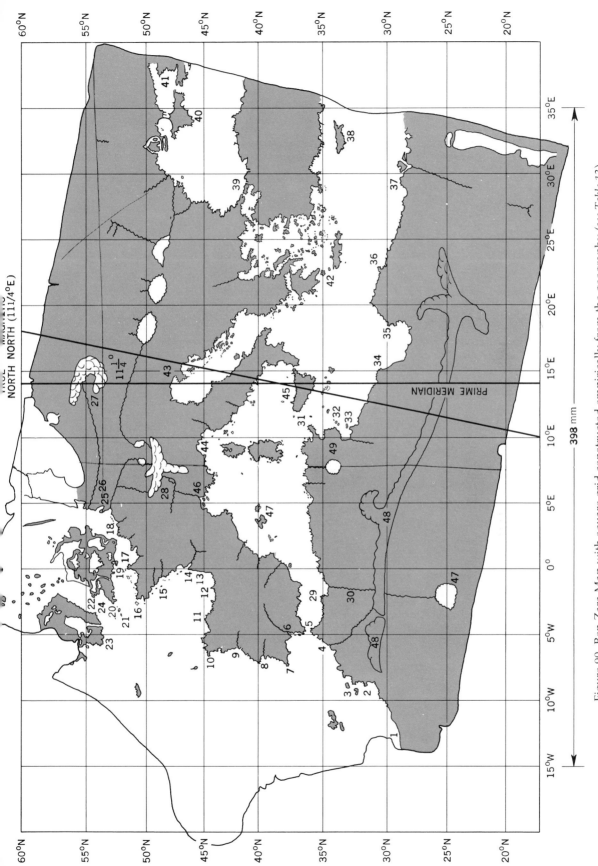

Figure 90. Ben Zara Map with square grid constructed empirically from the geography (*see Table 13*).

Germany, or are they run-off lakes from the melting glacier? Are those apparent islands really islands, or are they deglaciated tracts in the middle of the retreating ice cap? I was greatly intrigued by these possibilities, and considered the evidence very strong indeed when I observed that the general contour of the southern side of this "Baltic" followed very precisely the shape of the southern side of the Scandinavian ice cap as it stood about 8,000 B.C. (Fig. 88). Furthermore, the map shows the southern edge of the ice in the correct latitude of 57° or 58° N.

In all the maps that show this erroneous shape of the Baltic there appears a break in the Baltic coast. It seems that the accurate portolano in each case extends to Britain, and to the coast of the Netherlands. Then an entirely different source map has been used, and this map has been misinterpreted so that the coast of the Netherlands is mistaken for the coast of Denmark, which is thus placed about 250 miles too far west, much coastline being omitted. This apparently distorted map of the Baltic may have been circulating in southern countries—Portugal or Italy— where the true shape of the Baltic was less known. It is my suggestion that cartographers in those countries happened upon this old map, along with the others that had reached Europe from Constantinople or elsewhere, and combined it with the normal portolano.

Another possibility is provided by the consideration that there was a time in the post-glacial period when the Baltic may very well have had the shape shown on these maps. The northward extensions of the sea—the Gulfs of Bothnia and Riga—probably were covered by the ice long after the lower Baltic had become ice-free. Since they are both very shallow, they may even have been above sea level when the sea level was 50 or 100 meters lower.

## 4.   The Portolano of Iehudi Ibn ben Zara of Alexandria.

We have mentioned that Nordenskiöld considered all the portolan charts to be copies of one original. It seems to me that the portolano of Iehudi Ibn ben Zara of Alexandria (Fig. 89) may stand very close to this original.

I had been attracted to the study of this portolano because it seemed definitely superior to all the other portolan charts I had seen in the fineness of its delineation of the details of the coasts. As I examined these details in comparison with the modern maps, I was amazed that no islet, no matter how small, seemed too small to be noted. For example, on the French coast, along with the principal features, I found the mapmaker had drawn in the tiny islets, the Ile de Ré and the Ile d'Oléron, north of the mouth of the Gironde River. North of the mouth of the Loire he included Belle Ile and two other small islets. Off Brest, he drew in the Ile d'Ouessant. Similar fine details can be found all around the coasts.

The grid worked out for the map (Fig. 90) revealed, indeed, a most amazing accuracy so far as relative latitudes and longitudes were concerned. Total longitude between Gibraltar and the Sea of Azov was accurate to half a degree, total latitude from Cape Yubi to Cape Clear, Ireland, was accurate to a degree and a half. Average errors of latitude for the whole map were less than one degree; average

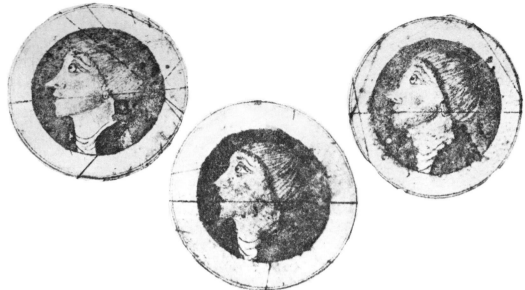

Figure 91. The faces of the Ibn ben Zara Map.

errors of longitude amounted to little more (see Table 13). As far as the map as a whole was concerned, there was no evidence of an oblong grid. Like the Benincasa Map, it seemed to have been drawn for a square grid. Yet a complication was to appear, as we shall see below.

Alfred Isroe, my student, drew my attention to one of the most remarkable features of the map. These were five tiny faces in medallions in its corners, where mapmakers of the Renaissance followed the custom of placing faces symbolizing the winds. Usually such faces are not found on the portolan charts. In Renaissance maps they are usually shown with their cheeks puffed out, obviously blowing vigorously in the appropriate direction.

The faces on the ben Zara Map are not typical of the cartography of the Renaissance. Their cheeks are not puffed out. The faces are calm and aristocratic in mien, and the clothing indicated does not seem characteristic of the contemporary styles.

Isroe suggested at first that the faces resembled faces found on icons of the Greek Orthodox Church, such as were, he said, produced by the famous iconographic school of Parnassus in the 7th and 8th centuries A.D. This was exciting indeed. Could it be that we had here an accurate copy of an ancient portolano that had come through a Greek monastery of the 8th century: Ibn ben Zara had, of course, added modern names to his chart, but perhaps he had made no other changes in his ancient source map. This matter required intensive examination.

I took the matter up with my aunt, Mrs. Norman Hapgood, who is a scholar and a translator with a knowledge of Russian and other eastern tongues. She said that, to her, the faces looked Coptic. I investigated Coptic art in Harvard's Fogg Museum and was well rewarded. A number of treatises gave me some light on the subject. Among these, two in particular were useful (80, 4).

Gruneisen, one of these scholars, describes the Coptic art born in Alexandria

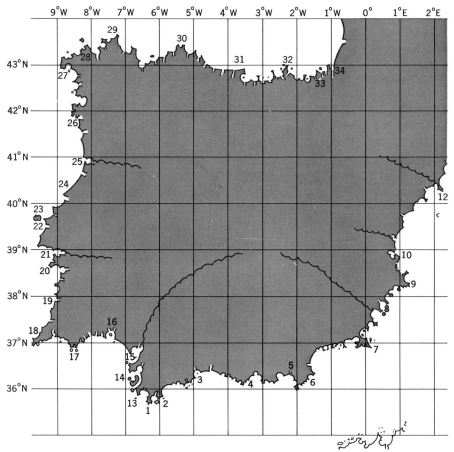

Figure 92. Spanish section of the Ibn ben Zara Map, with oblong grid constructed empirically from the topography. (*see Table 14*).

before the rise of Christianity as *"frivole, spirituel, profondement raffiné et aristocratique par excellence."** The reader may judge for himself how far the little faces agree with this description (Fig. 91). As I have already pointed out in connection with the Piri Re'is and other maps there is reason to believe that the portolan charts did in fact come through Alexandria and were copied and arranged by the geographers there, who may, indeed, have originated the flat portolan projection itself. In view of this, the Hellenistic-like faces may be quite significant.

I have mentioned that the grid worked out for this map indicated that a square grid, not an oblong one, was probably the sort of grid used in drawing the map, or at least in compiling it from local maps. Table 13 strongly suggests this.

I was profoundly surprised, therefore, when one of my students, Warren Lee, discovered that, in regards to Spain, the grid indicated by the topography was oblong, and not square (see Fig. 92 and Table 14). This is, indeed, astonishing. How can it be explained? Are we to suppose that the mapmaker who compiled the whole map, and did it so very well, made use of separate maps of different countries, and among these used a map of Spain that had been drawn earlier, perhaps on the same projection as the De Canerio Map?

* "Frivolous, intellectual, deeply refined, above all aristocratic."

Figure 93. Ptolemy's Map of Spain. *I*

Warren Lee is responsible for another interesting observation. In his study of the Spanish sector of the map he observed that it showed a large bay at the mouth of the Guadalquivir River. At this point the modern map shows a large delta, composed of swamps, about thirty miles wide and fifty miles long. The bay on the ben Zara Map might seem thus to represent the coastline before the growth of the delta of the Guadalquivir. Since the Guadalquivir is not an enormous river, and does not carry huge loads of sediment, it would have taken a considerable time indeed to build the delta. Several other maps we have examined carry indications of delta-building since they were originally drawn, but in no other case is the evidence so clear as this.

Another matter of importance to us was to determine whether, in the remarkably detailed representation of the islands, especially in the Aegean Sea, we might not have evidence of a change of sea level or a change in the elevation of the land since the original map was made. Comparison of the Aegean Sea on this map (Fig. 94) with the Aegean on a modern map (Fig. 95) suggests that many islands may have been submerged. There are many fewer islands on the modern map, and many of these are smaller than they are shown to be on the old map. One may ask, if the mapmaker was so conscientious in drawing in the smallest islands, and

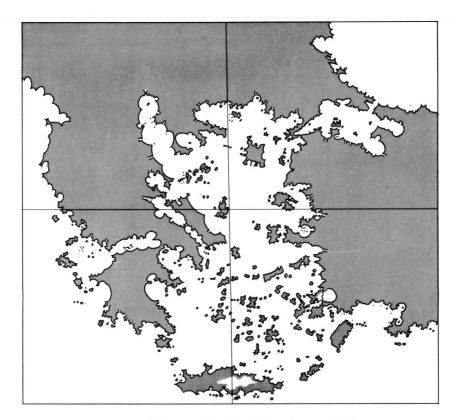

Figure 94. The Ibn ben Zara Map, Aegean Section.

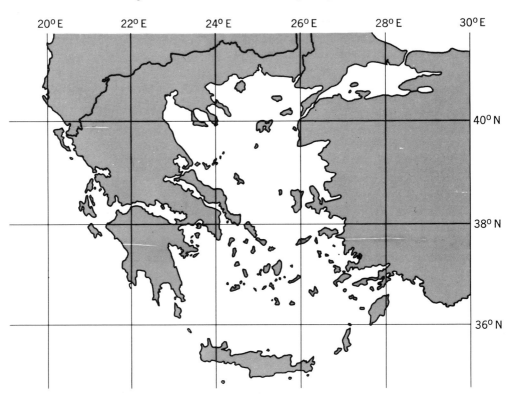

Figure 95. The Modern Map of the Aegean.

Figure 96. Thera on the Ibn ben Zara Map.

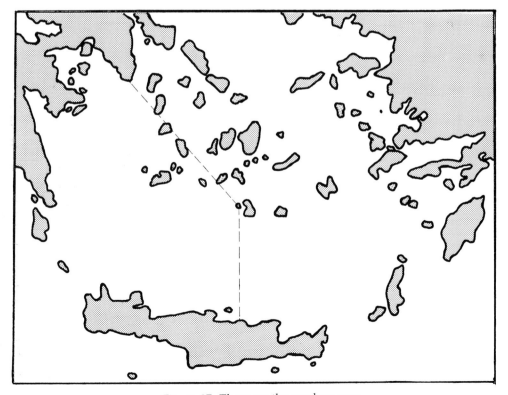

Figure 97. Thera on the modern map.

Figure 98. Ibn ben Zara Map, tracing of British Isles, possibly showing remnant glaciers.

showing all the features of the coast with the greatest accuracy possible, why in the Aegean should he suddenly take leave of his senses, and fill the sea with imaginary islands, *while still showing the real islands in their correct positions?*

This change in the Aegean may be connected with the great explosion of the island of Thera about 1400 B.C. Figs. 96 and 97 may show Thera before and after the explosion. Geologists have found that the island subsided half a mile after the explosion. The subsidence may have extended to the entire Aegean basin, and may have been a part of a more general geological change, evidence for which will be reviewed in Chapter VIII.

The reader will note that a corner of this map apparently shows the same feature we have discussed as a possible ice cap in the Benincasa Map. We had to admit that the evidence in that case was equivocal. Here, in this map, we have more of the same sort of evidence, in the form of features suggesting glaciers in central England and in central Ireland (see Fig. 98).

Here, at least, we can say the evidence all hangs together: the great lapse of time required for building the delta of the Guadalquivir, the evidence of a lower sea level at the time the map was drawn (which we know did exist at the end of the ice age), or land changes since, and these possible remnant glaciers in the British Isles.

# VII   The Hamy-King Chart of c. 1502

THE HAMY-KING Chart (Fig. 99), dated between 1502 and 1504, is based partly on Ptolemaic and partly on Portolan traditions, with some recently discovered lands added by one of the early explorers who is thought to have been Amerigo Vespucci.* The European section is based on one of the most accurate of the portolan charts, and is so important that it will be given treatment by itself in the final section of this chapter.

This world map provides evidence of numerous and extensive land changes since the first prototypes of its component local maps were drawn, probably many thousands of years ago. It supplements the evidences of land changes provided by the other maps examined in this book, as well as the evidence of climatic changes. These will be discussed in the following chapter.

Two features of special historical interest in the Mediterranean section of the map are the canal connecting the Mediterranean and Red Seas, supposedly built by Rameses II and restored by Persia after the Persian conquest of Egypt, and the site of the ancient city of Tyre, which is shown on its islet, connected with the coast by a causeway. The city and its causeway existed from about 2800 B.C. to the capture of Tyre by Alexander the Great shortly after 300 B.C. Its presence on this map is the clearest proof we have found of the antiquity of the Mediterranean portolano. (See Fig. 104.)

## 1.   The Construction of the Map.

The reader will remember that in our study of the Piri Re'is Map we found evidence that at one stage in its history another equator had been drawn four or five degrees to the north of the equator shown, and then erased. It eventually appeared that this upper equator had been, geometrically speaking, the correct equator of the portolan projection used in the map. It seemed there must have been an older map of Europe and Africa incorporated by Piri Re'is, possibly with-

* The original of this map is in the Huntington Library in San Marino, California. It was reproduced by Nordenskiöld in his *Periplus*.

152

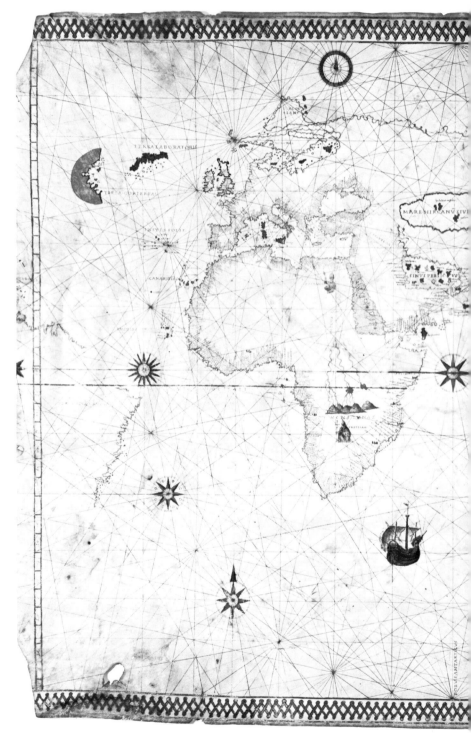

Figure 99. The Hamy-King Chart of 1502–4. (*H. E. Huntington Lib.*)

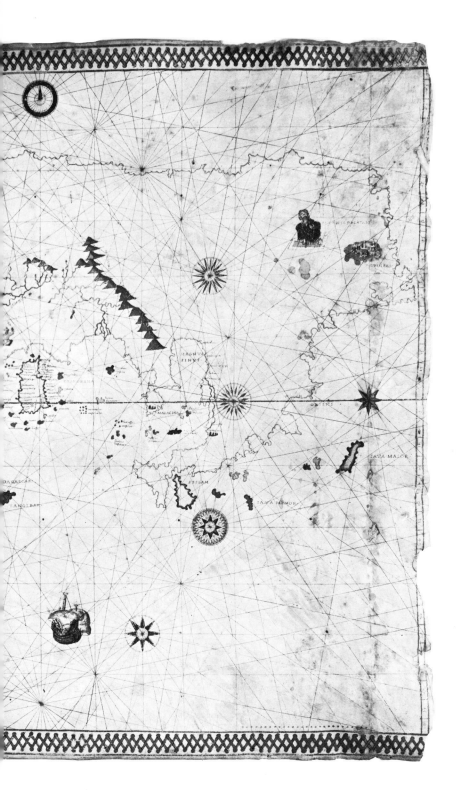

out change, into his world map, and by an error on this source map Europe and Africa had been placed about four or five degrees too far south. We have seen evidence of this upper equator on the Dulcert and Benincasa maps.

The Hamy-King Chart confirms this conjecture, for here the same two equators are seen actually drawn in. We see the upper equator, the equator of the projection, lying right on the coast of Guinea, which is a mistake. We see the lower equator lying about four or five degrees south of the coast, which is correct. It would seem that some cartographer discovered and tried to correct an error in an earlier compilation.

A brief discussion of another map must be inserted at this point. Evidence of two equators can be found on the Claudius Clavus Map of 1427.* There is a grid on the map, with registers of latitude and longitude, probably copied from Ptolemy. The register at the left counts latitude from a lower equator and the register on the right from an upper one, the difference between them being in this case four degrees.

It is a most interesting thing that the grid drawn on this map by Clavus shows the degree of latitude approximately twice the length of the degree of longitude. (Fig. 100.) A map of this area on the Mercator projection indicates that this is approximately the correct ratio of the degrees for the latitude of the Baltic in any projection where the meridians are straight lines parallel to each other. It seems inescapable that this grid must have been derived from the Ptolemy manuscript used by Clavus. We have seen that similar grids were used in drawing different parts of the Zeno Map of the North.

Another feature of the Clavus map should be noted in passing. Close examination reveals that this map shows the Baltic only as far as the Gulf of Finland; that is, as far north as the island of Saarmaa (Osel) off the Esthonian coast. The Gulfs of Finland and Bothnia are not shown.

This is peculiar considering the quantity of information contained by this map. It shows clearly enough the Danish island of Sjaelland, which contains Copenhagen, the three islands directly to the south of it (Lolland, Falster, and Moen), the island of Bornholm correctly placed 5° to the east, and the island of Gotland. On the German coast the estuaries of the Oder and Vistula Rivers are clearly shown. To the far north, the northernmost point of Norway, North Cape, is shown *in correct latitude*, 71° N, on the right hand scale.

One wonders how all this knowledge can be reconciled with the absences from this map of the two gulfs. Let us remember that Ptolemy drew upon and distorted many of the ancient maps he found in the Library of Alexandria. We have already seen that one of these maps (Fig. 83) seems to show extensive ice sheets in Scandinavia. As the ice age was a time of lowered sea levels, it is not beyond the possibilities that the Gulfs of Bothnia and Finland simply did not exist when the

---

* This map appeared as a modern version of Ptolemy's Baltic map in an early manuscript of Ptolemy's *Geographia*. It is now in the Bibliotheque Municipale of Nancy (France). (Information from Walter Ristow, Map Division of the Library of Congress.)

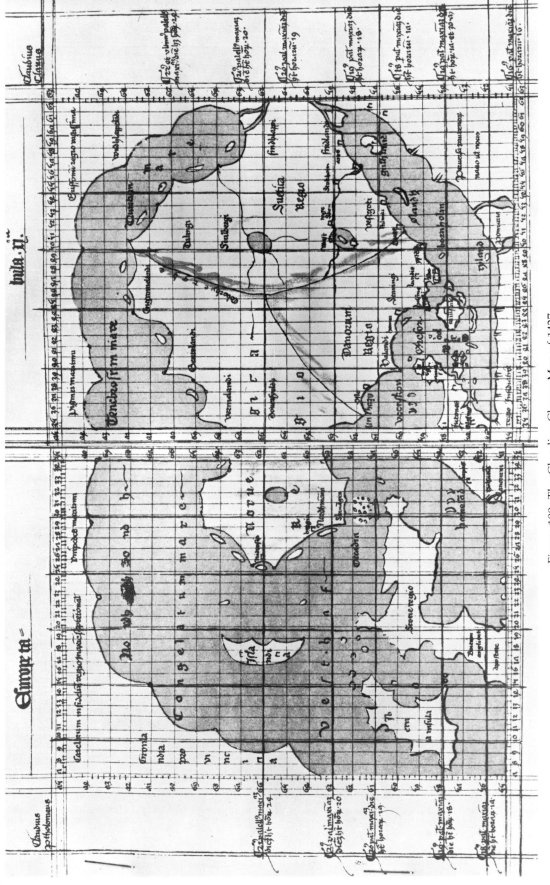

Figure 100. The Claudius Clavus Map of 1427.

prototype of this particular map was drawn.

Besides placing North Cape in correct latitude the Clavus Map also indicates the presence of many islands on the Arctic coast of Norway. Certainly nobody in Europe before 1427, even if he had explored and mapped the Arctic coast, could have accurately determined the latitude of North Cape.

When I began my study of the Hamy-King Chart in preparation for the present edition of this work I was pleased to see that the meridian through the center of the portolan projection was drawn *from pole to pole,* with the poles indicated, so that it was actually a complete meridian embracing 180°. (See Fig. 99). This offered the possibility of finding the length of the degree without going to the infinite pains required to discover the length of the degree for the Piri Re'is Map.

It was interesting to note that in placing the center of the portolan design in the Indian Ocean the cartographer had made it possible to construct a world map embracing all of Europe, Asia and Africa, and the Americas as well. It was a much broader design than we found in the Piri Re'is Map. We should note also that he used the eight-wind and not the older twelve-wind system.

As on the Clavus Map, there are two graduated scales of latitude on this map, at the right and left hand edges. The right hand scale has been badly damaged but enough of it remains so that it can be restored, and it can be seen that the length of the degree of latitude (in five degree units) is the same in both scales. However, the left hand scale is laid out from the lower equator, as in the Clavus Map while the right hand one is in both maps laid out northward and southward from the equator of the projection. As a result the two scales reach the top and bottom of the map with a difference of about 5°. There is thus clearly a close connection between the Clavus and Hamy-King Maps, a connection which extends also to the Piri Re'is, Dulcert and Benincasa Maps, and to the Vespucci world map of 1526 which we shall consider below.

At first it seemed that the length of the degree derived from division of the length of the meridian through the center of the Hamy-King Map was in fair agreement with the scales, though these were roughly drawn. A test layout of parallels indicated fair agreement with the true latitudes of many places. However, a count of the five-degree units revealed that two were lacking: each scale contained only 80° instead of 90°! This suggested that the cartographer who applied the scales had been guided by a correct knowledge of the latitudes of many places, rather than by the geometry of the projection. He had calculated the length of the degree of latitude from empirical knowledge of the geography and not by deduction from the portolan design.

In view of the fact that the scales were only approximately accurate I thought it best to check the length of the degree by the geography of the map itself. A measurement of the longitude difference between Alexandria and Gibraltar resulted in a very minor reduction of about one twenty-fifth in the length of the degree indicated by the scale. A measurement of the latitude difference between the northern tip of Scotland and the Cape of Good Hope showed that the degrees of latitude and longtiude were exactly the same, so we appeared to have a square grid for the map as a whole.

There were still several problems to be solved before I could draw a grid for the Hamy-King Map. Our base line for latitude was the equator, but we had two of them! It was necessary to find out how much of the map was based on each of these equators. At first I felt that the lower one would probably determine the latitudes for most of the map because it was obviously right for the Gulf of Guinea, as with the Piri Re'is Map. Later I thought that the meridian of Alexandria might be the dividing line, with everything to the east based on the upper equator and everything to the west on the lower. Finally I found that the entire map was based on the upper equator except the western coast of Africa from Dakar to the Cape of Good Hope, the Cape Verde Islands, and some interior points. (See Fig. 103.)

There now arose a problem about the degree of longitude. The map itself, as I have already remarked, suggested a square grid, but this finding was based on the parts of the map which seemed to derive directly from the pre-Ptolemaic portolan tradition. Most of the map suggested the influence of the Ptolemaic school. It occurred to me that if the compilation as a whole had originally been put together under the influence of Ptolemy's ideas then it would be likely that the map-maker would have accepted Ptolemy's estimate of the length of the degree.

It has been generally considered that the precise length of Ptolemy's degree and therefore his circumference of the earth are uncertain, and there have been differing estimates. Ptolemy said that 500 stadia equalled one degree but views have differed on the length of the stadium. The reader will remember our solution for this problem (pp. 27–28). It consisted of our finding the length of the stadium used by Eratosthenes who was head of the Alexandrian Library 300 years before Ptolemy held the same position. In considering the Hamy-King Map I thought it might be reasonable to assume that the stadium remained constant in that great center of learning for the intervening time. Ptolemy might not have agreed with Eratosthenes as to the circumference of the earth. He decidedly did not (and Eratosthenes was nearer the truth) but he expressed the difference not in the length of the stadium but in the number of stadia.

According to our finding of the length of the stadium Ptolemy's 500 stadia would make a degree one-sixth shorter than the one we use today. His circumference then would have been 18,000 instead of 25,000 miles. I reflected that if this were basically a Ptolemaic map I had better use his degree in finding longitude even though I knew that being based on error this would distort all longitudes with increasing distances from the prime meridian, for which I chose the meridian of Alexandria.*

In Fig. 102 I constructed a grid based on our empirically measured degree of latitude and on Ptolemy's degree for longitude. I extended the meridians to the eastern end of the map and found that the meridian there was 110° W longitude.

---

* I used this meridian, as the center of the Hamy-King design is in the Indian Ocean, and its precise longitude could not be determined.

Then I drew in the meridians westward to the Caribbean and found, to my shock, the same meridian, 110° W! In other words, this Ptolemaic map presumed to be a map of the whole circle of the globe! This map helps us to understand why Columbus thought he had found Asia. He knew a lot about maps and he might well have possessed a prototype of this one! This Hamy-King Map with this Ptolemaic grid is good visual evidence to support the ideas of Columbus' time. A version of it may have been the world map Columbus is reported to have presented to Ferdinand and Isabella. If he understood it himself this might explain why he succeeded in getting their support.

The designs along the top and bottom of the map at first sight appeared to be purely decorative. However, the makers of sea charts were not practitioners of the fine arts. They did not believe in art for art's sake. They wasted no time on embellishments. There might have been a practical utility to these apparently abstract designs. Eventually I compared the number of intervals between points in the designs with my grid based on Ptolemy's degree of longitude. I found that there were exactly three of these intervals for every 10° of Ptolemaic longitude. Counting the intervals in the designs across the top and the bottom of the map between the scales at east and west, I found that there were 110 of them, and they indicated a total longitude of 330°, lacking only 30° of the circle of the globe!

As already mentioned, the Hamy-King Map has been associated with the name of Vespucci. From what we have already said, however, it must be clear that the compilation of the map as a whole cannot have been Vespucci's work. He evidently used older maps for the entire Eastern Hemisphere. He could have been responsible only for the mapping of the coasts he actually explored himself. German Arciniegas, in his *Amerigo and the New World* (14a) furnishes maps of each of Amerigo's four voyages of exploration. On his first voyage (1497–1498) he explored the coasts of Costa Rica *or* Yucatan, the Gulf of Mexico, Florida, and the coast from Florida northward to Cape Hatteras or perhaps to Chesapeake Bay.

On his second voyage (1499–1500) Amerigo explored the northern coast of South America from Cape San Augustin (8° S) to Trinidad, and touched on some of the Caribbean islands. He did not, however, discover the mouth of the Amazon or the island of Marajo. The third voyage (1501–1502) took him down the eastern coast of South America from Cape San Roque as far as a river, probably the Rio Cananor, in Patagonia (50° or 51° S.) He discovered the River La Plata, but did not reach the Strait of Magellan. The fourth voyage (1503–1504) was not particularly important. He touched at Bahia on the eastern coast of South America, went a short way southward to San Vincente, and then recrossed the Atlantic to Sierra Leone in Africa.

The coasts Amerigo visited appear on the Vespucci World Map of 1526, (Fig. 102). There is little resemblance between the northern and eastern coasts of South America on these two maps, nor in the drawing of Cuba and Santo Domingo.

The title "Vespucci World Map of 1526" under which it is listed in the collections of the Spanish Historical Society of America, which contain the original, is somewhat of a misnomer. Vespucci himself died in 1512. He had, however, before his

Figure 101. Vespucci World Map of 1526. (*Hispanic Soc. of Amer.*)

death been appointed Pilot Major of Spain by King Ferdinand, and was entrusted with the preparation of a master map which was to be kept up to date with the addition of all new discoveries made by the explorers. After his death a committee was appointed to have charge of the continuing work, and thus, on the map itself we see all the discoveries reported down to the year 1526, including these of Balboa (1513) and Magellan (1520).

The differences in the drawing of the South American coasts on the King-Hamy Chart, and on the 1526 map, are very great. The map of 1502–4 shows many more indentations on the northern and eastern coasts than appear on the modern map, or on the map of 1526. It seems most unlikely that Amerigo would have invented these indentations. What would have been the point? And there is also the unexplained gap embracing a considerable amount of latitude and longitude. It looks very much as if the compiler of the King-Hamy map used ancient source maps for these coasts, rather than Vespucci's.

Amerigo claimed to be able to find his longitude by astronomical observations. Apparently using the method described by Morison (see pp. 34–5). However at one point he established his longitude as 150° west of the meridian of Alexandria, the longitude of Santa Barbara, California, much farther west than he ever got, which doesn't say much for the method!

A careful examination of this map, which unquestionably was compiled by Vespucci, reveals additional points of interest. He has used the ancient source maps for Africa and Europe. His map of the Mediterranean is a portolan chart, but not the version used in the Hamy-King Map. The center of his portolan design for his whole map is in East Africa, and it is observable that the equator of the projection is the upper equator of the Hamy-King, Piri Re'is and other maps we have mentioned. He has the Amazon aligned with the lower equator, which, however, is a degree or two too far south. In Central Africa there is similarity in the drawing of the tributaries of the Nile, but while the Hamy-King map shows the equatorial lakes, Albert and Victoria, located on the lower equator, the Vespucci Map shows them located on the upper one.

It was interesting to confirm the Ptolemaic construction of the map, but it was more important to discover how its geography would stand up with an accurate grid based on the true circumference of the earth. I therefore drew such a grid for each half of the map separately. (Fig. 103.)

After I completed the drawing of this grid for the whole Hamy-King Map I gave special attention to the European sector because I could see at a glance that it was probably a very accurate version of the original Mediterranean portolano. Moreover in the Scandinavian sector, derived from another very inaccurate source map, there seemed to be remnants of glaciers while in the most accurate part, in the Mediterranean itself, there seemed to be many islands not now existing, as in the Aegean section of the Ibn ben Zara Map. This encouraged me to think that perhaps here I had found a version of the portolano that dated from the time when the prototype of the Aegean part of the Ibn ben Zara Map had been compiled; that is, before the explosion of Thera. This in turn would indicate that the subsidence of the whole Aegean, indicated on the Ibn ben Zara Map, extended to the western Mediterranean as well.

My examination of this sector of the Hamy-King Map revealed two surprising facts. First, I discovered that the originally separate Mediterranean map had been oriented to magnetic and not to true north, and that the compiler had not understood this, and so he thus introduced an error into his own map. Secondly, I found that the grid of this separate map had actually been oblong and not square, as we had discovered in the Spanish sector of the Ibn ben Zara Map (see Fig. 92). I therefore re-oriented the portolano and drew a special grid for it (Fig. 103) but I will postpone detailed discussion of it to the final section of this chapter.

It is probable that the compilation of this portolano with the rest of the world map was made after the introduction of the compass into Europe in the 13th century, for it was only after this that a magnetic orientation was applied to many of the charts.

It now remains for us to discuss the geography of the world map as a whole.

## 2. The Geography of the Map.
### (a) The Americas

The mapping of the West Indies on the Hamy-King Chart appears to be the work of the early Renaissance discoverers, and may have been done by Vespucci himself. The fact that the islands are shown in correct longitude, however, is strange considering the fact that no one in that period could find correct longitude. The fact that the islands are placed some five degrees too far north, above rather than below the Tropic of Cancer, shows that (as we have already pointed out) they could not find accurate latitude either.

In Table 16 I have listed places on the northern and eastern coasts of South America, coasts that were explored by Vespucci. It is my impression that the accuracy of the mapping, while it does not compare with the accuracy of the mapping of the same coasts on the Piri Re'is Map, is too good to be ascribed to Vespucci, both as to latitude and longitude.

What is noteworthy in the drawing of these coasts is the uniformity of the longitude errors. They are all eastward and from the Orinoco nearly as far south as the Rio de la Plata, they vary only two degrees, from a minimum of 4° to a maximum of 6°. In other words, their longitudes relative to each other are extremely good. Latitudes on the east coast are even better, the errors varying only between 2° and 3°. It would seem to have been impossible for any 16th century navigator to survey and map a coast as well as this. We must not forget that the navigator of this period was essentially dependent upon dead reckoning. He navigated by estimating his speed, his net direction taking into account many changes in course dictated by the winds, and the effects of currents. He could not find longitude and it was next to impossible for him to find his latitude accurately with the instruments that existed. Furthermore, the northern and eastern coasts of

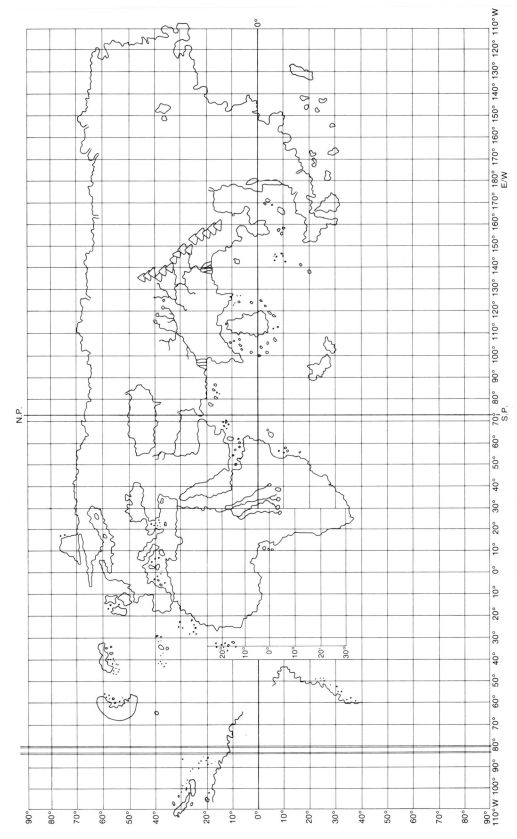

Figure 102. The Hamy-King Chart with Ptolemaic Grid.

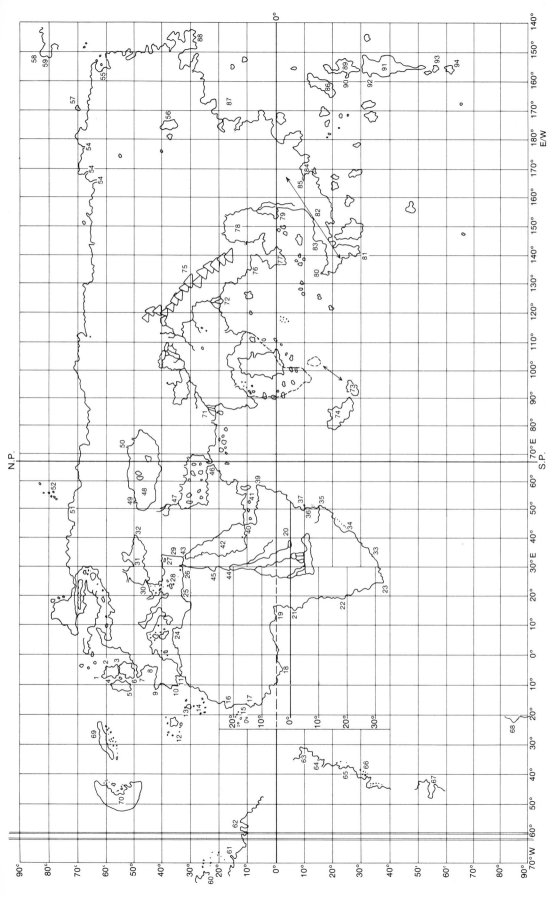

Figure 103. The Hamy-King Chart with Modern Grid.

South America are separated on the Hamy-King Map. The blank space represents more than ten degrees of latitude and longitude. If Vespucci or another explorer left the northern coast at 6° N, as the map suggests, how did he find the eastern coast at 6° S, and how could he have estimated its longitudes and its latitudes so correctly?

Longitude errors averaging 5° from the Orinoco southward may seem like good-sized errors, but we shall see that on the other side of the Atlantic, on the west coast of Africa from the mouths of the Niger to the Cape of Good Hope, there were eastward errors of longitude that average 7° on this same map. The width of the South Atlantic Ocean is therefore represented with an error of only 2°. A comparison with the other maps of this period will show that, except for the Piri Re'is Map, no other map of the Atlantic can approach this accuracy. I feel this accuracy cannot be dismissed as the result of accident. I feel that the Hamy-King compiler must have used an ancient map of the coasts.

The impression that no 16th century explorer could have mapped the coasts of South America as shown in the Hamy-King Map is strengthened by comparing them with some other features that another Renaissance cartographer did in fact add to the map. Two of these are seen in the middle of the Atlantic, floating freely in the ocean. One of these is labelled Labrador and the other is supposed to be Newfoundland. Somebody had visited these places, but did not know they were parts of North America. It is true that the latitude of Labrador is correct, but the latitude of Newfoundland is off about 15°, while the longitude errors for both features are enormous. Perhaps Vespucci depended upon hearsay for these two features and for the island of Madagascar which he places about 40° too far east.

While examining the photocopy of the map with a magnifying glass I saw what I thought represented erasures of some coastal features. I restored these and found items 67 and 68 of Table 16, which I have identified as the Strait of Magellan and the east coast of the Palmer or Antarctic Peninsula respectively. It would seem that these were probably features of the ancient source map used by the compiler.

## (b) The Siberian Coast and Alaska

After the double equator of the Hamy-King Map the feature that excited me most was the presence on it of the whole Arctic coast of Siberia from Lapland to Bering Strait and, as I found with my magnifying glass, a part of the coast of Alaska. The grid showed the coast of Siberia to be in correct latitude. A number of geographical features could be identified. It was amazing to find, for example, the three mouths of the Lena River indicated only two degrees south of their correct latitude. It was even more astonishing to find the Gulf of Anadyr, which opens into the Bering Sea, clearly indicated at its correct latitude of 60° to 65° N. When could the coasts of the Arctic Ocean and the Bering Sea have been mapped? Clearly not in the Renaissance. Clearly not in the Middle Ages. Certainly not by any geographers of Greece or Rome. Probably not by Cretans or Phoenicians. It would appear that this part of the Hamy-King Map preserves a tradition from that remote time when the Arctic

Ocean was warm and when Siberia supported vast populations of mammoths, deer, horses, and tigers, together with luxuriant forests on what is now the tundra. This will be dicussed more fully in the next chapter.

In Table 16 Wrangel Island as well as the Alaskan coast were features that had been erased and which I discovered by using a magnifying glass. I am not certain that a direct examination of the original map itself with a stronger glass would not reveal features I have not discovered. However, I can say that in each case I had no idea in advance of what the erased feature was.

## (c) Africa

The western coast of Africa falls clearly into two sections. The influence of the two equators and the attempts of cartographers to understand and reconcile them have distorted what was probably originally an accurate map, perhaps as accurate as the De Canerio map of Africa already discussed. Down as far as Cape Blanc the coast is aligned with the equator of the projection and is in correct relationship with the Mediterranean coast. From there southward the coast, including the Cape Verde Islands, are aligned with the lower equator. In order to accomplish this the coast between Gibraltar and Cape Blanc has been abbreviated by 4°. We confirm this by noting that while Gibraltar on the world projection is 2° too far south, Cape Blanc on the same projection is 2° too far north. On the other hand, from Cape Blanc to Cape Palmas the cartographer has added 3.5° of coastline and manages to reach the Cape of Good Hope only half a degree short. With the lower equator both the Guinea coast and the Cape are in correct latitude but the Mediterranean coast is four or five degrees too far north, while with the equator of the projection the situation is reversed.

On the east coast of Africa, which is in general in alignment with the upper equator, the cartographer made the mistake of aligning Cape Guardafui with the lower equator, thus placing it 5° too far south on the world projection. This forced him to save 5° of coastline to the southward and correspondingly lengthen the Red Sea. The result was a serious distortion of the east coast of Africa.

This question of the cartographer's knowledge of the latitude of Cape Guardafui is important from one point of view. We have already reviewed the state of exploration of the African coasts by the date of this map. (See pp. 105–6.) We know that the Portuguese had explored a little past the equator on the west coast by this time. They had not explored the west coast from there to the Cape and they had not explored the east coast at all. Therefore, the cartographer must have had information not available in Europe in the Renaissance. The data of the Clavus Map suggests that the problem of the two equators goes back to antiquity. A knowledge of the latitude of Cape Guardafui suggests the same thing.

As to longitude, on the west coast of Africa from Gibraltar to the Niger River errors average 1.2° E. Then they suddenly increase, and from the Niger to the Cape of Good Hope they average 6° E. On the east coast they average 9° E, so that the southern part of Africa has been given 3° too much longitude. This, however, still represents a remarkable achievement in cartographic science.

One of the most remarkable things in the Hamy-King Map is the evidence of ancient knowledge of the sources of the Nile; that is, of the great lakes that lie on or near the equator, especially the largest of them, Lake Victoria Nyanza. This lake is correctly placed in latitude (on the lower equator) and its longitude error, 5° E, is almost the same as the longitude error of the mouths of the Niger. The lake is therefore very accurately placed in longitude with reference to both the coasts. It is not reasonable to attribute this to accident. We have here a certain knowledge of central Africa in a map that was published 350 years before the 19th cetury "discovery" of the sources of the Nile. We have noted that the world map of Eratosthenes shows the course of the Nile down as far as the latitude of the entrance to the Red Sea.* Here is very sure evidence of the antiquity of the sources of the information on the Hamy-King Map.

As we cross the central meridian of the world projection at 67° E longitude there is an abrupt and very considerable increase of longitude errors. The map from here on eastward seems to have been stretched like a sheet of rubber. The consequence is a vast extension of the Caspian Sea and of the coast between the entrance to the Persian Gulf and the Indus River. We now find the mouths of the Indus 17.5° too far east and the Caspian Sea is extended 23.5° too far to the eastward, although as to latitude its location is correct to within about three degrees. The locations of the two rivers, the Volga and the Ural, are indicated. It is interesting that the longitude of the Volga in the western Caspian is only 5.5° too far east, while the Ural River in the eastern Caspian is 22.0° too far east. There has been a sudden addition to the longitude of 16.5°

## (d) India

We now come to one of the greatest puzzles of the Hamy-King Map: India. Here the map follows closely the tradition of Ptolemy. India is shown as a truncated peninsula, with a very large land mass lying as an island to the south. I am going to suggest that here we are not in the presence of bad cartography, but in the presence of an ancient tradition of a time when the northern plains of India were flooded and when the southern part of the peninsula, ancient Dravidia, was an island and perhaps the center of a great maritime civilization, and of the advanced culture of a civilization that was old when Egypt was young.

Let us consider the probabilities. In some ways the map we have here is quite accurate. The mouths of the Indus are very correctly placed in latitude. The mouths of the Ganges, across the whole extent of India, are correctly placed in latitude relatively to the Indus; that is, two degrees further south. The longitude between them has been stretched another 15.5°. To the far north, on the Arctic coast, the

---

* It is interesting to compare the map of Eratosthenes (Fig. 7) with the Hamy-King Chart with reference to the Gulf of Aden and the Persian Gulf.

same stretching can be observed, the mouths of the Lena River lying about 43° too far east. It should be noted that the mouths of the Lena are only ten degrees too far east as compared with the longitude of the Ganges.

Now let us consider the Himalayas. These mountains are shown on the map, but it is probable that the cartographer was dealing with the whole central Asian mountain complex, which includes the Himalayas, the Pamirs, and the Tien Shan Mountains of China. These mountains are in fact one system, as an examination of the modern map clearly shows. The different names reflect only the influence of the three great powers that have dominated the area in modern times.

If the mountain system is considered as a whole we find that the map represents its latitudes fairly well. The system actually extends through 20° of latitude; the map shows it extending through 33°. The error of latitude at the northern end of the system is only 3° N. As to longitude; surprisingly, the map is more accurate. It shows the full range of longitude for the mountain system to be 25° and this agrees perfectly with the modern map. There can be no question that there is real geographical knowledge here. There seems to be some real knowledge too of the tributaries of the Indus.

Now let us consider the probabilities. The Romans were remarkably bad geographers and they knew little of India. Ptolemy had no recent information on the geography of India. He had a source map, which he must have found in the Alexandrian library, showing southern India as an island, and he had no information to contradict it.

A comparison of his own map of India (Fig. 6) with the Hamy-King Map shows more realistic detail in Ptolemy's version. In the latter we see two large lakes in the island land mass. We see rivers flowing naturally from these lakes to the sea. We can also see rivers flowing from the northern mountains into the sea all along the continental coast as they must indeed have done when and if Dravidia was an island. The reader may note also that the islands shown surrounding the land mass, reproduced also on the Hamy-King Map, would, if united with the island and the continent represent pretty well the shape and the size of the India of today. I have indicated this in Fig. 103 by superimposing the present Indian coastline on the Hamy-King Map.

This presents us with a new possibility with regard to one of the two islands labelled "Madagascar" by the 16th century compiler. The smaller of the two looks suspiciously like Ceylon with a slightly wrong orientation. Let us remember that India on the Hamy-King Chart is too far east. The proper longitude for Ceylon is 80–82° E. The smaller island on the map is at 90–95° E. It is 10° too far east. The longitude error is about that of the east coast of Africa. The geographers who were "stretching" longitude between the Gulf of Aden and the Indus, and across India, may have just forgotten Ceylon. It is true that the latitude is wrong, but the 16th century compiler may have just moved it southward to agree with his ideas of the latitude of Madagascar.

There is some geological evidence for the flooding of the northern plains of India. This was presented by A. K. Dey of the Geological Survey of India in a paper entitled "The Shore Lines of India."* His paper does not establish the complete flooding of the northern plains, but he does follow the elevated beaches into the interior as far north as the estuaries of the Indus and the Ganges. The beaches might have met farther north.

There is also literary evidence. There are traditions in ancient Indian literature, the Vedas, of a time when Dravidia, the southern portion of the peninsular, was an island or connected with the mainland only by a narrow neck of land. A notable scholar of Vedic language and literature, Nilla Cram Cook, has found numerous references to an insular Dravidia.†

It must be admitted that there is an inconsistency about the reasonably good mapping of the Himalayas, the Ganges, and the tributaries of the Indus, and a complete departure from geographical reality in the peninusla to the south. It should be remembered that India was well known, if not to the Romans, then to the much earlier Phoenicians. They were trading in the ports of India as early as 2,000 B.C. We have shown that they must have possessed, even if they did not originally create, the fine maps we know as the Portolan Charts. Their maps of India must have been in the Alexandrian Library, along with those of the Mediterranean that have come down to us. But Ptolemy, knowing nothing of India, may have found and used a map that actually represented the India of ten thousand years ago.

As we travel further east on the Hamy-King Map we find additional evidence of vast land changes since the original prototypes of Ptolemy's maps came into existence, and again there is supporting geological evidence. A few places, such as Rangoon, the Malayan Peninsula, the Gulf of Siam, Cape Cambodia, are easily identified. However, east of these there is a vast southward extension of the Asian land mass which looks thoroughly imaginary. Within this land mass one can detect shapes that suggest Sumatra, Borneo, Korea. If such a land mass existed it might have included the Philippines.

Interestingly enough such a land mass is postulated by Alfred Russel Wallace, the co-discoverer of evolution, who studied the distribution of species in the islands of Indonesia and concluded that there was much evidence for a very recent connection between the islands of Java, Sumatra, and Borneo with the mainland or with Australia.* He also reported that there were native traditions that placed this connection only a few thousand years in the past.

There would be no point in even mentioning such apparently remote possibilities if we did not already have, in the maps studied in this book, ample proof of the vast antiquity of the cartographic tradition that has come down to us.

Along the eastern edge of the map, partly erased and covered with dirt, I discovered with the aid of the magnifying glass a number of islands which, when restored seemed to resemble rather strongly the islands of Japan. To be sure they

---

* *Quaternaria,* Vol. III, Rome, 1956, pp. 95–100.

† Unpublished manuscript.

* Wallace, Alfred Russel, *Island Life,* 3rd Rev., ed. London, Macmillan, 1902.

were located in the southern hemisphere, between 10° and 60° S latitude, but I assumed that this might be some guesswork of some 16th century or ancient cartographer. Then I made a comparison between these islands on the map and the Philippines. There were strong resemblances here too. The northern-most island on the Hamy-King Chart remarkably resembles the island of Luzon in the Philippines. The large island south of it remarkably resembles the Japanese island of Honshu, and the smaller islands farther south resemble the Japanese islands more than they do Mindanao in the Philippines. I can only suppose that some geographer, having prototype maps of both archipelagoes, may have thought they were the same islands. Obviously he was *trying* to draw a map of the Philippines, if we are to judge by the latitude in which we find the islands. The prototype maps would both have dated, of course, from a time subsequent to the subsidence of southeast Asia, but they are remnants just the same of the ancient cartographic tradition we have been following in this book.

## (e) The European Sector: An Ancient Portolan Chart.

As I have mentioned, it seemed to me that the European sector of the Hamy-King map (but not its Scandinavian portion) resembled the ancient portolan charts. It appeared that the compiler of the whole map must simply have incorporated an available portolan chart. At the same time this particular chart seemed to differ in some ways from the others I have examined in this book. There were the additional islands in the Mediterranean. There were numerous differences in the coastlines. These facts, combined with the suggestion of possible ice fields in Scandinavia, persuaded me that this version of the Mediterranean portolano might be one of the oldest to have survived. I therefore decided to construct a separate grid for it, to discover if possible the grid constructed by the original cartographers.

The first step, of course, was to check the orientation, and as I have mentioned I found that this part of the map was actually oriented about 7° east of true North, evidently toward magnetic North. I found the length of the degree of longitude by measuring the longitude difference between Alexandria and Gibraltar, and the length of the degree of latitude by measuring the latitude difference between Gibraltar and Cape Wrath, Scotland. The degree of latitude turned out to be somewhat longer, and so I found myslef with an oblong grid, such as we discovered on some of the maps already examined. In Table 17 I have listed a large number of geographical features that are clearly identifiable and have compared their positions on the modern map with their positions on the chart (Fig. 105).

As I compiled Table 17 I was astonished to find that here I had come across the most accurate of the portolan charts examined in this book. An analysis of the errors in position of 45 easily identifiable features revealed that they were well distributed over the whole map, with no noticeable general trends which might have indicated an error in the grid or in the orientation. There were a total of 35 errors in latitude, of which 15 were northerly and 20 southerly. There were 32

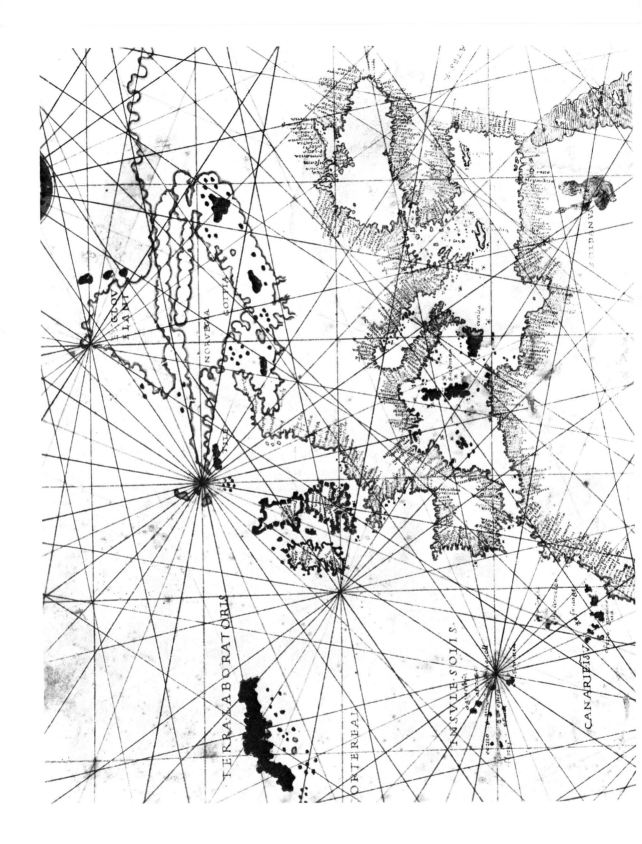

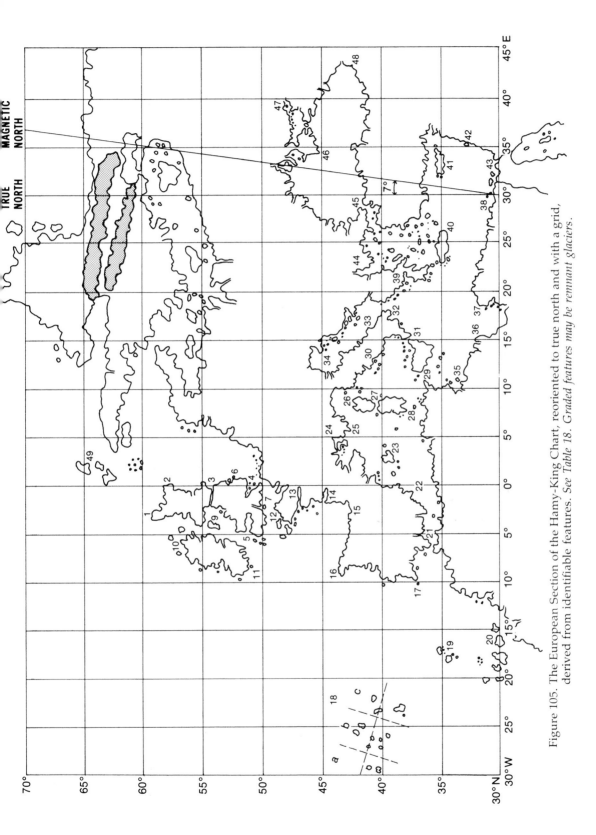

Figure 105. The European Section of the Hamy-King Chart, reoriented to true north and with a grid, derived from identifiable features. *See Table 18. Graded features may be remnant glaciers.*

errors in longitude, of which 16 were westerly and 16 easterly. Errors of latitude of the same magnitude at the eastern and western ends of the map indicated that the orientation I had found was correct. The amount of the average error in the latitudes of all forty-five features, was less than a degree, 0.7°, or about forty miles, and the errors of longitude averaged exactly the same. The fact that the errors of latitude and longitude were of equal average magnitude was an indication that the oblong grid I had constructed was probably very similar to the grid drawn by the original cartographers.

Some details of the portolan section are worth special attention. There is astonishing accuracy in the representation of major land areas. For example, the portolan chart gives the maximum latitude extent of Great Britain (excluding the Scilly Islands) as 8.5°, as compared with the correct 9°, and its maximum longitude extent as 4°, which is exactly right.

Ireland is a particularly interesting case. The chart gives Ireland 5.5° of extent in latitude, instead of the correct 3.8°, and 4° of longitude, which is exactly right. It is surprising that in both these cases the portolan chart is more accurate as to longitude than as to latitude. But the error in Ireland may have been the result of the use by the original cartographers of a slightly different ratio of latitude to longitude, that is of a longer latitude degree, in constructing the original grid. It is probable, of course, that the maps of the two islands were drawn at different times by different people and later combined, as was done with most maps of large areas in the early history of cartography.

Corsica and Sardinia together are another interesting case. Their total range in latitude is 4°. The portolan chart gives them 4.5°. Their total range in longitude is 1.4°. The chart gives them 2°. In other words, both islands are shown somewhat larger than they appear on the modern map. This difference may be connected with the general problem of land changes to be discussed in the following chapter.

Now we come up against a really tough problem. The great number of identifiable features (of which we have listed 45 in Table 17, though we could easily have listed three times as many) makes this the most accurate of all the portolan charts we have studied. At the same time, paradoxically, there are many more differences in the shorelines, as compared with the modern map, than appear on the other portolanos. These differences are very important. On any navigational chart such differences, if they were errors, would be lethal for ships and sailors. The portolanos were *navigational* charts. Nordenskiöld has pointed out how carefully they were all recopied from the 14th to the 16th centuries. Medieval and Renaissance cartographers knew very well that an error in a sea chart could mean death. The original portolan charts were so vastly superior to anything that could be drawn in the Middle Ages that navigators of ships, and cartographers, did not dare alter them. They were therefore slavishly recopied for 300 years.

But this particular portolan chart (and perhaps also that of Ibn ben Zara) may not have descended from Nordenskiöld's "normal portolano." Other versions of the ancient maps may have survived, including one that embodied more fully the geography of an earlier time. These differences do not look like the results of careless drawing. Many of them appear on the very coasts which would have been most familiar to Mediterranean sailors: the coasts of North Africa, Spain, France and Italy. If the Hamy-King map as a whole was compiled at some great center of ancient learning, such as the University of Cordova which flourished in Moslem Spain in the Middle Ages, geographers there may have been in possession of older versions of the portolano.

We should, therefore consider quite seriously the possibility that the prototype of this portolan chart was drawn before the great geological upheaval marked by the explosion of Thera in the Aegean about 1400 B.C., at which time most of Thera was destroyed and a part of the island subsided half a mile. The Ibn ben Zara Map indicated that the cataclysm changed the shorelines of the whole Aegean. Now in the portolan part of the Hamy-King Chart we have indications that the cataclysm extended to the whole Mediterranean, and even affected the Atlantic coasts. In the next chapter we will consider the evidence of all the maps as it bears on the problem of land changes.

If it is true that this portolan chart shows the Western Mediterranean and the Atlantic coasts as they were before the destruction of Thera, this is not true of the Aegean itself. Here we have not the map of the Aegean included in the Ibn ben Zara Map, but a redrawing of the map after the explosion, and not a good redrawing, either. Here the drawing seems to be typical of the lower standards of cartography that prevailed in the Ptolemaic school. The geographers of Alexandria in the time of Ptolemy were quite capable of realizing that the Aegean of their time did not resemble the geography we see on the Ibn ben Zara Map.

It must be added that the compilers of the world map, before the final additions made in the 16th century, do not appear to have been much interested in navigation per se. They were, it seems, academic geographers, men of learning, who thought major coastlines, major islands worth careful treatment, but were less concerned with the smaller islands highly important to the navigator. In many cases they indicated the positions of these smaller isands merely by circles. Such an attitude could be expected from the geographers of Cordova.

Finally, this portolan chart contains indications of the mouths of many more rivers than exist today in Europe and North Africa. This is a clue to a change of climate which we know actually did occur, and which we will discuss in the next chapter.

# VIII   Climatic and Land Changes Suggested by The Ancient Maps

## 1.   Geological Considerations

After World War II British scientists took the lead in developing a new technique for the investigation of the climates of the past,* and this technique has in fact already revolutionized our conceptions of the earth's history. It was a new approach to the study of rock magnetism.

It has long been known that particles of rocks made of iron-containing minerals take on the directions of the earth's magnetic field at the time of the formation of the rocks. Due to the iron in them they behave like tiny magnets, they are polarized and their north and south poles are aligned with the directions of the earth's magnetic field in that locality. They then tend to point toward the north and south magnetic poles of the earth. They can take on this magnetic orientation only when soft sediments are turning into rock or when molten rock is cooling and solidifying. Once a rock has solidified, the magnetic directions of the particles tend to be preserved indefinitely unless the rock is later subjected to extreme temperatures or pressures. By taking samples of rocks of the same age from different parts of the earth it is now possible to find the positions of the magnetic poles of the earth to within a small margin of error for different geological periods. It has been quite definitely established that the magnetic poles have tended to migrate around the earth's poles of rotation (the geographical poles) within a small radius, so that the positions of the magnetic poles in different periods can be considered true indicators of the approximate positions of the geographical poles.

In the last twenty years an immense quantity of research in this new field of paleomagnetism has revealed the astonishing fact that the positions of the geographical poles have changed at least 200 times during geological history, and that

---

* See, for example, P. M. S. Blackett, *Lectures on Rock Magnetism*, New York: Interscience Publications, 1956, or Arthur C. Munyan, editor, *Polar Wandering and Continental Drift*, Tulsa, Oklahoma: Society of Economic Minerologists Special Publication No. 10, 1963.

no fewer than 16 of these changes took place during the last geological period, the Pleistocene Epoch.**

At first it was thought that the different positions of the poles might be explained by the hypothesis of drifting continents, but it gradually became clear that while some of the various locations might be explained in this way many others could not. Geologists were forced to the conclusion that in addition to continental drift there had been displacements of the entire outer shell of the earth, the crystalline lithosphere, over the soft layers of magma below it. Such displacements would bring new areas into the polar regions. Their cause is still a matter for speculation and investigation, but it is likely that they result from the development of imbalances through the action of subcrustal currents in the magma of the earth's mantle.

In my book, *The Path Of The Pole,* I have given the results of this research in some detail, and have presented evidence of the occurrence of three displacements of the earth's crust in the last 100,000 years. According to my interpretation of the evidence Hudson Bay was located at the North Pole during the last ice age, and in this way I account for the ice age itself. The North American icecap, covering 4,000,000 square miles of the continent, and reflecting the sun's heat back into space, created a vast refrigerator from which cold winds blowing across the narrow North Atlantic brought about a lesser ice age in Europe, creating the Scandinavian ice sheet and many great mountain glaciers in Britain and in the mountainous regions of Europe.*

It is not ordinarily realized that causes of ice ages are not as yet understood. They are at present the greatest unsolved mystery of geology. A few years ago Professor J. K. Charlesworth, or Queen's University, Belfast, remarked:

> The cause of all these changes [ice ages], one of the greatest riddles of geology, remains unsolved; despite the endeavors of generations of astronomers, biologists, geologists, meteorologists and physicists, it still eludes us.†

According to my interpretation of much radiocarbon and other evidence, a great shift of the earth's crust began about 17,000 years ago. It was of course a slow movement, requiring perhaps as much as 5,000 years for its completion. North America was shifted southward, and with it the whole western hemisphere, while the eastern hemisphere was shifted northward. The effect was to cause the melting of the great ice cap in North America, while placing northern Siberia in deep freeze. This theory seems to succeed quite well in explaining not only the end of the ice age in North America and Europe but also the long-standing mystery of the quantities of frozen animals that have been found in the Siberian tundra.

Antarctica was of course affected by this shift of the crust. It was moved into the

---

** See Deutsch, in Munyan, *supra.*

* There was an earlier, much heavier glaciation in Europe, but this coincided, in my estimation, with a position of the North Pole in the Greenland Sea. See Fig. 107.

† Charlesworth, *The Ice Age and the Future of Man.* Science Progress (London), XLI:161, Jan., 1953.

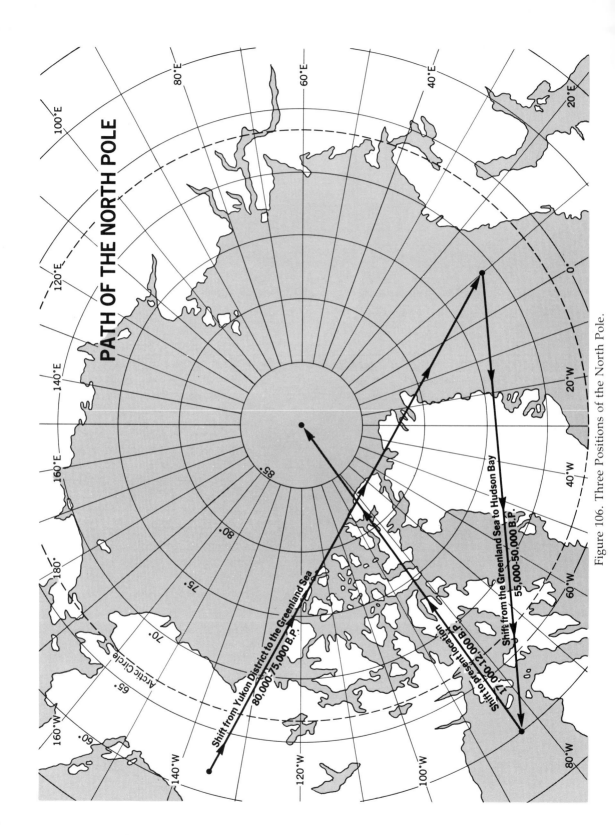

## PATH OF THE NORTH POLE

Shift from Yukon District to the Greenland Sea
80,000-75,000 B.P.

Shift from the Greenland Sea to Hudson Bay
55,000-50,000 B.P.

Shift to present location
17,000-12,000 B.P.

Figure 106. Three Positions of the North Pole.

Antarctic Circle. When the North Pole was in Hudson Bay the South Pole would have been located in the ocean off the Wilkes Coast (see Fig. 106), and as a result most of the continent would have been ice free. The displacement of the crust would have located the pole where it is now right in the center of the continent and brought about the vast expansion of any ice formations that might have been there before. At the same time, of course, the disappearance of the North American ice cap and the consequent warming of the Atlantic Ocean gradually melted the glaciers of Europe.

According to this theory, then, the Antarctic ice cap started its expansion about 17,000 years ago. We have seen, in the Ross Sea cores (Fig. 54) evidence that the Ross Sea became glacial only about 6,000 years ago. We can assume that by the latter date virtually all Antarctica was covered by the ice cap, though the evidence is that it has steadily gained in thickness since that time and is still growing. Certainly it is safe to assume that by that time human habitation and explorations for map-making had become impracticable.

In fact, we can place the probable inhabiting and mapping of Antarctica a good deal earlier than 6,000 years ago. It is true that the icecap itself took many thousands of years to cover the continent. For one thing it had to develop an enormous thickness before it could cross the coastal mountain ranges. But though the icecap developed slowly the climatic change was certainly much more rapid. This would depend on the temperature of the air, which is controlled by the sun. The temperature would have become polar by the time that the displacement of the crust had been completed. We have evidence that the displacement was completed not later than 12,000 years ago for in New England and in southern Canada the forests of a temperate climate had been re-established by that time. Antarctica must by then have become bitterly cold. We should assume, then, that it would probably have become uninhabitable several thousand years before that. It is a reasonable guess that Antarctica had become useless to man 15,000 years ago.

Yet the entire continent was mapped by man when the coasts at least were ice-free. The probabilities are not that the mapping was an enlightened scientific project undertaken by some people living in a temperate climate far away, but rather that there was material economic motivation, which would mean in one way or another the exploitation of the resources of Antarctica, both natural and human. By 12,000 years ago it would seem that such exploitation must have become impossible.

Let us now sum up the evidence contained in the maps we have studied for climatic changes in opposite directions in the northern and southern hemispheres at the end of the last ice age. We have already discussed the evidence of the Piri Re'is and Oronteus Finaeus Maps for a non-glacial epoch in Antarctica. I once asked Albert Einstein whether he could imagine any factor that could account for the phenomenon of simultaneous but opposite changes on entire continents other than a displacement of the earth's whole outer shell, and he replied that he could not. I asked the question, however, not relating to Antarctica but to East Asia, for I had just presented him evidence of the freezing up of Siberia simultaneously with the thawing of North America.

We have seen that a number of maps show stages of the withdrawal of the ice in Europe. The Ptolemy, Benincasa, Ibn ben Zara and Hamy-King maps, appear to contain evidences of a time when there were still great ice fields in Great Britain and in Scandinavia. We know the British ice fields had disappeared by 10,000 years ago, while by that time the southern front of the Scandinavian ice stood in the latitude indicated by what we have taken for an ice sheet on the Benincasa Map.

In general we have a good agreement between the map evidences for Europe and for Antarctia. The Antarctic map evidence is the strongest confirmation of our interpretation of the evidence of the European maps. They stand together to argue both for the vast antiquity of the maps and for the displacement of the earth's crust.

Following the ice age in Europe there was a climatic phase of which we find a good deal of evidence in our maps. This was a very rainy period which geologists call a "Pluvial" and and which lasted for several thousand years. It was described by Edward S. Deevey, a geologist, in a symposium entitled *Climatic Change* edited by Dr. Harlow Shapley, the director of the Harvard Observatory.* According to Deevey, who reflects the general opinion of geologists, this cold, wet period lasted until about 6,000 years ago, when it was succeeded by a period warmer and drier than now. While it lasted the large supply of moisture resulted in more and larger rivers and lakes not only in Europe but in Africa. The Sahara Desert was then very fertile, with wide grassy plains and great forests. There were large numbers of animals of all sorts, and there was human occupation.

In *The Path Of The Pole* I gave the reasons for believing that any general displacement of the earth's outer shell would result not only in climatic changes, but also in changes of land elevations relative to sea-level. Geophysical considerations indicated that because of the inequality of the polar and equatorial diameters of the earth there would be concomitant uplift of land in some parts of the earth and subsidence of land in other parts, together with much tectonic change (folding and fracturing of the crust.) We will now review the evidence for these and the climatic changes as they may be indicated in the ancient maps.

## 2.   The Evidence of the Maps

1. *The World Map of Eratosthenes* (Fig. 7). We have seen that the world map of Eratosthenes, which he drew in the 3rd century B.C., is a very poor map compared with the portolan charts which existed then and had existed for thousands of years. One wonders how he could know so little about geography, especially when he was able to measure the circumference of the earth so nearly correctly, and when he had at his command the resources of the Alexandrian Library. However, there is one detail of his map that is very significant. It shows the Caspian Sea

* Harvard University Press, 1953.

opening into the Arctic Ocean. This cannot be dismissed as a mere legend because we know that to this day there are arctic seals and other arctic marine species in the Caspian. These indicate beyond a reasonable doubt a former connection with the Arctic Ocean. If it were not for the map of Eratosthenes, and other maps influenced by it, one would naturally conclude that such an arctic connection could only have existed far back in geological time, because of the vast land changes involved. At present the Caspian is separated from the Arctic Ocean by the whole width of Siberia, that is, by about 1000 miles of land, and between the Caspian and the Ocean there is a great deal of high hilly country containing the sources of the Volga and Ural Rivers. A major difference in the slant of the land surfaces was required for this Arctic connection of the Caspian, and yet the map of Eratosthenes indicates it existed and came to an end within the memory of man.

Furthermore, the connection must have existed when the Arctic Ocean was cold, for otherwise there would have been no arctic seals there to migrate into the Caspian. But we have seen that with a pole in Hudson Bay there would have been a warm Arctic Ocean. The northern coast of Siberia would have been very warm. The arctic seals would then have been living in the Atlantic, perhaps birthing their young on the rocky islands off Norway. With the drastic temperature change resulting from the shift in the earth's crust, that I have assumed, they would have arrived on the coast of Siberia not much before 15,000 years ago, and perhaps not until 12,000 years ago, when the climatic revolution in the Arctic was complete. It is quite possible, therefore, that the land changes which destroyed the sea connection occurred as recently as 10,000 years ago. Then, in some way, the memory of the former sea connection persisted, was incorporated in ancient books, was handed down from age to age, and survived in manuscripts Eratosthenes saw in the Library of Alexandria. The same sea connection is found in the world map of Pomponius Mela, a later Roman geographer (Fig. 8.)

2. *The World Map of Ptolemy* (Fig. 6.) We have discussed that part of Ptolemy's world map that relates to India, and which was incorporated in the Hamy-King Map. I have pointed out that there are good reasons for taking the former existence of an insular Dravidia seriously. We must realize here again that anything that could depress the surface of the Indian sub-continent sufficiently to flood the valleys of the Indus and the Ganges was geologically far-reaching. It was not a local event. It had to be connected with changes of world-wide scope, for the balance of the whole earth's crust was involved. We would have to expect that there would be a balancing movement somewhere else.

This map contains some evidence of our rainy or Pluvial period. It shows one river that still enters the Mediterranean near the site of ancient Carthage. Then it shows a larger, now non-existent river, with a tributary, entering the Gulf of Skira almost due south of the heel of Italy, at about 19° E longitude, where today a dried-up river bed is indicated on the map. Other rivers are shown in the Sahara, flowing from mountains or lakes. These details may be as ancient as the details of Ptolemy s map of India.

Just north of the Gulf of Skira Ptolemy shows an island as large as Sicily where no island appears today. Moreover, neither does this island appear on the portolan charts. This is a most astonishing thing, considering the vast resources of geographical knowledge available to Ptolemy as director of the Library of Alexandria. He had the whole geographical literature of the world at his disposal. Moreover, to gather material for his maps he had collected a great number of itineraries of travels by officials and private persons all through the Roman Empire, from which he carefully calculated the longitudes of different places, making the most awful mistakes. None of these itineraries could have mentioned this island. No navigator who had spent his life piloting merchant ships to the ports of the Mediterranean could have failed to know that there was no such island. And that island would have been only a short distance from Alexandria itself! Obviously Ptolemy did not consult navigators. He had no use for the portolan charts. In fact, he spent a lot of time "correcting" and ruining the sounder maps in the portolan tradition that he got from the great Phoenician geographer, Marinus of Tyre.

Was Ptolemy a fool? the evidence is to the contrary. His great work, the *Geographia* is most readable and is written in the modern scientific spirit. It is simply that he was an academic man, a scholarly expert with a respect for ancient authorities. No doubt he found an ancient map with that island on it and put it on his map of the world convinced that it must have existed or it wouldn't be on that ancient map, and if it did once exist it must still exist. I am supposing that the island indeed must have existed, but so long ago that it was omitted from later editions of the portolan charts. It might have existed before the eruption of Thera in 1400 B.C.

3. *The World Map of Idrisi* (Fig. 5.) Although this map was drawn about a thousand years after Ptolemy it shows this same large island off the Gulf of Skira. This demonstrates the extremes of conservatism of which the academic mind is capable. Idrisi was a great Arab geographer who flourished in the brilliant age of classical learning in Baghdad in the Middle Ages. Ever since Ptolemy's day people had been voyaging in the Mediterranean. The Arabs were great sea-farers. They knew the Mediterranean intimately, and they also made long voyages in the Atlantic and Indian Oceans. Nobody had ever run into this island, for the reason that it didn't exist. Did this make any difference to Idrisi? None at all. But let us not be complaisant. Modern scholars, modern professors, modern historians of cartography are capable of the same feats of ignoring facts not supported by approved authority. Can anyone tell me why nobody has ever seriously tackled the problem of measuring the portolan charts to find out how scientific they are? Or why no scholar took seriously Nordenskiöld's suggestion that the charts were of ancient origin? It is really incredible that the foremost map scholars of the present day continue to regard the portolan charts as amateurish productions!

4. *The Piri Re'is Map.* The land and climatic changes indicated in this map are very numerous. The most significant ones are as follows:

(a) The climate of Africa and Spain. The facsimile colour reproduction of the map (see cover) has many details that suggest a well-watered Africa, including a number of lakes. Farther north, in Spain, there are indications of a large central lake which would have occupied the present valleys south and southeast of the Sierra de Guadarrama. (See Fig. 18).

(b) The Caribbean section. We have an interesting problem with respect to Cuba. The western half of the island is missing. Instead of the western half there is a coastline where the island is cut off, with some islands lying beyond. There is a strong suggestion here that when the prototype of this map was drawn the western half of the present island was below sea level. This is strengthened by a number of considerations. Let me begin by saying that details of the coasts and of the interior (Figs. 34, 35) leave no doubt as to the identification of the island. It is indeed the eastern half of Cuba, though Piri Re'is labelled it Santo Domingo. But we find that on the geometrical projection of the map this eastern section has been doubled in size so that it subtends exactly the right amount of longitude for the present island, but twice too much latitude. This is an enigma. How did the cartographers in far away Alexandria, or wherever they were, know how to orient the Caribbean grid of the map, and know Cuba's true length, and yet use a wrong source map for the island? Note that these geographers must have had information on the length of the island that now exists. Then they found a map that they knew was Cuba but which unknown to them had been drawn when western Cuba was below sea level, perhaps thousands of years earlier. To make it fit the longitude requirement they doubled its scale, but ignored the resultant distortion of latitude!

To verify the fact that this truncated version of Cuba is no figment of somebody's imagination we have only to observe its resemblance to the alleged maps of Cipango that were circulating in Europe before the discovery of America, and which have been supposed to represent Japan. Figure 36 clearly demonstrates that the map circulating in Europe before 1492 was nothing other than an ancient map of Cuba, in the truncated form shown on the Piri Re'is Map.

So here we have evidence of important land changes. This truncated Cuba represents a time when the geography of the Caribbean may have been radically different. But the land change suggested here does not appear to have been a gradual one. We are not dealing here with the slow pace of ordinary geological change. We seem, indeed, to be dealing here with one of the innumerable far-reaching effects of the last displacement of the earth's crust. And what this displacement may have done was to bring about an uplift of the Caribbean basin. Just as the half-mile subsidence of Thera in the Aegean suggests the probability of a general subsidence of the Aegean basin, so the uplift of Cuba suggests a raising of much or all of the Caribbean basin.

An uplift of the basin is rendered more believable because of evidence of other uplifts in the Americas in recent time. Some years ago I examined core evidence from the San Augustin Plains of New Mexico that seemed to me then to suggest a rather radical uplift of the highlands of the southwest late in the ice age.* More striking is a passage from Darwin's journal describing an elevated beach line on the

---

* See Clisby and Sears, *The San Augustin Plains—Pleistocene Climatic Changes. Science,* v. 124, No. 3221, Sept. 21, 1956.

western coast of South America, as summarized by Sir Archibald Geikie:

"On the west coast of South America, lines of raised terraces containing recent shells have been traced by Darwin as proofs of a great upheaval of that part of the globe in modern geological time. The terraces are not quite horizontal but rise to the south. On the frontier of Bolivia they occur from 60 to 80 feet above the existing sea-level, but nearer the high mass of the Chilean Andes they are found at one thousand, and near Valparaiso at 1300 feet. That some of these ancient sea margins belong to the human period was shown by Mr. Darwin's discovery of bones of birds, ears of maize, plaited reeds and cotton thread, in some of the terraces opposite Callao at 85 feet. Raised beaches occur in New Zealand and indicate a greater change of level in the southern than in the northern end of the country."†

Here we can see not only an uplift of the continent, but a change in the slant of the continental surface such as we have supposed to account for the interruption of the ocean connection of the Caspian, while both changes seem to have occurred recently. They may have occurred at the same time.

We have evidence of a drastic uplift in recent time of the Altiplano, the highland of Peru and Bolivia, which now stands at an elevation of about 12,500 feet above sea level. This highland contains Lake Titicaca, and the ruins of the ancient city of Tiahuanaco. There are high mountains surrounding the basin of the lake, and on the sides of these mountains the ancient inhabitants built terraces on which they raised crops. J. B. Delair and E. F. Oppé, in a chapter contributed to my book, *The Path Of The Pole,* spoke of these as follows:

Remarkable confirmation of the immensity of this uplift [of the Altiplano] is represented by the ancient agricultural stone terraces surrounding the Titicaca basin. These structures, belonging to some bygone civilization, occur at altitudes far too high to support the growth of crops for which they were originally built. Some rise to 15,000 feet above sea-level, or about 2,500 feet above the ruins of Tiahuanaco, and on Mt. Illimani they occur up to 18,400 feet above sea-level; that is, above the line of eternal snow.

Agricultural terraces above the snow line are of course sufficient evidence of the uplift of the area, considering the fact that it lies within the tropics. Even at the elevation of Tiahuanaco, at 12,500 feet, agricultural production is very sparse. According to our theory of displacement, this area, which now lies about 1,000 miles south of the equator lay 1,000 miles north of it 17,000 years ago, in a similar climate. The area was therefore displaced across the equator, but it always remained within the tropics. A change of latitude could not therefore be a reasonable explanation of the facts.

† Geikie, Sir Archibald, *Text Book of Geology,* 3rd ed., New York and London, Macmillan, 1893, page 288.

5. *The Zeno Map of the North.* We have shown that the Zeno Map could not have been drawn by the 14th century Zeno brothers, or by their descendant, for it is clearly a compilation of four different maps put together erroneously by a cartographer who nevertheless had good information as to the latitudes and longitudes of many coastal features of the North Atlantic. We can only suppose that the completed compilation must have been found in Venice by the earlier Zenos, and that it dates from ancient times.

This map is remarkable for the number and extent of the land changes it suggests. We have seen that there is good geological confirmation of these in the instance of Iceland. The map also suggests a subsidence in the region of the Faroe Islands. In place of them it shows a very large island extending about 150 miles north and south and about 300 miles east and west (2½° by 5° on the grid of the map.) Such an extreme exaggeration is improbable on a map that contains so much accurate information. The same consideration applies to a still larger island shown extending from 55 to 60° N., and from 20 to 30° W., in a part of the ocean where no land exists today. The details of this great island have a convincing look. There are also some smaller islands that don't look like imaginary islands.

The evidence we have is that the original prototypes of the four different component maps as well as the compilation itself were drawn when mathematics was applied to accurately ascertained data of latitude and longitude. When latitude was taken into account in finding the ratio of the degree of latitude to the degree of longitude, it is not reasonable to dismiss these islands as the product of the medieval imagination, fertile as that was. It is far more probable, in my view, that these islands really existed, as the greater Iceland did, and that they are further evidence of the subsidence of the Mid-Atlantic Ridge and the Atlantic basin suggested by the observations of Malaise. Submergence here makes a consistent pattern with submergence in the Azores, the submergence of the equatorial island shown on the Piri Re'is, Buache and Reinel Maps, and the submergence of other island groups suggested by the Buache Map.

6. *The Ptolemaic Map of the North.* Ptolemy's Map of the North (Fig. 83) is a bad map, owing to his ignorance of longitudes, but it was undoubtedly based on ancient prototypes and it contains some remarkable evidence of the climatic conditions that prevailed in the late ice age.

First we see clear evidence of the Greenland ice sheet. The map actually shows the sheen of the sunlight reflected from the ice surface. The appearance of Greenland on the map would be surprising enough, since the Ptolemy maps were recovered in the early 15th century, more than half a century before the discovery of America. The fact that the ice sheet covers only part of the island is far more surprising. For an explanation of this detail we have to go back to geological history, and reconsider the implications of my assumption that Hudson Bay lay at the North Pole during the last ice age. The reader may note by reference to a globe that this would have involved a warm Arctic Ocean (of which I presented numerous evidences in my *The Path Of The Pole*) and the deglaciation of much if not all of Greenland.

It is true that during the early Middle Ages there were unglaciated strips along the Greenland coast that were settled by the Norse. Then there came a refrigeration of the climate, a "little ice age" when lower temperatures prevailed from about 1550 to 1850. The Greenland ice cap expanded and overwhelmed the Norse settlements.

But this is not a Norse map. This is an ancient, Ptolemaic map. We can see, by comparison with the drawing of the Greenland ice, that it shows ice also in northern Scandinavia, with glaciers even in southern Sweden, and as I mentioned in our previous discussion of this map, there is evidence that when its original prototype was drawn the ice was melting. This is indicated by the rivers flowing from the apparent glaciers and converging on Lake Vänern, which still exists in southern Sweden. These features in southern Sweden are not mountains: (see Fig. 85) The enormous amount of water pouring from the melting glaciers is suggested by the broad outlet connecting Lake Vänern with the sea. And glaciers are also shown on the Südeten Mountains and on the Carpathians.

The evidence all hangs together: Ptolemy's source map, or its prototype, may have dated from a time when *simultaneously* the ice cap was advancing in Greenland as the Arctic Ocean became frigid with the movement of the pole to its very center, and the Scandinavian and German glaciers were melting with the disappearance of the North American ice cap. The conditions represented in the map suggest a time not later than 10,000 years ago.

There is still another interesting point about the Greenland ice cap on this Ptolemaic map. The ice cap is shown extending southward on the eastern rather than on the western coast of Greenland. This is what we would expect if the crust had shifted as we have supposed. In that case the very cold water from the now frigid Arctic Ocean would have been circulating in the North Atlantic, bringing low temperatures to the east coast of Greenland, while the western coast, facing Davis Strait, would have been feeling the warming influence of the now temperate continent of North America.

7. *The Maps and the History of the Sahara.* Strangely enough one of the most important confirmations of the antiquity of our cartographic tradition comes to us out of the Sahara Desert, and is connected with the Pluvial, or rainy period already mentioned.

When I lived for a summer on the Mediterranean coast of France, I became accustomed to the two prevailing winds, the Sirocco and the Mistral. The Sirocco is the south wind that blows out of the Sahara Desert. It is very hot indeed. When it blew it was possible to *smell* the desert across the whole width of the Mediterranean. The Mistral was the north wind, and when it was blowing it could chill you to the very bone.

In late glacial and post-glacial times, when great mountain glaciers still existed and were melting in Europe, the Mistral was a much wetter wind that it is now. From about 10,000 to about 6,000 years ago it bore great quantities of moisture across the Mediterranean and watered the Sahara. Consequently, as we have mentioned, the Sahara was covered with vegetation. Great numbers of wild

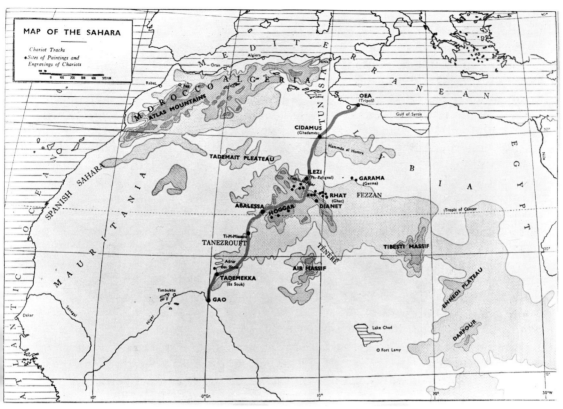

Figure 107. Henri Lhote's Map of the Sahara. (123a)

animals lived there and men built pastoral societies based on cattle raising.

It now appears that a succession of peoples occupied the Sahara from as early as 14,000 to as late as 6,000 years ago. Their ways of life are depicted in thousands of rock paintings that have been found in many parts of the desert. In 1956 a French expedition studied and copied as many of these paintings as possible. The leader of the expedition, Henri Lhote, published a book summarizing its findings (123a).

Lhote found much evidence of the ancient wet climate in the Sahara. Of the remains of animal life he wrote:

> The aquatic character of the predominant fauna indicates surroundings that were damp and the existence of numerous rivers in full flood. Such rivers, taking their rise in the great mountain masses such as the Hoggar, the Tassili and the Adrar of the Iforas, constituted a vast hydrographic system linked up with the Niger, with Lake Chad, and with those great lakes whose sunken remnants are to be seen in the *chotts* of the Tunisian south. It is still quite possible to plot out the courses of these streams . . . (123a:18).

We have seen that the Piri Re'is Map suggests an ample water supply in West Africa, and that other maps suggest the presence of lakes in the Sahara. We shall see that the maps give us even more information of that ancient time, but before we consider it we must mention a few more geographical facts. As Lhote says, there are mountains and highlands in the desert. The Tassily Mountains, which were the specific goal of his expedition, extend for about 500 miles from northwest to southeast in the Central Sahara, from about 6° to about 12° E longitude and from about 27° to about 22° N (see Fig. 107.) I mention this for the interesting reason that these mountains are accurately indicated on the Hamy-King Chart (Fig. 99). The Tassily Mountains, together with other mountain ranges and highlands, form a belt extending east and west across North Africa. During the Pluvial period animal and human life seem to have been concentrated in this belt. And this belt is shown on several of the maps.

About 6,000 years ago there set in a new climatic phase, warmer than now, called the climatic optimum or thermal maximum. Conditions in Europe became drier. The glaciers had, of course, disappeared. The Mistral carried less water to the Sahara, and slowly the modern desert came into existence. The thermal maximum itself came to an end about 2000 B.C., but the dessication of North Africa continued and by Roman times, as various historians (quoted by Lhote) tell us, desert conditions prevailed.

Now as to the maps. We have seen that the Dulcert portolano (Fig. 3) suggests this belt of highlands and mountains in about the same latitude in which they appear on the Lhote Map (Fig. 107.) The highland belt is shown on the Ptolemy Map (Fig. 6). It is beautifully shown on the Benincasa Map (Fig. 86) where forests are shown in the highlands, and hills are clearly indicated. The Ibn ben Zara Map (Fig. 89) shows the vegetation in more detail and indicates plenty of water in the areas south of the highlands.

These features are, if needed, further proof of the antiquity of these maps.

8. *Land Changes in the Ibn ben Zara and Hamy-King Maps.* We have already noted the vast difference between the modern map of the Aegean and the Aegean of the Ibn ben Zara Map (Figs. 94, 95), and we have noted the inconsistency of Ibn ben Zara's extreme accuracy every where else with his seeming inaccuracy in the Aegean. I have suggested that the difference may be accounted for by a subsidence of the whole Aegean basin in connection with the great explosion of Thera about 1400 B.C. There was an apparently simultaneous devastation of Crete, and it appears that about this time many of the temples of Egypt, including the great Temple of Karnak at Thebes, were destroyed by unparalleled earthquakes.

The portolan section of the Hamy-King charts (which shows the causeway of Ancient Tyre!) also suggests that the subsidence of the Aegean may have extended to the western Mediterranean. A number of islands are shown there that do not exist now, and many differences are indicated in the shorelines of the western Mediterranean and the Atlantic coast.

There is also evidence for the subsidence in the Caspian Sea area to the east. The Hamy-King chart shows islands in the Caspian that do not exist now, but these are not particularly convincing. What is convincing is that Soviet scientists have discovered a sunken city in the Caspian. This appears to lie near the island of

Pogorelaya Plita at the mouth of the Kura River, south of Baku, but as yet no detailed reports are available.

Returning to the Aegean, we have evidence of another submerged city, cited by Charles Berlitz (28a:102):

> . . . Heliké, in the Gulf of Corinth, was still visible from the surface in classical times, with its underwater streets and villas fairly intact, and was frequently visited by tourists in ancient times, who looked at it from boats, and free divers dove down to its submerged streets for sponges and occasionally retrieved "antiques."

Let us note that the Gulf of Corinth is quite a distance from Thera.

Perhaps we can now link up all the parts of the puzzle. Let us simply suppose that a world-wide geological upheaval took place about 1400 B.C., and that this was the final readjustment of the earth's outer shell to its new position after its last displacement. Simultaneously there could have been subsidence in the Aegean, in the western Mediterranean, in the North Atlantic, in the equatorial Atlantic and in the East Indies, where Sumatra and Java might then have been separated from Asia. Meanwhile, compensating uplifts were occurring in Siberia, in India, in the southwestern United States, in the Caribbean and in Peru and Bolivia.

It is interesting to note that the two areas affected by presumed subsidence—the Mid-Atlantic and Indonesia—lie almost opposite each other on the globe, while the two areas that may have undergone uplift—India and Middle America—also lie opposite each other. This is in agreement with the sort of major adjustments which I considered probable with a displacement of the earth crust, but the problem is so complex that here I must refer the reader to my work already mentioned, *The Path Of The Pole*.

A final remark about the maps. It seems extraordinary that we have found maps covering all parts of the world: Europe, Africa, Asia, the Arctic and the Antarctic, even a coastline of Australia: but no map of North America north of the Caribbean. An obvious reason for this suggests itself. It is simply that when the maps were being made America may have been covered down as far as New Jersey and Ohio by the continental ice cap of the last ice age. The coast south of the ice sheet as far down as Florida would have been bitterly cold. Who would have wanted to go there? Who would have wanted to map it? Nobody, of course. And it is possible that Florida was then below sea-level, like western Cuba. It is even possible that the truncated Cuba was once a center of imperial power—the legendary Antillia! What else would account for the preservation of a map of Cuba in medieval Europe?

# IX   A Civilization that Vanished

T
HE EVIDENCE presented by the ancient maps appears to suggest the existence in remote times, before the rise of any of the known cultures, of a true civilization, of an advanced kind, which either was localized in one area but had worldwide commerce, or was, in a real sense, a *worldwide* culture. This culture, at least in some respects, was more advanced than the civilizations of Greece, and Rome. In geodesy, nautical science, and mapmaking, it was more advanced than any known culture before the 18th century of the Christian Era. It was only in the 18th century that we first developed a practical means of finding longitude. It was in the 18th century that we first accurately measured the circumference of the earth. Not until the 19th century did we begin to send out ships for exploration into the Arctic or Antarctic Seas and only then did we begin the exploration of the bottom of the Atlantic. The maps indicate that some ancient people did all these things.

Mapping on a continental scale suggests both economic motivations and economic resources. Organized government is indicated. The mapping of a continent like Antarctica implies many exploring expeditions, many stages in the compilation of local observations and local maps into a general map under a central direction. Furthermore, it is unlikely that navigation and mapmaking were the only sicences developed by this people, or that the application of mathematics to cartography was the only practical application they made of their mathematical knowledge.

Whatever its attainments may have been, however, this civilization disappeared, perhaps suddenly, more likely by gradual stages. Its disappearance has implications we ought to consider seriously. If I may be permitted a little philosophizing, I would like to suggest that there are four principal conclusions to which we are led.

1. The idea of the simple linear development of society from the culture of the paleolithic (Old Stone Age) through the successive stages of the neolithic (New Stone Age), Bronze, and Iron Ages must be given up. Today we find primitive cultures co-existing with advanced modern society on all the continents—the Bushmen of Australia, the Bushmen of South Africa, truly primitive peoples in South America, and in New Guinea; some tribal peoples in the United States. We shall now assume that, some 20,000 or more years ago, while paleolithic peoples

held out in Europe, more advanced cultures existed elsewhere on the earth, and that we have inherited a part of what they once possessed, passed down from people to people.

2. Every culture contains the seeds of its own disintegration. At every moment forces of progress and of decay co-exist, building up or tearing down. All too evidently the destructive forces have often gained the upper hand; witness such known cases as the extinctions of the high cultures of ancient Crete, Troy, Babylon, Greece, and Rome, to which it would be easy to add twenty others. And, it is worth noting that Crete and Troy were long considered myths.

3. Every civilization seems eventually to develop a technology sufficient for its own destruction, and hitherto has made use of the same. There is nothing magical about this. As soon as men learned to build walls for defense, other men learned how to tear them down. The vaster the achievements of a civilization, the farther it spreads, the greater must be the engines of destruction; and so today, to counter the modern worldwide spread of civilization, we have atomic means to destroy all life on earth. Simple. Logical.

4. The more advanced the culture, the more easily it will be destroyed, and the less evidence will remain. Take New York. Suppose it was destroyed by a hydrogen bomb. After some 2,000 years, how much of its life could anthropologists reconstruct? Even if quite a few books survived, it would be quite impossible to reconstruct the mental life of New York.

When I was a youth I had a plain simple faith in progress. It seemed to me impossible that once man had passed a milestone of progress in one way that he could ever pass the same milestone again the *other* way. Once the telephone was invented it would stay invented. If past civilizations had faded away it was just because they had not learned the secret of progress. But Science meant *permanent* progress, with no going back, and each generation was pressing on further and further, rolling back the frontiers of the unknown. This process would go on forever.

Most people still feel this way, even in spite of two world wars, and the threat of universal annihiliation in a third. The two world wars shook the faith of many in progress, but even without the very sad story of the century we live in, there never was any good basis for the belief that progress is an automatic process. Progress or decline in civilization is just a balance sheet between what the human race creates in a given period and what it destroys. Sometimes for a while our race creates more than it destroys, and there is "progress"; then for a while it destroys more effectively—more scientifically, let us say—than it creates, and we have decline. Compare, for example, the time it took for saturation bombing by the American and British Air Forces in World War II to destroy most of the cities of Germany, including golden Dresden, and its priceless heritage of medieval architecture, with the time it took to build those cities. The destruction of Dresden involved the destruction of one of the greatest musical libraries in the world. Among uncounted unpublished manuscripts destroyed at this time were about 700 concertos of the great 17th century composer Vivaldi. Think of the destruction, in one instant, by American bombers, of the oldest monastery in the West, the Abbey of Monte Cassino.

But the sad story of destruction, whereby man destroys almost as much as he creates (even in the best of times), does not begin with the 20th century. Consider the question of libraries. There is something particularly upsetting about the burning of a library. Somehow it symbolizes the whole process. The ancient world of Rome and Greece had many libraries. The most famous of these was the Library of Alexandria, founded in Egypt by Alexander the Great three centuries before the Christian Era. Five hundred years later it is said to have contained about one million volumes, and into it was gathered the entire knowledge of the ancient western world—the technology, the science, the literature, and the historical records.

This library, the heritage of untold ages, was burned. The details are not very well known, but we think there were at least three burnings. The first happened when Julius Caesar captured Alexandria. The citizens resisted him, and in the battle about a third of the Library was destroyed. Caesar is said to have called a public meeting of the citizens and lectured them, sadistically accusing them of being guilty of the destruction—because they had resisted him! In his view Rome had a perfect right to conquer Egypt, and so the Alexandrians were guilty of misconduct in resisting him. This is the way people still think today.

There is evidence that most of the library—restored and enormously enlarged after the time of Julius Caesar—was destroyed by a Christian mob, inflamed by the preaching of a fanatical bishop, who pointed out to them—rightly, of course—that the library was no more than a repository of heathen teachings, and therefore a veritable timebomb, ticking away, preparing an explosion that could wreck the Christian world. But how can we afford to point the finger at the ignorant mob? We have had our book-burnings in the 20th century. And I don't refer only to Hitler's infamous Burning of the Books. The libraries of America are combed relentlessly by gimlet-eyed agents of various self-appointed saviours of morality and religion. The books just disappear off the shelves! Thousands of them, every year! And, of course, American libraries have recently been the particular objects of anti-American mobs in several countries. (59, 100, 159, 189, 205)

The final chapter in the destruction of the Library of Alexandria was a burning carried out by the Arabs after their conquest of Egypt in the 7th century. There are two stories. According to one, the conquering Caliph said, on being asked what to do with the library, that anything in it contrary to Islamic teaching should be destroyed, and everything else was in the Koran already. The library was therefore entirely destroyed (100:95–97). The other version is that the hot, dusty, dirty Arab legions, just out of the desert, found the enormous Roman baths of the capital city ready for use, but out of fuel for heating the water, and that the parchments from the library furnished the fuel. Sad as this reason for the destruction was, it was at least morally more justifiable than the others.

The Romans were guilty of another destruction of a library, which is important for our story. In the year 146 B.C. they burned the great city of Carthage, their ancient enemy and their incalculable superior in everything relating to science. The library of Carthage is said to have contained about 500,000 volumes, and these no doubt dealt with the history and the sciences of Phoenicia as a whole. We can add the destruction of Troy by the Greeks when they were still barbarians, about 1200 B.C. Troy was rich, civilized, it certainly had its great libraries with their records of ancient civilization. Troy was the last great city of the Cretan-Mycenean World. Its fall may have broken important links with the civilizations that produced the maps.

If the reader asks, how much of the total of ancient knowledge was lost by these and innumerable other acts of destruction, we will say 90 per cent or more. A few facts may give him a general idea. The most famous scientist of ancient times was Aristotle; his thought dominated the world for fifteen hundred years. He wrote many works, and it might be thought that these works, at least, would have been preserved from destruction. Not so. Only one work of his survives, the *Constitution of Athens*. All his other so-called "works" are only edited and re-edited versions of his students' notes. As I think of the kind of notes most of my students take in lectures, I shudder through and through, and wonder how much of Aristotle's real thought really does survive. Furthermore, Aristotle wrote many literary works that were considered marvels of style. All of these are lost.

Plato is an equally famous figure in the history of civilization. His dialogues, including his great *Republic*, have survived. But how many know that these were only his *popular* works? Every one of those he regarded as his serious scientific and technical works has been lost. With the great Greek tragedians, Aeschylus, Euripides, Sophocles, the story is the same. We possess only a handful—about 10 per cent—of the plays they wrote.

What we have, then, of ancient cultural products is only a sample and not necessarily a representative sample either. On the contrary, whole aspects of ancient culture have been consigned to oblivion. What fragments we have come from books considered of value to the people who dominated the Church and State in the centuries after the dissolution of the ancient civilization. The churchmen were interested in moral questions; the educated laymen—mostly aristocrats—continued to devote themselves to the great classics of arts and literature. Science, however, was neglected.

But if it is true that we have lost so much, still we have preserved much more than some people suppose. When I began this work I was aware of no definite evidence for the existence of an ancient advanced world civilization, though I was aware that others believed it had existed. Now that I have found, in the maps, evidence I accept as decisive in answering this question in the affirmative, I see additional evidence on every hand.

The reader will quite naturally wonder how, if once a great civilization existed over most of the earth, it could disappear leaving no traces except these maps? For an answer to this we must cite one of the best known principles of human psychology: *We find what we look for.* I do not mean by this that we never find anything by accident. But rather, we usually overlook, neglect, and pass by facts unless we have a motive to notice them. It was Darwin who said that to make new discoveries one had to have a theory (not a fixed dogmatic theory, of course, but an *experimental* hypothesis). With the theory of evolution people began to look in new directions, and they found new facts, by the thousands, which supported and verified the theory. The same thing had happened a half-century before with the geological theory of Sir Charles Lyell. It happened in the beginning of modern astronomy, when Copernicus proposed a new theory of the solar system. Hitherto people have not seriously believed that an advanced civilization could have preceded the civilizations now known to us. The evidences have been, therefore, neglected.

But if we take a glance at the history of archaeological research in the 19th century we see that it consists mainly of the rediscovery of lost civilizations. Jacquetta Hawkes, in her fascinating anthology of archaeological works covering all periods (86), devotes a section to "Lost Civilizations."

The story began in Mesopotamia, about 1811, when Claudius Rich began the rediscovery of Babylon. It continued with Paul Emile Botta, Henry Layard, and Henry Rawlinson who brought Assyria back into history. Egypt came back into history after Champollion solved the problem of Egyptian hieroglyphics, and in the fourth quarter of the century, Schliemann brought Troy out of the mists of legend, and Sir Arthur Evans gave substance to the myths of Crete. More recently still an advanced culture, with strangely modern luxuries, that flourished on the banks of the Indus River 5,000 years ago has joined the ranks of lost civilizations rediscovered. As recently as 1969 the world became aware of an even older civilization, with the publication of Geoffrey Bibby's *Looking For Dilmun* (30a), a fascinating account of the rediscovery of civilizations older than the Indus Culture, extending back at least 6,000 years.

But is this all? Is the process at an end? Are no more lost civilizations waiting to be discovered? It would be contrary to history itself if this were the case. Unimaginative people made fun of many of these discoveries and often hounded the discoverers. The same sort of person today accepts all that has been discovered in the past, but denies there is anything more to be discovered.

Let us start our review of the evidences with Egypt. Scholars are in disagreement about the particular achievements of the Egyptians in science, but they are in good agreement about some particular aspects of them. Egyptian knowledge of astronomy and geometry as early as the Fourth Dynasty has been shown to be remarkable. The Egyptians had a double calendar which has been described as "the most scientific combination of calendars that has yet been used by man" (77:7). This calendar system may have been in use as early as 4241 B.C. One historian of science writes:

> It may be, as some indeed suspect, that the science we see at the dawn of recorded history was not science at its dawn but represents the remnants of the science of some great and as yet untraced civilization. (77:12)

Some of the scientific knowledge possessed by ancient peoples can hardly be accounted for in view of the crudeness of the scientific instruments they are supposed to have possessed. The Mayans, for example, are supposed to have measured the length of the tropical year with incredible precision. Their figure was 365.2420 days, as against our figure of 365.2423 days. They are also supposed to have measured the length of a lunation, with an error of less than .0004 of a day (10:150). How did they achieve these results?

George Rawlinson, in a discussion of Babylonian science, made the statement: "The exact length of the Chaldean year is said to have been 365 days, 6 hours, and 11 minutes, which is an excess of two seconds only over the true length of the sidereal year" (173:II,576). He also remarked, "There is said to be distinct evidence that they [the Chaldeans] observed the four satellites of Jupiter and strong reason to believe that they were acquainted likewise with the seven satellites of Saturn. . ." (173:II,577)

This knowledge may, of course, have been derived by the Mayans, the Babylonians, the Egyptians by the use of instruments or methods of which we know nothing. But it is at least possible that such knowledge came to them as a heritage from the same ancient unknown people who made our maps.

The fact that vast areas of ancient science have remained unknown to us has recently been revealed in startling fashion by the discovery of a computer designed and built in ancient times. It was found by divers in 1901 in the wreck of a Greek galley that had been sunk off the Greek island of Antikythera in the 1st Century B.C. Transported to the National Museum at Athens, and carefully cleaned over a long period of time, it was finally examined by Professor Derek de Solla Price of Yale. He found it to be a planetarium, a machine to show the risings and settings of the known planets, and therefore very complicated. But what was particularly astonishing about it was the sophistication of the gearing system, which, Dr. Price said, was essentially modern. (167)

It is obvious, of course, that if this great tradition of technical and mechancial knowledge was lost to history, the same could well have happened to geographical and cartographical knowledge possessed by the Greeks, whether discovered by them or inherited from older peoples.

An Italian scholar, Professor Livio Stecchini, has now uncovered evidence of extremely advanced techniques of measurement and map-making in ancient Egypt. He has spent a lifetime in the investigation of ancient measurements. In a volume edited by Alfred de Grazia* he wrote:

> I was fortunate enough to come across a set of Egyptian documents, well known but neglected, that prove that by the time of the first dynasties the Egyptians had measured down to the minute the latitude and longitude of all the main points of the course of the Nile, from the equator to the Mediterranean Sea. Following this first result I have traced a series of texts (all earlier than the beginning of Greek science) which, starting from Egypt, provide positional data

---

* *The Velikovsky Affair*. New York: University Books, 1966.

that cover most of the Old World, from the rivers Congo and Zambesi to the Norwegian coast, from the Gulf of Guinea to the peaks of Switzerland and river junctions in central Russia. The data are so precise that they are a source of discomfort. I have tried desperately to ascertain errors, but I have never been able to establish an error of latitude greater than a minute or an error of longitude greater than possibly five minutes in ten degrees. Luckily the documentation is relatively simple and does not require the pursuit of detailed analyses of texts, such as the Sumerian tablets I have used in my general study of the ancient art of measurement (p. 167.)

Stecchini has found that the bias of scholars who have simply assumed ancient ignorance of science is responsible for the neglect of these ancient documents. He continues:

That this mass of data of mathematical geography had been gathered in Egypt should not come as a total surprise, since it is known that at the same time texts of mathematical astronomy were written by the tens of thousands in Mesopotamia. However, true Mesopotamiam texts have been denied any significance by an *a priori* argument that in those early times it would have been impossible to proceed to any accurate astronomical measurements. On the basis of this argument it is claimed that the astronomers of Mesopotamia through the centuries delighted, for the pure sake of number lore, in filling up tablets with ephemerides and calculations based on data that were imaginary. . . .

Speaking of ancient Sumerian cuneiform astronomical texts Stecchini says:

". . . these tablets have been almost completely neglected, with the result that less than one thousandth of what is available has been published. . . . The wealth of material that is available is such that it should occupy scores of scholars for several generations. . . ."

Here then we have a further explanation of why more evidence of the achievements of ancient civilization is not available. The fact that the first dynasties of Egypt possessed very precise measurements of a large part of the earth's surface does not necessarily mean that they originated the measurements. Why should they have been interested in measurements of the Alps, of the rivers of Russia or of the islands of Indonesia? It is quite likely that their knowledge of measurements was a heritage from the earlier peoples who mapped the whole earth, including the polar regions.

Dr. Stecchini has published a much more detailed report of his research in ancient measurements, including his studies of the measurements of Greek temples, in a contribution to a work by Peter Tompkins on the Great Pyramid.†

Perhaps it should be noted here in passing that the loss of ancient scientific knowledge was not confined to the period of the fall of ancient civilization. The

---

† *The Secrets of the Great Pyramid.* New York: Harper and Row, 1971.

Arabs preserved much of it, and much of it was undoubtedly passed on to medieval Europe. Perhaps we hear echoes of some of it in the remarkable mechanical ideas of the medieval monk Roger Bacon, or even in some of the ideas of Leonardo da Vinci. A considerable loss seems to have occurred in the Renaissance itself. This was partly because of the invention of printing. The printing presses in the 15th and 16th centuries were monopolized by two classes of books: religious tracts (Catholic and Protestant), and humanist books dealing with arts and letters. Science was of very little interest at the time, and scientific manuscripts just lay about and were allowed to rot away. Francis Bacon is supposed to have drawn attention to this deplorable neglect of scientific documents.

Another example of the possible loss of ancient knowledge has to do with the two moons of Mars, Deimos and Phobus. These moons were discovered by the American astronomer, Asaph Hall, in 1877. He had, however, been looking for them for six months because he knew that they had been known to the Greeks (who called them "the Steeds of Mars") and he gave them the same names given them by the Greeks.

Two hundred and fifty years before Asaph Hall the moons of Mars were described in detail by Jonathan Swift in *Gulliver's Travels.* In describing the scientists of Laputa Swift wrote:

> They have likewise discovered two lesser stars, or satellites, which revolve about Mars, whereof the innermost is distant from the center of the primary planet exactly three of the diameters, and the outermost five; the former revolves in a space of ten hours, and the latter in twenty-one and a half; so that the squares of their periodical times are very near in the same proportion with the cubes of their distances from the center of Mars, which evidently shows them to be governed by the same law of gravitation that influences the other celestial bodies.

Swift was familiar with Newton's Law of Gravitation and applied it to this information apparently derived from some ancient source. His source was wrong only in comparatively minor details. Phobus, the nearer moon, is distant from the center of Mars two rather than three of Mars' diameters, Deimos four rather than five diameters. Phobus revolves around Mars in seven hours rather than ten, and Deimos in thirty hours instead of twenty-one and a half.

Some people have dismissed Swift's statement as guesswork. One noted astronomer wrote: "Lucky guesser, Mr. Swift!" But an examination of the degree of probability of such coincidence makes it impossible to leave the matter there. We have four orders of improbability in this case: (1) that Swift guessed correctly that Mars had moons; (2) that he guessed correctly that Mars had *two* moons; (3) that he guessed to within a margin of 30% of accuracy the distances of *both* the moons from the center of Mars, and (4) that he guessed the periods of revolution of *both* of them in *hours,* again within a margin of 30% accuracy. It must be noted, as well, that this rate of revolution of satellites about their planet is *unique* in the solar system. It is clear that the ratio of probability against guessing all these points as accurately as this is millions or billions to one.

It has been reported that in 1610 Kepler predicted that Mars would be found to have two moons. I have not been able to find the reference, but in any case Kepler could only have based his prediction on his knowledge of the ancient legend. He could not have deduced their existence from perturbations of the orbit of Mars for two reasons. First, because the moons, being only five and ten miles in diameter, could not have observably affected the orbit of Mars, and second, because Newton's Law of Gravitation had not yet been formulated and so the effects of the moons on the orbit of Mars could not have been calculated.

In a letter to Dr. Silvio Begini of the Smithsonian Institution, dated September 15, 1962, I asked him as a specialist in the history of Optics, whether there was any record of the construction of a telescope capable of observing these moons, before the date of publication of *Gulliver's Travels.* He replied that there was no such record, but that he could not exclude the possibility that such an instrument could have been built but have remained unknown to science.

Here, again, we must consider the laws of probability. Such a telescope would have had to have a power capable of perceiving a football at a distance of 700 miles from earth. And we still have to account, of course, for the existence of knowledge of these moons in ancient Greece.

I am aware of a good many other indications of this kind, scattered all over the world, suggesting the ancient tradition of an advanced culture, but as yet their investigation is so incomplete that there is no point in mentioning them.* There is one matter, however, which I cannot forbear to mention, despite its rather controversial character, because I did investigate it myself.

Just outside Mexico City there is a round step pyramid, which, long ago, was swamped by lava from volcanoes not far off. This is the pyramid of Cuicuilco. The pyramid is not a mere mound, but a complex stone structure reflecting a comparatively advanced society. The lava flow swirled around three sides of the pyramid and covered about sixty square miles of territory to a depth of from five to thirty feet. The layer of volcanic rock thus formed is called the Pedrigal.

Geologists who examined the Pedrigal and tried to estimate, by the condition of its surface and the amount of loose sediment accumulated over it, how long ago it was formed, came up with a figure of about 7,000 years. This would have meant that the Mexican pyramid was older by far than the pyramids of Egypt, the oldest of which date back about 5,000 years. Archaeologists could not accept this, and generally took the view that the pyramid probably dated no earlier than the 7th or 8th centuries A.D. The development of the new technique of radiocarbon dating after World War II threw new light on this question.

Radiocarbon dating was developed by the nuclear scientist Willard F. Libby, of the University of Chicago. It was based on the discovery that a very small percen-

---

* Two recent developments of great interest have provided new evidence of scientific achievements in what we refer to as the Stone Ages. One consists of evidence of the use of an advanced lunar calendar as far back as 35,000 years ago (133), and the other is the discovery, by the use of a computer, that the builders of Stonehenge were really good astronomers. (87–88).

tage of the carbon contained in the carbon dioxide of the atmosphere is radio-active, and, like all radioactive substances, loses mass at a measurable rate. Radio-active carbon (Carbon 14) radiates away half its mass in about 5,000 years. All living things taking carbon dioxide from the air will, during their lifetimes, contain the same percentage of radiocarbon as the atmosphere, but after their death any new supply from the atmosphere is cut off, while the amount already absorbed continues to decay. After a time the percentage of radiocarbon in the body of the plant or animal will be less than that in the atmosphere, and by accurately measuring the difference it becomes possible to determine the lapse of time since the death of the plant or animal. This gives us a method of "absolute dating" for archaeological and geological materials. Despite many complexities, it is regarded as generally dependable, within a certain margin of error, for the period of the last sixty thousand years.

The first radiocarbon date for the Cuicuilco Pyramid was found by Dr. Libby (124). He used a sample of charcoal found under the Pedrigal in direct association with pottery fragments similar in style to the pottery of the known "Archaic Period" of the Indian civilization of Mexico. The result was a finding of an age of 2,422 years†, with a margin of error of 250 years either way. It appeared from this that the carbon came from a tree that died or was destroyed some time between 209 B.C. and 709 B.C. It was not certain, however, that this dated the lava flow, for the charcoal was not directly associated with the lava. The wood might have been burned by humans (perhaps for cooking) sometime before the lava flow. But the position of the charcoal directly under the lava suggested that no great period of time may have elapsed between the burning of the wood and the lava flow.

Additional radiocarbon dates subsequently amplified our information on Cuicuilco. Between 1957 and 1962 a number of samples of charcoal, collected from different depths beneath the Pedrigal, were dated in the radiocarbon laboratory of the University of Southern California (UCLA).* One of these samples was directly associated with the lava, and gave an age of about 414 A.D., but was considered by the archaeologists, in the light of other evidence, to be about 200 years older. The consensus of specialists was that the flow probably occurred about 200 A.D.

This would appear at first to demolish the claim that the pyramid was very old. It would appear that it might have been built by the same people who built other pyramids near Mexico City. There is, however, another aspect of the matter which would appear to have been overlooked. It seems that the archaeologists who have discussed the date of Cuicuilco have not, in some cases, attentively read the text of the report made by the man who excavated the pyramid for the Government of Mexico in 1920. He was Byron S. Cummings, an American archaeologist. (56)

Cummings dug down through the Pedrigal, below which he found a stratum of earth with fragments of pottery and figurines of the Archaic culture. He then dug further. At the bottom of the Archaic layer he found a deposit of volcanic ash. He

---

* "Radiocarbon," Supplement of the American Journal of Science, Vol. 5, pp. 12–13, and Vol. 6, pp. 332–334.
† The "Bristlecone pine adjustment" revises this to 2,664 years.

extended his excavation down through the ash, and below it found evidences of an entirely different culture, one that must have preceded the Archaic. He considered that the evidence of the pottery and figurines here showed a level of culture higher than the Archaic, but unconnected with it. As he sank his trenches deeper, he came to the bottom of this layer, and to another layer of volcanic ash. He dug through this, and came upon another layer of artifacts—fragments of pottery and figurines. These resembled those in the second layer, but they were cruder. Finally, at a depth of eighteen feet, Cummings came upon a pavement that had surrounded the Pyramid of Cuicuilco and which had evidently been built when the pyramid was built. (See Note 16).

Cummings made an estimate of the time required to accumulate the eighteen feet of sediment between the underside of the Pedrigal and the temple pavement. He estimated, first, the age of the Pedrigal lava flow at 2,000 years, and here came very close the truth. Then he measured the thickness of the sediments that have accumulated on the top of the Pedrigal since it was formed, and used this as a measuring stick to estimate the time required to accumulate the sediments below. He came to an estimate of 6,500 years for the time required to accumulate these eighteen feet of sediments.

In answer to the argument that the rate of accumulation of the sediments may have been different and more rapid in the period before the eruption of the volcano, Cummings pointed out that a great lapse of time was clearly indicated by the nature of the sediments themselves. The three culture layers are separated by two layers of volcanic ash, thick layers of sterile soil, with no indication of vegetation. In each case the development of a new layer of humus-rich top soil over the sterile layer probably took time on the order of centuries, and only after this process was completed did a new layer of artifacts appear. The evidence, according to Cummings, suggested that, first, the pyramid was abandoned, for some reason, by the people who built it; then, much later, a crude people with crude pots and tools occupied the region around the pyramid. After a lapse of time, an eruption of one or more of the neighboring volcanoes eliminated the occupation, depositing a layer of volcanic ash. A further considerable period elapsed, new top soil was formed, and the area was again occupied, this time by an advanced people whose artifacts suggested they were the descendants of the people preceding them. A process of cultural development would appear to have taken place in some other region perhaps nearby. Again, after a considerable time, another eruption of the volcanoes seems to have eliminated this advanced culture, and this time resulted in a complete culture break, for the third people to occupy the region, those of the Archaic culture, appear to have had no connection with their predecessors. Only after all these things had taken place was the Pedrigal formed.

A check on Cummings' estimate of 6,500 years, for the time required to accumulate all the sediments, is provided by the radiocarbon samples referred to above. They were taken at various depths below the Pedrigal, though at a distance of about 1,000 feet from the pyramid. They all consisted of charcoal. Arranged in the order of depth below the lava, their approximate dates were as follows:

**Table A: Cuicuilco Radiocarbon Dates**

| Sample Numbers | Depth (Approx.) | Age | Margin (± Yrs.) | Dendrological Correction* |
|---|---|---|---|---|
| UCLA-228, Cuicuilco A-2 | Associated with lava | 414 A.D. | 65 | 260 A.D. |
| UCLA-205, Cuicuilco B-1 | 4 ft. 6 in. | 160 A.D. | 75 | 19 B.C. |
| UCLA-206, Cuicuilco B-2 | 7 ft. 6 in. | 15 A.D. | 80 | 178 B.C. |
| UCLA-602, Cuicuilco B-17 | 7 ft. 6 in. | 240 B.C. | 80 | 459 B.C. |
| UCLA-208, Cuicuilco B-4 | 7 ft. 8 in. | 150 B.C. | 150 | 360 B.C. |
| UCLA-603, Cuicuilco B-18 | 7 ft. 11 in. | 280 B.C. | 80 | 503 B.C. |
| UCLA-207, Cuicuilco B-3 | 8 ft. 1 in. | 650 B.C. | 70 | 910 B.C. |
| UCLA-209, Cuicuilco B-5 | 8 ft. 8 in. | 350 B.C. | 70 | 580 B.C. |
| UCLA-594, Cuicuilco B-9 | 14 ft. 3 in. | 610 B.C. | 80 | 866 B.C. |
| UCLA-210, Cuicuilco B-6 | 15 ft. 0 in. | 2030 B.C. | 60 | 2428 B.C. |
| UCLA-595, Cuicuilco B-10 | 15 ft. 0 in. | 540 B.C. | 100 | 789 B.C. |
| UCLA-596, Cuicuilco B-11 | 15 ft. 4 in. | 610 B.C. | 100 | 866 B.C. |
| UCLA-597, Cuicuilco B-12 | 16 ft. 8 in. | 1870 B.C. | 100 | 2252 B.C. |
| UCLA-598, Cuicuilco B-13 | 16 ft. 8 in. | 1870 B.C. | 100 | 2252 B.C. |
| UCLA-211, Cuicuilco B-7 | 17 ft. 6 in. | 4765 B.C. | 90 | 5437 B.C. |
| UCLA-212, Cuicuilco B-8 | 19 ft. 0 in. | 2100 B.C. | 75 | 2505 B.C. |
| UCLA-600, Cuicuilco B-15 | 20 ft. 8 in. | 1980 B.C. | 100 | 2373 B.C. |
| UCLA-599, Cuicuilco B-14 | 21 ft. 6 in. | 1900 B.C. | 200 | 2285 B.C. |
| UCLA-601, Cuicuilco B-16 | 21 ft. 6 in. | 2160 B.C. | 120 | 2571 B.C. |

* These dates are calculated from a base line of 1950 A.D. Source: Table for Egyptian materials from: I.V. Olsson (ed) *Radiocarbon Variations in the Atmosphere* (1970).

If we disregard the samples out of chronological order (UCLA-602, 207, 210, 211), which suggest disturbances in the sediments through digging operations (or other causes) in ancient times, and compare the accumulation of sediments with the lapse of time between each pair of consecutive samples, we find there are very wide variations in the rate of accumulation.

## Table B: Rate of Sedimentation

| Sample Numbers | Accumulation | Time | Rate (Approx.) |
|---|---|---|---|
| UCLA-228, 205 | 4 ft. 6 in. | 254 yrs. | 1':56 yrs. |
| UCLA-205, 206 | 3 ft. 0 in. | 145 yrs. | 1':48 yrs. |
| UCLA-206, 208 | 0 ft. 2 in. | 165 yrs. | 1':990 yrs. |
| UCLA-208, 603 | 0 ft. 3 in. | 130 yrs. | 1':520 yrs. |
| UCLA-603, 209 | 0 ft. 9 in. | 70 yrs. | 1':93 yrs. |
| UCLA-209, 594 | 5 ft. 7 in. | 260 yrs. | 1':48 yrs. |
| UCLA-594, 596 | 1 ft. 1 in. | 00 | 0:00 |
| UCLA-596, 597 | 1 ft. 4 in. | 1,260 yrs. | 1':948 yrs. |
| UCLA-597, 212 | 2 ft. 4 in. | 230 yrs. | 1':100 yrs. |
| UCLA-212, 601 | 2 ft. 6 in. | 60 yrs. | 1':25 yrs. |

If we accept the dates of 414 A.D. and 2160 B.C. for the top and bottom of our column of sediments (Table A), we can suppose that 21½ feet of sediment accumulated in 2,574 years before the eruption of the Pedrigal, at an average rate of a foot in 119 years. The variations in the rate may mean simply that the sediments were much disturbed in ancient times, or they may reflect changes in the rate of accumulation related to periods of volcanic eruption, when the rate would have been rapid, and to periods following eruptions when there was no human occupation and very little vegetation, when it would be very slow. The samples were all taken from a human occupation site, that is, from mounds under the Pedrigal containing the ruins of buildings, where the rate of accumulation of sediment would naturally have been faster. The essential point is that while the radiocarbon samples taken near the pyramid give us approximate dates for various phases of the Archaic or Pre-Classical cultures in the area, they have not, so far, dated the pyramid. No excavation appears to have been made at a depth greater than that of the pavement mentioned by Cummings as surrounding the pyramid. It appears from the evidence that the structures near the pyramid under the Pedrigal, that have now been dated, were the work of people who occupied the region after the abandonment of the pyramid.

If this is the case, we have the date of 2160 B.C. as a minimum date for the abandonment of the pyramid. This does not date its construction. Cummings gives reasons to believe (see Note 16) that the structure was in use for a long period of time. Since its scale and advanced construction imply an advanced people possibly flourishing in Mexico four or five thousand years ago, we may have here a relic of the people who navigated the whole earth, and possessed the advanced sciences necessary to make our ancient maps.

I am not expecting that these remarks regarding the Pyramid of Cuicuilco will be regarded as final. I would only suggest that there should now be a re-examination of that pyramid, and of several other sites in Mexico and in South America, to determine whether, in fact, they may not be related to the ancient civilization which the maps so strongly indicate must once have existed, and which must have been worldwide, at least so far as exploration and mapmaking were concerned. Repeatedly, during the last hundred years, discoveries have been made, which were claimed by the discoverers to indicate the existence of an ancient advanced civilization. These alleged discoveries were disregarded or discredited by archaeologists as the products of sheer imagination or fakery. The task of disinterring and re-examining these old and perhaps mistakenly rejected discoveries will be a long one; that of finding new evidence in the field has not yet been begun. The research project is one for many hands, many years, and much money.

Outside the archaeological field there are two areas which warrant research for evidence of a united world culture. There is, first, the problem of the origin of the principal families of speech and the various groups of languages. Some scholars have claimed that most languages betray evidences of an original common language, ancestral to all the groups of language (such as the Indo-European, etc.). One of these was Arnold D. Wadler, who spent a lifetime on the problem. I do not know whether his conclusions are valid, but his book (214) shows, it seems to me, a scientific approach. It is interesting that a tradition of a universal language seems to be common in ancient literature. In Genesis we read, of course, "And the whole earth was of one language and one speech." Lincoln Barnett, in his *Treasure of Our Tongue*, remarks, "The notion that at one time all men spoke a single language is by no means unique to Genesis. It found expression in ancient Egypt, in early Hindu and Buddhist writings and was seriously explored by several European philosophers during the 16th century. . . ." (24:46.) Another linguistic investigation, this time of place names, has contributed impressive evidence of very early world voyages. The author, John Philip Cohane, in his book, *The Key*, (52a) has painstakingly established a persuasive body of evidence.

The other line of research is comparative mythology. For some years, with my anthropology classes, I have been pursuing research in mythology, and one concept that has emerged with great clarity from our studies, is the virtual identity of the great systems of mythology throughout the world. The same pattern, the same principal deities, appear everywhere—in Europe, in Asia, in North and South America, in Oceania. Table C below lists the Gods of the Four Elements—Air, Earth, Fire, Water—as they are found in mythologies all over the world.

There have been many theories of mythology. One of them attributed the similarities in the myths to a common origin in Egypt. This has been generally rejected, because there is insufficient evidence for the diffusion of Egyptian myths to America, India, China, and Oceania. If there was diffusion, the point of origin must lie farther back, in a culture earlier than Egypt. Another theory attributes the similarities to instinct. Its proponents argue that the myths derive from instincts that are the same in all men. This theory is weak because, in the first place, modern psychologists tend to doubt the existence of such instincts, and, secondly, insofar as they may exist they can apply ony to the most general themes, such as love, hate, mystical feeling, etc. The resemblances between the myths, as the table shows, are really too specific to be attributed to general instincts.

We have, then, a general conclusion. The evidence for an ancient worldwide civilization, or a civilization that for a considerable time must have dominated much of the world in a very remote period, is rather plentiful—at least potentially. We have manifold leads, which further research can hardly fail to develop.

### Table C

#### Gods of the Four Elements in Various Pantheons*

|  | FIRE | AIR | EARTH | WATER |
|---|---|---|---|---|
| EGYPT | Re | Shu | Geb, Gea | Nu, Nunu† |
| BABYLONIA | Girru | Anu | Enlil | Ea |
| HEBREW | Gabriel | Raphael | Raashiel | Rediyas |
| PHOENICIA | Ouranos | Aura | Gea | Ashera |
| PERSIA‡ | Atar | Ahura Mazda | Ameretet | Anahita |
| INDIA | Agni | Yayu | Prithivi | Varuna |
| CHINA | Mu-King | How-Chu | Yen-Lo-Wang | Mo-Hi-Hai |
| JAPAN | Ama-Terashu | Amida | Ohonamochi | Susa-No O |
| IRAN‡ | Asha; Atar Oeshma | Vohu Manah Oka Manah | Spenta Armati Bushyasta | Hauvatet Apaosha |
| NORSE | Thor | Tyr | Odin | Njord |
| INCA | Manco-Capac | Supay | Pachacamac | Viracocha |
| AZTEC | Ometecutli | Tezcatlipoca | Omeciuatl | Tlaloc |
| MAYAN | Kulkulcan | Bacabs | Voltan | Itzamna |
| SLAV | Swa | Byelun | Raj | Peroun |
| FINNS | Fire-Girl | Ukko | Ilmatar | Kul Uasa |

* Prepared by the anthropology class at Keene State College.

† The gods of the four elements in Egypt were different in different periods.

‡ Persian and Iranian mythologies were not the same; in Iranian mythology the four gods of the elements have their opposites, representing the good and evil aspects.

# Acknowledgments

I HAVE always felt that science is a social process. As a student of the history of science I have learned that every advance of science is the product of many minds working together, even if it may seem that only one individual is responsible. For this reason I wish to give credit here to the many people who have contributed to this work.

For the initiation of the project I am deeply indebted to Mrs. Ruth Verrill of Chiefland, Florida, who first drew my attention to the work of Captain Arlington H. Mallery.

From the beginning, my students took an active part in the investigation and many of them made important contributions. Among them were Ernest Adams, Ronald Bailey, Ruth Baraw, George Batchelder, Richard Cotter, Don Dougal, Clayton Dow, James D. Enderson, Leo Estes, Sidney B. Gove, William Greer, Larry Howard, Alfred Isroe, Warren Lee, Marcia Leslie, Loren Livengood, John F. Malsbenden, John Poor, Frank Ryan, Alan Schuerger, Robert Simenson, Lee Spencer, Margaret Waugh , Robert Jan Woitkowski, and my sons, Frederick and William. Many of them were mentioned in the book.

From the third year of the investigation we were fortunate to receive the co-operation of Captain Lorenzo W. Burroughs, chief of the Cartographic Unit of the 8th Reconnaissance Technical Squadron, at Westover Air Force Base, Westover, Massachusetts. Captain Burroughs and his commanding officer, Colonel Harold Z. Ohlmeyer, examined our findings regarding the Piri Re'is and Oronteus Finaeus Maps, and endorsed them in letters. Captain Burroughs, however, did much more than check our conclusions. His many suggestions were invaluable to us. In addition, he encouraged the members of his cartographic staff to contribute their own time to assisting us. The officers and men of the Air Force who contributed their work were: Captain Richard E. Covault, Captain B. Farmer, Chief Warrant Officer Howard D. Minor, Master Sergeant Clifton M. Dover, Master Sergeant David C. Carter, Technical Sergeant James H. Hood, Staff Sergeant James L. Carroll, Airman First Class Don R. Vance, and Airman Second Class R. Lefever.

Numerous individuals throughout the country took an interest in our work and contributed valuable information and advice. These include William Briesemeister, chief cartographer of the American Geographical Society, now retired, who read the manuscript of this book and contributed suggestions for the preparation of the various maps in it; David B. Ericson of the Lamont Geological Observatory, the late Archibald T. Robertson of Boston, Robert L. Merritt, of Cleveland, Ohio, who read the manuscript and contributed much scholarly information; Miss Elizabeth Kendall, of Washington, D.C., who very kindly provided me with translations of articles from the Soviet press relating to Piri Re'is; and to my aunt, Mrs. Norman Hapgood, for many suggestions. I am indebted also to Niels West, Dino Fabris, Mrs. Margaret Allen, Paul R. Swann; to Dr. Arch Gerlach, Walter Ristow, and Richard W. Stephenson, of the Library of Congress; to Miss Nordis Felland, librarian of the American Geographical Society, to E. Pognon and M. Hervé of the Bibliothèque Nationale in Paris; to I. Hatsukade of the National Diet Library in Tokyo, and to the staff of the Hispanic Society of America, in New York. In addition, I am grateful for the co-operation extended to me, in my search for ancient maps of the East, by the former Sultan of Zanzibar and by the late Emperor Haile Selassie of Ethiopia.

I am indebted to the United States Department of State for copies of the letters relating to the discovery of the Piri Re'is Map. Also, I wish to thank the American Geographical Society for making arrangements for me with the American Embassy in Ankara, Turkey, for special photographs of the Piri Re'is Map.

I must not forget a deep personal debt to Mr. and Mrs. Philip Martin of Keene, New Hampshire, my most excellent photographers, who bore with me through the innumer ble rephotographings of countless maps, for which I was always in a hurry, and to my typist, Miss Eileen Sullivan, who worked under equally bad conditions without ever losing her patience.

I am most deeply indebted to Dr. J. K. Wright, former director of the American Geographical Society, who, in addition to writing the Foreword to this book, read the entire manuscript and contributed many very valuable suggestions for improvements in both content and style, and to Charles W. Halgren, of Caru Studios in New York, who, in addition to preparing our drawings for reproduction, gave us much valuable advice on technical matters.

I am indebted to the following for their contributions to the present edition of this work: Professor Carl Weis for his collaboration in the study of the Vinland Map, Miss Barbara Beal for her research into the scales found on the Piri Re'is Map, Mr. Robert Merritt for his kindness in checking our tracing of the Piri Re'is Map with the original when the latter was on exhibit in the United States, Dr. John J. Shafer of Pesalozzi College, Ottawa, for his corrections of textual errors, Dr. Livio Stecchini for his kindness in granting permission to quote from his work, and many others whose suggestions have made it possible for me to correct weaknesses undetected in the first edition.

# List of Notes

# 1   The Piri Re'is Map of 1513

The Piri Re'is map of 1513 came to light in the old imperial palace at Istanbul in 1931. *The Illustrated London News* published a reproduction of it on 25th February 1932, which prompted a detailed letter by a prominent Turkish historian. The magazine published this letter by Yusuf Akura Bey, National Deputy and President of the Turkish Historical Society on 23rd July 1932, of which the following is an excerpt:

"The map in question is drawn on a gazelle skin by Piri Reis who had made a name for himself among the Western and Eastern Scholars through his detailed geographical book on the Mediterranean Sea entitled *Bahriye* ("On the Sea") and which testifies to his capacity and knowledge in his profession. Piri Reis is the son of the brother of the famous Kemal Reis who was the Turkish admiral in the Mediterranean Sea at the last quarter of the fifteenth century. History records Piri Reis Bey's last official post as admiral of the Fleets in the Red Sea and the Indian Ocean. Piri Reis wrote and completed the above-mentioned map in the city of Gelibolu (Gallipoli) in the year 1513, and four years after this date, i.e. in the year 1517, he presented personally to Selim I, the conqueror of Egypt, during the presence of the latter there.

"As the same thing will be noticed in the maps of ancient and mediaeval times, the map of Piri Reis contain [sic] important marginal notes regarding the history and the geographical conditions of some of the coasts and islands. *All these marginal notes* with hundreds of lines of explanation *were written in Turkish*. Three lines only, which from the title and head lines of the map, were written in Arabic; and this is done to comply with the usual traditional way which is noticed on all the Ottoman Turkish monuments up [to] the very latest centuries. These three lines in Arabic testify that the author is the nephew of Kemal Reis, and that the work [was] written and compiled of [sic] Gelibolu in the year 1513.

"The map in our possession is a fragment and it was out of from [sic] a world chart on large scale. When the photographic copy of the map is carefully examined, it will be noticed that the lines of the marginal noted [sic] on the eastern edges have been cut half away.

"In one of these marginal notes the author states in detail the maps he had seen and studied in preparing his map. In the marginal note describing the Antilles Islands, he states that he has used Christopher Columbus' chart for the coasts and islands. He sets forth the narratives of the voyages made, by a Spaniard a slave in the hands of Kemal Reis, Piri Reis' uncle, who under Christopher Columbus made three voyages to America. He also states, in his marginal notes regarding the South American coast that he saw the charts of four Portuguese discoverers. That he has made use of Christopher Columbus' chart is made clear in the following lines of his:

In order that these islands and their coasts might be known Columbus gave them these names and set it down on his chart. The coasts (the names of the coasts) and the islands are taken from the chart of Columbus.

"The work essentially was a world map. Therefore Piri Reis had made a study of some of the charts which represented the world, and according to his personal statement, he has studied and examined the maps prepared at the time of Alexander (the Great), the 'Mappa Mundis' and the eight maps in fragments prepared by the Muslims.

"Piri Reis himself plainly explains, in one of the marginal notes in his map, how his map was prepared:—

This section explains the way the map was prepared. Such a map is not owned by any body at this time, I, personally, drawn [sic] and prepared this map. In preparing this map, I made use of about twenty old charts and eight Mappa Mundis, i.e. of the charts called "Jaferiye" by the Arabs and prepared at the time of Alexander the Great and in which the whole inhabited world was shown; of the chart of [the] West Indies; and of the new maps made by four Portugueses [sic] containing the Indian and Chinese countries geometrically represented on them. I also studied the chart that Christopher Columbus drew for the West. Putting all these material [sic] together in a common scale I produced the present map. My map is as correct and dependable for the seven seas as are the charts that represent the seas of our countries.

"Piri Reis, in a special chapter in his book *Bahriye* mentions the fact that in drawing his map he has taken note of the cartographical traditions considered international at that time. The cities and citadels are indicated in red lines, the deserted places in black lines, the rugged and rocky places in black dots, the shores and sandy places in red dots and the hidden rocks by crosses."

There are in fact 207 charts drawn by Piri Re'is in his *Bahriye*.

The State Department, through their ambassador in Ankara, procured reproductions of the Piri Re'is map for the Library of Congress. The Library of Congress was particularly anxious also to obtain a copy of Columbus' maps upon which Piri Re'is claimed in part to have based his own map. At that time, Columbus was popularly believed to have "discovered" America. It was not widely recognised fifty years ago that Columbus died in the belief that he had discovered Japan. Nor was it known in the 1930's that other maritime explorers from Europe had sailed the Atlantic centuries before Columbus.

# 2   The Legends on the Piri Re'is Map*

I. There is a kind of red dye called vakami, that you do not observe at first, because it is at a distance ... the mountains contain rich ores ... There some of the sheep have silken wool.

II. This country is inhabited. The entire population goes naked.

III. This region is known as the vilayet of Antilia. It is on the side where the sun sets. They say that there are four kinds of parrots, white, red, green and black. The people eat the flesh of parrots and their headdress is made entirely of parrots' feathers. There is a stone here. It resembles black touchstone. The people use it instead of the ax. That it is very hard ... [illegible]. JPe saw that stone.

[NOTE: Piri Reis writes in the "Bahriye": "In the enemy ships which we captured in the Mediterranean, we found a headdress made of these parrot feathers, and also a stone resembling touchstone."]

IV. This map was drawn by Piri Ibn Haji Mehmed, known as the nephew of Kemal Reis, in Gallipoli, in the month of muharrem of the year 919 (that is, between the 9th of March and the 7th of April of the year 1513).

V. This section tells how these shores and also these islands were found.

These coasts are named the shores of Antilia. They were discovered in the year 896 of the Arab calendar. But it is reported thus, that a Genoese infidel, his name was Colombo, he it was who discovered these places. For instance, a book fell into the hands of the said Colombo, and he found it said in this book that at the end of the Western Sea [Atlantic] that

---

* From "The Oldest Map of America," by Professor Dr. Afet Inan. Ankara, 1954, pp. 28–34. The Roman numerals refer to the key map.

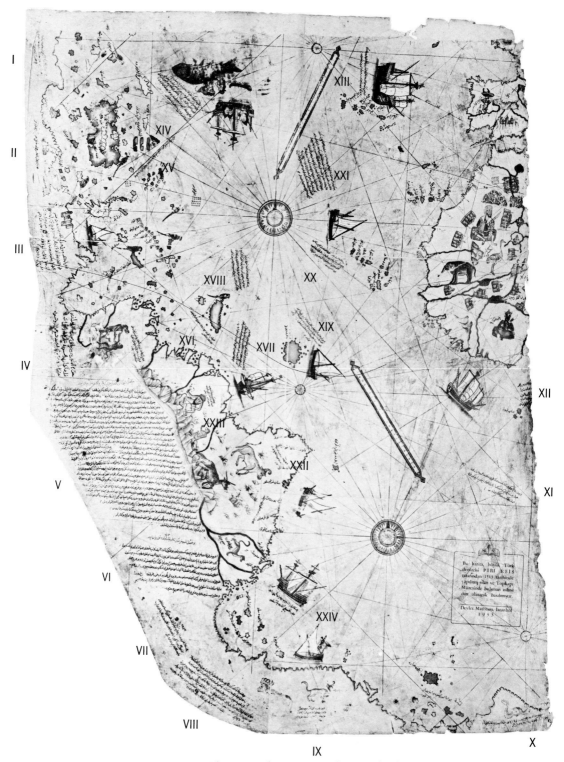

Figure 108. The Piri Re'is Map with numerals corresponding to the legends translated in Note 2.

is, on its western side, there were coasts and islands and all kinds of metals and also precious stones. The above-mentioned, having studied this book thoroughly, explained these matters one by one to the great of Genoa and said: "Come, give me two ships, let me go and find these places." They said: "O unprofitable man, can an end or a limit be found to the Western Sea? Its vapour is full of darkness." The above-mentioned Colombo saw that no help was forthcoming from the Genoese, he sped forth, went to the Bey of Spain [king], and told his tale in detail. They too answered like the Genoese. In brief Colombo petitioned these people for a long time, finally the Bey of Spain gave him two ships, saw that they were well equipped, and said:

"O Colombo, if it happens as you say, let us make you kapudan [admiral] to that country." Having said which he sent the said Colombo to the Western Sea. The late Gazi Kemal had a Spanish slave. The above-mentioned slave said to Kemal Reis, he had been three times to that land with Colombo. He said: "First we reached the Strait of Gibraltar, then from there straight south and west between the two ... [illegible]. Having advanced straight four thousand miles, we saw an island facing us, but gradually the waves of the sea became foamless, that is, the sea was becalmed and the North Star—the seamen on their compasses still say star—little by little was veiled and became invisible, and he also said that the stars in that region are not arranged as here. They are seen in a different arrangement. They anchored at the island which they had seen earlier across the way, the population of the island came, shot arrows at them and did not allow them to land and ask for information. The males and the females shot hand arrows. The tips of these arrows were made of fishbones, and the whole population went naked and also very ... [illegible]. Seeing that they could not land on that island; they crossed to the other side of the island, they saw a boat. On seeing them; the boat fled and they [the people in the boat] dashed out on land. They [the Spaniards] took the boat. They saw that inside of it there was human flesh. It happened that these people were of that nation which went from island to island hunting men and eating them. They said Colombo saw yet another island, they neared it, they saw that on that island there were great snakes. They avoided landing on this island and remained there seventeen days. The people of this island saw that no harm came to them from this boat, they caught fish and brought it to them in their small ship's boat [filika]. These [Spaniards] were pleased and gave them glass beads. It appears that he [Colombus] had read—in the book that in that region glass beads were valued. Seeing the beads they brought still more fish. These [Spaniards] always gave them glass beads. One day they saw gold around the arm of a woman, they took the gold and gave her beads. They said to them, to bring more gold, we will give you more beads, [they said]. They went and brought them much gold. It appears that in their mountains there were gold mines. One day, also, they saw pearls in the hands of one person. They saw them when; they gave beads, many more pearls were brought to them. Pearls were found on the shore of this island, in a spot one or two fathoms deep. And also loading their ship with many logwood trees and taking two natives along, they carried them within that year to the Bey of Spain. But the said Colombo, not knowing the language of these people, they traded by signs, and after this trip the Bey of Spain sent priests and barley, taught the natives how to sow and reap and converted them to his own religion. They had no religion of any sort. They walked naked and lay there like animals. Now these regions have been opened to all and have become famous. The names which mark the places on the said islands and coasts were given by Colombo, that these places may be known by them. And also Colombo was a great astronomer. The coasts and island on this map are taken from Colombo's map.

VI. This section shows in what way this map was drawn. In this century there is no map like this map in anyone's possession. The—hand of this poor man has drawn it and now it is constructed. From about twenty charts and Mappae Mundi—these are charts drawn in the days of Alexander, Lord of the Two Horns, which show the inhabited quarter of the world; the Arabs name these charts Jaferiye—from eight Jaferiyes of that kind and one Arabic map of Hind, and from the maps just drawn by four Portuguese which show the countries of Hind, Sind and China geometrically drawn, and also from a map drawn by Colombo in the western region I have extracted it. By reducing all these maps to one scale this final form was arrived at. So that the present map is as correct and reliable for the Seven Seas as the map of these our countries is considered correct and reliable by seamen.

VII. It is related by the Portuguese infidel that in this spot night and day are at their shortest of two hours, at their longest of twenty two hours. But the day is very warm and in the night there is much dew.

VIII. On the way to the vilayet of Hind a Portuguese ship encountered a contrary wind [blowing] from the shore. The wind from the shore ... [illegible] it [the ship]. After being driven by a storm in a southern direction they saw a shore opposite them they advanced towards it [illegible]. They saw that these places are good anchorages. They threw anchor and went to the shore in boats. They saw people walking, all of them naked. But they shot arrows, their tips made of fishbone. They stayed there eight days. They traded with these people by signs. That barge saw these lands and wrote about them which.... The said barge without going to Hind, returned to Portugal, where, upon arrival gave information.... They described these shores in detail.... They have discovered them.

IX. And in this country it seems that there are white-haired monsters in this shape, and also six-horned oxen. The Portuguese infidels have written it in their maps....

X. This country is a waste. Everything is in ruin and it is said that large snakes are found here. For this reason the Portuguese infidels did not land on these shores and these are also said to be very hot.

XI. And these four ships are Portuguese ships. Their shape is written down. They travelled from the western land to the point of Abyssinia [Habesh] in order to reach India. They said towards Shuluk. The distance across this gulf is 4200 miles.

XII. ... on this shore a tower ... is however ... in this climate gold
        ... taking a rope
        ... is said they measured
[NOTE: The fact that half of each of these lines is missing is the clearest proof of the map's having been torn in two.]

XIII. And a Genoese kuke [a type of ship] coming from Flanders was caught in a storm. Impelled by the storm it came upon these islands, and in this manner these islands became known.

XIV. It is said that in ancient times a priest by the name of Sanvolrandan (Santo Brandan) travelled on the Seven Seas, so they say. The above-mentioned landed on this fish. They thought it dry land and lit a fire upon this fish, when the fish's back began to burn it plunged into the sea, they reembarked in their boats and fled to the ship. This event is not mentioned by the Portuguese infidels. It is taken from the ancient Mappae Mundi.

XV. To these small islands they have given the name of Undizi Vergine. That is to say the Eleven Virgins.

XVI. And this island they call the Island of Antilia. There are many monsters and parrots and much logwood. It is not inhabited.

XVII. This barge was driven upon these shores by a storm and remained where it fell.... Its name was Nicola di Giuvan. On his map it is written that these rivers which can be seen have for the most part gold [in their beds]. When the water has gone they collected much gold [dust] from the sand. On their map....

XVIII. This is the barge from Portugal which encountered a storm and came to this land. The details are written on the edge of this map. [NOTE: see VIII.]

XIX. The Portuguese infidels do not go west of here. All that side belongs entirely to Spain. They have made an agreement that [a line] two thousand miles to the western side of the Strait of Gibraltar should be taken as a boundary. The Portuguese do not cross to that side but the Hind side and the southern side belong to the Portuguese.

XX. And this caravel having encountered a storm was driven upon this island. Its name was Nicola Giuvan. And on this island there are many oxen with one horn. For this reason they call this island Isle de Vacca, which means, Ox Island.

XXI. The admiral of this caravel is named Messir Anton the Genoese, but he grew up in Portugal. One day the above-mentioned caraval encountered a storm, it was driven upon this island. He found much ginger here and has written about these islands.

XXII. This sea is called the Western Sea, but the Frank sailors call it the Mare d'Espagna. Which means the Sea of Spain. Up to now it was known by these names, but Colombo, who opened up this sea and made these islands known, and also the Portuguese, infidels who have opened up the region of Hind have agreed together to give this sea a new name. They have given it the name of Ovo Sano [Oceano] that is to say, sound egg. Before this it was thought that the sea had no end or limit, that at its other end was darkness. Now they have seen that this sea is girded by a coast, because it is like a lake, they have called it Ovo Sano.

XXIII. In this spot there are oxen with one horn, and also monsters in this shape.

XXIV. These monsters are seven spans long. Between their eyes there is a distance of one span. But they are harmless souls.

# 3 Blundeville's Directions for Constructing the Portolan Design* *"Of the Mariners Carde and of the marking thereof."*

"First drawe with a pair of compasses a secrete circle which may be put out, so great as you shall think meet for your carde, which circle shall signifie the Horizon, then divide that circle into foure equall quarters, by drawing two Diameters crossing one another, in the center of the foresaide circle with right angles, whereof the perpendicular line is the line of North and South, and the other crossing the same is the line of East and West, at the foure ends of which crosse Diameters you must set downe the foure principall windes, that is, East, West, North, and South, making the North parte with a flower deluce in the toppe, and the East parte with a crosse, as you may see in the figure following. Then divide everie quarter of the saide circle with your compasses into two equal partes, setting down pricks in the middest of everie quarter, through which pricks, and also through the centre of the circle drawe two other crosse lines, which must extende somewhat beyond the circumference of the Horizon, which two crosse lines together with the first two crosse lines shall divide the circle into 8 partes, and thereby you shall have the eight principall windes. That done, divide everie eight part of the saide Horizon into two equall partes by drawing other two crosse lines through the centre and extending somewhat beyond the circumference of the Horizon as before, whereby the whole circle shall be divided into 16 partes, which shall suffice without making anie more divisions, which woulde cause a confusion of lines, and at the end of every one of these 16 lines you must drawe a little circle, whose center must stande upon the circumference of the Horizon, everie one whereof must bee also divided into 16 partes by the helpe of 16 lines, diversely drawne from the center of one little circle to another, in such order as the figure here placed more plainely sheweth to the eie, than I can

* Heathecote (89) quotes the directions given by Blundeville in "Blundeville his Exercises," 1594, for constructing the portolano design.

expresse by mouth. And these little circles do signifie 16 little Mariners Compasses, the lines whereof signifying the winds, do shew how one place beareth from another, and by what winde the shippe hath to saile. But besides these little circles there is woont to be drawne also another circle somewhat greater than the rest upon the verie center of the Horizon, which circle by reason of the 16 lines that were drawne passing through the same, is divided into 16 parts, and the Mariners doe call this circle the mother compas."

# 4   Dr. Richard Strachan on Map Projections

Richard W. Strachan discusses here the features of a number of projections that appear to have been involved with one or more of the ancient maps. The reader may be reminded that map projections are mechanical and mathematical devices for transferring points from the round earth to flat paper, and they are therefore artificial and complex. The earth is virtually a sphere, and only a globe can correctly represent all of it in correct proportion. Various projections may represent parts of the earth on flat paper with sufficient accuracy for practical purposes, but they all have their faults, and they all distort the earth very badly in one way or another. The mapmaker tries to select the particular projection that is best for mapping the area he wants to map, the projection that has the most advantages and the fewest disadvantages. Strachan here defines five projections, but there are many more. For more detailed discussions the reader may consult Deetz and Adams (60).

AZIMUTHAL: An azimuthal projection is one in which the earth is projected onto a flat plane held tangent to it at one point. The tangent point may be at a pole, on the equator, or anywhere else desired. The class of azimuthal projections includes several of interest, namely the stereographic, gnomonic and azimuthal equidistant, which are described below.

STEREOGRAPHIC: A stereographic projection results if the earth is projected onto a plane from a point on the earth opposite to the point of tangency. The advantages of this projection are that it can show a whole hemisphere without great distortion, and that great circles through the tangent point plot as straight lines.

[A "great circle" is a circle about the earth that equals the full circumference. For example, the equator is a great circle, but it is the only parallel of latitude which is a great circle. All other parallels are shorter, and are therefore not great circles. A great circle actually describes a plane that cuts the earth in half, and may be drawn about the earth in any direction.]

GNOMONIC: A gnomonic projection is obtained when the projection of the earth onto a tangent plane is done from the center of the earth. The advantage of this projection is that any great circle plots a straight line.

AZIMUTHAL EQUIDISTANT: This projection is one in which the distance scale along any great circle through a tangent point is constant. A polar azimuthal equidistant projection shows the meridians of longitude as straight radial lines, and the parallels as equally spaced concentric circles. It cannot be visualized as being projected, but rather as being constructed, by setting up a scale and transferring the features of the earth onto this scale point by point. It has the great advantage that the whole earth may be shown. Also it has a constant distance scale from the point of tangency (or "pole"); and, like all other azimuthal projections, all angles measured from the point of tangency are true.

CORDIFORM: No recent literature describes the cordiform projection, and to get some sort of definitive statement on it, it was necessary to refer to Nordenskiöld. He lists three cordiform projections (147:86–92). The first he ascribes to the cartographer Sylvanus, noting its similarity to Ptolemy's "homeother" projection. The second, also similar to

Ptolemy's homeother projection, was used by the geographer Apianus in a map he drew in 1520. The third was described by Johannes Werner in 1514 as an invention of his own. The second of these projections was the one used by Oronteus Finaeus, and later by Mercator. It is often referred to as "Werner's Second Projection" since he discussed all three. The details of this projection are as follows:

(a) The pole is the center for the parallels of latitude, which are concentric circles or portions of concentric circles.

(b) The size (diameter, circumference, spacing) of the parallels is adjusted to give the true proportion between the length of the degree of longitude at the equator and at other latitudes. That is, the sizes of the parallels are changed to give the right length of a degree of longitude at any latitude.

(c) At the equator, the length of the degree of latitude is equal to the length of the degree of longitude.

MERCATOR PROJECTION: This projection is of the cylindrical type, in which a cylinder, placed around the earth and touching it along a circle, has projected onto it (from inside outwards) a representation of the earth's surface. The cylinder is then cut lengthwise, and flattened out to form a map. If the cylinder is tangent to the earth at the equator, the meridians become vertical, parallel, equidistant, straight lines; and the equator becomes a horizontal straight line across the center of the map.

The Mercator Projection is of the cylindrical type, but is not constructed by geometric projection. The parallels of latitude are derived mathematically. Its main feature is that the parallels of latitude are spaced ever farther apart with increasing distances from the equator, so as to maintain, at every point, the correct ratio between the degree of latitude and the degree of longitude; which, of course, actually grows shorter toward the poles. The advantage of this projection is that it is "conformal"—that is to say angles may be measured correctly at any point, and distances may be measured directly over small changes in latitude. For purposes of navigation, course lines are straight lines, whose directions may be directly measured from the chart.

# 5   Plane v. Spherical Trigonometry in the Piri Re'is Map

Strachan a number of times calculated the positions of the five projection points on the Piri Re'is Map both by plane and by spherical trigonometry. Each time it seemed that the calculations by spherical trigonometry were at variance with the geography of the map. The following comparison will illustrate the point. It was made in 1960, on the assumptions that the center of the map was at Syene, on the Tropic of Cancer in Long 32½° E, that the radius of the circle was drawn from this point to the North Pole, and that the base line for latitude was the Piri Re'is Equator.

| Plane Trigonometry | Spherical Trigonometry |
|---|---|
| 1. 50.9 N; 30.5 W | 1. 28.1 N; 46.1 W |
| 2. 25.7 N; 36.4 W | 2. 18.7 N; 42.0 W |
| 3.  0.0 N; 34.4 W | 3.  0.0 N; 34.0 W |
| 4. 22.1 S; 18.5 W | 4. 18.2 S; 23.1 W |
| 5. 37.0 S;  2.6 E | 5. 32.9 S; 07.1 W |

We see that by plane trigonometry the maximum spread of latitude is 87.9 degrees, and that of longitude is 39 degrees. By spherical trigonometry, on the other hand, the spread of latitude is only 71 degrees while the spread of longitude is 53.2 degrees. Thus the effect of the use of spherical trigonometry would be to compress latitude and exaggerate longitude in a way that apparently does not fit the map at all.

# 6   Strachan on the Construction of the Piri Re'is Grid

"I just received your letter (of 7-30-60), and thought that I'd better write and clear up some misunderstandings on your part. You seem to feel that the grid which Frank [Ryan] drew lines up pretty closely with the locations of the points which I figured out, *which is true*, but that the grid was figured pretty independently of the latitudes and longitudes of the points, *which is false*. The fact is, that the grid was *derived* from the latitude and longitude of the points. They are directly related, and had the Piri Re'is chart [the parchment on which the map is drawn] not stretched or shrunk some, they would coincide. And quite probably, some of the discrepancies are due to the relative inaccuracy of my math; that is, I worked only to slide rule accuracy which is not extremely precise. The mathematicians have a name for what was done to finally draw the grid; it is a conversion from polar (or circular) to rectangular (or grid-like) coordinates. The actual conversion was in changing the locations of our five points as expressed on the circumference of a circle to their locations on a rectilinear grid, as in latitude and longitude by plane sailing. Let me go through the steps leading to the formation of the grid so that you will see what I mean.

1. We are given the locations of the five points with respect to another point (Syene). These positions are given in terms of distance (radius of circle) and in terms of angles. This relationship in terms of angles and distances is called *polar* (Syene being the pole here). We also know the location of Syene in latitude and longitude—the rectangular system. This is the key to our finding the latitude and longitude locations of the five points; it is the starting point.

2. As seen in the figure, we are able to find the latitude and longitude of each point in turn using our known distance and angle from Syene and applying a little trigonometry. If you don't follow the math or my notation system, just take my word for it. This gives us then the latitude and longitude of the five scattered points.

3. If we consider these points to be on a chart, as they are, we may draw a network of latitude and longitude lines through the points to the top and bottom and to the sides of the chart to our (now) blank latitude and longitude scales. Thus, we have five latitudes located on our latitude scale and five longitudes on our longitude scale. Now we are in business. We next measure with a ruler the distance on the chart between any two points on the latitude scale. Now we set up a simple proportion to find the chart length of one degree of latitude:

$$\text{Length of one degree} = \frac{\text{length between measured points}}{\text{degrees between measured points}}$$

And so we find the length of a degree of latitude on our latitude scale. We do the exact thing over again with the longitude scale to find the length of one degree of longitude on the chart.

4. Now, knowing the length of a degree of latitude and longitude on the chart scale, and knowing the latitudes and longitudes of five points, we can start at any point and draw in our latitude and longitude grid with spacing to suit our purposes. The latitudes and longitudes of our original five points should be the same as they actually are when we use the

grid which we have just constructed to find them.

Why do we find some discrepancies on the Piri Re'is chart between the actual (calculated) positions of the points and the positions of these points as found using the grid which Frank has drawn, after I have just proven that they must be the same? Well, if the assumptions which we used to find the positions of the five points are accurate, and if the points were originally drawn on the chart correctly, then either the chart has physically distorted (shrunk, warped, etc.) through the centuries, or the precision of the mathematics is not good enough. Actually, any of these errors may be suspect:

> *a*)   original assumptions inaccurate
> *b*)   chart not drawn accurately
> *c*)   chart distorted through age
> *d*)   insufficient mathematical precision

We can only hope to find where the error lies by comparing the positions of known points are given on the chart with the actual positions of these points. In my opinion, we will be able to find the cause of the error *if enough such positions are compared*.

After working with these minor problems and eventually solving them we hope, the BIG QUESTION still remains; who drew the original chart(s)? I wonder if we ever will know.''

# 7   Nordenskiöld on the Projection of Marinus of Tyre

Referring to the projection of Marinus of Tyre, which he identifies with Ptolemy's equidistant-rectangular, or equidistant-cylindrical projection, Nordenskiöld remarks:

> For the sake of brevity I shall name this projection after Marinus of Tyre, who, according to Ptolemy, used if for his charts, but I suppose that it had already been employed earlier, unknown cartographers. The meridians and parallels are equidistant straight lines, forming right angles to each other, and so drawn that the proper ratio between the degrees of latitude and longitude are maintained on the map's mean or main parallel. When the equator is selected for this purpose the net of graduation becomes quadratic. The 26 special maps in an older manuscripts of Ptolemy are drawn on this projection. . . . (147:85)

There may well be some connection between the oblong grids found by us on the Piri Re'is and Chinese maps, and in the Spanish sector of the ben Zara Map, and the projection described here by Nordenskiöld. In this connection our solution of the De Canerio Map raises a problem, for in its case a solution by spherical trigonometry yielded a similar oblong grid.

# 8   Route of the Norwegian-British-Swedish Queen Maud Land Expedition

The expedition, with equipment for taking depth soundings through the ice cap, left Maudheim, on the coastal ice shelf, at 71° S. Lat., and 11° W. Long. (just northeast of Cape Norvegia). They crossed some shelf ice in an east-southeasterly direction, and reached the 500-meter contour line of the continental ice cap at 71.5° S., and 7° W. Directly east of here, at distances of 4 and 5 degrees were the Witte Peaks and Stein's Nunataks. Slightly to the northeast, at a distance of 3 degrees of longitude were the Passat and Boreas Nunataks. These were all comparatively low features. Here the expedition was 150 kilometers from

Maudheim. The profile showed that for another fifty kilometers the surface of the continent was below sea level. At one point (A, in Fig. 45) the ice extended 1,000 meters below sea level.

Just before the expedition reached the 1,000-meter contour, they passed over a subglacial "island" rising a couple of hundred meters above sea level. This island would be at 6° W. and 71° 40′ S. and would measure about 30 km. across. Beyond this, to the 1,000-meter contour, the surface was again below sea level, for about 40 km. (B on Fig. 45).

Just after the 1,000-meter contour, the subglacial surface rose steeply above sea level, reaching an altitude under the ice of about 750 meters, or about half a mile. The expedition was now (when the surface came above sea level) about 225 km. from Maudheim. At 280 km. from Maudheim the surface again dipped below sea level (C on Fig. 45). The subglacial mountain, or mountain range, indicated here lay approximately in Lat. 72° S., and Long. 5–6° W., and was about 55 km. across from northwest to southeast. A relatively slight change in sea level (about 200 meters) from depression of the land or rise of the sea could have divided this land mass into two islands.

About 120 km. farther on, the group began to pass over a higher submerged mountain range. They established an advance base at a point where a mountain peak just reached the surface of the ice cap, still at an altitude of about 1,000 meters. This was in 72.3° S. Lat., and 3.5° W. Long. About 20 miles beyond this point the Regula Mountains were reached, with peaks rising to elevations of about two miles. The submerged mountains were certainly a part of the Regula Mountains covered by the ice. Three times more, after this, the surface dipped below sea level, indicating subglacial "islands." Naturally, the part traveled on the surface of the ice cap, and did not climb the peaks that showed above the surface of the ice eastward and westward of their line of march. At one point they were forced to detour to the west to avoid a high mountain, Shubert Peak (2,710 meters). To the west of them they passed Mount Ropke (2,280 meters), and farther on they passed Speiss Peak (2,420 meters) about 20 miles to the west. After this they reached Penck Trough, where again the surface dipped below sea level, and then reached the Neumeyer Escarpment, at an elevation of 2,500 meters, the beginning of the interior plateau. They had crossed New Schwabenland. The route ended in 74.3° S. and 0.5° E. at a point where the ice surface was about 2,700 meters above sea level.

If the southern part of the Piri Re'is Map represents this coast, then it shows terrain a considerable distance in both directions from this line. It shows the sea advanced to the base of the Neumeyer Escarpment, and the various mountains as islands. Toward the east a number of inland mountain ranges are shown, while to the west a peninsula may represent what is now Cape Norvegia or Maudheim (A in Fig. 45). If the inland mountain ranges are the Muhlig–Hofmann and Wholthat Ranges, then the Piri Re'is Map shows the Antarctic coast from about 10° W. to 15° E. Long.

# 9    Strachan on the Oronteus Finaeus Projection

"I was very interested to have the opportunity to see for the first time a picture of the Oronteus Finaeus Map of 1531. The chart projection, as Nordenskiöld clearly states, and again as noted by Captain Burroughs, is the Cordiform Projection. This projection appears to be some modified form of the simple conic projection; the parallels of latitude are circles centered at the pole and equally spaced as in the conic; however, the meridians are curved (with the exception of the 90th) in the Finaeus while being straight in the simple conic. The meridional curvature is designed to minimize the area distortion of the projection. Nordenskiöld credits Ptolemy's "homeother" projection as the basis for the cordiform. In any event the Cordiform Projection is probably derived mathematically, requiring the use of geometry and trigonometry to transcribe accurately the features of the earth (i.e., a sphere) onto it.

"Coming to the main question at hand, we ask how did Oronteus Finaeus draw his map? It is apparent that Oronteus used some earlier source map. This we must concede. We must presume that the source map was equipped with a grid of some sort; it must have had one to have been drawn originally and there would seem to be no reason to have removed it. The simplest method of transferring a map or figure from one grid to another is by point to point transference. This is to say, a point located at a given latitude and longitude on the source map must be relocated to the same latitude and longitude on the secondary grid, regardless of the relative shapes of the grids. This process does not require knowledge of cartography or mathematics; any child can do it. This appears to me to be a logical method of transcription, and is the way that I would do it. Notice that this neither involves nor introduces in any way any new knowledge. It is merely a way of transplanting data from one grid to another and does not depend upon the shapes of the grids, or upon any method by which the original intelligence was placed upon the primary grid. By this theory, Oronteus Finaeus could not have correctly located the South Pole as nearly as he did by his own knowledge. He merely placed it as shown on his source map. And he need not have known a bit of mathematics to have accomplished this job.

# 10 Nordenskiöld on the First World Map of Oronteus Finaeus

Several years before the publication of the cordiform map [his map of 1538] Oronteus Finaeus had constructed another map also on Werner's second projection, but modified in such a manner that the map of the world here is divided into two parts, the one embracing the northern hemisphere, with the North Pole for a centre of the parallel circles, and the other, the southern hemisphere, with the South Pole as a centre. It is of this map that a facsimile is given on Pl. XLI [our Fig. 48]. It is dated 1531, but is generally found inserted in *Novus Orbis Regionem ac Insularum veteribus incognitarum, Parisiis, 1532*. It was afterwards reprinted from the same block, but with a new title legend from which the name of Oronteus was omitted, in the edition of the Geography of Glareanus printed Brisgae 1536, and in an edition of *Pomponius Mela, Parisiis apud Christianum Wechelum 1540*.

"The map of Oronteus Finaeus finally had the honour of being copied, although with some modifications, by Gerard Mercator, for one of his first maps, of which I give a facsimile on Plate XLIII. . . . (147)

# 11 Attempts to Adapt the Twelve-Wind System to the Compass

N. H. de Vaudry Heathecote, B.S., University College, London, in an essay on *Early Nautical Charts* (89) found references to the use of the twelve-wind system on the compass. After discussing the usual 32-point compass card he says:

"Another system appears to have been in use in which the 'wind' was divided, not into four quarter-winds, but into six 'sixth winds', so that there were *two* points on the compass card between, for example, N.W. and N.N.W. instead of the single point corresponding to N.W. by N. I have myself seen only one chart marked according to this division of the compass; it is contained in a collection of charts by various Venetian cartographers of the second half of the 15th century (British Museum MS, Egerton 73, fol. 36). Breusing says (Breusing, 'La Toleta de Martelio', Zeitsch, f. wiss. Geog. 2, 129) that this was the French system. It strikes me as less convenient than the Mediterranean system and certainly does not appear to have been in very wide use."

# 12   Hough's Interpretation of the Ross Sea Cores

The log of core N-5 shows glacial marine sediment from the present to 6,000 years ago. From 6,000 to 15,000 years ago the sediment is fine-grained with the exception of one granule at about 12,000 years ago. This suggests an absence of ice from the area during that period, except perhaps for a stray iceberg 12,000 years ago. Glacial marine sediment occurs from 15,000 to 29,500 years ago; then there is a zone of fine-grained sediment from 30,000 to 40,000 years ago, again suggesting an absence of ice from the sea. From 40,000 to 133,500 years ago there is glacial marine material, divided into two zones of coarse- and two zones of medium-grained texture.

The period 133,000–173,000 years ago is represented by fine-grained sediment, approximately half of which is finely laminated. Isolated pebbles occur at 140,000, 147,000, and 156,000 years. This zone is interpreted as recording a time during which the sea at this station was ice free, except for a few stray bergs, when the three pebbles were deposited. The laminated sediment may represent seasonal outwash from glacial ice on the Antarctic continent.

Glacial marine sediment is present from 173,000 to 350,000 years ago, with some variation in the texture. Laminated fine-grained sediments from 350,000 to 420,000 years ago may again represent rhythmic deposition of outwash from Antarctica in an ice-free sea. The bottom part of the core contains glacial marine sediment dated from 420,000 to 460,000 years by extrapolation of the time scale from the younger part of the core (96:257–59).

# 13   Gerard Mercator

Gerard Kramer (1512–1594), who took the name of Gerardus Mercatorius, and is known as Mercator, was the leading cartographer of the 16th century and the founder of scientific cartography. He deserves this title because of his invention of the famous "Mercator Projection," still the most widely used of all map projections, especially for purposes of navigation.

According to Asimov (16:58–59) Mercator was at first under the influence of Ptolemy. However, he seems to have abandoned the Ptolemaic ideas sometime after he established a center for geographical studies at Louvain in 1534. From a comparison of his maps with the portolan charts, it is my impression that he probably abandoned Ptolemy because he realized the superiority of the protolanos. It seems evident, not only from his maps of the Antarctic, but also from his maps of South America, that he made use of the ancient maps. It would seem, in the latter case, that he used an ancient map in 1538, but abandoned it in favor of the explorers' accounts in his 1569 Atlas.

Mercator's maps were unique in their artistry. They incorporated, however, the 16th century misconception of the size of the earth, as we have seen. In consequence, his distances are in fact less accurate than those of the ancient maps, which were based on a comparatively accurate estimate of the circumference. Mercator, then, while he laid the basis for modern scientific cartography, did not attain the technical level of the ancients.

It would be a matter of great interest to discover his source maps. In the hope of doing so, my student, Alfred Isroe, transferred from Keene State College to the University of Amsterdam, and spent a considerable time during the academic year 1964–1965 in a search of them. Despite the excellent cooperation of the Dutch authorities, the search was fruitless, and it appears that the source maps may have perished. If so, this would be only one more instance of the careless treatment of ancient manuscripts of practical or scientific value in the Renaissance. The humanists devoted themselves to collecting and restoring the manuscripts of ancient classical literature, but their interest rarely extended to physical science. Between the religious frenzy of the Reformation and the aristocratic bias of the humanists, the printing presses, as already mentioned, were largely monopolized by non-scientific material. Thus, the Renaissance was not only an age of recovery of ancient learning, but also possibly a period in which a large part of the scientific heritage of the past was lost.

# 14   The Twelve-Wind System

It appears that there may be a connecting link between the body of ancient maps we have discussed and the remote civilization from which they may have been derived; that link is the so-called "twelve-wind system." This system appears to stem from the farthest antiquity.

To begin with, scholars have long been aware of the fact that the type of portolan design known as the "eight-wind system" and used in the portolan charts of the Middle Ages and the Renaissance was preceded, in antiquity, by another type, the twelve-wind system, which we have discussed. No portolano based on the twelve-wind system was known until we discovered that system in the Venetian Chart of 1484.[1] The presence of the twelve-wind system in this chart, plus the fact that it proved to have been constructed by trigonometry, is good evidence of its origin in antiquity.

Now, from the standpoint of the history of science, the twelve-wind system is of very special importance. This system involved, as we have previously pointed out, the division of the circle into twelve arcs of 30 degrees each, or six arcs of 60 degrees. (See Fig. 65.) It involved the division of the circle into 360 degrees. This fact relates the system, in most interesting fashion, to Babylonian science. The Babylonians had a numbering system based on sixty, and on decimals. They are supposed to have invented the 360-degree circle, and the divisions of time we still use today.

The Babylonians also had a zodiac, and this was divided into twelve signs of 30 degrees each. The constellations of the zodiac did not precisely coincide with the twelve signs, as was natural enough, since the latter were mathematical divisions.

Now the stars were used in ancient times, in navigation, as E. G. R. Taylor points out (199:40), and so the zodiac and the other constellations of the northern and southern hemispheres (Note 18) were a sort of map written in the sky.* The relationships of the Babylonians and Phoenicians in ancient times were very close, and we can easily imagine that the Phoenicians might have applied these basic elements of Babylonian science to mapmaking. The result of any such effort would have been the twelve-wind system.

We must not allow ourselves to be confused by the fact that the 360-degree circle is used in modern navigation. This method of dividing the circle is not modern; it is the oldest way of dividing the circle known to man. Furthermore, since it involves counting by tens, it alone can explain how the ancient source map of the Antarctic, probably drawn ages before

1. But see Note 16.
* This idea was laborated by a little-known 19th century writer, W. S. Blacket (32).

either Phoenicians or Babylonians existed, had on it the circle that Oronteus Finaeus took for the Antarctic Circle, but which was have shown coincides with the 80th parallel. The implication from this is that the 360-degree circle and the twelve-wind system were ancient before the rise of Babylonia and long before Tyre and Sidon were built by the Phoenicians. Babylonian science was thus, perhaps, a heritage from a much older culture.

There are curious connections and comparisons that can be made between the ancient sciences of Greece, Egypt, Babylonia, and China, not to neglect either India or Central America. I have assembled some passages referring to these connections, showing particularly that both the Babylonians and the Chinese had numbering systems that could fit in very well with decimals of the twelve-wind system (see Note 15).

# 15   Dr. Marshall Clagett on Science in Antiquity

On Egyptian Geometry:

> The most advanced of the Egyptian mathematical achievements were in geometry....
> The Egyptians knew how to determine the areas and volumes of a number of figures; they could find the area of a triangle and a trapezium, the volume of a cylindrical granary and of the frustrum of a square pyramid, and perhaps even the area of the surface of a hemisphere (although the last is doubtful). Their proficiency in geometry was certainly fostered by their high development in architectural engineering and surveying. (52:26)

On Babylonian Mathematics:

> When we turn to Mesopotamia, we find from at least 1800 B.C. a Babylonian mathematics more highly developed than the Egyptian. Although it too had strong empirical roots that are clearly present in most of the tablets that have been published, it certainly seems to have tended to a more theoretical expression. The key to the advances made by the Babylonians in mathematics appears to have been their remarkably facile number system, which demands brief characterization.
> (1) Although it had certain features of both the decimal and sexagesimal systems, it was primarily a sexagesimal system. That is to say, it was based on sixty and powers of sixty.
> (2) It was a system highly general and abbreviatory in character. All numbers could be made with only two symbols. $\triangle = 1$ and $\triangleleft = 10$. Using these symbols the numbers from 1 to 59 can be represented thus: $\triangle \triangle = 2$; $\triangleleft \triangleleft \triangle = 21$; etc. Numerous tricks were used to save writing all the symbols out in a string. Not only could these symbols be used to represent numbers from 1 to 59, but they could also be used to write the numbers 1 to 59 times any power of 60. Thus, unless one knew what order of magnitude was being considered from the details of the problem being worked, he could not know whether the two symbols $\triangleleft \triangleleft$ by themselves on a tablet without supporting text equalled 20, or $20 \times 60$, or $20 \times 60^2$, or $20 \times 60^{-1}$, etc.
> What is more, these same symbols changed their value as their position changed; that is to say, this system was a place-value system, as is our own decimal system. In our system as the symbol changes position in the following numbers it changes its value in that it stands for a higher power of ten: 00.1, 1, 10, 100, etc. So in the number $\triangle \triangleleft \triangle$ the symbol $\triangle$ has the value of 1 in the last position and sixty the first position, the whole number being 71 (if the $\triangle$ in the last position represents 60, then the $\triangle$ in the first position represents $60^2$ and the whole number is $4260:60^2$ plus $11 \times 60$).

It was not until very late that the Babylonian system developed what in the decimal system is called zero—i.e., a sign for the absence of any units of a given power of ten indicated by position; thus in our system 101 means of course one hundred, no tens, and one unit. Instead of using that sign we could agree that we would simply leave a space, writing 1 1. This was done until the very last stages of the Babylonian system, when a zero sign or its equivalent was developed. . . .

Freed from the drudgery of calculation by this really remarkable system of calculation . . . the Babylonians made extraordinary advances in algebra. . . . (52:28–30)

B. L. van der Waerden sums up the characteristics of Babylonian astronomy thus:

. . . The fundamental ideas of Babylonian Astronomy are: the idea of the periodical return of celestial phenomena, the artificial division of the Zodiac into 12 signs of 30 degrees each, the use of longitude and latitude as coordinates of stars and planets, and the approximation of empirical functions by linear, quadratic and cubic functions, computed by means of arithmetical progressions of first, second, and third order. (216:50)

Needham notes the early appearance in China of a number system with affinities to the Babylonian:

. . . Decimal place-value and blank space for the zero had begun in the land of the Yellow River earlier than anywhere else, and decimal metrology had gone along with it. By the first century B.C. Chinese artisans were checking their work with sliding calipers decimally graduated. Chinese mathematical thought was always profoundly algebraic; not geometrical. . . . (145:118–119)

We see here suggestions that Babylonian and Chinese science were linked, either through contemporary contacts or through inheritance from a common source.

Taking Babylonian, Chinese, Egyptian, and Greek science together, we may note that there was a very considerable development of geometry in Egypt, but apparently no algebra. There was a remarkable development of algebra in Babylonia and in China, but no special development of geometry. Remarkable likenesses existed in the number systems of Babylonia and China, but this number system had no similarity to that of Egypt.

We have seen that the science reflected in the maps implies, however, the possession of all of these elements by *one culture*. Geometry is present in the portolan design; the Babylonian division of the Zodiac is present in the twelve-wind system; so are the units of sixty (six units of sixty in the circle). The included decimal system for counting the 360 degrees of the circle are present in the Oronteus Finaeus Map (for, as we have seen, the 80th parallel must have been drawn on that map by the people who mapped Antarctica).

It is possible that what we have here is evidence that all these different scientific achievements were once the possessions of the unknown people who originally drew these maps, and that, in the dissolution of their culture, various remnants survived, some in one place, some in another? Let us suppose that a "carrier people"—an intermediary people (like the seafaring Phoenicians)—were the ones to inherit all these aspects of science from the ancient source. Let us further suppose that the "carrier people" brought this science, by trade contacts, separately to our known civilizations of antiquity; the Babylonians and the Chinese took some elements of this ancient heritage, the Egyptians others, and American Indian peoples perhaps still others. We must not, of course, omit India. It is here, apparently, that our symbol for zero appeared, and it is in India more than in any other country on earth that the traditions of an ancient great world civilization are still preserved.

# 16   Cummings on the Pyramid of Cuicuilco

In his report (56:40) Cummings, after describing the excavation of successive pavements about the Pyramid of Cuicuilco, writes:

... "These six pavements, with their six corresponding shrines, all lying at different levels below the carbonized stratum that indicates the time of the eruption of Xitli and the coming of the Pedrigal, speak in a language that is clear and convincing. The lowest pavement lies more than 18 feet below the surface. Eighteen feet of gradual fill on top and 12 to 20 feet of debris overlying the base, all accumulated probably before the Christian era, and the composite condition of the structure itself, bespeak a lapse of time that pushes its builders back into the dim beginnings of things in the Valley of Mexico."

Cummings' further comments on the probable age of the pyramid should be quoted in full.

### The Great Age of the Temple

"Cuicuilco tells its own story quite clearly. Its crude cyclopean masonry without mortar of any kind, its massive conical form, and its great elevated causeways for approach instead of staircases, all demonstrate that the structure was the work of primitive men, and that its builders hardly knew the rudiments of architecture. Its base lies buried beneath from 15 to 20 feet of accumulated debris, which in turn was covered with three lava flows that have crowded around its slopes and piled up upon each other in rapid succession to the depth of 10 to 20 feet. The old temple has been so completely covered with rock and soil, volcanic ash and pumice in successive strata that the noses of the lava streams as they pushed around the mound and crawled up its slopes were nowhere able to touch the walls of the ancient structure. Centuries must have elapsed and several eruptions of old Ajusco must have buried its platforms and slopes under successive mantles of ash and pumice before Xitli poured fourth its baptisms of fire. Two and a half to 3 feet of surface soil have accumulated above this scorched and blackened stratum that marks the footprints of Xitli's consuming blasts. Careful measurements were taken in several places of this accumulation since the eruption of Xitli, and of the accumulation directly beneath between the pavement surrounding the temple and the blackened stratum just underlying the lava, and the story was always the same. If it has taken 2,000 years for the deposit to form since the eruption of Xitli, then by the same yardstick it took some 6,500 years for the debris beneath the lava to have accumulated, and so Cuicuilco fell into ruins some 8,500 years ago. But some will say, 'What evidence have we that the deposit overlying the structure beneath the lava did not form rapidly on account of successive showers of volcanic ash?' True, volcanic deposits played their part, but the presence of three strata of rock and organic soil containing stone implements, pottery and figurines of three quite different types of workmanship, and separated by two thick barren strata of volcanic ash and pumice mingled with streaks of sand, indicates the passing of centuries rather than months or years. The two massive enlargements of the temple, and the repeated reinforcement of the great causeways leading to the top of the structure, represent no brief period of the active use of this ancient center of religious ceremonials. The presence of 18½ feet of deposit on top of the original platform, and the six successive pavements with their corresponding platforms or altars, all buried therein before Xitli erupted, demonstrates further the long use of this lofty pile as a sacred gathering place. The late Mrs. Nuthall, a noted Aztec scholar, found that the word Cuicuilco, signified a place for singing and dancing. Everything about the structure bears out that interpretation. Here men and women met to pay tribute to the great spirits who, they thought, controlled their lives and their destinies. Here they danced and sang in honor of their gods and for the benefit of their fellow men seemingly through many centuries of time. Cuicuilco stands out as a monument to the religious zeal and to the organized power and perserverance of the earliest inhabitants of the Valley of Mexico. It is a great temple that records devotion to their gods and subservience to the will of great leaders. It shows the beginning of that architecture that developed into the pyramids and altars of Teotihuacan. It certainly gives evidence of being the oldest temple yet uncovered on the American continent. Everything about it so far revealed bears out its great antiquity, and it should serve as a strong incentive to the further investigation of the archaic culture of Mexico."

There has been much speculation as to the possible connections of the pyramids of Mexico, Egypt and China. If the Pyramid of Cuilcuilco is as old as Cummings suggests it may be linked with the world-wide culture of the ancient time when the maps we have studied were first composed. It is astonishing that archeologists have as yet taken no notice of Cummings' report, which was published 45 years ago. I have never met a specialist in American archeology who is familiar with it.

# 17  Brogger on an Ancient "Golden Age" of Navigation

Vilhjalmur Stefansson (192) mentioned a reference by a Norwegian historian to a great age of navigation in ancient times:

"To those of us brought up in the pedagogic tradition of forty and more years ago, where navigation of the high seas was supposed to have started with the Phoenicians, it is more than a little against the grain to believe that man swarmed over at least three of the oceans, the Atlantic, Indian, and Pacific, during remote periods. In fact, about the only group of scholars to whom that type of thinking appears to be natural or ingrained is the archaeologists, particularly those who devote themselves to the late Stone and various Bronze ages. . . .

"Professor A. W. Brogger created no great stir, or at least aroused no storm of protest, when at an international congress of archaeologists at Oslo in 1936 he lectured, as president of the congress, about a golden age of deep-sea navigation which he thinks may have been at its height as much as three thousand years before Christ and which was on the decline after 1500 B.C., so that the very period which we used to selected as the beginning of real seamanship, the Phoenician, is shown as having been (by that theory) at the bottom of a curve, which thereafter rose slowly until it attained a new high in the navigational cycle of the Viking Age which started less than fifteen hundred years ago.

"That man of the Old World discovered the Americas, from Brazil to Greenland, during Brogger's golden age of navigation five thousand years ago, and perhaps earlier, rests merely on possibilities and probabilities. As yet we cannot prove it certain, though we can prove it likely."

NB. In the course of research on the maps, much attention was paid to ancient navigation and ship building, particularly to the influence that the Phoenicians may have exerted on the Greeks in these areas. For reasons of space it seemed best to eliminate a detailed discussion of them in this volume, but some of the references have been retained in the Bibliography (Nos. 34, 38, 41, 49, 86, 99, 102, 114, 190, 211–3).

# 18   The Constellations as Denoters of Latitude on the Piri Re'is Map

In the light of the apparent connection of the twelve-wind system with the signs of the ancient Babylonian zodiac, and because of various evidences that sailors in ancient times used the constellations in navigation, it would not be particularly strange to find that the representations of the constellations were used on ancient maps. Some of these representations seem to be suggested by the ships and animals on the Piri Re'is Map.

This suggestion was first made to me by the late Archibald T. Robertson, of Boston, a scholar in the esoteric lore of ancient navigation and astronomy. He suggested that Piri Re'is might have copied (and misinterpreted) some of his animals and ships from the ancient source maps he used, adding others to suit his fancy.

Robertson suggested that the great snake shown in what we take to be Queen Maud Land, Antarctica, may have originally been intended to represent the constellation Hydra (the Snake), a constellation which is visible in the southern sky (during the spring equinox of the Northern Hemisphere) only in Lat 70°–72° S, the correct latitude of the Queen Maud Land coast. The ship lying off the coast of what looks like Argentina, he suggested, might represent the constellation Argo (the Ship), visible at that season in Lat 55° S, as would be correct. Following this line of reasoning, we might suggest that other ancient constellations might be represented by the bull in the center of Brazil (Taurus) and the wolf-like creature in the south (Lupus). The bull is shown in the equatorial region of Brazil, which would be correct, since Taurus is an animal of the Zodiac.

It would be natural for Piri Re'is, or any other Arab, Medieval, or Renaissance mapmaker, to misunderstand these figures on the ancient source maps, and to take them for references to historical events or local fauna. It would be natural for them to add others of their own, which, as we have seen, Piri Re'is did. For the unfamiliar ships on the source maps, he might have quite naturally substituted those he knew, the ships of the 16th century, connecting them with known or presumed historical events, such as the voyages of St. Brendan and Diaz. He seems also to have drawn upon the medieval bestiaries for fabulous animals, in accordance with the habits of mapmakers of his day.

# 19   Endorsement by Officers of the Cartographic Staff of Strategic Air Command

"Your request for evaluation of certain unusual features of the Piri Reis World Map of 1513 by this organization has been reviewed.

"The claim that the lower part of the map portrays the Princess Martha Coast of Queen Maud Land Antarctica, and the Palmer Peninsula is reasonable. We find this is the most logical and in all probability the correct interpretation of the map.

"The geographical detail shown in the lower part of the map agrees very remarkably with the results of the Seismic profile made across the top of the ice cap by the Swedish-British-Norwegian Antarctic Expedition of 1949.

"This indicates the coastline had been mapped before it was covered by the ice cap.

"The ice cap in this region is now about a mile thick. We have no idea how the data on this map can be reconciled with the supposed state of geographical knowledge in 1513."
HAROLD Z. OHLMEYER *Lt. Colonel, USAF*
*Commander, 8th Reconnaissance Technical Squadron (SAC),*
*Westover, Mass.*

"It is not very often that we have an opportunity to evaluate maps of ancient origin. The Piri Reis (1513) and Oronteus Fineaus [*sic*] (1531) maps sent to us by you, presented a delightful challenge, for it was not readily conceivable that they could be so accurate without being forged. With added enthusiasm we accepted this challenge and have expended many off duty hours evaluating your manuscript and the above maps. I am sure you will be pleased to know we have concluded that both of these maps were compiled from accurate original source maps, irrespective of dates. The following is a brief summary of our findings:

*a*. The solution of the portolano projection used by Admiral Piri Reis, developed by your class in Anthropology, must be very nearly correct; for when known geographical locations are checked in relationship to the grid computed by Mr. Richard W. Strachan (MIT), there is remarkably close agreement. Piri Reis' use of the portolano projection (centred on Syene, Egypt) was an excellent choice, for it is a developable surface that would permit the relative size and shape of the earth (at that latitude) to be retained. It is our opinion that those who compiled the original map had an excellent knowledge of the continents covered by this map.

*b*. As stated by Colonel Harold Z. Ohlmeyer in his letter (July 6, 1960) to you, the Princess Martha Coast of Queen Maud Land, Antarctica, appears to be truly represented on the southern sector of the Piri Reis Map. The agreement of the Piri Reis Map with the seismic profile of this area made by the Norwegian-British-Swedish Expedition of 1949, supported by your solution of the grid, places beyond a reasonable doubt the conclusion that the original source maps must have been made before the present Antarctic ice cap covered the Queen Maud Land coasts.

*c*. It is our opinion that the accuracy of the cartographic features shown in the Oronteus Fineaus [*sic*] Map (1531) suggests, beyond a doubt, that it also was compiled from accurate source maps of Antarctica, but in this case of the entire continent. Close examination has proved the original source maps must have been compiled at a time when the land mass and inland waterways of the continent were relatively free of ice. This conclusion is further supported by a comparison of the Oronteus Fineaus [*sic*] Map with the results obtained by International Geophysical Year teams in their measurements of the subglacial topography. The comparison also suggests that the original source maps (compiled in remote antiquity) were prepared when Antarctica was presumbaly free of ice. The Cordiform Projection used by Oronteus Fineaus [*sic*] suggests the use of advanced mathematics. Further, the shape given to the Antarctic continent suggests the possibility, if not the probability, that the original source maps were compiled on a stereographic or gnomonic type of projection (involving the use of spherical trigonometry).

*d*. We are convinced that the findings made by you and your associates are valid, and that they raise extremely important questions affecting geology and ancient history, questions which certainly require further investigation.

We thank you for extending us the opportunity to have participated in the study of these maps. The following officers and airmen volunteered their time to assist Captain Lorenzo W. Burroughs in this evaluation: Captain Richard E. Covault, CWO Howard D. Minor, MSgt Clifton M. Dover, MSgt David C. Carter, TSgt James H. Hood, SSgt James L. Carroll, and AlC Don R. Vance."

LORENZO W. BURROUGHS
*Captain, USAF*
*Chief, Cartographic Section*
*8th Reconnaissance Technical Sqdn (SAC)*
*Westover, Mass.*

## 20    Biographical Note on Piri Re'is from the Turkish Embassy, Washington

"In reply to your letter of October 16, 1964, I am pleased to enclose a photocopy of the Piri Reis Map received recently from Ankara.

"To the best of our knowledge the original map has been drawn on gazelle hide.

"A short biographical information on Piri Reis is given below which we think might be of interest to you.

"He was born at the town of Karaman, near Konya, Turkey. The exact date of his birth is unknown. In his early youth he joined his uncle Kemal Reis, a well known pirate. He distinguished himself during the operations of his uncle's small fleet on French and Venetian coasts. When Kemal Reis had abandoned piracy and joined the Imperial Ottoman Fleet during the reign of Beyazit II (1481–1512) Piri Reis followed suit and was appointed captain. The battles of Modon and Inebahti (Lepanto) made him famous. According to historian Von Hammer, 'he gained an awesome fame' for his deeds in these expeditions.

"Piri Reis, whose real name was Ahmet Muhiddin, stayed with the Ottoman Fleet during the reigns of Yavuz Selim (1512–1520) and Suleiman the Magnificent (1520–1566). He served as an aide to Barbaros Hayrettin Pasha, Great Admiral of the Imperial Ottoman Fleet. In 1551 he was elevated to the rank of Commander in Chief of the Fleet of Egypt, then a dependency of the Ottoman Empire. In an expedition launched the same year with 31 vessels he seized the port of Masqat on the Arap peninsula and laid siege to the islands of Hurmuz in the Persian Gulf. The islanders offered him treasures, which he accepted as spoils of war and lifted the siege. On his way back, news reached him that a powerful Portuguese fleet had blockaded the entrance to the Persian Gulf. He loaded up all the treasures he had gotten from the islanders on three ships and leaving the remaining 28 in Basra he sailed to Istanbul. While passing through the Portuguese blockade he lost one of his vessels but managed to return safely to Egypt with the other two. The Governor of Egypt, one of his political opponents, misrepresented the facts to the Emperor in Istanbul reporting that 'Piri Reis had returned with only 2 ships though he sailed at the beginning with 31,' without mentioning the treasures he had brought with him. Emperor Suleiman flew into a rage and in a fit of anger ordered his execution, thus committing one of the very few fateful mistakes of his 46 years rule. Piri Reis was executed in Egypt in 1554.

" 'Kitabi Bahriye—The Navy's Book,' which is the most famous of his works, is considered as an excellent geography book of his times. He also prepared a map of the world which has been reproduced in recent years. He wrote many poems too."

## 21    The "Lost Map" of Columbus?

Admiral Morison, the historian, is authority for the statement that all of Columbus' maps, except possibly one of Santo Domingo, were lost. However, the late James H. Campbell, who collaborated with me in the research for *Earth's Shifting Crust*, may actually have seen the famous "lost map" that persuaded the sovereigns, Ferdinand and Isabella, to finance Columbus' trip to the western ocean. Campbell's statement, written in April, 1960, describes an event of his youth, as follows:

"The Spanish Government built and sent over to this country for exhibition at the

Columbian Exhibition at Chicago in 1893, three replicas of Columbus' vessels. There was the *Santa Maria*, which was the largest of the three; then there was the *Pinta*, and I think the third one was the *Nina*. They came to Chicago by way of the St. Lawrence River and the Great Lakes, and as they were passing through Lake Ontario they stopped at Toronto. My brother, who was on the reception committee of the Royal Canadian Yacht Club, met the officers and they made him promise that when he went to Chicago to see the Fair, he would call on them. The Fair was open for six months, and as near as I can remember my brother came to Chicago about the end of July or the first week of August. My father was living in Chicago at the time, and was employed by one of the publishing houses.

"When my brother came to Chicago to visit the Exhibition my father and I went along with him, as he was going to pay a visit to the officers of the caravels.

"The caravels were tied up alongside of the Agricultural Building and right next to the boathouse of the Electric Launch and Navigation Co. Since I was in charge of the electric launches I was able to guide them directly to the caravels.

"We went aboard the *Santa Maria*, and my brother introduced my father and me to the officers. When the officers learned that my father was a geographer and the author and publisher of geographies and other school books in Canada, they became much interested and asked my Dad if he would like to see Columbus' map. Up to this time my Dad had left the conversation to my brother and me, but after that the conversation was carried on between the officers and my Dad, and what made it worse when the Spaniards were at a loss to find words in English to express their thoughts, my Dad invited them to speak in French, and to their surprise they found out a little later that he could also speak Spanish, so that cut both my brother and me out of the conversation for the remainder of the visit.

"The officers invited us into the Chart Room, and took out a large map. As I remember it now, it was about four feet square. It covered most of the table that was situated in the center of the Chart Room. My Dad was very short sighted, so he pored over the chart with his nose almost touching the paper. He was tremendously pleased, but he didn't say very much, until we got home again, and then he said he had difficulty reading the map, not in understanding the language as he was a Spanish scholar, and had one time published a Spanish journal, and he also understood navigation, but he said he didn't have enough time to study the map. Nevertheless, he was overjoyed at having seen it. I might add that by father was an enthusiastic yachtsman, and at one time had contemplated making a trip around the world on his yacht, the *Oriole*. I am sorry I don't remember the names of the officers who showed us the map, but it is most likely that they signed the log at the Club House, and this has probably been preservd."

This fascinating and veridical account persuaded me to investigate this question. I wrote President Eisenhower, enclosing a photostatic copy of Campbell's statement, and later learned that the State Department had made an inquiry of the government of Spain. As nothing came of this I corresponded with the American Geographical Society, forwarding a copy of the statement. It was forwarded to the Society's Curator of Maps, who was then in London. She showed it to the Curator of Maps of the British Museum, Mr. R. A. Skelton, who suggested that I write to Admiral Julio F. Guillén, Director of the Museo Naval in Madrid. I did so but recieved no reply.

It seems to me quite possible that the Government of Spain has preserved a Columbus Map without imparting that information to scholars. This is unfortunate but similar cases are by no means unusual in the history of bureaucracy. It is to be hoped that someday this matter may be properly investigated.

From the foregoing account it does not seem likely that the map Campbell saw was the portolan-type chart of the Atlantic coasts of Europe and Africa which De la Roncière ascribed to Columbus, for this chart shows no land in the west.

# 22   The Scales of the Piri Re'is Map

When we started on the investigation of the Piri Re'is map it seemed best to ignore the scales placed upon it by Piri Re'is. We thought these were probably based on some contemporary measure of length and were not of ancient origin. However, early in 1972 I received a letter from a highly intelligent science student, Miss Barbara Beal, who inquired about these scales and I encouraged her to make them the subject of a research paper. She devoted a great deal of time to this project, and it has now led to some surprising results.

Miss Beal began by selecting ten pairs of clearly identifiable localities on the Piri Re'is Map, and finding the true air distance between these same pairs on the modern map. Taking the length of the unit shown in the Piri Re'is scales, she divided the true air distances by this unit. In this way she discovered that while there were differences in the value of the unit as found from the ten different pairs of localities on the Piri Re'is Map, differences due, in all probability, to inaccuracies in drawing or to stretching of the map after it was completed, nevertheless these differences were comparatively minor, and they averaged out to a length for the Piri Re'is unit of 48.82 or roughly 49 English statute miles of 5,280 feet.

Next, Miss Beal checked the scales against the Portuguese nautical mile of 6,758.7 feet, and from this found that each unit on the scales would equal about 40 Portuguese nautical miles.

Finally, she checked the scales against the Turkish nautical mile of 3,000 feet, and this resulted in a finding of 88 sea miles for each of the units. It is highly probable that Piri Re'is, as an admiral of the Turkish navy in an age when the Ottoman Empire was the leading power in Europe, would have used the Turkish sea mile. However, the scales do not conform to that sea mile, any more than they do to the Portuguese. It seems reasonable, therefore, to suppose that Piri Re'is simply transferred to his map the scales he found on one or another of his ancient maps, without understanding in the least what the unit represented.

We have seen that the Hamy-King Map, which has two equators, betrays evidence of having been put together from a number of ancient source maps by geographers of the Ptolemaic school. The fact that the Piri Re'is Map also has indications of two equators (and the same two) suggests that it also at one stage of its development went through the hands of the Ptolemaic school. We have seen that in the Hamy-King map, these geographers made use of Ptolemy's value for the length of the degree, one sixth shorter than the correct length.

Now let is suppose that the units in the Piri Re'is scales represent *degrees* rather than units of length. The length of the degree of longitude at the latitudes where the scales are shown equals about 60 miles. Miss Beal has shown that the unit in the scales equals about 48 miles or four-fifths of this degree of longitude. This comes very close to the length of the Ptolemaic degree, as we saw it applied in the Hamy-King Map.

On the other hand, there is another possibility. It looks almost as if the scales were placed so as to indicate True North in the Northern and Southern Hemispheres on the spherical surface of the earth, in which case they may be units of length used by some ancient and perhaps unknown people. Piri Re'is never put scales on any of the maps he drew for his *Bahriye*, and he could have had no reason to place the scales as we see them, for so far as he could he oriented his map to True North on a flat and not on a spherical projection.

# 23  Possible Polar Origin of the Vedic People

In 1898 Houghton Mifflin & Co. of Boston published the 11th edition of a work by Dr. William F. Warren, President of Boston University, entitled *Paradise Found: The Cradle of the Human Race at the North Pole*. Dr. Warren's book is not a piece of sensationalism or pseudo-science; it is a very serious systematic work for which he drew upon a very rich knowledge of ancient languages and literatures as well as on scientific studies in geography, geology, climatology, paleontology and anthropology. He cites evidence from Japanese and Chinese literature, and from Iranian, Akkadian, Assyrian, Babylonian, Egyptian and Greek thought. It looks as if he must have conscripted the assistance of a large part of the Boston College faculty! In its extraordinary range of evidence his book suggests the method and organization of Donnelly's famous work on Atlantis.

The book was widely circulated and helped to inspire a work by an accomplished Vedic scholar, B. G. Tilak. Tilak's book was entitled *The Arctic Home of the Vedas*. It was first published in 1903 and then republished in 1925 and 1956, at Poona, India, by a descendant, Shri J. S. Tilak. The author examines the Vedic evidence in full detail, and shows that it contains excellent descriptions of *polar* conditions, including the lengths of the polar day and polar night. This is, of course, very remarkable because we have no evidence of any polar explorations by the peoples of India.

Tilak appears to have been inspired originally by Warren in placing the home of the Vedas at the North Pole, and he never appears to have considered any alternative hypothesis. His argument is that the Vedic people were forced to abandon their polar home because of the coming of the ice age, that is the last ice age in North America, called the "Wisconsin Glaciation". In my book, *The Path of the Pole*, I have shown by radiocarbon and other evidence, that this ice age began at least 50,000 years ago, and this, of course, would imply an enormous age for the Vedic literary tradition. There is also the geological difficulty that there is at present no land at the North Pole.

If we assume, however, that original home of the Vedas was at the *South* Pole, that is, in Antarctica, the difficulties vanish, for there is plenty of land there, and the coming of the present great ice sheet, as I have shown both in this book and in *The Path of the Pole*, can be dated at between 10,000 and 15,000 years ago. Moreover, if a population possessing an advanced culture was emigrating from Antarctica, a voyage from the Antarctic coast to the tip of India (where India's oldest culture, the Dravidian was centered) across the Indian Ocean would have been much easier than crossing the continent of Asia from north to south, and crossing the vast Himalayan ranges, on foot, confronting on the way innumerable hostile tribes. The maps in this book show that an ancient advanced culture mapped virtually the whole earth (glaciated North America excepted), that its cartographers mapped a mostly deglacial Antarctica; for such a people crossing the Indian Ocean to the tip of India would have been no problem.

Although Warren's book is by no means negligible, Tilak's work is more scholarly because, except for its first three chapters, which are a rehash of outdated geology, he deals with material within his own special field of life-long study, the Vedic literature.

# 24   The Vinland Map

Before the recent controversy over the authenticity of the Vinland Map I had observed some interesting details of it. First, the European sector was a good copy of the Andrea Bianco Map of 1436, and second, the Far Eastern sector was a good representation of the coasts of the Sea of Japan, which gave evidence of having been originally drawn on a spherical projection of considerable sophistication. The so-called "Vinland" sector bore no relationship in style to the other two, being to all appearances a crudely drawn Norse sketch. It is my impression that the three parts of the map are authentic, but how or when they were combined and by whom I do not know.

# 25   Derek Allan on Knowledge of the Arctic

*Extracts of a letter to the Author:*
  "It is becoming increasingly clear that there is something drastically wrong with present theories regarding the antiquity of the Ice Age. It would seem to be quite a recent event. This is amply borne out by the maps. Here we have two maps (Finaeus, Ahmed), each showing the area to be ice free, and one drawn later, showing an ice cap (Mercator). (It is missing part of the North American coast due to there having been only ice there?)
  "I have compiled a composite map of the Arctic from these three maps, of the areas which roughly conform with the coastal outline as it is today. There has been no 'monkeying about' to make it fit, other than longitudinal adjustments—and a correction in latitude for Hudson Bay, and for Mercator. In fact, with further adjustments in latitude, the maps could be made even more accurate (e.g. Spitzbergen). I think the results are quite surprising, and suggest that the whole area must have been mapped—probably on more than one occasion.
  "By chance I compared the Hadji Ahmed map of the Americas with an azimuthal equidistant projection, centred on London; the resemblance is quite astonishing—they are almost identical. I rotated Hudson Bay on the Ahmed map into its original position. It is possible that the west coasts of Canada and Labrador were distorted to cover the missing parts of the Arctic.
  "It appears that a date can be placed before which the maps of North America could not have been drawn. Dr. J. Mansell Valentine, the marine archeologist of Miami, who has recently discovered many constructions on the sea bed off Bimini and Andros Island, places the date of these (by C-14) to 10,000—9,600 BPE—a significant date. There seems to be mounting evidence pointing at a catastrophic global disaster at the time. (E.g. the glaciation of Antarctica, the raising of the Andean Altiplano (Lake Titicaca, Tiahuanacu), the extinction of Toxodon and other exotics at Lagoa Santa, Brazil (*Cahiers de'archeologie d'Amerique de Sud*).)
  "As none of the maps of the Florida area show this as being above sea level, one must assume that the 'mapmakers' must have existed after this date. This leads one to speculate that perhaps the 'mapmakers' may have remapped the world after the disaster, which might account for different maps of the Arctic."

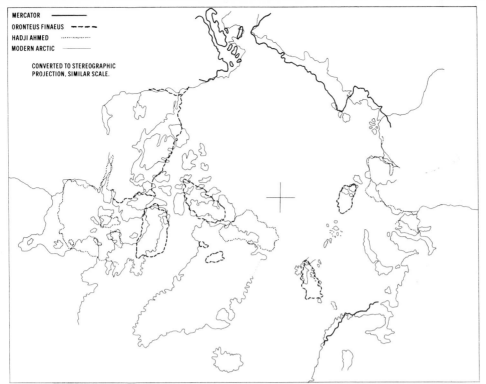

Figure 109. The Arctic as a compilation of Mercator, Oronteus Finaeus, Hadji Ahmed and a modern sterographic projection.

# 26   Advanced science in traditions of the Dogon

A recent work by Robert Temple, *The Sirius Mystery* (203a) illustrates the survival in an African tribe of astonishingly advanced scientific knowledge derived from an unknown source in remote antiquity. The Dogon, a people living in the Mali Republic near Timbuktu, are shown to have had a knowledge, from ancient tradition, of the dark companion of the star Sirius, a tiny star invisible to us. Mr. Temple has interpreted the evidence as indicating ancient extra-terrestial visits to earth, without considering a possible alternative. It seems, however, that it can be just as easily (and more convincingly) explained as knowledge surviving from the sciences of the advanced people who originated the maps studied in this book. The maps cannot be used as evidence of ancient extra-terrestrial visits to earth. They could have been drawn from the ground, using only spherical map projections, trigonometry, and accurate instruments for determining the latitudes and longitudes of places.

It appears that the invisible companion of Sirius (now called Sirius B) has very special importance to the Dogon, being central to their religious beliefs and rites. Their knowledge includes the fact that Sirius B travels in an elliptical orbit with Sirius as one of the foci of the ellipse. It seems that the Dogon also know the period of the revolution of Sirius B in its orbit, which is fifty years, and the fact that it rotates on its axis! Moreover, they know it's relative density, calling it the heaviest thing in the universe. It is in fact a white dwarf star.

The Dogon consider the moon to be dry and dead, that Saturn has a ring, that the planets revolve about the sun, and that the Milky Way is composed of distant stars. They know of four of the moons of Jupiter. They know of the circulation of blood and of the existence of red and white blood corpuscles. They believe that Sirius is the star where the souls of the dead go, and they believe space visitors from there brought all this knowledge to earth. However, these visitors were not human, but had tails. They were amphibious!

Temple has traced the Dogon's traditions back to pre-dynastic Egypt. Perhaps we can trace them to the much older civilization that produced the maps.

# The Mathematics of the Piri Re'is Map

## by Richard W. Strachan

Trigonometric projection based on the equator

### I

The Piri Re'is Map of 1513 is a typical portolano in appearance. The usual portolan chart is characterized by groups of eight, sixteen, or thirty-two lines radiating from one or more centers on the chart, like the spokes of a wheel. These lines, or rhumbs, are equally spaced at angles of 45, 22½ or 11¼ degrees apart. It has hitherto been supposed that this system of radial lines originated as actual course lines between various ports, that is, compass courses. It has not been supposed that any mathematical system underlay these portolan charts.

It is this assumption that has now been destroyed by the discoveries made by Professor Hapgood and his students. They have proved that, in the cases of several of these maps, the portolan design is based on geometry and may be translated by plane or spherical trigonometry into the terms of modern latitudes and longitudes.

### II

In the case of the Piri Re'is Map, Hapgood found that the five minor projection centers shown on the surviving fragment (its western section) evidently had been placed on the perimeter of a circle with a center somewhere to the eastward of the torn edge. Rhumbs from these points, when projected to the east, proved to meet in Egypt at the intersection of the Tropic of Cancer with the Meridian of Alexandria. It appeared from this that the complete map (which included Asia) may have had sixteen of these minor projection centers (22½ degrees apart) on the perimeter of the circle.

A mathematician would consider this graphically as a polar (or circular) type of construction. The problem was to convert this polar projection into the rectangular coordinate system which is used today. Reference points used in the rectangular coordinate system are located by intersection of lines of latitude and longitude, the lines which form the type of grid with which we are all familiar. It is not difficult to convert from polar to rectangular coordinates provided several points, angles, distances, or a combination of these factors are known. Hapgood made the following assumptions:

1. The center of the portolan grid was located at the intersection of the Tropic of Cancer and the Meridian of Alexandria, that is, at 23° 30′ N, 30° E.

2. The radius from this center to the perimeter of the circle on which the minor projection points are located is 69.5°, or 3° longer than the distance from the Tropic of Cancer to the North Pole. The drawing of the projection involved, then, an overestimate of the circumference of the earth amounting to about 4.5°.

3. Projection Point III on the map was presumed to lie precisely on the Equator.

With these assumptions, we have enough information to solve for the geographical positions (latitude and longitude) of all five projection points.*

Sketching in the knowns and unknowns on a triangle as shown below, we have:

---

* It appeared, after a trial, that as between plane and spherical trigonometry, plane trigonometry gave better results in terms of a grid fitting the geography. Therefore, in this case, we have used plane trigonometry. (See Note 5)

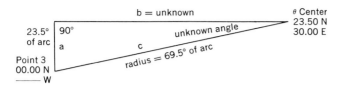

As seen in the figure, we know the length of the two sides of the triangle (which is a right triangle by construction). We may solve for the unknown angle, $\theta$, first, and knowing $\theta$ and the length of one side, we can find the length of side X, which you can see is the latitude difference between the center and Point III. We may solve as follows:

$$\text{Sin } \theta = \frac{a}{c} = \frac{23.50}{69.50} = .3381 \qquad \theta = 19.75$$

$$\text{Then } \cos \theta = \frac{b}{c} \qquad b = c \cos \theta = (69.5)(\cos 19.75)$$

$$b = (69.5)(.94108) = 65.41° \text{ of arc}$$

Subtracting the longitude of the center (since it is east Longitude) from the length of side b, we find the longitude of Point 3.

So:
$$\begin{array}{r} 65.41 \\ -30.00 \text{ E} \\ \hline 35.41 \text{ W} \end{array}$$

Thus we have the position of Point 3 to be:

**00.00 N** (given)
**35.41 W** (calculated)

The calculations for the other points are slightly different. For these calculations we know the length of one side of a triangle (which we construct), and the angle $\theta$, which we find by addition or subtraction knowing the original $\theta$, and knowing that the angles between the rhumb lines are $22\frac{1}{2}°$. The solution for Point II is illustrated.

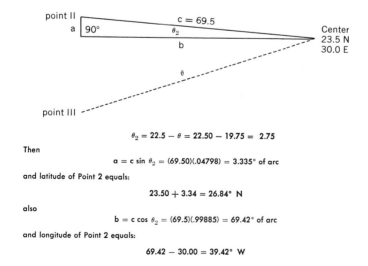

$$\theta_2 = 22.5 - \theta = 22.50 - 19.75 = 2.75$$

Then

$$a = c \sin \theta_2 = (69.50)(.04798) = 3.335° \text{ of arc}$$

and latitude of Point 2 equals:

$$23.50 + 3.34 = 26.84° \text{ N}$$

also

$$b = c \cos \theta_2 = (69.5)(.99885) = 69.42° \text{ of arc}$$

and longitude of Point 2 equals:

$$69.42 - 30.00 = 39.42° \text{ W}$$

The positions of the remaining points are:

| Point | Latitude | Longitude |
|-------|----------|-----------|
| 1 | 53.15 N | 32.86 W |
| 2 | 26.84 N | 39.42 W |
| 3 | 00.0 | 35.41 W |
| 4 | 23.09 S | 21.45 W |
| 5 | 39.36 S | 0.35 E |

III

Knowing the positions of the five points, it is necessary to know only one more thing to be able to construct the rectangular coordinate grid. This is the direction of True North on the Piri Re'is Map. Once Hapgood and his co-workers had established the North direction, it was a simple matter to draw in a grid, merely using the lines indicated on the map itself, which intersect the five projection points, running North-South or East-West.

*Supplement to Mathematical Considerations*: In calculating the positions of the five Projection Points on the Piri Re'is Map, based on the pole [see Fig. 17] we would proceed as follows for the new grid:

(1) Assume center position 23.5 N, 30.0 E.
(2) Assume length of radius, 69.5 degrees.
(3) Assume (decide from geometry I should say) point II to be on same latitude as tropic and center, i.e., rhumb from pt II goes through center, must be same latitude.
(4) Find longitude of *point II*.

$$\text{radius length} = 69.5$$

pt II ———————————————— 23.5 N
23.5 N                                    30. E
? longitude

$$\text{longitude } (\lambda) = 69.5° - 30° E = \boxed{39.5° W}$$

$$\boxed{L = 23.5° N \text{ from map}}$$

(5) Do other points similar to last time:

pt I — radius 69.5 — c
b
pt II — a — 23.5 N / 30.0 E
b
radius 69.5 — c
pt III

point I: $\sin \theta = \dfrac{b}{c}$; $b = c \sin \theta$
$$b = 69.5 \sin 22.5 = (69.5)(.3825)$$
$$b = 26.65$$

$$L = 23.5 + 26.65 = \boxed{50.15° N}$$

$$\cos = \dfrac{a}{c}; a = c \cos \theta$$
$$a = 69.5 \cos 22.5 = (69.5)(.9245)$$
$$a = 64.14$$

$$\lambda = 64.14 - 30.00 = \boxed{34.14° W}$$

point III: same calculation for a & b; they are the same (triangle for pt III is upside down from pt I)

thus b = 26.65

L = 26.65 − 23.50 = | 3.15° S |

a = 64.14

λ = 64.14 − 30.00 = | 34.14° W |

point IV:

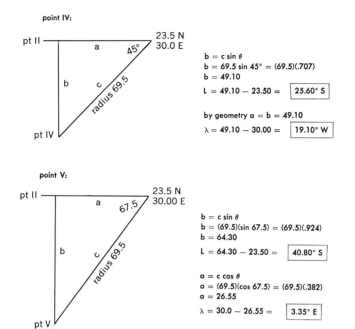

b = c sin θ
b = 69.5 sin 45° = (69.5)(.707)
b = 49.10
L = 49.10 − 23.50 = | 25.60° S |

by geometry a = b = 49.10
λ = 49.10 − 30.00 = | 19.10° W |

point V:

b = c sin θ
b = (69.5)(sin 67.5) = (69.5)(.924)
b = 64.30
L = 64.30 − 23.50 = | 40.80° S |

a = c cos θ
a = (69.5)(cos 67.5) = (69.5)(.382)
a = 26.55
λ = 30.0 − 26.55 = | 3.35° E |

These calculations are more accurate than those of my last letter. Note some small changes.

| Pt | L | |
|----|------|------|
| I | 50.15° N | 34.14° W |
| II | 23.50° N | 39.50° W |
| III | 3.15° S | 34.14° W |
| IV | 25.60° S | 19.10° W |
| V | 40.80° S | 3.35° E |

These figures, of course, had to be adjusted to take account of the Eratosthenian error of 4½% in the circumference of the earth. This was done by adding 4½% to latitudes from the North Pole and to longitudes from the meridian of Alexandria.

For the De Canerio Map

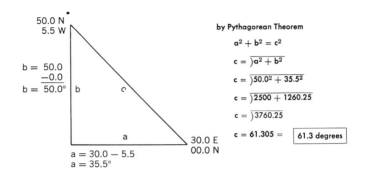

From the spherical trigonometry:

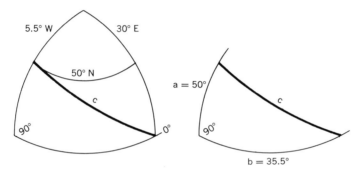

$$\cos c = \cos a \cos b$$

$$\log \cos a = 9.80807 - 10$$
$$\log \cos b = 9.91069 - 10$$
$$\overline{\log \cos c = 58 \quad 26'40''}$$
$$\text{(or about 58.4)}\dagger$$

---

* Calculation by E. A. Wixson.
† An independent calculation by Dr. John M. Frankland, of the Bureau of Standards, gave a closely similar result of 58° 27'.

# List of Geographical Tables

In some cases the identifications of geographical features in the following tables are merely suggestive. They are rendered probable by their positions on the grids rather than by strict physical resemblances. Fractions of degrees are given in decimals rather than in minutes for ease in computing averages.

## Table 1  Piri Re'is Map of 1513

| Locality | True Position | Piri Re'is Map | Errors |
|---|---|---|---|
| (a) AFRICA | | | |
| 1. Annobon Islands | 2.0 S 6.0 E | 2.0 S 0.0 | 0.0 6.0 W |
| 2. Cavally River | 4.0 N 8.0 W | 5.0 N 2.5 W | 1.0 N 5.5 E |
| 3. Cape Palmas | 7.0 N 11.0 W | 6.0 N 7.5 W | 1.0 S 3.5 E |
| 4. St. Paul River | 7.5 N 12.0 W | 6.0 N 9.0 W | 1.5 S 3.0 E |
| 5. Mano River | 8.5 N 15.5 W | 7.5 N 12.0 W | 1.0 S 3.5 E |
| 6. Freetown | 11.0 N 16.0 W | 10.0 N 15.0 W | 1.0 S 1.0 E |
| 7. Bijagos Islands | 13.5 N 16.5 W | 13.0 N 16.0 W | 0.5 S 0.5 E |
| 8. Gambia River | 15.0 N 17.0 W | 14.0 N 17.5 W | 1.0 S 0.5 W |
| 9. Dakar | 16.0 N 16.5 W | 15.0 N 16.0 W | 1.0 S 0.5 E |
| 10. Senegal River | 21.0 N 17.0 W | 21.0 N 18.0 W | 0.0 1.0 W |
| 11. Cape Blanc | 28.0 N 13.0 W | 25.5 N 15.0 W | 2.5 S 2.0 W |
| 12. Cape Juby | 34.3 N 9.0 W | 32.0 N 8.0 W | 2.3 S 1.0 E |
| 13. Sebu River | | | |
| (b) EUROPE | | | |
| 14. Gibraltar | 36.0 N 5.5 W | 35.0 N 7.0 W | 1.0 S 1.5 W |

| Locality | True Position | Piri Re'is Map | Errors |
|---|---|---|---|
| 26. Andros Island | 23–25 N 76–77 W | 26.0 N 92–96 W  −4.0 | 2.0 N 12.0 W |
| 27. San Salvador (Watling) | 24.0 N 74.5 W | 26.5 N 84.5 W  −4.0 | 2.5 N 6.0 W |
| 28. Isle of Pines | 22.0 N 83.0 W | 16.0 N 91.0 W  −4.0 | 6.0 S 4.0 W |
| 29. Jamaica | 18.0 N 77.0 W | 15–16 N 86.0 W  −4.0 | 2.5 S 5.0 W |
| 30. Hispaniola (Santo Domingo, Haiti) | 18–20 N 68–74 W | 16–19 N 74–76 W  −4.0 | 1.0 S 0.0 |
| 31. Puerto Rico | 18–19 N 66–67 W | 21.0 N 74.0 W  −4.0 | 1.5 N 3.5 W |
| (e) SOUTH AND CENTRAL AMERICAN COASTS ON GRID B | | | |
| 32. Rio Moroni? | 6.0 N 54.0 W | 11.0 N 59.0 W  −4.0 | 5.0 N 1.0 W |
| 33. Corantijn River? | 6.0 N 57.0 W | 10.0 N 60.0 W  −4.0 | 4.0 N 1.0 E |
| 34. Essequibo River? | 7.0 N 58.0 W | 10.0 N 61.5 W  −4.0 | 3.0 N 1.0 E |
| 35. Orinoco River | 9–10 N 61–63 W | 14.0 N 67.0 W  −4.0 | 4.5 N 1.0 W |
| 36. Gulf of Venezuela | 11–12 N 71.0 W | 13.0 N 76.0 W  −4.0 | 1.5 N 1.0 W |
| 37. Pt. Gallimas | 12.5 N 72.5 W | 14.5 N 77.5 W  −4.0 | 2.0 N 1.0 W |
| 38. Magdalena River? | 11.0 N 75.0 W | 12.5 N 79.5 W  −4.0 | 1.5 N 0.5 W |
| 39. Gulf of Uraba | 8.0 N 77.0 W | 10.5 N 79.0 W  −4.0 | 2.5 N 2.0 E |

| No. | Name | | | | | | | |
|---|---|---|---|---|---|---|---|---|
| 15. | Guadalquivir River | 37.0 N | 6.3 W | 37.0 N | 7.0 W | | 0.0 | 0.7 W |
| 16. | Cape St. Vincent | 37.0 N | 9.0 W | 36.0 N | 11.0 W | | 1.0 S | 2.0 W |
| 17. | Tagus River | 38.5 N | 9.0 W | 38.0 N | 11.0 W | | 0.0 | 2.0 W |
| 18. | Cape Finisterre | 43.0 N | 9.0 W | 43.0 N | 12.0 W | | 0.0 | 3.0 W |
| 19. | Gironde River | 45.5 N | 1.0 W | 45.0 N | 3.0 W | | 0.5 S | 2.0 W |
| 20. | Brest | 48.0 N | 5.0 W | 48.0 N | 8.0 W | | 0.0 | 3.0 W |
| (c) | NORTH ATLANTIC ISLANDS | | | | | | | |
| 21. | Cape Verde Islands | 15–17 N | 22–25 W | 14–19 N | 23–29 W | | 0.0 | 0.0 |
| 22. | The Canary Islands | 27–29 N | 13–17 W | 26–28 N | 14–20 W | | 1.0 S | 1.0 W |
| 23. | Madeira Islands | 36.6 N | 17.0 W | 31.0 N | 17.0 W | | 5.6 N | 0.0 |
| 24. | The Azores | 37–39 N | 25–31 W | 36–40 N | 25–32 W | | 0.0 | 0.0 |
| (d) | THE CARIBBEAN ON GRID B | | | | | | | |

The northward shifting of the geography of the main grid by 4.4° to agree with the line through Point III as the equator, pushed the geography of the Caribbean about 4° *west*. This error is taken account of in the following table.

| No. | Name | | | | | | | |
|---|---|---|---|---|---|---|---|---|
| 25. | Cuba | | | | | | | |
| (a) | Gulf of Guacanayabo | 20.5 N | 77.5 W | 18.0 N | 88.0 W | −4.0 | 2.5 S | 7.5 W |
| (b) | Guantanamo Bay | 20.0 N | 75.0 W | 18.0 N | 86.0 W | −4.0 | 2.0 S | 7.0 W |
| (c) | Bahia de Nipe | 21.0 N | 77.5 W | 21.5 N | 85.0 W | −4.0 | 0.5 N | 3.5 W |
| (d) | Bahia de la Gloria | 22.0 N | 77.5 W | 22.0 N | 88.0 W | −4.0 | 0.0 | 6.5 W |
| (e) | Camaguey Mountains | 21.0 N | 77–79 W | 20.0 N | 85–89 W | −4.0 | 1.0 S | 4.0 W |
| (f) | Sierra Maestra Mountains | 20.0 N | 76–77 W | 18.0 N | 84–86 W | −4.0 | 2.0 S | 4.0 W |

| No. | Name | | | | | | | |
|---|---|---|---|---|---|---|---|---|
| 40. | Honduras (Cape Gracias a Dios) | 15.0 N | 83.0 W | 13.0 N | 86.0 W | −4.0 | 2.0 S | 1.0 E |
| 41. | Yucatán | 21.0 N | 88.0 W | 15.0 N | 96.0 W | −4.0 | 6.0 S | 4.0 W |
| (f) | SOUTH AND CENTRAL AMERICAN COASTS (on the main grid of the map on the inset grid, Grid C) | | | | | | | |
| 42. | Cape Frio | 23.0 S | 42.0 W | 23.0 S | 38.0 W | | 0.0 | 4.0 E |
| 43. | Salvador | 13.0 S | 39.0 W | 13.5 S | 38.0 W | | 0.5 S | 1.0 E |
| 44. | San Francisco River | 11.5 S | 36.5 W | 10.5 S | 37.0 W | | 1.0 N | 0.5 W |
| 45. | Recife (Pernambuco) | 8.0 S | 35.0 W | 7.0 S | 34.5 W | | 1.0 N | 0.5 W |
| 46. | Cape Sao Rocque | 5.0 S | 36.0 W | 6.5 S | 36.0 W | | 1.5 S | 0.0 |
| 47. | Rio Parahyba | 3.0 S | 42.0 W | 4.0 S | 40.0 W | | 1.0 S | 2.0 E |
| 48. | Bahia Sao Marcos | 2.5 S | 44.0 W | 4.0 S | 45.0 W | | 1.5 S | 1.0 W |
| 49. | Serras de Gurupi, de Desordam, de Negro | | | | | | | |
| 50. | The Amazon (No. 1) (Grid C) | 0.5 S | 48.0 W | 0.5 S | 48.0 W | | 0.0 | 0.0 |
| 51. | The Amazon (No. 2) Pará River | 0.5 S | 48.0 W | 2.0 N | 50.0 W | | 3.0 N | 2.0 W |
| 52. | The Amazon (No. 2) western mouth | 0.0 | 50.0 W | 0.0 | 53.0 W | | 0.0 | 3.0 W |
| | [On the trigonometric projection] | | | | | | | |
| 53. | Island of Marajó | | | | | | | |
| 54. | Essequibo or Demarara River | 7.0 N | 58.5 W | 5.0 N | 60.0 W | | 2.0 S | 1.5 W |
| 55. | Mouths of the Orinoco | 9–10 N | 61–63 W | 6.5–7.5 N | 62.5 W | | 2.5 S | 0.0 |
| 56. | Peninsula of Paria | 10.5 N | 62–63 W | 7–9 N | 61.0 W | | 2.5 S | 1.5 E |
| (g) | CARIBBEAN ISLANDS ON THE MAIN GRID | | | | | | | |
| 57. | Martinique | 14.5 N | 61.0 W | 14.5 N | 59.0 W | | 0.0 | 2.0 E |

| Locality | True Position | Piri Re'is Map | Errors |
|---|---|---|---|
| 58. Guadaloupe | 16.3 N 61.5 W | 17.0 N 60.0 W | 0.7 N 1.5 E |
| 59. Antigua | 17.0 N 62.0 W | 19.0 N 59.0 W | 2.0 N 3.0 E |
| 60. Leeward Islands | 17–18 N 61–63 W | 17–21 N 60–63 W | 0.0 0.0 |
| 61. Virgin Islands | 18.5 N 64.5 W | 26–29 N 62–65 W | c. 9.0 N 0.0 |

(h) CENTRAL AMERICAN COAST

Between the Peninsula of Paria and the Gulf of Venezuela there is a break in the map, and the coast between these points has been omitted, resulting in a loss of about 4½° of west longitude. This has been compensated for by adding 4½° to each finding of west longitude.

| Locality | True Position | Piri Re'is Map | Errors |
|---|---|---|---|
| 62. Gulf of Venezuela | 11–12 N 71.0 W | 10–11 N 65.0 W +4.5 | 0.0 1.5 E |
| 63. Magdalena River | 11.0 N 75.0 W | 10.0 N 68.0 W +4.5 | 1.0 S 2.5 E |
| 64. Atrato River | 8.0 N 77.0 W | 8.0 N 73.0 W +4.5 | 0.0 0.5 W |
| 65. Honduras (Cape Gracias a Dios) | 15.0 N 82.5 W | 17.0 N 72.0 W +4.5 | 2.0 N 6.0 E |
| 66. Yucatán | 21.0 N 88.0 W | 24.0 N 77.0 W +4.5 | 3.0 N 6.5 E |

(i) THE LOWER EAST COAST OF SOUTH AMERICA AND SOME ATLANTIC ISLANDS (on the main grid of the map)

Here a mistake of compilation has resulted in the omission of all of the coast between Cape Frio and Bahia Blanca. About 900 miles of coastline is missing, with a net loss of 16° of latitude going south, and 20° of longitude going west. The table includes adjustment for these errors.

| Locality | True Position | Piri Re'is Map | Errors |
|---|---|---|---|
| 67. Bahia Blanca | 39.0 S 62.0 W | 22.0 S +16 40.0 W +20 | 1.0 N 2.0 E |
| 68. Rio Colorado | 40.0 S 62.0 W | 22.5 S +16 41.0 W +20 | 1.5 N 1.0 E |
| 69. Gulf of San Mathias | 42.5 S 64.0 W | 25.0 S +16 42.5 W +20 | 1.5 N 1.5 E |

| Locality | True Position | Piri Re'is Map | Errors |
|---|---|---|---|
| 86. Vorposten Peak | 71.5 S 16.0 E | 42.5 S +25 6.0 E +10 | 3.0 N 0.0 |
| 87. Boreas, Passat Nunataks | 71.5 S 4.0 W | 37–38 S +25 11–14 W −10 | 4.0 N 0.0 |

(k) SOUTH ATLANTIC ISLANDS (on the main grid of the map)

| Locality | True Position | Piri Re'is Map | Errors |
|---|---|---|---|
| 77. South Georgia | 54.5 S 37.0 W | 36.0 S 37–38 W | 18.5 N 0.0 |
| 95. Fernando da Naronha | 4.0 S 31.0 W | 10.0 S 30.0 W | 6.0 S 1.0 E |

The latitude error suggests that the island was placed on the map with reference to Amazon No. 1, but on the scale of the main grid.

(l) PACIFIC COAST OF SOUTH AMERICA

90a, 90b. Coastal ranges of the Andes
91. Peninsula of Paracas
92. Valparaiso

(m) NON-EXISTENT ISLANDS

93. Island over Mid-Atlantic Ridge
94. Island labeled "Antillia" by Piri Re'is

# Table 2   Oronteus Finaeus World Map of 1531

| Geographical Localities | True Position | Oronteus Finaeus Position | Errors |
|---|---|---|---|
| (a) QUEEN MAUD LAND | | | |
| 1. Cape Norvegia | 71.5 S 12.0 W | 66.5 S 6.0 W | 5.0 N 6.0 E |
| 2. Regula Range | 72–73 S 2–5 W | 68–69 S 0–3 E | 4.0 N c. 5.0 E |

| No. / Place | Modern position (lat / long) | Piri Re'is Map (lat / long) | Error (lat / long) |
|---|---|---|---|
| 3. Penck Trough | 71– 74 S / 3.0 W | 66– 69 S / 4.0 E | c. 3.0 N / 7.0 E |
| 4. Neumeyer Escarpment | 68– 69 S / 0.5 E | 73.0 S / 0– 4 W | 4.0 N / c. 4.0 E |
| 5. Muhlig–Hofmann and Wohlthat Mountains | 70– 71 S / 10– 15 E | 71– 73 S / 0– 15 E | 0.0 / 0.0 |
| 6. Sor Rondanne and Belgica Mts. | 72– 73 S / 20– 30 E | 72.0 S / 22– 33 E | 0.0 / 0.0 |
| 7. Prince Ha ald Coast, Lützow–Holm Bay, Shirase Glacier | 70.0 S / 35– 37 E | 69– 70 S / 35– 40 E | 0.0 / 0.0 |
| 8. Queen Fabiola Mountains | 73.0 S / 30– 40 E | 76– 77 S / 35– 36 E | c. 3.0 N / 0.0 |
| **(b) ENDERBY LAND** | | | |
| 9. Casey Bay (Lena Bay) or Amundsen Bay | 70.0 S / 48.0 E | 67.0 S / 48– 50 E | 3.0 N / 0.0 |
| 10. Nye Mountains, Sandercook Nunataks | 72– 73 S / 50.0 E | 73.0 S / 49.0 E | 0.0 / 1.0 E |
| 11. Edward VIII Bay (Kemp Coast) | 69– 70 S / 55.0 E | 66– 67 S / 58– 60 E | 3.0 S / 4.0 W |
| 12. Schwartz Range, Rayner Peak, Dismal Mountains, Leckie Range, Knuckley Peaks, etc. | 71– 73 S / 60– 75 E | 71– 74 S / 54– 57 E | 0.0 / 12.0 E |
| 13. Amery Ice Shelf, MacKenzie–Prydz Bays | 67.0 S / 73.0 E | 73– 78 S / 70– 75 E | c. 8.5 N / 0.0 |
| 14. Prince Charles Mountains and adjacent peaks | 68– 70 S / 70– 75 E | 72– 74 S / 60– 69 E | c. 4.0 N / c. 5.0 E |
| **(c) WILKES LAND** | | | |
| 15. Philippi Glacier, Posadowsky Bay | 66.0 S / 77.0 E | 67.0 S / 88– 89 E | 1.0 N / 11.5 W |
| 16. Denman–Scott Glaciers (Shakleton Ice Shelf) | 66.0 S / 85.0 E | 66– 67 S / 99– 101 E | 0.0 / 15.0 W |
| 18. Vincennes Bay | 65.0 S / 105.0 E | 66– 67 S / 109 E | 1.5 N / 4.0 W |
| 19. Totten Glacier | 66.0 S / 112.0 E | 67.0 S / 115– 117 E | 1.0 N / 4.0 W |
| 20. Porpoise Bay | 67.0 S / 122.0 E | 67.0 S / 128– 130 E | 0.0 / 7.0 W |
| 21. Merz Glacier | 70.0 S / 140.0 E | 68.0 S / 144– 145 E | 2.0 S / 4.5 W |

| No. / Place | Modern position (lat / long) | Piri Re'is Map (lat / long) | Correction (lat / long) | Error (lat / long) |
|---|---|---|---|---|
| 70. Rio Neg[r]o (Argentina) | ? / 63.0 W | ? / 43.0 W | ? / +20 | 0.0 / 0.0 |
| 71. Rio Chubua | 44.0 S / 65.0 W | 27.0 S / 47.5 W | +16 / +20 | 1.0 N / 2.5 W |
| 72. Gulf of San Gorge | 47.0 S / 66.0 W | 27.5 S / 45.0 W | +16 / +20 | 3.5 N / 1.0 E |
| 73. Bahia Grande | 50– 52 S / 69.0 W | 30.0 S / 47.0 W | +16 / +20 | 5.0 N / 2.0 E |
| 74. Cape San Diego (near the Horn) | 55.0 S / 65.0 W | 35.0 S / 46.5 W | +16 / +20 | 4.0 N / 1.5 W |
| 75. Falkland Islands | 52.0 S / 60.0 W | 30– 32 S / 43– 45 W | +16 / +20 | 5.0 N / 4.0 W |

At this point there appears to be another break in the map, with the omission of of Drake Passage. This involves a further loss of about 9° of latitude. The total latitude adjustment now amounts to 25°.

| No. / Place | Modern position (lat / long) | Piri Re'is Map (lat / long) | Correction (lat / long) | Error (lat / long) |
|---|---|---|---|---|
| 76. The South Shetlands | 61.0 S / 60.0 W | 33– 34 S / 40– 43 W | +25 / +20 | 2.5 N / 0.0 |
| 77. South Georgia | Anomalous. See below. | | | |
| **(i) ANTARCTICA** | | | | |
| 78. The Palmer Peninsula | 65.0 S / 60.0 W | 36.0 S / 40.0 W | +25 / +20 | 4.0 N / 0.0 |
| 79. The Weddell Sea | 67– 75 S / 20– 60 W | 37.0 S / 30– 40 W | +25 | c. 8.0 N |

At this point the deficiency of west longitude is compensated for by a large error in the total longitude covered by the Weddell Sea. On the modern map this amounts to 40°; on the Piri Re'is Map only to about 10°. We therefore now subtract 10° from the west longitude readings.

| No. / Place | Modern position (lat / long) | Piri Re'is Map (lat / long) | Correction (lat / long) | Error (lat / long) |
|---|---|---|---|---|
| 80. Mt. Ropke, Queen Maud Land | 72.5 S / 4.0 W | 42.5 S / 15.0 W | +25 / –10 | 5.0 N / 1.0 W |
| 81. The Regula Range | 72.5 S / 2.5 W | 42.5 S / 12.5 W | +25 / –10 | 5.0 N / 0.0 |
| 82. Muhlig–Hofmann Mountains | 71– 73 S / 1– 6 E | 41– 43 S / 7– 10 W | +25 / –10 | 4.0 N / 0.0 |
| 83. Penck Trough | 73.0 S / 2.5 W | 44.0 S / 12.0 W | +25 / –10 | 4.0 N / 0.0 |
| 84. Neumeyer Escarpment | 73.5 S / 2.0 W | 45.0 S / 12.0 W | +25 / –10 | 3.5 N / 0.0 |
| 85. Drygalski Mountains | 71– 73 S / 8– 14 S | 40.0 S / 2.0 E | +25 / +10 | 7.0 N / 0.0 |

## Table 3　The Hadji Ahmed Map of 1559, Exclusive of the Antarctic

| Geographical Localities | Oronteus True Position | Finaeus Position | Errors |
|---|---|---|---|
| 22. McLean, Carroll Nunataks, Aurora Peak, Medig n Nunatak, etc. | 67–68 S 143–145 E | 70–71 S 132–134 E | 3.0 S 11.0 W |
| 23. Pennell Glacier, Lauritzen Bay | 69.0 S 157–158 E | 70.0 S 150.0 E | 1.0 S 7.5 W |
| (d) VICTORIA LAND and THE ROSS SEA | | | |
| 24. Rennick Bay | 70.5 S 162.0 E | 72.5 S 155.0 E | 2.0 S 7.0 W |
| 25. Arctic Institute Range | 70–73 S 161–162 E | 74–75 S 150–155 E | 3.5 S 7.0 W |
| 26. Newnes Iceshelf and Glacier | 73.5 S 167.0 E | 74.5 S 170.0 E | 1.0 S 3.0 E |
| 27. Ross I. (Mount Erebus) | 77.5 S 168.0 E | 76.5 S 172.0 E | 1.0 S 4.0 E |
| 28. Ferrer Taylor Glacier | 77–78 S 159–163 E | 77.0 S 160–170 E | 0.0 0.0 |
| 29. Boomerang Range and adjacent peaks (Escalade Peak, Portal Mt., Mt. Harmsworth, etc.) | 77–78 S 159–163 E | 77–79 S 142–152 E | 0.0 14.0 E |
| 30. Mountain group: Mt. Christmas, Mt. Nares, Mt. Albert Markham, Pyramid Mountains, Mt. Wharton, Mt. Field, Mt. Hamilton | 80–82 S 157–160 E | 79–80 S 140–150 E | 1.5 N c. 13.5 W |
| 31. Queen Alexandra Range | 84–85 S 160–165 E | 84–87 S 145–155 E | 0.0 c. 10.0 W |
| 32. Queen Maud Range | 87.0 S 140 W–180 E/W | 81–82 S 140–160 E | 5.5 N c. 20–40 E |
| 33. Nimrod Glacier | 82.5 S 157–163 E | 81.0 S 160–175 E | 1.5 S c. 0.0 |
| 34. Beardmore Glacier | 84–85 S 170.0 E | 82–85 S 170 E–170 W | 0.0 c. 0.0 |
| 36. Leverett Glacier | 85.5 S 150.0 W | 81–82 S 140–160 W | 4.0 N c. 0.0 |
| 37. Supporting Party Mountain, or Mt. Gould | 85.3 S 150.0 W | 80.0 S 160.0 W | 5.3 N 10.0 W |
| 38. Thiel and Horlich Mts. | 86.0 S 90–130 W | 83–85 S 130–150 W | 3.0 N c. 30.0 W |

| Locality | True Position | Turkish Map | Errors |
|---|---|---|---|
| (a) POSITIONS CLOSE TO THE PRIME MERIDIAN | | | |
| Magellan Strait | 54 S 68–73 W | 49 S 68–73 W | 5.0 S 0.0 |
| Cape Horn | 55 S 65 W | 51 S 70 W | 4.0 S 5.0 W |
| Amazon River | 1 S 50 W | 1 S 50 W | 0.0 0.0 |
| Rio de la Plata | 35 S 55 W | 35 S 51 W | 0.0 4.0 E |
| Cape Frio | 23.5 S 43 W | 23 S 43 W | 5.0 N 0.0 |
| Peninsula of Paria | 10.5 N 62 W | 10 N 70 W | 0.5 N 8.0 W |
| Hudson River | 41 N 72 W | 51 N 72 W | 10.0 N 0.0 |
| Gibraltar | 35 N 7 W | 31 N 10 W | 4.0 S 3.0 W |
| (b) POSITIONS DISTANT FROM THE PRIME MERIDIAN | | | |
| Chile Coast | 25–50 S 72 W | 40–49 S 80 W | c. 7.5 S 9.0 W |
| Haiti | 19–20 N 70 W | 19–20 N 80 W | 0.0 10.0 W |
| Coast of Texas | 29 N 99 W | 29 N 110 W | 0.0 11.0 W |
| Ceylon | 6 N 80 E | 9 N 110 E | 3.0 N 30.0 E |
| Aden | 12 N 60 E | 12 N 45 E | 0.0 15.0 W |
| Gulf of California | 23.5 N 130–140 W | 30 N 110 W | 6.5 N 25.0 E |

## Table 4  Mercator's World Map of 1569 (Antarctic coast on a polar projection)

| Locality | True Position | Mercator | Errors |
|---|---|---|---|
| 1. Cape Dart (Mt. Siple) (Marie Byrd Land) | 73.5 S 121.0 W | 63.0 S 95.0 W | 10.0 N 26.0 E |
| 2. Cape Herlacher (Marie Byrd Land) | 74.0 S 114.0 W | 65.0 S 92.0 W | 11.0 N 22.0 E |
| 3. Amundsen Sea | 72.0 S 90–104 W | 69–71 S 90–100 W | 1.0 N 0.0 |
| 4. Thurston Island (Eights Coast) (Ellsworth Land) | 72.0 S 88–93 W | 70.0 S 81–84 W | 2.0 N c. 7.0 E |
| 5. Fletcher Islands (Bellingshausen Sea) | 71–82 S 71–82 W | 72–75 S 70–80 W | 0.0 0.0 |
| 6. Alexander I Island | 72.5 S 67.0 W | 72.5 S 58.0 W | 0.5 S 9.0 E |
| 7. Palmer (Antarctic) Peninsula (Truncated) | 70.0 S 60.0 W | 72.0 S 47.0 W | 1.5 S 13.0 E |
| 8. Weddell Sea* | 71–73 S 35–50 W | 72–75 S 34–40 W | 0.0 0.0 |

\* Longitudes of places west of the Weddell Sea may be off 10° because of an error in the width of the Weddell Sea; the same error is found on the Piri Re'is Map.

| Locality | True Position | Mercator | Errors |
|---|---|---|---|
| 9. Cape Norvegia (Queen Maud Land) | 71.0 S 28.0 W | 75.0 S 20.0 W | 4.0 S 8.0 E |
| 10. Regula Range (Queen Maud Land) | 72.0 S 4.0 W | 77.0 S 5.0 W | 5.0 S 1.0 W |
| 11. Muhlig–Hofmann Mts. (Queen Maud Land) | 72.0 S 3– 8 E | 77.0 S 2– 7 E | 5.0 S 0.0 |
| 12. Prince Harald Coast | 70.0 S 20–31 E | 74.0 S 30–40 E | 4.0 S 10.0 E |
| 13. Shirase Glacier (Prince Harald Coast) | 70.0 38–40 E | 73.5 S 45.0 E | 3.5 S 6.0 E |
| 14. Padda Island (Lützow–Holm Bay) | 69.5 S 35.0 E | 71.0 S 42.0 E | 1.5 S 7.0 E |
| 15. Prince Olaf Coast (Enderby Land) | 68.5 S 33–40 E | 73.0 S 45–50 E | 4.5 S 11.0 E |

| Locality | True Position | Mercator | Errors |
|---|---|---|---|
| 39. Bay, unnamed, west coast of Ross Sea | 80– 81 S 150.0 W | 77.5 S 150–160 W | 3.0 N 0.0 |
| 40. Prestrude Inlet, Kiel Glacier | 78.0 S 157–159 W | 74.0 S 160.0 W | 4.0 N 2.0 W |
| 42. Edward VII Peninsula | 77– 78 S 155–158 W | 72– 73 S 158–165 W | 5.0 N c. 4.0 W |
| 43. Sulzberger Bay | 77.0 S 146–154 W | 73.5 S 150–155 W | 3.5 S c. 0.0 |
| 44. Land now submerged? | | | |

**(e) MARIE BYRD LAND**

| Locality | True Position | Mercator | Errors |
|---|---|---|---|
| 45. Edsel Ford Range | 76– 78 S 142.0 W | 73– 75 S 135–143 W | 3.5 S 0.0 |
| 46. Executive Committee Range | 77.0 S 125–130 W | 73.0 S 130–135 W | 4.0 N c. 5.0 W |
| 47. Cape Dart, Wrigley Gulf, and Getz Ice Shelf | 75.0 S 130.0 W | 70.5 S 130.0 W | 4.5 N 0.0 |
| 48. Cape Herlacher, Martin Peninsula | 74.0 S 114.0 W | 72.0 S 108.0 W | 2.0 N 6.0 E |
| 49. Kohler Range and Crary Mountains | 76– 77 S 111–118 W | 74– 75 S 108–115 W | 2.5 N 0.0 |
| 50. Canisteo Peninsula | 74.0 S 102.0 W | 74.0 S 98.0 W | 0.0 4.0 E |
| 51. Hudson Mountains | 74– 75 S 99.0 W | 72– 74 S 105–110 W | 1.0 N c. 8.0 W |

**(f) ELLSWORTH LAND**

| Locality | True Position | Mercator | Errors |
|---|---|---|---|
| 52. Jones Mountains | 73.5 S 94.0 W | 74.0 S 100.0 W | 0.5 S 6.0 W |
| 53. Inlet in Ellsworth Land, indicated to exist under the present ice cap | 73– 80 ?S 80– 95 W | 72– 74 S 85– 95 W | 0.0 0.0 |
| 54. Base of the Antarctic (Palmer) Peninsula? | | | |
| 55. The Weddell Sea, shown almost connected with the Ross Sea? | | | |
| 56. Duplicated coastline of Ellsworth Land? | | | |
| 57. Duplicated base of Antarctic Peninsula? | | | |
| 58. Berkner Island in the Weddell Sea shown extending over the continental shelf to the north? | | | |

## Table 5 Mercator's World Map of 1538

| Identified Localities | True Longitudes | Mercator's Longitudes |
|---|---|---|
| (a) ANTARCTICA | | |
| 1. Antarctic (Palmer) Peninsular, truncated at 70° S. | 60–70 W | 74.0 W |
| 2. Weddell Sea | 25–55 W | 26–42 W |
| 3. Caird Coast | 20–30 W | 10–18 W |
| 4, 5. Princess Martha and Princess Astrid Coasts, Queen Maud Land | 20 W–20 E | 0.0 |
| 6. Prince Harald Coast | 30–35 E | 6 W–6 E |
| 7. MacKenzie-Prydz Bays | 70–80 E | 38–46 E |
| 8. Denman Glacier and Ice Tongue | 100.0 E | 68.0 E |
| 9. Vincennes Bay | 110.0 E | 78.0 E |
| 10. Beardmore Glacier, Ross Sea | 170.0 E | 142.0 E |
| 11. Robert Scott Glacier, Ross Sea | 150.0 W | 150.0 E |
| 12. Amundsen Sea | 110–120 W | 162–170 W |
| 13. Alexander Island | 70–75 W | 82.0 W |
| (b) SOUTH AMERICA | | |
| 14. The Chile Coast | 70–75 W | 74.0 W |
| 15. Falklands? (as one large island) | 60.0 W | 58.66 W |
| 16. Gulf of San Gorge, Argentina | 65–67 W | 50.0 W |
| 17. Gulf of San Mathias, Argentina | 64–65 W | 42.0 W |
| 18. Arica (Peru-Bolivia) | 70.0 W | 66.0 W |
| 19. Pt. Aguia | 81.0 W | 74.0 W |
| 20. Gulf of Guayaquil (Ecuador) | 80.0 W | 74.0 W |
| 21. Ensenada di Tumaco (Colombia) | 79.0 W | 71.0 W |
| (c) NEW ZEALAND | | |
| 22. New Zealand: "Los roccos Insula" | 165–180 E | 102–110 E |

| Locality | True Position | Dulcert Portolano | Errors |
|---|---|---|---|
| 13. Brest | 48.5 N 4.5 W | 47.5 N 4.0 W | 1.0 S 0.5 E |
| 14. Belle Isle | 47.2 N 3.0 W | 46.2 N 3.0 W | 1.0 S 0.0 |
| 15. The Loire River | 47.2 N 2.0 W | 46.2 N 2.5 W | 1.0 S 0.5 W |
| 16. La Gironde River | 45.5 N 1.0 W | 44.0 N 2.0 W | 1.5 S 1.0 W |
| 17. Cape Finisterre, Spain | 43.0 N 9.0 W | 42.5 N 8.5 W | 0.5 S 0.5 W |
| 18. Tagus River, Portugal | 39.0 N 9.0 W | 37.0 N 7.0 W | 2.0 S 2.0 E |
| 19. Guadalquivir River | 37.0 N 6.3 W | 35.5 N 7.0 W | 1.5 S 0.7 W |
| 20. Gibraltar | 36.0 N 5.5 W | 34.9 N 5.0 W | 1.1 S 0.5 E |
| 21. Sebu River | 35.0 N 6.0 W | 32.0 N 7.5 W | 3.0 S 1.5 W |
| 22. Madeira Islands | 32.5 N 16–17 W | 30.0 N 13.0 W | 2.5 S 3.5 E |
| 23. Cape Juby | 27.0 N 13.0 W | 27.0 N 11.5 W | 0.0 2.0 E |
| 24. Fuerteventura (Canary Islands) | 28.0 N 14.0 W | 30.0 N 13.0 W | 2.0 N 1.0 E |
| 25. Cartagena, Spain | 37.5 N 1.0 W | 36.5 N 0.5 W | 1.0 S 0.5 E |
| 26. Majorca (Mallorca) | 39.9 N 3.0 E | 39.0 N 3.0 E | 0.9 S 0.0 |
| 27. Marseilles | 42.0 N 5.0 E | 44.0 N 6.0 E | 2.0 N 1.0 E |
| 28. Cape Corse, Corsica | 43.5 N 9.3 E | 43.5 N 9.5 E | 0.0 0.2 E |
| 29. Cagliari, Sardinia | 39.0 N 9.0 E | 37.0 N 9.5 E | 2.0 S 0.5 E |
| 30. Cape Bon, Tunisia | 37.0 N 11.0 E | 36.0 N 11.5 E | 1.0 S 0.5 E |
| 31. Cape Passero, Sicily | 36.5 N 15.0 E | 35.5 N 15.0 E | 1.0 S 0.0 |

**(d) AFRICA**

| | | |
|---|---|---|
| 23. Cape of Good Hope | 18.5 E | 22.0 E |
| 24. St. Helena Bay | 18.0 E | 21.0 E |
| 25. Walvis Bay | 15.0 E | 12.0 E |
| 26. Laurence Marques Bay | 22.0 E | 36.0 E |
| 27. Cape San Sebastian | 35.0 E | 42.0 E |
| 28. Madagascar | 45.0 E | 46– 50 E |

| Locality | True Position | Dulcert Portolano | Errors |
|---|---|---|---|
| 32. Bengazi, Libya | 32.0 N 20.0 E | 30.0 N 20.0 E | 2.0 S 0.0 |
| 33. Trieste, Italy | 46.0 N 14.0 E | 47.5 N 14.5 E | 1.5 N 0.5 E |
| 34. Corfu | 40.2 N 20.0 E | 40.0 N 20.0 E | 0.2 S 0.0 |
| 35. Kalamai, Peloponnesus | 37.0 N 22.0 E | 37.0 N 22.5 E | 0.0 0.5 E |
| 36. The Bosphorus | 41.0 N 29.0 E | 44.0 N 28.5 E | 3.0 N 0.5 W |
| 37. Danube River | 45.0 N 34.5 E | 50.0 N 29.5 E | 5.0 N 5.0 W |
| 38. Sevastopol | 44.5 N 33.5 E | 49.3 N 33.5 E | 4.8 N 0.0 |
| 39. Rostov | 47.3 N 39.5 E | 53.0 N 38.0 E | 5.7 N 1.5 W |
| 40. Don River bend | 49.0 N 44.0 E | 52.5 N 44.5 E | 3.5 N 0.5 E |
| 41. Stalingrad (Volga River) | 49.0 N 44.5 E | 55.0 N 47.0 E | 6.0 N 2.5 E |
| 42. Batum | 41.5 N 41.5 E | 45.0 N 41.5 E | 3.5 N 0.0 |
| 43. Cape Andreas (Cyprus) | 36.0 N 34.5 E | 37.0 N 35.5 E | 1.0 N 1.0 E |
| 44. Crete, South Coast | 37.5 N 24.5–26 E | 35.0 N 24–26 E | 2.5 S 0.0 |
| 45. Rhodes | 36.0 N 28.0 E | 37.0 N 28.0 E | 1.0 N 0.0 |
| 46. Antalya, Turkey | 37.0 N 30.7 E | 37.5 N 31.5 E | 0.5 N 0.8 E |
| 47. Alexandria | 31.0 N 30.0 E | correct by assumption 32.0 E | 2.0 E |
| 48. Aswan | 24.0 N 33.0 E | 24.0 N 34.0 E | 0.0 1.0 E |
| 49. Ras Muhammad (Sinai) | 27.5 N 34.0 E | 27.5 N 35.5 E | 0.0 1.5 E |
| 50. Coast of India?* | | | |

* Appears to resemble the coast of India from about 25° North Latitude, 62° East Longitude, to about 22° North Latitude, 70° East Longitude.

## Table 6   Dulcert Portolano of 1339

| Locality | True Position | Dulcert Portolano | Errors |
|---|---|---|---|
| 1. Malin Head, Ireland | 55.2 N 7.0 W | 56.5 N 7.0 W | 1.3 N 0.0 |
| 2. Galway, Ireland | 53.0 N 9.0 W | 53.0 N 8.0 W | 0.0 1.0 E |
| 3. Cape Clear, Ireland | 51.5 N 9.0 W | 50.5 N 8.0 W | 1.0 S 1.0 E |
| 4. The Hebrides | 57–58.5 N 6– 7 W | 57–58 N 4– 5 W | 0.0 2.0 E |
| 5. Moray Firth, Scotland | 57.7 N 3.5– 4 W | 57.0 N 1.5 W | 0.7 S c. 2.0 E |
| 6. Solway Firth | 55.0 N 3– 4 W | 55.0 N 3.5 W | 0.0 c. 0.0 |
| 7. Lands End, England | 50.0 N 6.0 W | 50.0 N 4.5 W | 0.0 1.5 E |
| 8. Scilly Islands | 50.0 N 6.5 W | 50.0 N 5– 6 W | 0.0 1.0 E |
| 9. The Wash | 53.0 N 0.3 E | 53.5 N 1.0 W | 0.5 N 1.3 W |
| 10. Thames River | 51.3 N 0.5 E | 51.5 N 0.5 W | 0.2 N 1.0 W |
| 11. Isle of Wight | 50.6 N 1.3 W | 50.4 N 2.0 W | 0.2 S 0.7 W |
| 12. Calais, France | 50.7 N 2.0 E | 50.4 N 0.0 | 0.3 S 2.0 W |

| Geographical Localities | True Position | De Canerio Map | Errors |
|---|---|---|---|
| 37. Al Hadd, Oman* | 22.5 N<br>60.0 E | 19.0 N<br>79.5 E | 3.5 S<br>19.5 E |

\* Ptolemaic part of the map.

## Table 8   The Venetian Map of 1484

Shown are the positions of identified geographical points, as found on a grid worked out empirically. The length of the degree of latitude was found between Villa Cisneros, at 24° N., and the equator as found by comparison with the geography. The length of the degree of longitude was found from the longitude distance between Dakar and Cape Lopez. These degrees turned out to be practically the same. For the grid, longitude was based on the longitude of Dakar, and latitude on the equator as found. The map was reoriented to True North from its former magnetic orientation.

| Localities | True Position | Venetian Map | Errors |
|---|---|---|---|
| 1. Villa Cisneros | 24.0 N<br>16.0 W | 24.0 N<br>16.0 W | by assumption<br>0.0 |
| 2. Cape Blanc | 21.0 N<br>17.0 W | 21.5 N<br>17.0 W | 0.5 N<br>0.0 |
| 3. Cape Minik | 19.3 N<br>16.0 W | 20.0 N<br>16.0 W | 0.7 N<br>0.0 |
| 4. Senegal River | 16.0 N<br>17.0 W | 16.0 N<br>17.0 W | 0.0<br>0.0 |
| 5. Dakar | 14.0 N<br>17.5 W | 15.5 N<br>17.5 W | 1.5 N<br>by assumption |
| 6. Gambia River | 12.5 N<br>17.0 W | 14.5 N<br>17.0 W | 2.0 N<br>0.0 |
| 7. Sao Nicolau, Cape Verde Islands | 16.5 N<br>24.0 W | 18.5 N<br>23.0 W | 2.0 N<br>0.0 |
| 8. Sao Tiago, Cape Verde Islands | 16.0 N<br>24.0 W | 17.0 N<br>23.0 W | 1.0 N<br>1.0 E |
| 9. Cape Roxe | 12.5 N<br>17.0 W | 13.0 N<br>17.0 W | 0.5 N<br>0.0 |
| 10. Bijagos Islands | 11.0 N<br>16.0 W | 12.0 N<br>16.0 W | 1.0 N<br>0.0 |

## Table 7   De Canerio Map of 1502
(grid drawn by spherical trigonometry. See page 235)

| Geographical Localities | True Position | De Canerio Map | Errors |
|---|---|---|---|
| 1. Cape of Good Hope | 35.5 S<br>18.5 E | 37.0 S<br>14.0 E | 1.5 S<br>4.5 W |
| 2. Gt. Paternoster Pt. | 33.0 S<br>18.0 E | 35.5 S<br>14.0 E | 2.5 S<br>4.0 W |
| 3. Walvis Bay, Pelican Point | 23.0 S<br>15.0 E | 22.5 S<br>10.0 E | 0.5 N<br>5.0 W |
| 4. Congo River | 6.0 S<br>12.2 E | 13.0 S<br>14.0 E | 7.0 S<br>1.8 E |
| 5. Cap Lopez | 1.0 S<br>9.0 E | -5.0 S<br>10.0 E | 4.0 S<br>1.0 E |
| 6. Sao Tomé (island) | 0.0<br>6.0 E | 4.0 S<br>8.0 E | 4.0 S<br>2.0 E |
| 7. Niger Delta | 4.0 N<br>6.0 E | 1.0 N<br>8.0 E | 3.0 S<br>2.0 E |
| 8. Cape Three Points | 5.0 N<br>2.0 W | 3.5 N<br>5.0 W | 1.5 S<br>3.0 W |
| 9. Cap Palmas | 4.5 N<br>8.0 W | 4.0 N<br>9.0 W | 0.5 S<br>1.0 W |
| 10. Freetown | 8.0 N<br>13.5 W | 10.0 N<br>17.5 W | 2.0 N<br>4.0 W |
| 11. Dakar | 15.0 N<br>17.0 W | 17.0 N<br>20.0 W | 2.0 N<br>3.0 W |
| 12. Cap Blanc | 21.0 N<br>17.0 W | 24.0 N<br>20.0 W | 3.0 N<br>3.0 W |
| 13. Cap Yubi | 28.0 N<br>13.0 W | 28.0 N<br>15.5 W | 0.0<br>2.5 W |
| 14. Gibraltar | 36.0 N<br>5.5 W | 34.5 N<br>5.5 W | 1.5 S<br>0.0 |
| 15. Cap Bon | 37.0 N<br>11.0 E | 34.0 N<br>11.0 E | 3.0 S<br>0.0 |
| 16. Bengazi | 32.0 N<br>20.0 E | 28.0 N<br>19.5 E | 4.0 S<br>0.5 W |
| 17. Alexandria | 31.0 N<br>30.0 E | 26.5 N<br>30.0 E | 4.5 S<br>assumption |

| | Localities | True Location | Portuguese Map | Errors |
|---|---|---|---|---|
| 11. | Freetown | 8.5 N 13.0 W | 8.5 N 13.5 W | 0.0 0.5 W |
| 12. | Cape Palmas | 4.5 N 7.5 W | 5.0 N 7.5 W | 0.5 N 0.0 |
| 13. | Cape Three Points | 5.0 N 2.0 W | 5.0 N 2.5 W | 0.0 0.5 W |
| 14. | Volta River Estuary | 6.0 N 0.5 E | 6.0 N 0.5 E | 0.0 0.0 |
| 15. | Lagos | 6.5 N 3.5 E | 7.0 N 4.0 E | 0.5 N 0.5 E |
| 16. | Niger River Delta | 4.5 N 6-7 E | 5.0 N 6-7 E | 0.5 N 0.0 |
| 17. | Fernando Po Island | 3.5 N 9.0 E | 3.5 N 9.5 E | 0.0 0.5 E |
| 18. | Sao Tome | 0.0 7.0 E | 0.0 6.0 E | by assumption 1.0 W |
| 19. | A non-existent island, possibly a duplicate of Sao Tomé. | | | |
| 20. | Cape Lopez | 1.0 S 9.0 E | 1.0 S 9.0 E | 0.0 by assumption |
| 21. | Congo Estuary | 6.0 S 12.0 E | 9.0 S 12.0 E | 3.0 S 0.0 |
| 22. | Benguela | 12.5 S 13.0 E | 16.0 S 11.0 E | 3.5 S 2.0 W |

# Table 9  Reinel Map of the Indian Ocean

| Localities | True Location | Portuguese Map | Errors |
|---|---|---|---|
| 1. Rocks of St. Paul | 0.0 29.0 W | 0.0 33.0 W | 0.0 4.0 W |
| 2. Ascension Island | 8.0 S 14.5 W | 16.0 S 15.0 W | 8.0 S 0.5 W |
| 3. Sao Tomé | 0.0 0.0 | 0.0 7.0 W | 0.0 7.0 W |
| 4. Tristan d'Achuna | 37.0 S 12.5 W | 40.0 S 8–13 W | 3.0 S 0.0 |
| 5. The Congo River | 6.0 S 12.0 E | 6.0 S 8.0 E | 0.0 4.0 W |

| | Localities | True Location | Portuguese Map | Errors |
|---|---|---|---|---|
| 18. | Cyprus | 35.0 N 32-34 E | 35.0 N 32-34E | 3.0 S 0.0 |
| 19. | Crete | 35.0 N 24-26 E | 35.0 N 25.0 E | 3.0 S 0.0 |
| 20. | Lesbos (Aegean Sea) | 39.0 N 26.0 E | 36.0 N 26.5 E | 3.0 S 0.5 E |
| 21. | Bosphorus | 41.0 N 29.0 E | 39.0 N 29.5 E | 2.0 S 0.5 E |
| 22. | Sevastopol (Crimea) | 44.5 N 34.5 E | 41.0 N 35.0 E | 3.5 S 0.5 E |
| 23. | Batum (Caucasus) | 42.0 N 42.0 E | 38.0 N 43.0 E | 4.0 S 1.0 E |
| 24. | Sicily | 36-37 N 13-15 E | 34.0 N 15.0 E | 2.5 S 0.0 |
| 25. | Sardinia | 39-41 N 8-10 E | 35-38 N 9-10 E | 3.0 S 0.0 |
| 26. | Cape St. Vincent | 37.0 N 11.0 W | 36.0 N 10.0 W | 1.0 S 1.0 E |
| 27. | Cap Finisterre | 43.0 N 9.0 W | 42.0 N 9.0 W | 1.0 S 0.0 |
| 28. | Brest | 48.0 N 5.0 W | 47.0 N 4.0 W | 1.0 S 1.0 E |
| 29. | Cape Clear (Ireland) | 52.0 N 10.0 W | 49.5 N 8.0 W | 2.5 S 2.0 E |
| 30. | Londonderry | 55.0 N 7.5 W | 54.5 N 6.5 W | 0.5 S 1.0 E |
| 31. | Denmark (northern coast) | 50-53 N 8-10 E | 56.0 N 7.5 E | 4.5 N 2.5 W |
| 32. | Gulf of Riga | 57.5 N 23-24 E | 52.5 N 25.0 E | 5.0 S 1.5 E |
| 33. | Saarma Island (Gulf of Riga) | 57.5 N 22.5 E | 55.0 N 24.0 E | 2.5 S 1.5 E |
| | AFRICAN EAST COAST | | | |
| 34. | Laurenço Marques | 25.0 S 33.0 E | 27.0 S 35.0 E | 2.0 S 2.0 E |
| 35. | Beira* | 20.0 S 35.0 E | 15.0 S 45.0 E | 5.0 N 10.0 E |
| 36. | Capo Guardafui* (Ras Assir) | 12.0 N 51.0 E | 1.0 N 69.0 E | 11.0 S 18.0 E |

| Localities | True Position | Venetian Map | Errors |
|---|---|---|---|
| 6. Cape Town | 34.5 S / 18.5 E | 35.0 S / 15.0 E | 0.5 S / 3.5 W |
| 7. Cape St. Marie, Madagascar | 25.5 S / 45.0 E | 26.0 S / 45.0 E | 0.5 S / 0.0 |
| 8. Dar es Salaam (Tanganyika) | 7.0 S / 39.5 E | 9.0 S / 40.0 E | 2.0 S / 0.5 E |
| 9. Zanzibar | 6.0 S / 35.9 E | 5.0 S / 41.0 E | 1.0 N / 5.1 E |
| 10. Comore Islands | 11–13 S / 43–45 E | 10–16 S / 41–46 E | 0.0 / 0.0 |
| 11. Cape St. André (Madagascar) | 16.0 S / 44.5 E | 17.0 S / 44.5 E | 1.0 S / 0.0 |
| 12. Cape d'Ambre | 12.0 S / 49.5 E | 12.0 S / 53.0 E | 0.0 / 3.5 E |
| 13. Cape Guardafui (Ras Assir) | 12.0 N / 51.0 E | 12.0 N / 57.0 E | 0.0 / 6.0 E |
| 14. Seychelles and Amirante Islands | 4–7 S / 53–56 E | 3–5 S / 55–59 E | 0.0 / 2.0 E |
| 15. Al Hadd (Arabia) | 27.5 N / 60.0 E | 22.0 N / 70.0 E | 5.5 S / 10.0 E |
| 16. Reunion Island | 21.0 S / 55.5 E | 21–25 S / 72–74 E | 0.0 / 17.0 E |
| 17. Mauritius | 20.0 S / 57.0 E | 23–24 S / 78.0 E | 3.5 S / 21.0 E |
| 18. Mouth of Indus R. (no delta shown) | 24.0 N / 68.0 E | 23.0 N / 81.0 E | 1.0 S / 13.0 E |
| 19. Laccadive Islands | 10–13 N / 72–74 E | 23.0 N / 81.0 E | 1.0 S / 13.0 E |
| 20. Maldive Islands | 1–6 N / 73–74 E | 4 N–5 S / 80–85 E | 0.0 / 10.0 E |
| 21. Ceylon | 6–8 N / 80–82 E | 7–10 N / 89–90 E | 2.0 N / 9.0 E |
| 23. Cape Leeuwin, Australia | 34.5 S / 115.0 E | 17.0 S / 104.0 E | 17.5 N / 11.0 W |
| 24. Northwest Cape, Australia | 22.0 S / 114.0 E | 1.0 S / 106.0 E | 21.0 N / 8.0 W |
| 25. Caroline Islands (Central: Ulul, Truk) | 7–10 N / 147–150 E | 5 N–5 S / 133–140 E | c. 8.0 N / c. 10.0 W |

| Locality | True Position | 1137 Map | Errors |
|---|---|---|---|
| 42. Mouth of the R. Yangtze | 31.5 N / 122.0 E | 32.0 N / 121.0 E | 0.5 N / 1.0 W |
| 43. Lake Hungtze Hu | 33.2 N / 118.5 E | 32.0 N / 118.0 E | 1.2 S / 0.5 W |
| 44. Taku, former mouth of the R. Hwang (1852–1938) | 37.7 N / 118.8 E | 37.8 N / 117.5 E | 0.1 N / 1.3 W |
| (c) SOUTHWEST QUADRANT | | | |
| 8. Junction of R. Kwei and R. Yu at Kwei Ping | 23.5 N / 110.0 E | 23.3 N / 113.0 E | 0.2 S / 3.0 E |
| 21. Chungking, at junction of R. Yangtze and R. (Fow) | 29.3 N / 106.0 E | 29.3 N / 106.5 E | 0.0 / 0.5 E |
| 23. Junction of the R. Yangtze and the R. Wu (Kweichow Province) | 30.0 N / 107.5 E | 29.5 N / 106.5 E | 0.5 S / 1.0 W |
| 24. Westward bend of the R. Wu | 28.0 N / 106.2 E | 26.7 N / 107.5 E | 1.3 S / 1.3 E |
| 27. Junction of the R. Changti and the R. Chu | 27.9 N / 110.1 E | 27.1 N / 111.9 E | 0.8 S / 1.8 E |
| 35. Junction of the R. Yangtze and R. Min near Ipin | 29.7 N / 104.5 E | 27.5 N / 104.5 E | 2.2 S / 0.0 |
| 36. Chengtu on the R. Min | 30.5 N / 104.0 E | 28.5 N / 104.5 E | 2.0 S / 0.5 E |
| 25. Junction of the R. Yangtze and the R. Yalung | 26.5 N / 101.7 E | 27.7 N / 103.2 E | 1.2 N / 1.5 E |
| 50. Source of R. Tzu | 26.5 N / 110.5 E | 25.3 N / 112.2 E | 1.2 S / 1.7 E |
| (d) SOUTHEAST QUADRANT | | | |
| 9. Lake Tung Ting Hu | 29.0 N / 112–113 E | 28–29 N / 113.5–114.5 E | 0.0 / 1.5 E |
| 10. Junction of R. Yangtze and R. Han at Hankow | 30.5 N / 114.0 E | 30.7 N / 115.0 E | 0.2 N / 1.0 E |
| 4. Mouth of R. Fushun | 30.4 N / 121.0 E | 29.7 N / 121.0 E | 0.7 S / 0.0 |
| 6. Mouth of the R. Kwei | 22.0 N / 113.0 E | 22.6 N / 115.5 E | 0.6 N / 2.5 E |

| | True Position | 1137 Map | Errors |
|---|---|---|---|
| 39. Mouth of the R. Wu (Chekiang Province) | 23.0 N 121.0 E | 25.7 N 122.5 E | 2.7 N 1.5 E |
| 46. Lake Pohang Hu | 29.0 N 116.5 E | 30.0 N 117.5 E | 1.0 N 1.0 E |
| 49. Kanhsien, Kiang Prov. | 25.8 N 115.0 E | 26.7 N 116.5 E | 0.9 N 1.5 E |

## Table 10b  Latitude Errors on Yü Chi Fu Map

The averages of these errors of the northernmost and southernmost positions, about 0.4° of latitude on the north (some northerly and some southerly), and a little more than one degree on the south, about equally distributed northward and southward, suggest that we have approximately the right length for the degree of latitude.

| | Errors |
|---|---|
| NORTHERN MOST POSITIONS: NORTH of 35TH PARALLEL | |
| 18. Junction of the R. Tatung and the R. Sining | 0.6 N |
| 15. Bend of the R. Hwang near Ningsia | 1.5 S |
| 16. Junction of R. Hwang and R. Tsingshui | 0.0 |
| 17. Junction of R. Hwang and R. Fen | 0.2 S |
| 47. Junction of R. Hwang and R. Tao | 0.0 |
| 1. Penglai | 0.0 |
| 2. Chenchan Tow | 0.3 N |
| 11. Lake Tunga | 0.0 |
| 13. Southward turn of R. Hwang | 0.0 |
| 22. Junction of R. Hwang and R. Chin | 0.2 N |
| 26. Source of R. Tzeya | 0.4 S |
| 44. Taku, former mouth of the Hwang | 0.1 N |
| SOUTHERNMOST POSITIONS: SOUTH OF 28TH PARALLEL | |
| 8. Junction of R. Kwei and R. Yu | 0.2 S |
| 25. Junction of the R. Yangtze and R. Yalung | 1.0 N |
| 50. Source of the R. Tzu | 1.2 S |
| 24. Westward bend of R. Wu | 1.3 S |
| 27. Junction of R. Yangtze and the R. Chu | 0.8 S |

## Table 10a  Yü Chi Fu Map

| Locality | True Position | 1137 Map | Errors |
|---|---|---|---|
| (a) THE NORTHWEST QUADRANT | | | |
| 18. Junction of the Tatung and Sining Rivers | 36.4 N 103.0 E | 37.0 N 103.3 E | 0.6 N 0.3 E |
| 15. Bend of the R. Hwang near Ningsia | 38.5 N 107.2 E | 37.0 N 107.5 E | 1.5 S 0.3 E |
| 16. Junction of R. Hwang and R. Tsingshui | 38.0 N 106.0 E | 38.0 N 105.5 E | 0.0 0.5 W |
| 17. Junction of R. Hwang and R. Fen | 35.5 N 110.5 E | 35.3 N 110.5 E | 0.2 S 0.0 |
| 19. Eastward turn of R. Hwang at Tali | 34.5 N 110.0 E | 34.5 N 110.5 E | 0.0 0.5 E |
| 20. Junction of R. King and R. Wei (Siking Province) | 34.4 N 109.0 E | 35.0 N 109.0 E | 0.6 N 0.0 |
| 28. Bend in the R. Tao | 34.5 N 104.0 E | 35.0 N 103.0 E | 0.5 N 1.0 W |
| 47. Junction of the R. Hwang and the R. Tao | 36.0 N 103.0 E | 36.0 N 103.0 E | 0.0 0.0 |
| (b) THE NORTHEAST QUADRANT | | | |
| 1. Penglai | 37.7 N 120.6 E | 37.7 N 119.5 E | 0.0 1.1 W |
| 2. Chenshan Tow (tip of Shantung Peninsula) | 37.4 N 122.5 E | 37.7 N 122.0 E | 0.3 N 0.5 W |
| 11. Lake (Tunga) on former course of the R. Hwang | 36.0 N 116.0 E | 35– 36 N 116.0 E | 0.0 0.0 |
| 13. Southward turn of the Hwang at Tokoto (Suiyuan P.) | 40.0 N 111.2 E | 40.0 N 111.6 E | 0.0 0.4 E |
| 22. Junction of R. Hwang and R. Chin | 35.0 N 113.3 E | 35.2 N 113.3 E | 0.2 N 0.0 |
| 26. Source of the R. Tzeya | 37.0 N 113.2 E | 36.6 N 113.3 E | 0.4 S 0.1 E |
| 29. Island in Lake Tai Hu | 30.7 N 120.5 E | 31.0 N 120.3 E | 0.3 N 0.2 W |

| | Errors |
|---|---|
| 6. Mouth of River Si | 0.6 N |
| 39. Mouth of R. Wu (Chekiang Prov.) | 2.5 N |
| 49. Kanhsien, Kiang Prov. | 0.9 N |

# Table 10c  Longitude Errors on Yü Chi Fu

These longitude positions suggest that we have approximately a correct length for the degree of longitude and, therefore, that the lengths of the degrees of latitude and longitude differ, according to the Mercator Projection, although we have not computed the projection mathematically.

| | Errors |
|---|---|
| POSITIONS IN SOUTH, 104TH MERIDIAN OR FARTHER WEST | |
| 18. Junction of R. Tatung and R. Sining | 0.3 E |
| 28. Bend in R. Tao | 1.0 W |
| 47. Junction of R. Hwang and R. Tao | 0.0 |
| 35. Junction of the Yangtze and R. Min | 0.0 |
| 36. Chengtu | 0.5 E |
| 25. Junction of the Yangtze and R. Yalung | 1.5 E |
| POSITIONS ON 116TH MERIDIAN OR FARTHER EAST | |
| 1. Penglai | 1.1 W |
| 2. Chenshan Tow | 0.5 W |
| 11. Lake Tunga | .0 |
| 29. Island in Lake Tai Hu | 0.2 W |
| 4. Mouth of R. Fushun | 0.0 |
| 39. Mouth of R. Wu (Chekiang) | 1.5 E |
| 46. Lake Pohang Hu | 1.0 E |
| Longitude errors on west: | 0.3 E |
| on east: | 1.1 W |

| Locality | True Position | Zeno Map | Errors |
|---|---|---|---|
| 11. Cape Brewster | 70.2 N 22.0 W | 70.0 N 25.0 W | 0.2 S 3.0 W |
| 12. Jameson Land (as island) | 70.5–71.5 N 22.0 W | 72.5 N 18–22 W | 1.0 N 0.0 |
| 13. Scoresby Sound | 71.0 N 25.0 W | 73.0 N 22.0 W | 2.0 N 2.0 E |
| 14. Cape Broer Ruys | 73.5 N 20.5 W | 74.0 N 4.0 W | 0.5 N 16.5 E |
| ICELAND | | | |
| 15. Reykjanes Point | 64.0 N 23.0 W | 64.0 N 29.0 W | 0.0 6.0 W |
| 16. Dyrholaey Point | 63.4 N 19.0 W | 64.2 N 25.0 W | 0.8 N 6.0 W |
| 17. Seydhisfjorder | 65.3 N 14.0 W | 66.5 N 19.0 W | 1.2 N 5.0 W |
| 18. Rifstangi | 66.5 N 16.3 W | 69.5 N 19.0 W | 3.0 N 2.7 W |
| EUROPE | | | |
| 19. Trondheimsfiord, Norway | 63.5 N 10.0 E | 67.5 N 1.0 E | 4.5 N 9.0 W |
| 20. Nordfiord, Norway | 61.9 N 5.0 E | 62.5 N 3.0 W | 0.6 N 8.0 W |
| 21. Mandal (The Naze (C. Lindesnes), Norway | 58.0 N 7.5 E | 59.0 N 4.0 E | 1.0 N 3.5 W |
| 22. Oslo, Norway | 60.0 N 10.5 E | 60.0 N 10.5 E | correct by assumption |
| 23. Copenhagen, Denmark | 55.6 N 12.5 E | 55.0 N 14.0 E | 0.5 S 1.5 E |
| 24. Lolland Island (Denmark) | 54.5 N 11.5 E | 52.0 N 9.0 E | 2.5 S 2.5 W |
| 25. Cape Wrath, Scotland | 58.6 N 5.0 W | 54.0 N 9.0 W | 4.6 S 4.0 W |
| 26. Shetland Islands (as one island) | 60–61 N 1.0 W | 60–62 N 7–10 W | 0.0 c. 8.0 W |

| | |
|---|---|
| 1.0 W | 0.5 W |
| 0.0 | 0.0 |
| 0.0 | 0.2 W |
| 0.5 E | 0.0 |
| 1.5 E | 1.5 E |
| | 1.0 E |

## Table 11a The Zeno Map of the North: Polar Projection

| *Locality* | *True Position* | *Zeno Map* | *Errors* |
|---|---|---|---|
| WEST COAST OF GREENLAND | | | |
| 1. Cape Farewell | 60.0 N<br>44.0 N | correct by assumption | |
| 2. Godthaab | 64.0 N<br>52.0 W | 64.0 N<br>50.0 W | 0.0<br>2.0 E |
| 3. Kangatsiak Island | 68.3 N<br>53.5 W | 66.5 N<br>51.0 W | 1.8 S<br>2.5 E |
| 4. Egedesminde Island | 68.7 N<br>52.7 W | 69.0 N<br>49.0 W | 0.2 N<br>3.7 E |
| 5. Christianshaab | 68.7 N<br>51.0 W | 70.0 N<br>46.0 W | 1.3 N<br>5.0 E |
| 6. Jacobshavn | 69.3 N<br>51.0 W | 73.0 N<br>40.0 W | 3.7 N<br>9.0 E |
| 7. Svantenhuk Point | 71.5 N<br>55.8 W | 74.0 N<br>45.0 W | 2.5 N<br>13.8 E |
| 8. Island 1° East of Upernavik Island | 72.7 N<br>55.5 W | 76.0 N<br>37.0 W | 3.3 N<br>18.5 E |
| EAST COAST OF GREENLAND | | | |
| 9. Angmagssalik Island | 65.6 N<br>38.0 W | 66.0 N<br>38.5 W | 0.4 N<br>0.5 W |
| 10. Kangerdlugssuaq Bay | 68.0 N<br>32.0 W | 69.5 N<br>29.0 W | 1.5 N<br>3.0 E |

## Table 11b The Zeno Map with Four Different Grids

| *Locality* | *True Position* | *Zeno Map* | *Errors* |
|---|---|---|---|
| WEST COAST OF GREENLAND: An Oblong Grid; a different north | | | |
| 1. Cape Farewell | 60.0 N<br>44.0 N | 60.0 N<br>47.0 | assumption<br>3.0 W |
| 2. Godhaab | 64.0 N<br>52.0 W | 62.5 N<br>52.0 W | 1.5 S<br>0.0 |
| 3. Kangatsiak Island | 68.3 N<br>53.5 W | 64.5 N<br>53.5 W | 3.8 S<br>?.? |
| ½. Egedesminde Island | 68.7 N<br>52.7 W | 67.0 N<br>53.0 W | 1.7 S<br>0.3 W |
| 5. Christianshaab | 68.7 N<br>51.0 W | 68.5 N<br>50.5 W | 0.2 S<br>0.5 E |
| 6. Jacobshavn | 69.3 N<br>51.0 W | 70.5 N<br>50.0 W | 1.2 N<br>1.0 E |
| 7. Svantenhuk Point | 71.5 N<br>55.8 W | 71.0 N<br>52.0 W | 0.5 S<br>3.8 E |
| 8. Island 1° East of Upernavik Island | 72.7 N<br>55.5 W | 70.0 N<br>50.0 W | 2.7 S<br>5.5 E |
| EAST COAST OF GREENLAND: on a larger scale | | | |
| 1. Cape Farewell | 60.0 N<br>44.0 W | 59.0 N | 1.0 S |
| 9. Angmagssalik Island | 65.6 N<br>38.0 W | 64.3 N | 0.3 S |
| 10. Kangerdlugssuaq Bay | 68.0 N<br>32.0 W | 67.0 N | 0.0 |
| 11. Cape Brewster | 70.2 N<br>22.0 W | 69.0 N | 0.0 |
| 12. Jameson Land (Island) | 70.5–71.5 N<br>22.0 W | 69.5–70.5 N | 0.0 |
| 13. Scoresby Sound | 71.0 N<br>25.0 W | 70.0 N | 0.0 |
| 14. Cape Broer Ruys | 73.5 N<br>20.5 W | 72.7 N | 0.2 N |

| Locality | True Position | Zeno Map | Errors |
|---|---|---|---|
| **ICELAND: on the same scale of latitude, but not related in longitude** | | | |
| 15. Reykjanes Point | 64.0 N 23.0 W | 63.7 N 20.5 W | 0.3 S 2.5 E |
| 16. Dyrholaey Point | 63.4 N 19.0 W | 63.6 N 19.0 W | 0.2 N 0.0 |
| 17. Seydhistjerder Point | 65.3 N 14.0 W | 66.6 N 14.0 W | 1.3 N 0.0 |
| 18. Rifstangi Point | 66.5 N 16.3 W | 68.5 N 17.0 W | 2.0 N 0.7 W |
| **EUROPE: on a special grid** | | | |
| 19. Trondheimsfjord, Norway | 63.5 N 10.0 E | 62.0 N 9.0 E | 1.5 S 1.0 W |
| 20. Nordfiord, Norway | 61.9 N 5.0 E | 59.5 N 5.5 E | 2.4 S 0.5 E |
| 21. Mandal (The Naze) (C. Lindesnes, Norway) | 58.0 N 7.5 E | 57.0 N 8.0 E | 1.0 S 0.5 E |
| 22. Oslo, Norway | 60.0 N 10.5 E | 58.9 N 11.5 E | 1.1 S 1.0 E |
| 23. Copenhagen, Denmark | 55.6 N 12.5 E | 54.0 N 13.5 E | 1.6 S 1.0 E |
| 24. Island of Lolland | 54.5 N 11.5 E | 53.0 N 11.5 E | 1.5 S 0.0 |

| Localities | True Position | Benincasa Map | Errors |
|---|---|---|---|
| 25. The Danube runs an entirely fictitious course from the Alps to the Black Sea, only the terminal points being correct; it may be a medieval addition to the source map. | | | |
| 26. The Alps are drawn in the medieval tradition, and probably were added by the modern geographer (as also the mountains in Farica). | | | |
| **THE MEDITERRANEAN AND BLACK SEA** | | | |
| 27. River Moulouya | 35.0 N 2.5 W | 34.0 N 2.5 W | 0.0 0.0 |
| 28. Cape Bon | 37.0 N 11.0 E | 36.5 N 10.0 E | 0.5 N 1.0 W |
| 29. Ile Djerba | 34.0 N 11.0 E | 34.0 N 11.0 E | 0.0 0.0 |
| 30. Cape Misurata | 32.5 N 15.3 E | 31.0 N 15.0 E | 1.5 S 0.3 W |
| 31. Bengazi | 32.0 N 20.0 E | 30.5 N 19.0 E | 1.5 S 1.0 W |
| 32. Alexandria | 31.0 N 30.0 E | 31.0 N 31.0 E | 0.0 [by assumption] 1.0 E |
| 33. Cyprus | 34.5–35.5 N 32.5–34.5 E | 36–37 N 32–34.5 E | 1.5 N 0.0 |
| 34. Crete (southern coast) | 35.0 N 23–27 E | 35.0 N 23–34.5 E | 0.0 1.0 W |
| 35. The Bosphorus | 41.0 N 29.0 E | 44.0 N 28.5 E | 3.0 N 0.5 W |
| 36. Yalta | 44.5 N 34.0 E | 49.0 N 33.0 E | 4.5 N 1.0 W |
| 37. Batum | 41.5 N 41.5 E | 45.5 N 42.0 E | 4.0 N 0.5 E |
| **CENTRAL MEDITERRANEAN (NORTH COAST)** | | | |
| 38. Trieste | 46.0 N 14.0 E | 48.0 N 13.0 E | 2.0 N 1.0 W |
| 39. Marseilles | 43.0 N 5.0 E | 44.0 N 5.0 E | 2.0 N 0.0 |
| 40. The Red Sea is shown without the Gulf of Aqaba or the Gulf of Suez. Latitude 28° N (northern end) and Longitude 35–40° E. Correct. | | | |

## Table 12   Benincasa Portolano of 1508

| Localities | True Position | Benincasa Map | Errors |
|---|---|---|---|
| 1. Cape Yubi | 28.0 N 13.0 W | 26.0 N 15.0 W | 2.0 S 2.0 W |
| 2. Cape Guir | 30.5 N 10.0 W | 29.5 N 10.0 W | 1.0 S 0.0 |
| 3. Mojador | 31.5 N 10.0 W | 31.0 N 10.0 W | 0.5 S 0.0 |

# Table 13 The Map of Iehudi Ibn ben Zara

| Locality | True Position | Zara Map | Errors |
|---|---|---|---|
| 1. Cape Yubi | 28.0 N / 13.0 W | c. 28.0 N / c. 14.0 W | 0.0 / 1.0 W |
| 2. Cape Guir | 30.5 N / 10.0 W | 31.5 N / 10.0 W | 1.0 N / 0.0 |
| 3. Majador | 31.5 N / 10.0 W | 32.5 N / 9.0 W | 1.0 N / 1.0 E |
| 4. Mazagan (Oum er Rbia River) | 33.5 N / 8.5 W | 34.0 N / 7.0 W | 0.5 N / 1.5 E |
| 5. Gibraltar | 36.5 N / 5.5 W | 35.5 N / 4.5 W | 1.0 S / 1.0 E |
| 6. Guadalquivir | 37.0 N / 6.5 W | 37.0 N / 5.0 W | 0.0 / 1.5 E |
| 7. Cape St. Vincent | 37.5 N / 9.0 W | 37.5 N / 7.5 W | 0.0 / 1.5 E |
| 8. Tagus River (Lisbon) | 38.5 N / 9.5 W | 39.5 N / 7.0 W | 1.0 N / 2.5 E |
| 9. Oporto (Douro River) | 41.0 N / 8.5 W | 41.5 N / 6.0 W | 0.5 N / 2.5 E |
| 10. Cap Finisterre | 43.0 N / 9.5 W | 44.0 N / 7.0 W | 1.0 N / 2.5 E |
| 11. Cape de Penas | 43.5 N / 6.0 W | 45.0 N / 4.0 W | 1.5 N / 2.0 E |
| 12. Cape Machichaco | 43.5 N / 3.0 W | 44.0 N / 1.5 W | 1.5 N / 1.5 E |
| 13. Arcachon, France | 44.5 N / 1.0 W | 45.0 N / 0.0 | 0.5 N / 1.0 E |
| 14. Gironde River | 45.5 N / 1.0 W | 46.0 N / 0.0 | 0.5 N / 1.0 E |
| 15. Loire River | 47.0 N / 3.0 W | 48.5 N / 0.5 W | 1.5 N / 2.5 E |
| 16. Isle d'Ouessant (off Pointe de St. Mathieu) (Brest) | 48.5 N / 5.0 W | 50.0 N / 3.0 W | 1.5 N / 2.0 E |
| 17. Cherbourg | 49.5 N / 1.5 W | 51.5 N / 0.0 | 2.0 N / 1.5 E |
| 18. Calais | 51.0 N / 2.0 E | 52.0 N / 2.5 E | 1.0 N / 0.5 E |

| Locality | | | |
|---|---|---|---|
| 4. Mazagan (Oum er Rbia River) | 33.5 N / 8.5 W | 33.0 N / 6.5 W | 0.5 S / 2.0 W |
| 5. Gibraltar | 36.5 N / 5.5 W | 35.0 N / 6.0 W | 1.5 S / 0.5 W |
| 6. Guadalquivir | 37.0 N / 6.5 W | 36.0 N / 6.5 W | 1.0 S / 0.0 |
| 7. Cap St. Vincent | 37.5 N / 9.0 W | 36.5 N / 9.0 W | 1.0 S / 0.0 |
| 8. Lisbon | 38.5 N / 9.5 W | 38.5 N / 8.5 W | 0.0 / 1.0 E |
| 9. Cap Finisterre | 43.0 N / 9.5 W | 43.5 N / 9.0 W | 0.5 N / 0.5 E |
| 10. Cape de Penas | 43.5 N / 6.0 W | 44.0 N / 6.0 W | 0.5 N / 0.0 |
| 11. Brest | 48.5 N / 5.0 W | 50.0 N / 5.0 W | 1.5 N / 0.0 |
| 12. Cherbourg | 49.5 N / 1.5 W | 51.0 N / 2.5 W | 1.5 N / 1.0 W |
| 13. Calais | 51.0 N / 2.0 E | 52.5 N / 2.0 E | 1.5 N / 0.0 |
| 14. Lands End | 50.0 N / 5.5 W | 52.0 N / 5.5 W | 2.0 N / 0.0 |
| 15. Cape Clear, Ireland | 51.5 N / 9.5 W | 53.0 N / 9.0 W | 1.5 N / 0.5 E |
| 16. Malin Head, Ireland | 55.0 N / 7.5 W | 58.0 N / 7.5 W | 3.0 N / 0.0 |
| 17. Firth of Forth | 56.0 N / 3.0 W | 56.5 N / 1.0 W | 0.5 N / 2.0 E |
| 18. Kinnard's Head | 57.5 N / 2.0 W | 60.5 N / 1.5 W | 2.5 N / 0.5 E |
| 19. The Rhine | 52.0 N / 4.0 E | 53.0 N / 2.5 E | 1.0 N / 1.5 W |
| 20. The Elbe | 54.0 N / 9.0 E | 55.0 N / 2.0 E | 1.0 N / 7.0 W |
| 21. Erz Gebirge (Mts.) | 50-51 N / 12-16 E | 55-57 N / 13-15 E | 4.0 N / 0.0 |
| 22. Swedish Coast (south coast) | c. 58.0 N / 5-10 E | 62.0 N / 2 W-3 E | 4.0 N / 6.0 W |
| 23. The Wash (England) | 53.0 N / 0.0 | 55.0 N / 1.0 W | 2.0 N / 1.0 W |

| Locality | True Position | Zara Map | Errors |
|---|---|---|---|
| 19. Isle of Wight, England | 50.5 N 1.0 W | 52.5 N 0.5 E | 2.0 N 1.5 E |
| 20. Lands End | 50.0 N 5.5 W | 52.5 N 2.5 W | 2.5 N 3.0 E |
| 21. Scilly Islands | | | |
| 22. St. Bride's Bay | 52.0 N 5.0 W | 54.5 N 2.0 W | 2.5 N 3.0 E |
| 23. Cape Clear, Ireland | 51.5 N 9.5 W | 53.0 N 7.0 W | 1.5 N 2.5 E |
| 24. Carnsore Point, | 52.3 N 6.5 W | 54.0 N 4.0 W | 1.7 N 2.5 E |
| 25. The Rhine | 52.0 N 4.0 E | 52.5 N 4.0 E | 0.5 N 0.0 |
| 26. The Elbe River | 54.0 N 9.0 E | 55.0 N 5.0 E | 1.0 N 4.0 W |
| 27. Erz Gebirge (Mts.) | 50–51 N 12–16 E | 53–56 N 13–16 E | c. 2.0 N 0.0 |
| 28. The Alps | 44–48 N 6–16 E | 46–50 N 6–16 E | 2.0 N 0.0 |
| THE MEDITERRANEAN | | | |
| 29. Cape Tres Forcas, Morocco | 35.5 N 3.0 W | 35.0 N 2.0 W | 0.5 S 1.0 E |
| 30. River Moulouya | | | |
| 31. Cape Bon | 37.0 N 11.0 E | 36.0 N 10.5 E | 1.0 S 0.5 W |
| 32. Iles Kerkennah | | | |
| 33. Ile Djerba | 34.0 N 11.0 E | 33.0 N 10.5 E | 1.0 S 0.5 W |
| 34. Cape Misurata | 32.5 N 15.3 E | 31.0 N 15.0 E | 1.5 S 0.3 W |
| 35. Bengazi | 32.0 N 20.0 E | 30.0 N 19.0 E | 2.0 S 1.0 W |
| 36. Ras et Tin | 32.5 N 23.0 E | 31.0 N 22.5 E | 1.5 S 0.5 W |
| 37. Alexandria | 31.0 N 30.0 E | 29.0 N correct by assumption | 2.0 S |

| Locality | True Position | Zara Map | Errors |
|---|---|---|---|
| 5. Almeria | 36.8 N 2.5 W | 36.3 N 2.2 W | 0.5 S 0.3 E |
| 6. Cape of Gata | 36.7 N 2.2 W | 36.1 N 2.0 W | 0.6 S 0.2 E |
| 7. Cape of Palos | 37.7 N 0.7 W | 36.9 N 0.0 | 0.8 S 0.7 E |
| 8. Alicante | 38.2 N 0.5 W | 37.5 N 0.3 E | 0.7 S 0.8 E |
| 9. Cape of Nao? | 38.7 N 0.2 E | 38.2 N 1.2 E | 0.5 S 1.0 E |
| 10. Valencia | 39.5 N 0.2 W | 39.0 N 0.8 E | 0.5 S 1.0 E |
| 12. Cape of Tortosa | 40.7 N 0.2 E | 40.3 N 2.3 E | 0.4 S 2.1 E |
| 13. Cape Trafalgar | 36.2 N 6.0 W | 36.0 N 6.7 W | 0.2 S 0.7 W |
| 14. Cádiz | 36.5 N 6.2 W | 36.2 N 6.7 W | 0.3 S 0.5 W |
| 15. Guadalquiver Delta | 36.7 N 6.2 W | 36.7 N 6.7 W | 0.0 0.5 W |
| 16. Huelva | 37.2 N 7.0 W | 37.2 N 7.5 W | 0.0 0.5 W |
| 17. Faro | 37.0 N 8.0 W | 36.8 N 8.7 W | 0.2 S 0.7 W |
| 18. Cape of Sao Vicente | 37.0 N 9.0 W | 37.0 N 9.7 W | 0.0 0.7 W |
| 19. Cape Sines | 38.0 N 8.7 W | 38.0 N 9.0 W | 0.0 0.3 W |
| 20. Cape Espichel | 38.5 N 9.2 W | 38.6 N 9.2 W | 0.1 N 0.0 |
| 21. Lisbon | 38.7 N 9.2 W | 38.8 N 9.2 W | 0.1 N 0.0 |
| 22. Cape Carvoeiro | 39.5 N 9.5 W | 39.7 N 9.3 W | 0.2 N 0.2 E |
| 23. Farilhoes Is. | 39.5 N 9.7 W | 39.7 N 9.6 W | 0.2 N 0.1 E |
| 24. Cape Mondego | 40.2 N 9.0 W | 40.2 N 8.9 W | 0.0 0.1 W |

| # | Locality | True Position | Zara Map | Errors |
|---|----------|---------------|----------|--------|
| 25. | Oporto | 41.2 N / 8.7 W | 41.0 N / 8.2 W | 0.2 S / 0.5 E |
| 26. | Vigo | 42.2 N / 8.7 W | 42.0 N / 8.6 W | 0.2 S / 0.1 E |
| 27. | Cap Finisterre | 42.7 N / 9.2 W | 43.0 N / 8.9 W | 0.3 N / 0.3 E |
| 28. | La Coruna | 43.5 N / 8.3 W | 43.2 N / 7.8 W | 0.3 S / 0.5 E |
| 29. | Cape Ortegal | 43.7 N / 7.7 W | 43.7 N / 7.4 W | 0.0 / 0.3 E |
| 30. | Cape of Penas | 43.7 N / 6.0 W | 43.5 N / 5.3 W | 0.2 S / 0.7 E |
| 31. | Santander | 43.5 N / 3.7 W | 42.9 N / 3.7 W | 0.6 S / 0.0 |
| 32. | Cape Machichaco | 43.5 N / 2.7 W | 43.0 N / 2.3 W | 0.5 S / 0.4 E |
| 33. | San Sebastian | 43.2 N / 2.7 W | 42.8 N / 1.3 W | 0.4 S / 1.4 E |
| 34. | Biarritz | 43.5 N / 1.5 W | 42.9 N / 1.0 W | 0.6 S / 0.5 E |

*Analysis of Errors in the ben Zara Map of Spain*

This suggests that a slight error in the length of the degree of longitude may have produced errors in the longitudes of places across Spain amounting to about 20 miles, while a smaller error in the length of the degree of latitude may have accounted for latitude errors averaging about six miles.

| | Latitude | Longitude |
|---|----------|-----------|
| (a) East Coast | 0.5 S* | 0.2 E |
| (b) West Coast | 0.0 | 0.1 E |
| (c) Northern Coast | 0.4 S | 0.4 E |
| (d) Southern Coast | 0.3 S† | 0.0 |

Error in Long. Distance, East and West coasts: 0.3°
Error in Lat. Distance, North and South coasts: 0.1°

\* Two localities anomalous, not averaged.
† One locality anomalous, not averaged.

| # | Locality | True Position | Errors |
|---|----------|---------------|--------|
| 38. | Cyprus | 34.5–35.5 N / 32.5–34.5 E | 1.5 S / 0.0 |
| 39. | The Bosphorus | 41.0 N / 29.0 E | 0.0 / 0.5 W |
| 40. | Yalta | 44.5 N / 34.0 E | 1.5 N / 0.5 E |
| 41. | Dolzhanskaya (Sea of Azov) | 46.0 N / 38.0 E | 2.0 N / 0.0 |
| | THE CENTRAL MEDITERRANEAN | | |
| 42. | Kythera (Cythera) Island (s. of Peloponnesus) | 36.3 N / 23.0 E | 1.3 S / 0.5 W |
| 43. | Trieste | 46.0 N / 14.0 E | 1.5 N / 1.0 E |
| 44. | Genoa | 44.3 N / 9.0 E | 0.2 N / 0.0 |
| 45. | Sicily, northern coast | 38.0 N / 12.5–15.5 E | 1.0 S / 0.0 |
| 46. | The Rhone River | 43.5 N / 5.0 E | 1.0 N / 0.0 |
| 47. | Mallorca | 39.5–40 N / 3.0 E | 0.0 / 0.0 |
| 48. | High and well-watered areas | | |
| 49. | Lake, no longer existent | | |
| 50. | Lake, no longer existent | | |

## Table 14  Ibn ben Zara (Spanish section)

| Locality | True Position | Zara Map | Errors |
|----------|---------------|----------|--------|
| 1. Tarifa | 36.0 N / 5.5 W | 35.8 N / 6.4 W | 0.2 S / 0.9 W |
| 2. La Linea | 36.2 N / 5.3 W | 35.8 N / 6.0 W | 0.4 S / 0.7 W |
| 3. Málaga | 36.7 N / 4.3 W | 36.2 N / 5.0 W | 0.5 S / 0.7 W |
| 4. Motril | 36.7 N / 3.5 W | 36.1 N / 3.7 W | 0.6 S / 0.3 E |

## Table 15 Alternative Grid for the East Coast of South America (Piri Re'is Map)

| Locality | True Position | Alternative Grid | Errors |
|---|---|---|---|
| 1. The Amazon (Para River) | 0.0 48.0 W | 0.0 48.0 W | correct by assumption |
| 2. Bahia de Sao Marcos | 2.0 S 44.0 W | 3.0 S 44.0 W | 1.0 S 0.0 |
| 3. Parnaiba | 3.0 S 42.0 W | 3.0 S 44.0 W | 0.0 1.0 E |
| 4. Fortaleza | 3.5 S 38.5 W | 3.0 S 37.5 S | 0.5 N 1.0 E |
| 5. C. de Sao Roque | 5.0 S 35.5 W | 2.5 S 36.0 W | 2.5 N 0.5 W |
| 6. Recife | 8.0 S 35.0 W | 4.5 S 34.5 W | 3.5 N 0.0 |
| 7. Rio Sao Francisco | 10.5 S 36.5 W | 7.5 S 36.5 W | 3.0 N 0.0 |
| 8. Salvador | 13.0 S 38.5 W | 10.0 S 38.0 W | 3.0 N 0.5 E |
| 9–11. Ponta de Baleia | 17.6 S 39.0 W | 16.0 S 39.0 W | 1.6 N 0.0 |
| 12. C. de Sao Tomé (and Rio Paraiba) | 22.0 S 41.0 W | 19.0 S 40.0 W | 3.0 N 1.0 E. |
| 13. C. Frio | 23.0 S 42.0 W | 22.0 S 41.0 W | 1.0 N 1.0 E |
| 14a. Rio de Janeiro | 23.0 S 43.0 W | 23.0 S 44.0 W | correct by assumption 1.0 W |
| 14b. Bahia de Ilha Grande | 23.0 S 44.5 W | 24.0 S 45.0 W | 1.0 S 0.5 W |

| Locality | True Position | Hamy-King Chart | Errors |
|---|---|---|---|
| 16. Cape Blanc | 21.0 N 17.5 W | 23.0 N 17.5 W | 2.0 N 0.0 |
| 17. Dakar | 15.0 N 18.0 W | 15.0 N 17.0 W | 0.0 1.0 E |
| 18. Cape Palmas | 4.5 N 7.5 W | 2.0 N 4.0 W | 1.5 S 2.5 E |
| 19. Mouths of the Niger | 4.5 N 5.5–7.0 E | 5.0 N 12–13 E | 0.5 N 6.0 E |
| 20. Lake Victoria Nyanza | 0.0 33.0 E | 0.0 38.0 E | 0.0 5.0 E |
| 21. Cape Lopez | 0.5 S 9.0 E | 1.0 S 16.0 E | 0.5 S 7.0 E |
| 22. Cape Fria | 18.0 S 12.0 E | 20.0 S 20.0 E | 2.0 S 8.0 E |
| 23. Cape of Good Hope | 34.5 S 18.0 E | 34.0 S 25.5 E | 0.5 N 7.5 E |
| THE MEDITERRANEAN, BLACK SEA, AND AFRICA ON THE EQUATOR OF THE PROJECTION | | | |
| 24. Cape Bon | 37.0 N 11.0 E | 37.0 N 10.0 E | 0.0 1.0 E |
| 25. Bengasi | 32.0 N 20.0 E | 32.0 N 18.5 E | 0.0 1.5 E |
| 26. Alexandria | 31.5 N 30.0 E | 32.5 N 30.0 E | 1.0 N correct by assumption |
| 27. Cyprus | 35.0 N 33.0 E | 38.0 N 32.0 E | 3.0 N 1.0 W |
| 28. Crete | 35.0 N 25.0 E | 37.0 N 25.0 E | 2.0 N 0.0 |
| 29. Lebanon | 34.0 N 35.5 E | 36.0 N 34.0 E | 2.0 N 1.5 W |
| 30. The Bosporus | 41.0 N 29.0 E | 45.5 N 25.0 E | 4.5 N 4.0 W |
| 31. Sevastopol | 44.5 N 34.0 E | 50.0 N 32.0 E | 5.5 N 2.0 W |
| 32. Batum | 41.5 N 41.5 E | 49.0 N 40.0 E | 7.5 N 1.0 W |

## Table 16 The Hamy-King Chart of 1502–4*

| Locality | True Position | Hamy-King Chart | Errors |
|---|---|---|---|
| 1. Cape Wrath, Scotland | 58.5 N / 5.0 W | 61.0 N / 6.0 W | 2.5 N / 1.0 W |
| 2. Duncansby Head, Scotland | 58.6 N / 3.0 W | 60.0 N / 3.0 W | 1.4 N / 0.0 |
| 3. The Humber River, England | 53.5 N / 0.0 | 54.0 N / 0.0 | 0.5 N / 0.0 |
| 4. Malin Head, Ireland | 55.3 N / 7.4 W | 58.0 N / 9.0 W | 2.7 N / 1.6 W |
| 5. Cape Clear, Ireland | 51.5 N / 9.5 W | 51.5 N / 10.0 W | 0.0 / 0.5 W |
| 6. Land's End, England | 50.5 N / 4.8 W | 50.0 N / 7.5 W | 0.5 S / 2.2 W |
| 7. Brest, France | 48.5 N / 5.0 W | 49.0 N / 7.0 W | 0.5 N / 2.0 W |
| 8. Gironde River, France | 45.5 N / 1.0 W | 45.0 N / 2.0 W | 0.5 S / 1.0 W |
| 9. Cape Finisterre, Spain | 43.0 N / 9.4 W | 42.5 N / 10.5 W | 0.5 S / 1.1 W |
| 10. Cape San Vincent, Spain | 37.0 N / 9.0 W | 35.0 N / 9.5 W | 2.0 S / 0.5 W |
| 11. Gibraltar, Strait of | 36.0 N / 5.5 W | 34.0 N / 6.0 W | 2.0 S / 0.4 S |
| 12. The Azores | 38.0 N / 28.0 W | 38.0 N / 24.0 W | 0.0 / 4.0 E |
| 13. Madeira Islands | 33.0 N / 17.0 W | 31.0 N / 16.0 W | 2.0 S / 1.0 E |
| 14. Canary Islands | 28.0 N / 16.0 W | 25.0 N / 15.0 W | 3.0 S / 1.0 E |

\* Based on the upper Equator (the correct equator for the projection) except where otherwise indicated.

THE WEST AFRICAN COAST AND INTERIOR ON THE LOWER EQUATOR

| Locality | True Position | Hamy-King Chart | Errors |
|---|---|---|---|
| 15. Cape Verde Islands | 15.0 N / 24.0 W | 15.0 N / 22.0 W | 0.0 / 2.0 E |

| Locality | True Position | Hamy-King Chart | Errors |
|---|---|---|---|
| 33. Port Elizabeth | 34.0 S / 25.5 E | 33.0 S / 34.0 E | 1.0 S / 8.5 E |
| 34. Laurence Marques (Delagoa Bay) | 26.0 S / 33.0 E | 23.0 S / 41.5 E | 3.0 N / 8.5 E |
| 35. Save River | 22.0 S / 35.0 E | 15.0 S / 50.0 E | 7.0 S / 15.0 E |
| 36. Cape Delgado | 10.5 S / 40.3 W | 10.5 S / 50.0 E | 0.0 / 9.7 E |
| 37. Mozambique | 15.0 S / 40.5 E | 10.0 S / 50.0 E | 5.0 N / 9.5 E |
| 39. Cape Guardafui | 12.0 N / 51.0 E | 7.0 N / 58.0 E | 5.0 S / 7.0 E |
| 40. Strait of Mandeb | 12.5 N / 43.0 E | 11.0 N / 44.5 E | 1.5 S / 1.5 E |
| 41. Gulf of Aden | 11– 15 N / 43– 53 E | 6– 14 N / 45– 58 E | 1.0 S / 5.0 E |
| 42. Red Sea | 13– 26 N / 34– 43 E | 9– 31 N / 32– 45 E | Latitude ratio = 13:22 / 2.0 E |
| 43. Canal said built by Rameses II, restored by Cyrus of Persia | | | |
| 44. Blue Nile (Kartoum) | 15.5 N / 32.5 E | 17.0 N / 31.0 E | 1.5 N / 1.5 W |
| 45. Abu Hamad | 19.5 N / 33.0 E | 22.0 N / 33.0 E | 2.5 N / 3.0 W |
| 46. Dibba (Entrance to Persian Gulf) | 25.5 N / 51.0 E | 24.0 N / 65.0 E | 1.5 S / 14.0 E |
| 47. Tigris-Euphrates River | 30.0 N / 48.0 E | 34.0 N / 51.5 E | 4.0 N / 3.5 E |
| 48. Caspian Sea | 36.5–47.5 N / 47– 53.5 E | 40– 50 N / 50– 77 E | c. 3.0 N / * |
| 49. Volga River | 47.0 N / 47.0 E | 48.0 N / 52.5 E | 1.0 N / 5.5 E |
| 50. Ural River | 48.0 N / 52.0 E | 50.0 N / 74.0 E | 2.0 N / 22.0 E* |

\* Stretching of longitude—see text.

SIBERIA AND ALASKA

| Locality | True Position | Hamy-King Chart | Errors |
|---|---|---|---|
| 51. Kanin Peninsula, Barents Sea, Arctic Ocean | 68.0 N / 45.0 E | 72.0 N / 52.0 E | 4.0 N / 7.0 E |

| Locality | True Position | Hamy-King Chart | Errors |
|---|---|---|---|
| 52. Kolguyev Island, Barents Sea (as an archipelago) | 69.0 N 50.0 E | 78.0 N 55.0 E | 9.0 N 5.0 E |
| 53. Baydaratskaya Bay, Kara Sea | 70.0 N 65.0 E | 68.0 N 72.0 E | 2.0 S 7.0 E |
| 54. Mouths of the Lean River | 72.0 N 123–130 E | 70.0 N 164–176 E | 2.0 S 43.0 E |
| 55. Gulf of Anadyr | 62– 66 N 180–175 W | 65.0 N 155.0 W | 0.0 20.0 E |
| 56. Lake Baikal | 52– 56 N 105–110 E | 36– 42 N 180 E/W | 14.0 S 70.0 E |
| 57. Wrangel Island | 71.0 N 180 E/W | 72.0 N 170.0 W | 1.0 N 10.0 E |
| 58. Alaska, Cape Lisburne | 69.0 N 167.0 W | 86.0 N 170.0 W | 17.0 N 15.0 E |
| 59. Alaska, Point Hope | 68.5 N 167.0 W | 82.0 N 152.0 W | 13.5 N 15.0 E |
| 60. Cape Engano, Dominican Republic | 18.5 N 72.0 W | 25.0 N 72.0 W | 6.5 N 0.0 |
| 61. Cape Gallinas, Colombia | 12.5 N 72.5 W | 17.0 N 70.0 W | 4.5 N 2.5 E |
| 62. Orinoco (estuary) | 9.0 N 62.0 W | 14.0 N 56.0 W | 5.0 N 6.0 E |
| 63. Cape Sao Roque | 5.2 S 35.0 W | 8.0 S 30.0 W | 2.8 S 5.0 E |
| 64. Salvador | 13.0 S 38.0 W | 15.0 S 34.0 W | 2.0 S 4.0 E |
| 65. Cape Frio (Rio de Janeiro) | 23.0 S 42.0 W | 25.0 S 37.0 W | 2.0 S 5.0 E |
| 66. Porto Alegre | 30.0 S 51.0 W | 33.0 S 45.0 W | 3.0 S 6.0 E |
| 67. Strait of Magellan? | 52.0 S 69.0 W | 55.0 S 45.0 W | 3.0 S 24.0 E |
| 68. Palmer or Antarctic Peninsula? | 63– 70 S 60.0 W | 80– 90 S 20.0 E | 20.0 S 80.0 E |
| 69. Labrador | 50– 60 N 55– 65 W | 58– 63 N 22– 33 W | c. 5.0 N c. 33.0 E |
| 70. Newfoundland | 47– 52 N 55– 60 W | 48– 65 N 42– 52 W | c. 6.0 N c. 10.0 E |

| Locality | True Position | Hamy-King Chart | Errors |
|---|---|---|---|
| RESTORED ERASURE: the islands of Japan apparently taken for the Philippines | | | |
| 89. Hokkaido | | | |
| 90. Cape Shanotan | | | |
| 91. Honshu | | | |
| 92. Noto Peninsula | | | |
| 93. Skikoku | | | |
| 94. Kyushu | | | |

## Table 17  The European Sector of the Hamy-King World Chart

| Feature | True Position | Hamy-King Position | Errors |
|---|---|---|---|
| 1. Cape Wrath, Scotland | 58.6 N 5.0 W | 58.9 N 3.0 W | 0.3 N 2.0 E |
| 2. Duncansby Head, Scotland | 58.6 N 3.0 W | 58.0 N 0.0 | 0.6 S 3.0 E |
| 3. Humber River, England | 53.5 N 0.0 | 54.0 N 0.0 | 0.5 N 0.0 |
| 4. North Foreland, England | 51.3 N 1.4 E | 50.0 N 0.7 E | 1.3 S 0.7 W |
| 5. St. David's Head, England | 51.8 N 5.3 E | 52.0 N 4.5 W | 0.2 N 0.8 E |
| 6. The Wash, England | 51.0 N 0.3 E | 52.5 N 1.0 E | 1.5 N 0.7 E |
| 7. Isle of Wight, England | 50.6 N 1.3 W | 49.5 N 2.0 W | 1.1 S 0.7 W |
| 8. Land's End, England | 50.0 N 5.7 W | 50.0 N 5.0 W | 0.0 0.7 E |
| 9. Isle of Man, Britain | 54.3 N 4.5 W | 53.5 N 4.0 W | 0.8 S 0.5 E |
| 10. Malin Head, Ireland | 55.3 N 7.4 W | 56.5 N 6.0 W | 1.2 N 1.4 E |

## SOUTHEAST ASIA

| | | | | | |
|---|---|---|---|---|---|
| 71. Indus River | 24.0 N | 67.5 E | 22.0 N | 85.0 E | 2.0 S / 17.5 E |
| 72. Ganges River | 22.5 N | 91.0 E | 20.0 N | 124.0 E | 2.5 S / 33.0 E |
| 73. Ceylon | 3– 10 N | 80– 82 W | 12– 17 S | 90– 95 E | 15.0 S / 10.0 E |
| 74. Madagascar | 12– 25 S | 43– 50 W | 20– 28 S | 79– 90 E | c. 6.0 S / c. 40.0 E |
| 75. Himalaya, Pamirs, Tien Shan Mountain System | 25– 45 N | 70– 95 E | 15– 48 N | 115–140 E | Ratio: 20:33* / Ratio: 25:25° |
| 76. Cape Negrais (Rangoon) | 16.0 N | 94.0 N | 8.0 N | 134.0 E | 8.0 S / 40.0 E |
| 77. Malayan Union | 1– 5 N | 100–103 E | 4 S–4 N | 135–141 E | 1.0 S / 36.0 E |
| 78. Gulf of Siam | 8– 13 N | 100–105 E | 0– 18 N | 145–154 E | 0.0† / 46.0 E |

* The total latitude covered by the mountain system is exaggerated, but is correct at the north. The total longitude covered is correct.
† Error in scale, not in latitude.

| | | | | | |
|---|---|---|---|---|---|
| 79. Cape Mui Bai Bung, South Vietnam | 8.5 N | 105.0 E | 2.0 S | 152.0 E | 10.5 S / 47.0 E |
| 80. Cape Djambuair, Sumatra | 8.5 N | 105.0 E | 2.0 S | 152.0 E | 10.5 S / 47.0 E |
| 81. Rata, Sumatra (Sunda Strait) | 6.0 S | 105.0 E | 31.5 S | 140.0 E | 25.5 S / 35.0 E |
| 82. A land mass embracing Sumatra, Malaysia, Thailand, and Cambodia. (Malaysia is duplicated.) | | | | | |
| 83. Phuket (Peninsula and island, Malay Peninsula) | 6.0 N | 99.0 E | 15.0 S | 144.0 E | 21.0 S / 45.0 E |
| 84. Gulf of Tonkin | 20.0 N | 106–110 E | 10– 15 S | 167–173 E | c. 30.0 S / c. 60.0 E |
| 85. Red River mouth | 20.2 N | 106.5 E | 10.0 S. | 165.0 E | 30.2 S / 58.5 E |
| 86. Taiwan? | | | | | |
| 87. Yellow Sea? | | | | | |
| 88. Korea? | | | | | |

| | | | | | |
|---|---|---|---|---|---|
| 11. Cape Clear, Ireland | 51.5 N | 9.5 W | 51.0 N | 8.5 W | 0.5 S / 1.0 E |
| 12. C. de La Hague, France | 49.6 N | 2.0 W | 48.5 N | 2.5 W | 1.1 S / 0.5 W |
| 13. River Loire, France | 47.2 N | 2.0 W | 46.0 N | 2.0 W | 1.2 S / 0.0 |
| 14. River Gironde, France | 45.5 N | 1.0 W | 45.0 N | 1.0 W | 0.5 S / 0.0 |
| 15. San Sebastien, Spain | 43.4 N | 2.0 W | 42.5 N | 2.5 W | 0.9 S / 0.5 W |
| 16. C. Finisterre, Spain | 43.0 N | 9.2 W | 43.5 N | 9.0 W | 0.5 N / 0.2 E |
| 17. C. St. Vincent, Spain | 37.0 N | 9.0 W | 37.0 N | 9.5 W | 0.0 / 0.5 W |
| 18. The Azores | 37–40 N | 25–31 W | 38–43 N | 21–29 W | 2.0 N / 3.0 E |
| 19. Madeira | 32.5 N | 17.0 W | 34.5 N | 17.5 W | 2.0 N / 0.5 W |
| 20. The Canaries | 28–29 N | 14–18 W | 30–31 N | 14–19 W | 2.0 N / 0.0 |
| 21. Gibraltar | 36.0 N | 5.5 W | 36.0 N | 5.5 W | 0.0 / 0.0 |
| 22. C. Nao, Spain | 40.0 N | 0.3 E | 38.5 N | 0.7 E | 1.5 S / 0.4 E |
| 23. Mallorca | 39.5 N | 3.0 E | 39.5 N | 3.0 E | 0.0 / 0.0 |
| 24. River Rhone, France | 43.0 N | 4.7 E | 44.0 N | 5.0 E | 1.0 N / 0.3 E |
| 25. Toulon, France | 43.0 N | 6.0 E | 42.5 N | 6.0 E | 0.5 S / 0.0 |
| 26. C. Corse, Corsica | 43.0 N | 9.3 E | 42.5 N | 9.0 E | 0.5 S / 0.3 W |
| 27. Strait of Bonifacio (Corsica-Sardinia) | 41.2 N | 9.2 E | 40.5 N | 8– 8.7 E | 0.7 S / 0.5 W |
| 28. C. Toulada, Sardinia | 39.0 N | 8.7 E | 38.0 N | 8.0 E | 1.0 S / 0.7 W |
| 29. C. Bon, Tunisia | 37.0 N | 11.0 E | 36.5 N | 11.0 E | 0.5 S / 0.0 |
| 30. Bay of Naples, Italy | 40.8 N | 14.0 E | 40.7 N | 13.5 E | 0.1 S / 0.5 W |
| 31. Strait of Messina, Italy | 38.0 N | 15.5 E | 37.5 N | 15.5 E | 0.5 S / 0.0 |

| Feature | True Position | Hamy-King Position | Errors |
|---|---|---|---|
| 32. C. Santa Maria de Leuca, Italy | 39.7 N<br>18.5 E | 39.0 N<br>18.0 E | 0.7 S<br>0.5 W |
| 33. C. Vieste, Italy | 41.8 N<br>16.3 E | 41.5 N<br>16.5 E | 0.3 S<br>0.2 E |
| 34. Istrian Peninsula, Yugoslavia | 45.0 N<br>14.0 E | 45.0 N<br>14.0 E | 0.0<br>0.0 |
| 35. Djerba, Tunisia | 34.0 N<br>11.0 E | 33.7 N<br>11.0 E | 0.3 S<br>0.0 |
| 36. C. Misratan, Libya | 32.5 N<br>15.2 E | 32.4 N<br>15.5 E | 0.1 S<br>0.3 E |
| 37. Bengazi, Libya | 32.0 N<br>20.0 E | 32.0 N<br>19.0 E | 0.0<br>1.0 W |
| 38. Alexandria, Egypt | 32.0 N<br>30.0 E | 31.0 N<br>30.0 E | 1.0 S<br>by assumption |
| 39. The Piraeus, Greece | 38.0 N<br>23.0 E | 38.0 N<br>22.5 E | 0.0<br>0.5 W |
| 40. Crete | 35.0 N<br>25.0 E | 35.0 N<br>25.0 E | 0.0<br>0.0 |
| 41. Cyprus | 35.0 N<br>33.0 E | 35.0 N<br>25.0 E | 0.0<br>0.0 |
| 42. Site of Ancient Tyre (Lebanon) | 33.3 N<br>35.5 E | 33.0 N<br>35.0 E | 0.3 S<br>0.3 W |
| 43. Ancient Mediterranean-Red Sea Canal | | | |
| 44. Salonika, Greece | 40.7 N<br>23.0 E | 42.0 N<br>22.5 E | 1.3 N<br>0.5 W |
| 45. The Bosphorus | 41.0 N<br>29.09 E | 41.5 N<br>29.0 E | 0.5 N<br>0.0 |
| 46. Sevastopol, Crimea, USSR | 46.5 N<br>34.0 E | 45.0 N<br>34.5 E | 1.5 S<br>0.5 E |
| 47. Taganrog, USSR | 47.0 N<br>39.0 E | 48.0 N<br>39.5 E | 1.0 N<br>0.5 E |
| 48. Batum, Caucasus, USSR | 41.5 N<br>41.5 E | 42.5 N<br>43.0 E | 1.5 N<br>1.5 E |
| 49. Shetland islands | 60.0 N<br>2.0 W | 62–65 N<br>1– 2 E | c. 3.0 N<br>c. 3.0 E |
| 50. North Cape (Norway) | 71.0 N<br>25.0 E | 72.0 N<br>20.0 E | 1.0 N<br>5.0 W |

# Table 18   The Azores

A comparison of the Maximum Extent of each island in minutes of latitude and longitude on the Piri Re'is and modern maps (approximate figures).

| | Modern Map | Piri Re'is | Ratio | Multiplier |
|---|---|---|---|---|
| 1. Corvo | Lat. 4'<br>Long. 2' | 30'<br>30' | 4:30<br>2:30 | 7.0<br>15.0 |
| 2. Flores | Lat. 11'<br>Long. 8' | 84'<br>42' | 11:84<br>8:42 | 7.5<br>5.0 |
| 3. Faial | Lat. 9'<br>Long. 8' | 60'<br>60' | 9:60<br>13:60 | 6.5<br>2.0 |
| 4. Pico | Lat. 11'<br>Long. 26' | 48'<br>48' | 11:48<br>26:48 | 4.5<br>2.0 |
| | (Two islets are considered to be part of Pico) | | | |
| 5. Sao Jorge | Lat. 18'<br>Long. 33' | 40'<br>48' | 18:40<br>33:48 | 2.0<br>1.5 |
| 6. Graciosa | Lat. 7'<br>Long. 7' | 30'<br>40' | 7:30<br>7:40 | 4.0<br>6.0 |
| 7. Terceira | Lat. 11'<br>Long. 20' | 50'<br>48' | 11:50<br>20:48 | 4.5<br>2.5 |
| 8. Sao Miguel | Lat. 12'<br>Long. 42' | 48'<br>90' | 12:48<br>42:90 | 4.0<br>2.0 |
| 9. Santa Maria (Anomalous, shown as four small islands) | | | | |

*The Scale of the Archipelago*

Despite the fact that all the islands are shown greatly magnified, the archipelago occupies approximately correct amounts of latitude and longitude, as shown by the positions of the northwesternmost and southeasternmost islands.

| | Modern Map | Piri Re'is Map | Errors |
|---|---|---|---|
| 1. Corvo | 39.7° N<br>31.1° W | 40.0 N<br>32.0 W | 0.3 N<br>0.9 W |
| 2. S. Maria | 37.0° N<br>25.0° W | 36.0 N<br>25.0 W | 1.0 S<br>0.0 |

# Bibliography

This list includes not only works referred to in the text, but a selection of the relevant literature (with no attempt at comprehensiveness). It is hoped that it may be helpful at least as a starting point for those wishing to pursue further studies.

1. "A Columbus Controversy" (Piri Re's Map), *Illustrated London News*, February 27, 1932.
2. Afet Inan, Dr. *The Oldest Map of America, Drawn by Piri Re'is*. Translated by Dr. Leman Yolac. Ankara: the National Library, 1954.
3. *Afrique* [Physical map of Africa]. (Sheets 1 and 3: Northwest Africa and West Africa to the Gold Coast.) Paris: Institut Géographique Nationale, 1940–1941.
4. Ainalov, D. V. *The Hellenistic Origins of Byzantine Art*. Translated from the Russian by E. and S. Sobolovitch. New Brunswick, N.J.: Rutgers University Press, 1961.
5. Akçura, Yusuf. *Piri Re'is Haritasi hakkinda izahname*. "Turk Tarihi Arastirma Kurumu yayinlarindan," No. 1. Istanbul, 1935.
6. ———. "Turkish Interest in America in 1513: Piri Re'is' Chart of the Atlantic," *Illustrated London News*, July 23, 1932.
7. Amalgia, Roberto, ed. See *Monumenta Cartographica Vaticana*.
8. *American Encyclopedia of History*, ed. Ridpath, J. C., *et al*. Vol. I. Philadelphia: Encyclopedia Publishing Company, 1919.
9. *American Oxford Atlas*. New York; Oxford University Press, 1951.
10. Andrews, E. Wylls. "Chronology and Astronomy in the Maya Area," *The Maya and Their Neighbors*. Memorial volume to Prof. Alfred M. Tozzer. New York and London: D. Appleton Century, n.d.
11. Andrews, M.C. "The British Isles in the Nautical Charts of the 14th and 15th Centuries," *Geographical Journal*, LXVIII (1926), 474–481.
12. ———. "The Study and Classification of Medieval Mappae Mundi," *Archeologia*, LXXXV (1926), 61–76.
13. ———. "Scotland in the Portolan Charts," *Scottish Geographical Magazine*, XLII (1926), 129–153, 193–213.
14. Anthiaume, l'Abbé A. *Cartes marines, Constructions navales, Voyages de découvertes chez les Normandes, 1500–1650*. Paris: Dumont, 1916.
14a. Arciniegas, German. *Amerigo and the New World*. New York, Knopf, 1955.
15. Ashe, Geoffrey. *Land to the West*. New York: The Viking Press, 1962.
16. Asimov, Isaac. *Asimov's Biographical Encyclopedia of Science and Technology*. Garden City, N.Y.: Doubleday, 1964.
17. *Atlas of Mountain Glaciers of the Northern Hemisphere*. (Technical Report EP-92.) Headquarters, Quartermaster Research and Engineering Command, U.S. Army, Natick, Mass., n.d.
18. *Atlas Över Sverige*. (Utgiven av Svenska Sallskapet For Anthropologi och Geografi.) Loose sheets.
19. d'Avezac-Macaya, Marie Armand Pascal. *Note sur un Mappemonde Turke du XVI° Siècle, conservée à la bibliothèque de Saint-Marc à Venise*. Paris: Imprimerie de E. Martinet, 1866.
20. Ayusawa, Shintaro. "The Types of World Maps Made in Japan's Age of National Isolation," *Imago Mundi*, X (1953), 125–128.

21. Babcock, William H. *Legendary Islands of the Atlantic*. ("American Geographical Society Research Series," No. 8.) New York: American Geographical Society, 1922.

22. Bagrow, Leo. *The History of Cartography*, ed. R. A. Skelton. Cambridge, Mass.: The Harvard University Press, 1964.

23. ———. "A Tale from the Bosphorus. Some Impressions of My Work at the Topkapu Saray Library, Summer of 1954," *Imago Mundi*, XII (1955).

24. Barnett, Lincoln, *Treasure of Our Tongue*. New York: Knopf, 1964.

25. Beazley, Charles Raymond. *The Dawn of Modern Geography*. 3 vols. London: J. Murray, 1897–1906.

26. ———. *Prince Henry the Navigator*. New York and London, 1895.

27. Belov, M. "Mistake or Intention?" (translated for E. A. Kendall), *Priroda*, No. 1 (November, 1960). (Moscow: Soviet Academy of Sciences.)

28. ———. "A Windfall Among Manuscripts" (translated for E. A. Kendall), *Vednyi Transport* (August 17, 1961).

28a. Berlitz, Charles. *Mysteries from Forgotten Worlds*. New York: Doubleday, 1972.

29. Bernardini-Sjoestedt, Armand. *Christophe Colomb*. Paris: Les Sept Couleurs, 1961.

30. Bibby, Geoffrey. *The Testimony of the Spade*. New York:Knopf; London: Collins, 1956.

30a. ———. *Looking for Dilmun*. New York: Knopf, 1969.

31. Bigelow, John. "The So-Called Bartholomew Columbus Map of 1506," *Geographical Review*, October, 1935, pp. 643–656.

32. Blacket, W. S. *Lost Histories of America* [etc.]. London: Trübner and Co., 1883. Now obtainable from University Microfilms, Ann Arbor, Mich. (Xerox).

33. Blundeville [Blundivile], M. *Blundeville His Exercises . . . A New and Necessarie Treatise of Navigation . . .* London, 1594.

34. Boland, Charles Michael. *They All Discovered America*. New York: Doubleday, 1961; Permabook Edition, 1963.

35. Boyd, William C. *Genetics and the Races of Man*. Boston: Little, Brown, 1952.

36. Braunlich, Erick. *Zwei turkischen Weltkarten aus dem Zeitalter der grossen Entdeckungen*. Leipsic: S. Hirzel, 1937.

37. Brooks, C. E. P. *Climate through the Ages*. New York: McGraw-Hill, 1949.

38. Brosses, C. de. *Histoire des Navigations aus Terres Australes*. 2 vols. Paris: Durand, 1756.

39. Brown, Lloyd Arnold. *The Story of Maps*. Boston: Little, Brown, 1950.

40. Bunski, Hans-Albretch von. "Kemal Re'is, ein Betrag zur Geschichte der turkischen Flotte." Bonn, 1928. (Ph.D. thesis.)

41. Calahan, Harold Augustin. *The Sky and the Sailor*. New York: Harper, 1952.

42. Callis, Helmut G. *China, Confucian and Communist*. New York: Henry Holt, 1959.

43. Caras, Roger A. *Antarctica—Land of Frozen Time*. Philadelphia: Chilton Books, 1962.

44. Carli, Carlo Giovanni Dinaede. *Lettres Americaines*. (French translation of his Italian work.) 2 vols. Boston, 1788.

45. *Cartografia de Ultramar*. Vol. I, 1949; Vol. II, 1953; Vol. III, 1955; Vol. IV, 1957. Madrid: Ejercito Servicio Geographico.

46. Cary, M., and E. H. Warmington. *The Ancient Explorers*. London: Methuen, 1929; New York: Pelican Books, 1963.

47. Chamberlin, Wellman. *Round Earth on Flat Paper*. Washington, D.C.: National Geographic Society, 1950.

48. Charlesworth, J. K. *The Quarternary Era with Special Reference to Its Glaciation*. 2 vols. London: Edward Arnold, Ltd., 1957. Vol. II.

49. Chatterton, E. Keble. *Sailing Ships and Their Story*. New ed. London: Sidgewick and Jackson, Ltd., 1923.

50. Chevallier, M. "L'Aimantation des lavas de l'Etna et l'orientation du champ terrestre en Sicile du XIIe au XVIIe Siècle," *Annales de Physique*, IV, 1925, pp. 5–162.

51. *China, Map of, Compiled and Drawn in the Cartographic Section of the National Geographic Society, for the National Geographic Magazine*. Washington, D.C.: National Geographic Society, 1945.

52. Claggett, Marshall. *Science in Antiquity*. New York: Collier Books, 1963.

52a. Cohane, John Philip. *The Key*. New York: Crown Publishers, 1969; Turnstone Press, London, 1973.

53. Commision on the Bibliography of Ancient Maps, International Geophysical Union. 2 vols. Paris, 1952. Pp. 63, 93.

53a. Cook, James. *Explorations in the Pacific,*

ed. Sir A. G. Price. New York: Dover, 1972.

54. Cortesao, Armand. *The Nautical Chart of 1424 and the Early Discovery and Cartographical Representation of America*. Coimbra, Portugal: University of Coimbra, 1954.

55. Crombie, A. C., ed. *Scientific Change*. London: Heinemann, 1963.

55a. Crone, J. R. *The Vinland Map Cartographically Considered*. Geographical Journal. Vol. 132, Part 1. March 1966, pp. 75–80.

56. Cummings, Byron S. "Cuicuilo and the Archaic Culture of Mexico," *Bulletin*, University of Arizona, IV, No. 8, Nov. 15, 1933.

57. ———. "Obituary," *Science*, CXX, No. 3115, Sept. 10, 1954, pp. 407–408.

58. Dampier, Sir William. *a History of Science* (3rd ed. rev.). New York: The Macmillan Company, 1944.

59. Davis, H. T. *Alexandria, the Golden City*. 2 vols. Evanston, Ill.: The Principia Press of Illinois.

60. Deetz, Charles H., and Oscar Adams. *Elements of Map Projection with Applications to Map and Chart Construction*. (U.S. Coast and Geodetic Survey "Special Publication," No. 68, Serial no. 146.) Washington, D.C.: Government Printing Office, 1921.

61. Deissmann, A. *Forschungen und Funde im Serai*. Berlin-Leipsic: 1933.

62. Denuce, Jean. Les Origines de la Cartographie portugaise et les Cartes de Reinel. Ghent: E. van Goethem, 1908.

63. Diller, Aubrey. "The Ancient Measurements of the Earth," *Isis*, XL (1948), pp. 6–9.

64. *Directory of Special Libraries and Research Centers*, ed. Anthony T. Kruzas. Detroit, Mich.: Gale Research Company, 1963.

65. Durand, Dana B. "The Origins of German Cartography in the 15th Century." 3 vols. and portfolio. (Thesis, Harvard University.)

66. ———. *The Vienna-Klosterneuburg Map Corpus of the 15th Century*. Leiden: E. J. Brill, 1952.

67. Eames, Wilberforce. *A List of the Editions of Ptolemy's Geography, 1475–1730*. New York, 1886.

68. *Encyclopedia Britannica* (11th ed.). VII, p. 869.

69. *Encyclopedia of Islam*, ed. M. Th. Houtsma, *et al*. Leiden: E. J. Brill, 1936.

70. *Expéditions Polaires Françaises, Missions Paul-Emile Victor*. "Campagne au Groenland, 1950, Rapports Préliminaires." "Campagne au Groenland, 1951, Rapports Préliminaires." Paris, 1953.

71. *Facsimiles of Portolan Charts*. Publication No. 114 of the Hispanic Society of America (Introduction by Edward Luther Stevenson). New York: The Hispanic Society, 1916.

72. Fairbridge, Rhodes, E. "Dating the Latest Movements of the Quarternary Sea Level." *Transactions*, New York Acad. Sci., Ser. II, XX, No. 6, pp. 471–482, April, 1958.

73. Finé, Oronce (Oronteus Finaeus). *Sphaera mundi* ... Lvtetiae Parisorum apud Michaëlem Vascasanum, 1551.

74. Fischer, Teobald. (Atlas-Series.) Venice: Ferd. Ongania, editore, 1881–1886.

75. ———. *Sammlung Mittelalterlicher Welt und Seekarten italienischen Ursprungs und aus italienischen Bibliotheken und Archiven*. Venice: F. Ongania, 1886.

76. Gallois, Lucien. *De Orontio Finaeo Gallico Geographo*. Paris: E. Lerous, 1890.

77. Glanville, S. R. K., ed. *The Legacy of Egypt*. Oxford: The Clarendon Press, 1957 (reprint).

78. Goodwin, William A. Letter to James A. Robertson, May 26, 1933 (analysis of the Piri Re'is Map). (Unpublished: Library of the American Geographical Society.)

79. Gordon, Cyrus H. "The Decipherment of Minoan," *Natural History*, LXXII, No. 9, November, 1963.

80. Gruneisen, W. de. *Les caractéristiques de l'art Copte*. Florence, Italy: Instituto di Edizione Artistiche Fratelli Alinari, 1922.

81. Guest, Edwin. *Origines Celticae and other contributions to the History of Britain*. 2 vols. London: The MacMillan Co., 1883. (Caesar's destruction of the Druid library.)

82. *A Guide to Historical Cartography*. Washington: Map Division, Library of Congress, 1954. Revised, 1960.

83. Hakki, Ibrahim. *Topkapi Sarayinde deri uzerine yapilmis eski Haritalar*. Istanbul, 1936.

84. Hamy, Jules Theodore Ernest. *La Map-*

*pemonde d'Angelino Dulcert de Majorque*, 1339 (2nd ed.). Paris: H. Champion, 1903.

85. Hapgood, Charles H. *Earth's Shifting Crust*. New York: Pantheon, 1958.

86. Hawkes, Jacquetta. The World of the Past. New York: Knopf, 1963.

87. Hawkins, Gerald S. "Stonehenge: A Neolithic Computer," *Nature*, CCII, No. 4939 (June 27, 1964), 1258–1261. Reprinted by the Smithsonian Astrophysical Observatory, Cambridge, Mass.

88. ———. "Stonehenge Decoded," *Nature*, CC, No. 4909 (October 26, 1963), 306–308. Reprinted by the Smithsonian Astrophysical Observatory, Cambridge, Mass.

89. Heathecote, N. H. de V. "Early Nautical Charts," *Annals of Science*, I (1963), 13–28.

90. ———. "Christopher Columbus and the Discovery of Magnetic Variation," *Science Progress*, XXVII (1932), 82–103.

91. Heidel, William. *The Frame of the Ancient Greek Maps*. American Geographical Society Research Series No. 20. New York: The Society, 1937.

92. Heizer, R. F., and J. A. Bennyhoff. "Archaeological Investigation of Cuicuilco, Valley of Mexico, 1957," *Science*, v. 127, No. 3292, pp. 232–233.

93. Hobbs, William H. "The Fourteenth Century Discoveries by Antonio Zeno," *The Scientific Monthly*, January, 1951, pp. 24–31.

94. ———. "Zeno and the Cartography fo Greenland," *Imago Mundi*, VI.

94a. Holand, Hjalmar R. *Explorations in America Before Columbus*. New York: Twayne Publishers, Inc., 1956.

95. Holtzscherer, J. J., and G. de Q. Robin. "Depth of Polar Ice Caps," *Geographical Journal*, CXX, Part 2, June, 1954, pp. 193–202.

96. Hough, Jack. "Pleistocene Lithology of Antarctic Ocean Bottom Sediments," *Journal of Geology*, LVIII, 257–259.

97. Humboldt, Alexander von. *Cosmos: A Sketch of a Physical Description of the Universe* (trans. E. C. Otte). New York: Harpers, 1852.

98. *Idrisi, World Map*. (1150 A.D.in Arabic.) Map Division, Library of Congress, 1951 (six sheets).

99. Irwin, Constance. *Fair Gods and Stone Faces: Ancient Seafarers and the World's Most Intriguing Riddle*. New York: St. Martin's Press, 1963.

100. Jeans, Sir James. *The Growth of Physical Science*. A Premier Book: Fawcett World Library, 1958.

101. Jervis, W. W. *The World in Maps*. London: George Philip and Son, 1936.

102. Johnston, Thomas Crawford. *Did the Phoenicians Discover America? Embracing the origin of the Aztecs, with some further light on Phoenician civilization and colonization. The Story of the Mariner's Compass*. San Francisco, 1892. 2nd ed. London: James Nisbet, 1913.

103. Jomard, Edme Francois. *Les Monuments de la Géographie*. Paris: Du Prat, 1862.

104. Kahle, Paul. "La Carte Mondiale de Piri Re'is." *Actes du XVIII Congress international des orientalistes*. Leiden, 1932.

105. ———. "Die Verschollene Columbus-Karte von Amerika von Jahre 1498 in einer turkischen Weltkarten von 1513," *Forschungen und Fortschritte*, 8 Jahrg. No. 19 (1 Juli 1932), pp. 248–249.

106. ———. "The Lost Map of Columbus," *The Geographical Review*, XXIII, No. 4 (1933).

107. Kamal, Prince Youssouf. *Hallucinations Scientifiques (Les Portulans)*. Leiden: E. J. Brill, 1937.

108. ———. *Monumenta Cartographica Africae et Aegypti*. 16 vols. in 5. Cairo, 1926–1951. (Vol. IV: Epoque des Portulans.)

109. Ketman, Georges. "The Disturbing Maps of Piri Re'is," *Science et Vie* (Paris), September, 1960.

110. Keuning, Johannes. "The History of Geographical Map Projection until 1600," *Imago Mundi*, XII (1955).

111. Kimble, George Herbert Tinsley. *Geography in the Middle Ages*. London: Methuen, 1938.

112. Kitson, Arthur. *Capt. James Cook, the Circumnavigator*. London: L. Murray, 1907.

113. Koeman, Cornelis. *Collections of Maps and Atlases in the Netherlands*. Leiden: E. J. Brill, 1961.

114. Konjnenburg, E. van. *Shipbuilding from Its Beginnings*. 3 vols. Brussels: Permanent International Association of Congresses of Navigation, Executive Committee, 1913.

115. Krachkovsky, J. "The Columbus Map of America, Worked in Turkish," *Isvestia*

(Moscow), VGO, XVI (1954), pp. 184–186.

116. Kretschmer, Konrad. *Die italienischen Portolane des Mittelalters; ein Beitrag zur Geschichte der Kartographie und Nautik*. Berlin: E. S. Mittler, 1909.

117. ———. "Die verschollene Kolumbuskarte von 1498 in einer turkischen Weltkarte von 1513" (A. Petermans), *Mitteilungen*, LXXX (1934).

119. La Roncière, Charles de. *La Découverte de l'Afrique au Moyen Age: Cartographie et Explorateurs*. 3 vols. (in Memoires of the Royal Society of the Geography of Egypt, Vols. V, VI, VII).

119a. Layng, T. E. *The King-Hamy Chart, 1502–1504, in Sixteenth Century Maps Relating to Canada*. Ottawa: Public Archives of Canada, 1956, No. 8.

120. Leithauser, Joachim G. von. *Mappae Mundi: die geistige Eroberung der Welt*. Berlin: Safari-Verlag, 1958.

121. Lelewel, Joachim. *Géographie du Moyen Age accompagné d'Atlas et de cartes dans chaque Volume*. Brussels: V. et J. Pilliet, 1850–1852.

122. ———. *Pytheas de Marseille et la géographie de son temps*. Paris: Straszéwicz, 1836.

123. Lewis, W. N. *The Splendid Century. Life in the France of Louis XIV*. Garden City, N.Y.: Doubleday, Anchor Books, 1957.

123a. Lhote, Henri. *The Search for the Tassili Frescoes*. New York: Dutton; London: Hutchinson, 1959.

124. Libby, Willard F. *Radiocarbon Dating*. Chicago: The Chicago University Press, 1952.

125. Lucas, Fred W. *Annals of the Brothers Niccolo and Antonio Zeno*. London: H. Stevens, Son and Stiles, 1898.

126. Lynam, Edward. *The Map-Maker's Art*. London: The Batchworth Press, 1953.

127. McElroy, John W. "The Ocean Navigation of Columbus on His First Voyage," *The American Neptune*, Vol. I, No. 3 (July, 1941).

128. Maggiolo, Visconte de. *Atlas of Portolan Charts*. New York: The Hispanic Society of America, 1911.

129. Major, R. H. *Voyages of the Zeno Brothers*. London: The Hakluyt Society, 1873; Boston: The Massachusetts Historical Society, 1875.

130. Mallery, Arlington H. *Lost America*. Washington, D.C.: The Overlook Printing Co., 1951.

131. Mallery, Arlington H., *et al*. "New and Old Discoveries in Antarctica," Georgetown University Forum of the Air, August 26, 1956 (mimeographed verbatim).

132. *Mapas Espanoles de America, Siglos XV–XVII*. Vorwick Jacobo Maria del Pilar Carlos Manuel Stuart, Duque de Fitz-James, ed., 1878. Madrid, 1941.

133. Marshak, Alexander. "Lunar Notation on Upper Paleolithic Remains," *Science*, CXLVI (November 6, 1964).

134. Means, Philip Ainsworth. "Pre-Spanish Navigation off the Andean Coast,"*American Neptune*, II, No. 2 (April, 1942).

135. Mercator, Gerardus. *Correspondence Mercatorienne*, ed. M. van Durme. Anvers: De Nederlandsche Boekhandel, 1959.

135a. Mertz, Henriette, *Pale Ink: Two Ancient Records of Chinese Exploration in America*. Chicago: Swallow Press, 1972. (*Recently republished as Gods from the Far East*).

136. Miller, Konrad, ed. *Mappae Arabicae*. Stuttgart (privately printed), 1926–1929.

137. ———. *Mappaemundi: Die altesten Welkarten*. 6 vols. Stuttgart: Roth, 1895–1898.

138. *Monumenta Cartographica Africae et Aegypti*, see Kamal.

139. *Monumenta Cartographica Vaticana*, ed. Roberto Amalgia. 5 vols. Vatican City, 1944.

140. Morison, Samuel E. *Admiral of the Ocean Sea*. Boston: Little, Brown, 1942.

141. ———. *Christopher Columbus, Mariner*. Mentor Books, 1956.

143. Motzo, Bacchisio R., ed. *Il compasso da navigare; opera italiana della metà del secolo XIII* [etc.]. Cagliari: Universita, 1947.

144. Needham, Joseph. "Poverties and Triumphs of Chinese Scientific Tradition." (In Crombie.)

145. ———. *Science and Civilization in China*. 3 vols. Cambridge University Press, 1959.

146. Nordenskiöld, A. E. *Facsimile-Atlas to the Early History of Cartography, with Reproductions of the Most Important Maps printed in the XVth and XVIth Centuries*. Translated from the Swedish original by J. A. Ekelbf and C. R. Markham. Stockholm, 1889.

147. ———. *Periplus: An Essay in the Early History of Charts and Sailing Directions*. Translated from the Swedish original by

F. A. Bathev. Stockholm: Norstedt, 1897.

148. Norlund, Niels Erick. *Islands Kortlaegning en Historisk Fremstilling*. (Geodaetsk Instituts Publication VII.) Copenhagen: Ejnar Munksgaard, 1944.

149. "Notice of a British Discovery of Antarctica in 1819," *Blackwood's Magazine*, VII (August, 1920), p. 566.

150. *Nouvelle Biographie Universelle*. Paris: Firmin Didot Frères, 1858.

151. Nowell, Charles E. *The Great Discoveries and the First Colonial Empires*. Ithaca, N.Y.: Cornell Univ. Press, 4th Printing, 1964.

152. Nunez, Pedro. *Tratado da Sphera*. Lisbon, 1537.

153. Nunn, George E. *The Geographical Conceptions of Columbus*. New York: American Geographical Society, 1924.

154. Oberhummer, A. K. "Eine turkische Karte zur Endeckung Amerikas," *Anzeiger der Akademie der Wissenschaften* (Vienna), Philos-histor-Kl 68, 1931, pp. 99–112.

155. *Oceanographic Atlas of the Polar Seas*. (U.S. Hydrographic Office Publication No. 705.) Part I, "Antarctica," 1957.

156. Oronteus Finaeus. Biography. See Finé, Orance, in *Nouvelle Biographie Universelle*, Paris: Firmin Didot Frères, 1858.

157. —— *Cartes Géographiques dessignées par O. Finé: Galliae totius nova descriptio*. Paris, 1525, 1557; Venice, 1561, 1566; Cosmographia universalis: Paris, 1536, 1566 (lost?).

158. Parry, J. H. *The Age of Reconnaissance*. Mentor Books (No. 597), 1963.

159. Parsons, Edward Alexander. *The Alexandrian Library*. Amsterdam, London, New York: The Elsevier Press, 1952.

160. Pauvels, Louis, and Jacques Bergier. *The Dawn of Magic*. Trans. Rollo Myers. London: Anthony Gibbs and Phillips, 1963.

161. Pears, Edwin. *The Destruction of the Greek Empire and the Story of the Capture of Constantinople by the Turks*. New York: Longmans, Green and Co., 1903.

162. Penrose, Boies. *Travel and Discovery in the Renaissance, 1420–1620*. Cambridge, Mass.: Harvard University Press, 1955.

163. Petermans, A. *Mitteilungen aus Justis Perthes' Geographischer Anstalt*. XXXIX, No. 182 (Mercator). Gotha: Justus Perthes, 1915.

164. Piri Re'is (Muhiddin ibn Mahmud or Ahmet Muhiddin). *Kitabe Bahriye*. 2 vols. Berlin: De Gruyter, 1926.

165. Pohl, Frederick, J. *Atlantic Crossings Before Columbus*. New York: W. W. Norton, 1961.

166. *Portugaliae Monumenta Cartographica*, ed. Armando Cortesao and Avelino Teixeiro da Mota. 4 vols. (Portuguese and English.) Lisbon, 1960.

167. Price, Derek de Solla. "An Ancient Greek Computer," *The Scientific American*. CC, No. 6 (June, 1959).

168. Ptolemy, Claudius. *The Geography*, translated and edited by Edward Luther Stevenson, with reproductions of the maps. New York: The New York Public Library, 1932.

169. Pullè, Francesco Lorenzo. *La Carographia antica dell'India*. (Vol. I: Byzantine and Arab; Vol. II: Medieval and Early Renaissance; Vol. II, Supplement: The Orient; Vol. III: The Century of the Discovery.) 1901–1902.

170. "Radiocarbon": *Supplement of the American Journal of Science*, I–VII (1959–1965). New Haven: The Yale University Press.

171. Rainaud, Armand. *Le Continent Austral, hypothèses et découvertes*. Paris: Armand Colin, 1893.

172. Ravenstein, E. G. *Martin Behaim, His Life and Works*. London: George Philip and Son, 1908.

173. Rawlinson, George. *The Five Great Monarchies of the Ancient Eastern World*. 4th ed., 3 vols. New York: Scribner and Welford, 1880.

175. Reymond, Arnold. *History of the Sciences in Graeco-Roman Antiquity*. Trans. Ruth de Bray. New York: E. P. Dutton, 1932.

175a. Richy, M. W. *The Vinland Map*. Journal of The Institute of Navigation. Vol. 19, No. 1, January, 1966, pp. 124–125.

176. Ristow, W. W., and C. E. Legear. A Guide to Historical Cartography (2nd rev. ed.). Washington, D.C.: The Library of Congress, 1960.

177. Robbins, Roland W., and Evan Jones. *Hidden America*. New York: Knopf, 1959.

178. Roncière. See La Roncière (119).

179. Rotz, John. *John Rotz: His Books of Hydrography (1542)*. (Brit. Mus. Ms. 20. E.IX.)

180. Rouse, Irving. "Prehistory of the West Indies," *Science*, CXLIV, no. 3618, May 11, 1964.

181. Salinari, Marina Emiliani. "An Atlas of the 15th Century Preserved in the Library of the former Serail in Constantinople," *Imago Mundi*, Vol. III, 1951, pp. 101–102.

182. Santarem, Vicomte de. *Atlas Composé de Mappemondes, de portulans et de cartes hydrographiques et historiques depuis le VI° jusqu'au XVII° Siècle* [etc.].

183. Sarton, George. *A Guide to the History of Science*. New York: The Ronald Press Co., 1952.

184. ———. *Hellenistic Science and Culture in the Last Three Centuries B.C.* Cambridge, Mass.: Harvard University Press, 1952.

185. Schulmberger, Gustave. *Le siège, la prise et le sac de Constantinople par les turcs en 1453*. Paris: Librarie Plon, 1913 (reprinted with slight changes—no date—before 1935).

186. Schütt, Gudmund. *Ptolemy's Maps of Northern Europe: A Reconstruction of the Prototypes*. (Royal Danish Geographical Society.) Copenhagen: H. Hagerup, 1917.

187. Selen, H. Sadi. *Piri Re'is in Simali Amerika*. Haritasi Bulletin, No. II'den ayri basim Istanbul: Devlet Basimevi, 1937.

189. Sharpe, Samuel. *Alexandrian Chronology from the Building of the City until Its Conquest by the Arabs (A.D. 640)*. London, 1857 (no publisher).

190. Silverberg, Robert. *Lost Cities and Vanished Civilizations*. Philadelphia: Chilton Books, 1962.

190a. Skelton, R. A., Thomas E. Marston, and George D. Painter. *The Vinland Map and The Tartar Relation*. Yale University Press, 1965.

191. Stahl, William Harris. *Ptolemy's Geography: A select bibliography*. New York: The New York Public Library, 1953.

192. Stefansson, Vilhjalmur. *Greenland*. New York: Doubleday, Doran and Company, 1942.

193. Steger, Ernst. *Untersuchungen über italienische seekarten des mittelalters auf grund der kartometrischen methode*. Gottingen: W. F. Kaestner, 1896.

194. Stevens, Henry. *Johann Schöner: a reproduction of his globe of 1523 long lost*. London: H. Stevens & Son, 1888.

195. Stevenson, Edward Luther. *Marine World Chart of Nicolo de Canerio Januensis (1502)*. New York: The De Vinne Press, 1908.

196. ———. *Terrestrial and Celestial Globes, Their History and Construction* [etc.]. 2 vols. New Haven: published for the Hispanic Society of America by the Yale University Press, 1921.

197. Strabo. *The Geography of Strabo*. (Trans. by Horace Leonard Jones.) The Loeb Classical Library. London: Heinemann; New York: Putnam, 1923–1928.

199. Taylor, E. G. R. *The Haven-Finding Art: A History of Navigation from Odysseus to Captain Cook*. New York: Abelard-Schuman Ltd., 1957.

200. ———. "Jean Rotz and the Marine Chart," *Journal of the Institute of Navigation*, VII, No. 2 (April, 1954), pp. 136–143.

201. ———. "The Navigating Manual of Columbus," *Journal of the Institute of Navigation*, V, No. 1 (January, 1952), pp. 42–54.

202. ———. "The Oldest Mediterranean Pilot (Carta Pisana)," *Journal of the Institute of Navigation*, IV, 81 (1951).

203. Teleki, Paul. *Atlas zur Geschichte der Kartographes der japonischen Inseln*. Budapest, 1909; Leipsic: K. W. Hiersemann, 1909.

203a. Temple, Robert. *The Sirius Mystery*, London: Sidgwich & Jackson; New York: St. Martins, 1976.

204. Thalamas, A. *La Géographie* [de Eratosthenes]. (Ph.D. Thesis, Harvard University, 1921.)

205. Thompson, James W. *Ancient Libraries*. University of California Press, 1940.

206. Tooley, R. V. *Maps of Antarctica: A list of early maps of the South Polar Regions*. Map Collectors' Circle, Durrant House, Chiswell Street, London E.C.1.

207. ———. *Maps and Map Makers*. London: B. T. Batsford, Ltd., 1949, 1952.

208. True, David O. "Correspondence relating to the Piri Re'is Map." (In files of the American Geographic Society, New York City.)

209. Tseukernik, David. (An article entitled "Did Columbus Discover America?" summarizing an article written by this author and previously published in the Soviet publication *Novy Mir* was published in the English language paper, USSR, October, 1963.)

210. Uhden, Richard. "The Oldest Original Portuguese Chart of the Indian Ocean, A.D. 1509," *Imago Mundi*, III, 1939.

210a. Vance, Adrian. *UFOs: The Eye and the Camera*. New York: Barlenmir, 1977.

211. Verrill, A. Hyatt. *America's Ancient Civilizations*. New York: Putnam, 1953.

212. Villiers, Alan John. *Men, Ships and the Sea*. Washington, D.C.: National Geographic Society, 1962.

213. ———. *Wild Ocean*. New York: McGraw-Hill, 1957.

214. Wadler, Arnold D. *The Origin of Language*. New York: The American Press for Art and Science, 1948.

215. Waltari, Mika. *The Wanderer*. New York: Putnam, 1951; Pocket Books, 1964. (Chapter on Piri Re'is.)

216. Waerden, B. L. van der. *Basic Ideas and Methods in Babylonian and Greek Astronomy* (in Crombie).

217. Wieder, F. C., ed. *Monumenta Cartographica: Reproductions of Unique and Rare Maps*. 5 vols. The Hague: Nijhoff, 1925–1933.

218. Wilson, A. Tuzo. "Continental Drift," *Scientific American*, CCVII, no. 4, April 1963, pp. 2–16.

219. Winsor, Justin. *A Bibliography of Ptolemy's Geography*. Cambridge, Mass.: Harvard University Press, 1884.

220. ———. *Narrative and Critical History of America*. Boston and New York: Houghton Mifflin & Co., 1889.

221. Winter, Heinrich. "Catalan Portolan Maps and Their Place in the Total View of Cartographic Development," *Imago Mundi*, XI (1954).

222. ———. "A Late Portolan Chart of Madrid, and Late Portolan Charts in General," *Imago Mundi*, VII (1950).

223. ———. "The Origin of the Sea-Chart," *Imago Mundi*, XII (1951), pp. 39 ff. (See also *Imago Mundi*, Vol. V, for his reply to Richard Uhden [Vol. I] on question of compass.)

224. ———. "The True Position of H. Wagner in the Controversy of the Compass Chart," *Imago Mundi*, V (1948).

225. Worcester, Donald E., and Wendell C. Schaeffer. *The Growth and Culture of Latin America*. New York: Oxford University Press, 1956.

226. *World Map, Miller Cylindrical Projection, 1 Degree Grid Prepared by the American Geographical Society for the U.S. Geographical Society for the U.S. Department of State*. "Outline Series No. 7." Drawn by William Briesemeister.

227. Wright, Helen S. *The Seventh Continent*. Boston: Richard G. Badger; New York: The Gorham Press, 1918.

228. Wright, John Kirtland. *The Geographical Lore of the Time of the Crusades*. New York: The American Geographical Society, 1925.

229. ———. *The Leardo Map of the World, 1452–1453*. "American Geographical Society Library Series," No. 4, 1928.

230. Wright, John Kirtland, and Elizabeth T. Platt. *Aids to Geographical Research*. New York: American Geographical Society Research Series, No. 22, 1947.

231. Wytfleet, Cornielle. *Descriptionis Prolemaicae Augmentum*. Louvain: Ionannis Bogardi, 1598 (Antarctic map, pp. 100–101). Republished 1964 in Amsterdam and Israel with introduction by R. A. Skelton.

# Index